Praise for the Novels of Carrie Vaughn

After the Golden Age

"More than a superhero story, this is a tale of finding your true self and realizing that good and evil often come in various shades. Vaughn has written an adventurous story that is much more about the emotions than the ability to fly or read minds."
—*RT Book Reviews* (4½ stars, a Top Pick!)

"Vaughn tells a good tale. I thoroughly enjoyed the read and recommend it without hesitation." —*SFFWorld*

"A satisfying read that realistically depicts superheroes."
—*SF Signal*

Discord's Apple

"Melds a near-future world torn by war with the legend of the fall of Troy in this brilliantly structured, beautifully written stand-alone . . . Vaughn brings together mythology, fairy tales, and very human lives, immersing readers in the stories these complex characters tell themselves to make sense of their war-torn worlds." —*Publishers Weekly* (starred review)

"*Discord's Apple* is an apocalypse that belongs on the same shelf as *American Gods* and the best of Charles de Lint." —Daniel Abraham, author of *A Betrayal in Winter*

"Carrie Vaughn weaves a gorgeous tapestry of the human condition in a postapocalyptic world filled with mystery, magic, and immortals. Her world-building is masterful!"—L. A. Banks, *New York Times* bestselling author of *The Thirteenth*

TOR BOOKS BY CARRIE VAUGHN

Kitty Goes to War
Kitty's Big Trouble
Kitty's Greatest Hits
Kitty Steals the Show
Kitty Rocks the House
Kitty in the Underworld
Low Midnight (forthcoming)
Kitty Saves the World (forthcoming)

Discord's Apple
After the Golden Age
Dreams of the Golden Age

DREAMS
OF THE
GOLDEN
AGE

CARRIE
VAUGHN

TOR®

A TOM DOHERTY ASSOCIATES BOOK
NEW YORK

DREAMS OF THE GOLDEN AGE

Edited by David G. Hartwell

A Tor Book
Published by Tom Doherty Associates, LLC
175 Fifth Avenue
New York, NY 10010

www.tor-forge.com

Tor® is a registered trademark of Tom Doherty Associates, LLC.

ISBN 978-0-7653-7010-5

Tor books may be purchased for educational, business, or promotional use. For information on bulk purchases, please contact the Macmillan Corporate and Premium Sales Department at 1-800-221-7945, extension 5442, or write to specialmarkets@macmillan.com.

First Edition: January 2014
First Mass Market Edition: December 2014

Printed in the United States of America

0 9 8 7 6 5 4 3 2 1

To George, Melinda, and the Wild Cards Consortium,
for showing that superheroes can live in prose
(and then making me stay up way too late
reading about them)

DREAMS
OF THE
GOLDEN
AGE

ONE

Celia West sat alone in her office, a corner suite in the family penthouse at West Plaza. She kept her wide, preternaturally slick desk neat, the few files stacked in a corner, pens lined up, computer screen conveniently placed, laptop dock accessible. Everything else was put away in drawers and filing cabinets. Anyone standing before her wouldn't be able to tell a thing about her, except that she kept her office tidy. People might make assumptions based on that. They might even be right about some of them.

On the computer, she clicked on an encrypted file she'd been sent.

A video played, dark and grainy feed from a security camera outside a jewelry store on the south side of downtown. The camera looked down at the front doors from a corner of the building, creating a foreshortened image, as if the walls had shrunk. Time stamp read 1:23 a.m. A trio approached: men in ski masks, overcoats, baggy jeans, shit-kicking boots. Hoodlums of one flavor or another. One carried a backpack, one carried a baseball bat, the third a crowbar. Standard smash and grab.

Before they could get started on the window and grating, though, a masked vigilante walked into the frame. Words were probably exchanged, but the camera didn't record audio.

The vigilante was just a kid. Male, tall in that impossibly lanky way of teenage boys. All limbs and chaotic movement. He wore a black T-shirt and sweatpants and a homemade mask, probably a bandana with eyeholes cut out, covering most of his hair and the top half of his face. His chin was smooth, youthful. He stood with his fists clenched at his sides, bouncing a little on worn sneakers. He was nervous, excited—this was obviously a first outing. Too young and stupid not to know he couldn't save the world.

The robbers didn't have any patience for this. They stood back a moment, glancing at one another as if confirming this was really happening. Then the guy with the baseball bat stepped forward and swung, aiming for the kid's head.

The vigilante vanished. Blinked out of existence, there . . . and then not.

Celia used the laptop's touch pad to back up the video and leaned forward to watch the scene again. The average person might think the trick was a special effect, some editing cut made on the video. But the frame didn't skip, nothing else in the image changed. The boy was there one frame, gone the next.

The guy with the baseball bat stumbled, thrown off balance when his blow didn't connect. All three crooks looked around in obvious confusion. Then the baseball bat jerked out of the guy's hands, swung apparently of its own volition, and caught its former owner on the chin. He fell back and lay writhing on the concrete sidewalk.

The kid hadn't vanished, then—invisible, along with what he was wearing.

The other two lunged at the bat hanging in midair. The bat fell—wisely, the kid dropped it and wasn't there when the two crooks attacked the spot where he should have been. One of them bent double, from what looked like a kick in the crotch. The other stumbled at a strike to his knees. Kid wasn't doing too badly, really.

It couldn't last, however much Celia might want it to. The guy with the crowbar might have just gotten lucky, but he swung in a likely spot, and connected. The kid flickered back to visibility, cringing and holding his shoulder. Pain, maybe any distraction, interrupted his powers. He had to focus to stay invisible.

Now that he had a target, the guy with the crowbar punched him, fist connecting to cheek. The kid's head whipped around, and he stumbled, his chest heaving to catch his breath. Still visible—he hadn't pulled himself back together.

Celia had a sinking feeling about how the rest of this was going to go, but the kid turned out to be smarter than she expected. He picked up the bat and shoved it through the bars of the security grating to smash the window of the jewelry store. Celia could tell the alarm went off by the way the crooks flinched. The two still standing hauled up their fallen partner and ran. The kid hesitated a moment, rubbing his face where he'd been struck, shaking his head as if to clear it. He looked down the street—at the approaching police sirens, Celia guessed. He disappeared, turning invisible again before presumably running away. Preserving his secret identity.

As a first outing for a vigilante went, it wasn't an unmitigated success, but it wasn't a disaster, either. More interesting to her, though—he was a new guy. She didn't know who he was. But she had a good guess.

Celia kept a file folder in a locked safe that lived underneath her desk. Inside the folder was a list of a dozen names. The people the names belonged to were all dead, but most of them had descendants who lived on, and she kept a list of those names as well. A third generation was coming up. If she traced down the family trees of that original list of names, she'd find the invisible kid. She wondered what he called himself—not the Invisible Kid, she was pretty sure.

And there it was—several teenage boys on the list, all but one of whom she was already tracking. The remaining one had a question mark by his name: Theodore Donaldson. Grandson of Lawrence Donaldson, whose son hadn't exhibited any sign of superhuman abilities, which didn't mean anything. The trait often skipped generations, as she very well knew. But *his* son . . .

She crossed out the question mark, wrote a note, and put the file back in the safe. Then she picked up her phone and made a call. A standard receptionist voice answered.

"I'd like to speak to Captain Paulson, please," Celia said.

"I'm sorry, he's in a meeting now."

"Tell him it's Celia West."

The receptionist didn't say anything to that, which made Celia smile. That one name had so much power didn't seem right, somehow. How had it come to this, again? Once upon a time, she'd just wanted to stay anonymous.

"Captain Paulson will speak to you now," the receptionist said curtly, maybe even offended. Gatekeeper duties overridden. Sorry, honey.

Mark's voice came on the line. "Celia?"

"Hi, Mark. I watched that video you sent over."

"Yeah? What did you think?"

"I think he's one to keep an eye on."

"Do you know who he is?"

"Let's give the kid some room, okay?"

"Celia—"

"Did you catch the three crooks?"

"No, but we're canvassing the neighborhood and we've got a few leads."

"You canvassing for the kid, too?"

The police captain sighed. "I can't discuss an ongoing investigation with you."

"Why don't you drop it and let me keep an eye on

him? You wouldn't have sent me the video if you didn't want me to know about him, right?"

"I just thought you might have a name."

"I can get it if we need it. But let's see what he does next. This may have shaken him up, he may back off."

"Not likely—I know how these guys operate."

"So do I, Mark. Better than you."

"Yeah. Well." He cleared his throat, avoiding an uncomfortable change of subject. "You'll let me know if you hear anything through the grapevine?"

"You know I'm always here for you," she said.

"That's exactly what I need, for people to think I'm in the pocket of the president of West Corp."

"No, they'll know better than that. Take care of yourself, Mark."

"You, too."

The complicated phone unit—the thing had more controls than a jet fighter—beeped an incoming call. She punched the button, which summoned her own receptionist to the line.

"Ms. West? There's a call from Elmwood Academy on line three."

She suppressed a groan. This was about one of the girls. But which one, and was it good news or bad? She could just make the caller leave a message . . .

"Right, okay, put it through." The line clicked, and she announced, "This is Celia West."

"Ms. West, this is Director Benitez, I'm so sorry to bother you"—Celia was pretty sure other parents didn't get apologies from the headmistress of the city's most exclusive private school—"but I thought you should know that Anna came to school significantly tardy today."

"Define significantly tardy."

"She didn't arrive until after lunch."

That late, Celia wondered why Anna bothered showing up at all, but she didn't say so.

"Did she have a good excuse?"

"I'm not sure what would be a good excuse in this case . . ."

"Oh, you know, saving orphans from a burning building, that sort of thing."

"Um. Well. No, I don't think she had a good excuse. She said she got held up and lost track of time. She wouldn't go into details. But as you know, Ms. West, attendance is an essential component of success here at Elmwood Academy, and Anna's attendance may come under review if there's another similar incident."

She wondered if Benitez had checked the records to see that Celia had dropped out of Elmwood when she was seventeen. Probably not.

"Yes, Director, I understand. We'll straighten this out at home."

"Thank you." The woman sounded relieved.

"Thank *you*, for letting me know. Anna and I will have a talk."

The woman hung up quickly. Celia smiled at the phone a moment before putting it away.

Something was definitely up with Anna, but Celia refused to get too worked up about it. It couldn't possibly be worse than the kinds of things Celia got up to at her age. Well, it could, realistically speaking. Imagination always failed to provide all the possible scenarios.

The security cameras in the lobby and elevator let Celia know when the kids arrived home. That meant they'd be in her office in about five minutes, checking in, giving the report for the day. Her little minions, returning to home base. They grumbled when she talked like that.

Her daughters. How the hell did she get far enough

along in her life to have two teenage daughters? She ought to get some kind of medal for it. *Wait to see if either one of them turns out to be a mass murderer.* Ah, yes, there was that.

She timed it well and set aside the spreadsheet she'd been studying so that she was waiting, back straight, hands folded on the desk in front of her, when they walked into her office. Sullen, they held their backpacks slung over their shoulders, and afternoon weariness marred their features. Their neat uniforms—navy skirts, white shirts, maroon cardigans—always looked rumpled by this time of the day.

She greeted them. "Girls."

They muttered hellos and trudged forward to sit in the two chairs that might have been put there for the purpose.

"How was your day?"

Thirteen-year-old Bethy went first. "We had a quiz today, you know that quiz I told you about, and I think I did okay, but I don't really know. You won't be mad if I flunk it, right? 'Cause you saw me studying for it, right?"

"I know you studied. I don't think you flunked."

She went on for another minute about gym class, about how she needed a new pair of gym shoes because her old ones were too small, and so on, and on one hand Celia wanted to shake her and tell her stop with the minutiae. But really, the greater impulse was to sit back, smile, and let her go on all day long, just to hear the sound of her not-quite-mature voice tumbling forth. Right now, Celia could fool herself that Bethy was still a little girl, with round cheeks, hair in a ponytail, foot swinging to kick at her chair leg. In a couple of years, she'd be like Anna, slouched in her seat, her mind a million miles away, on boys or school or the problems of the world, or maybe just wanting to get out of her mother's crummy office and back to the sanctity of her own private life.

Bethy was strawberry blond, but Anna had inherited Celia's own flame red hair, which she in turn had inherited from her mother. The West redheads. God help her.

Bethy finally wound down and let out a sigh. Amused, Celia said, "I know you're not going to believe me, kid, but you shouldn't worry so much. You'll have plenty to worry about soon enough, don't spend it all on a math quiz."

Her youngeest pouted, clearly not believing her, but Celia didn't expect her to.

"Grandma's cooking dinner tonight. You guys'll be ready for it in a couple of hours?"

They brightened at that, which was a comfort. Family still held some attraction for them, for however long that lasted. Gathering their bags, they stood to make their exit.

Celia said, "Anna, you mind talking to me for just a minute?"

Bethy looked at her sister with a wide-eyed expression, like someone rubbernecking at a car accident. Anna herself put on a blank face, a prisoner walking into a courtroom, and returned to her seat.

Eggshells. Celia couldn't pinpoint the moment when dealing with Anna had become like walking on eggshells, or handling fine china. The change had happened slowly, and then one day she looked up and her oldest daughter wasn't a little girl anymore, and Celia didn't know what to say to her.

Treat her with respect. First rule. Celia remembered being that age, how she felt when people didn't take her seriously. She wouldn't inflict that on her own kids if she could help it.

"Hi, Anna," she said.

"Hi, Mom," the teenager answered, her thin smile a mask. Her hair was chin length, loose, the color bringing out the faint freckles on her nose. She let Celia catch her gaze, but her expression was neutral.

"I got a call from Director Benitez today. You were late to school. Very late."

Anna sighed and looked at the ceiling. "It wasn't that big a deal. It *shouldn't* have been, I wasn't hurting anything."

"You sure about that?"

She didn't answer.

"So, where were you this morning?"

Her mouth worked, as if chewing over words. "A friend of mine needed help. I couldn't ignore that, could I?"

Celia believed her, because neither of the girls was a practiced liar. They were smart enough to know that lying wouldn't get them anywhere, with their father the telepath around. That was something, at least.

"No, of course not. If your friend was really in trouble and if you were really the only person who could help."

"I was." She stated it as a challenge.

Celia leaned forward and asked, "Was this friend of yours Teddy Donaldson by any chance?"

Anna gaped. "How—" She clamped her mouth shut, then changed her mind about talking. "Did Dad tell you that?"

"I don't think Dad knows anything about it. You haven't seen him since this morning, have you? So how would he know?"

She went into full shutdown mode, as Celia expected, but that was okay. She had her confirmation.

"I applaud your efforts to help your friend. But next time, call me first. We can get you a permission slip or something. Don't go haring off just because you think something's a good idea. Got it?"

"Fine."

"You're still grounded for skipping school, but just for the weekend instead of till the end of the month, like you would have been if you were off smoking or something. Okay?"

No response, not that Celia needed one.

"And for the next three weeks Tom's going to be dropping you off in the town car and watching you go through the front doors."

"Oh, come on!" Anna said.

"Three weeks. Then we renegotiate."

"Two weeks."

"Three. Argue again and I'm riding in the car with you."

"You wouldn't."

Celia glared. Anna wilted.

"Agreed?" Celia said.

Her daughter slumped in the chair, looking sullen. Looking trapped, really. A familiar expression lately. Celia risked a further prompt, stepping gently. "How was the rest of your day? School, classes . . . anything else you want to talk about?"

She grimaced. "The usual. It's fine, I shouldn't complain, but it's so . . . It feels like I'm just going through the motions."

"Jumping through hoops," Celia added. "I guarantee you, jumping through the hoops now will make things easier later on. You just have to stick with it."

Oh, that sigh she gave would power wind turbines. "Then I should get started on my homework, shouldn't I?" She gathered her things, edging off the chair.

One of these days, Celia feared, Anna was going to walk out of the office and never come back. "Okay. I love you."

"Love you, too," she muttered perfunctorily, stalking to the door with her bag over her shoulder.

Celia spent a moment indulging in blind panic, convinced that she'd failed as a mother, her children hated her and were destined to become terrorists or trophy wives, that her entire life would come crashing down around her any day now. The moment passed.

She pulled herself together and finished up a last bit of work, reviewing company financials and arranging her task list for the next day.

"Celia? Your mother has dinner ready."

A man in his fifties stood in the doorway. He wore tailored slacks, and the top button of his dress shirt was undone. His brown hair needed a trim. He seemed like he would be most at home at a university, standing before a chalkboard, lecturing—studious, upstanding. In fact, he was a practicing psychiatrist and a semiretired superhuman vigilante, Dr. Arthur Mentis.

"Hey." Celia smiled at her partner of twenty years. "How was your day?"

"Calm. Saw a couple of patients, did some record keeping. Nothing else to report. You?" He spoke with a mild British accent, which added to his intellectual air. He approached her desk and sat on the edge to look down at her. The only person who could get away with that.

"Something's up with Anna," she said.

"Being seventeen is what's up with Anna."

"Something a little more specific."

"I couldn't say what it might be," he said, shrugging oh so innocently.

"You're not even tempted to pry?"

"No, because I have a good idea of what else I'd find in that stew of a mind. There are so many things fathers are not meant to know about their daughters, I'm terrified at what she might let slip out."

What she already had let slip, Celia suspected. Arthur Mentis was very good at picking up stray thoughts, and though Anna had by sheer force of necessity become very good at keeping her thoughts to herself, she wasn't perfect. But Arthur was also one of the most discreet and understanding men Celia had ever met.

Fathers and daughters, yes. Not that Celia was anything of an expert on the subject. She winced and rubbed at a crick in her neck. She'd been sitting here too long. She seemed to get tired earlier and earlier these days.

"Would she tell us if she had powers?" Celia asked. If Anna had powers, Arthur probably already knew, but he wouldn't say a word about it until Anna did, no matter how much Celia wheedled. It was one of the things they'd agreed on when they became parents. The girls deserved to keep their secrets, as long as no one got hurt.

Arthur nodded. "I think she would. We have to have faith in her."

"She ditched school this morning to help out a friend."

"You see? She has her priorities straight. I think."

"Tell you what: Next time, you can talk to the headmistress."

"The headmistress hangs up the phone whenever I answer her calls. She won't stay in the same room with me, did you know that?"

Arthur had been open and public with his powers for a long time. Everyone knew he was a telepath, and people usually got very nervous around him.

Celia never had.

"I'd noticed, yes. I think it's funny."

"It makes me wonder what she's hiding," he said.

Indeed. She patted his hand. "Faith, Arthur."

TWO

Anna rushed out of the sleek black town car before Tom could walk around to open the door for her. Bad enough that everyone would see the limo dropping her off. She could try to lessen the association, keep some of her dignity. Usually, she took the city bus to school, to try to blend in. She didn't like being noticed.

It would be easier if she could *act* like one of the richest girls at school, showing off ultra-expensive phones and gadgets, driving her own sports car, wearing diamond studs with her school uniform. Other girls did that, forming their own cliques based on brand names and spending in excess rather than on any real friendship, and Anna did everything she could to separate herself from that. She got enough attention as it was, being Anna West-Mentis, daughter and granddaughter of superheroes, and of wealth and influence. And when would she develop superpowers and don a mask to fight crime?

Someday. Someday soon. But no one would know because she wasn't going to tell them. She was going to do it on her own terms, and she didn't want everyone—and with her family involved that meant *everyone*—watching.

Bethy was still in the middle school, and Tom would drop her off a block up the road at the next building. She didn't seem to care what people thought of her or the company car or the superfamily in West Plaza. At least not yet. She got straight A's and shrugged off the attention, while Anna felt like she was constantly walking through minefields.

Anna had to talk to Teddy before class started, and he wasn't where he should have been, on the front steps or in the fountain courtyard with the rest of their friends—Teia, Lew, Sam. The certainty of her power confirmed their presences. She imagined it as a compass in the back of her mind, exerting pressure as it pointed the way. She could find people. She wanted to find Teddy, and she knew exactly where he was: in the nurse's office, which couldn't be good. The news websites had a story on him today—someone had leaked a still image from the security footage at the jewelry store. Anna had hoped this would pass under the radar of anyone who cared. Fat chance, it turned out. Seriously, what was the point of *having* a secret identity if you got your picture in the paper on your first outing?

She put her head down and marched, hoping to get inside quickly, but didn't make it past the front steps.

"Oh my God, Anna, what's up with Teddy?"

Reluctantly, she stopped to answer. Izzy, the girl who'd called her, was tall and loud and way too nosy. One of the girls with a sports car who *wanted* to be noticed. Anna decided to play dumb. "Why? What's the matter?"

"He looked like he got hit by a truck. Is that why he wasn't in school yesterday?"

"I can't say anything until I've talked to him."

"But—"

Anna walked off and through the front doors.

Elmwood prided itself on not looking like a school but more like some hundred-year-old English manor, with carpeted halls, polished wood doors, manicured courtyards, and so on. Like they weren't students at a school but guests in someone's mansion. But who made guests take midterms? It was all vaguely ridiculous.

She would have reached the end of the corridor without interruption, but Teia and Lew had moved inside from the courtyard and were waiting to ambush her. They'd probably been watching for her. She'd have avoided them if there was another way out of the corridor and to the nurse's office. They were twins; Lew's brown skin was a shade or two darker than Teia's, but they had the same round dark eyes and sharp features. Teia wore her curly hair back with a headband, making a halo around her face. Lew kept his cropped short. They both blocked her path and studied her like they were about to dissect her.

"What happened to Teddy?" Teia whispered as Lew took her arm and pulled her into a corner. Unlike Izzy, they were in on the whole thing and wouldn't let her just walk away.

"He did it, didn't he?" Lew said. "He went out on patrol. He really did it." His eyes gleamed with excitement. Maybe even with envy.

"And then got the shit beat out of him," Teia said.

Anna sighed. "And he got his freaking picture in the paper."

"I know!" Teia exclaimed. "It's great!"

"Be quiet!" Anna hissed. They were supposed to be keeping this secret. "I have to go talk to him before class starts."

Lew pointed a thumb over his shoulder and said, "He got called to the nurse's office—"

"I know that. Can I go now?" She pulled her arm out of his grip and marched on.

"Anna—" they called after her, but she ignored them.

Yesterday, Teddy had called her before school and begged her to come help. He'd had a run-in the night before. She thought he was crazy for going out at all, for thinking he could battle crime, right wrongs, whatever, all by himself. That was why they were practicing as a team, but he just couldn't wait, could he? Over the phone he kept insisting that the expedition had been successful. He'd stopped a real-live, honest-to-God robbery. He'd just gotten a little banged up was all, and he didn't want his folks to know. She'd taken the bus to his town house, where he'd been hiding in the garden shed out back.

He'd been more than a little banged up. Anna wanted him to go to the hospital. But no, he'd made it through the night, he'd be fine. He'd turned invisible to get ice packs and aspirin without his parents knowing, staying in his bedroom long enough to convince them he was sick and couldn't go to school. Somehow, they'd bought it. They went to work, so it was just Teddy at home.

He wanted her to help him wash the blood out of his outfit.

She just about killed him for that. She didn't wash his outfit, but they ended up spending a couple of hours talking about what had happened, what he'd done right, and how it could have gone better. Her opinion: He should wait for the team to go with him next time. One against three were terrible odds, and sometimes even an invisible kid who could walk through walls needed someone to watch his back. He had to learn to phase out when someone hit him, the way he phased through walls. She told him that, and he defended himself, saying he couldn't focus on so many things at once. Well then, he shouldn't be trying to fight crime yet, should he?

That should have been the end of it, but then she had that talk with her mother. Her apparently omniscient mother.

She reached the nurse's office just as he was walking out, closing the door behind him.

"Teddy!" she called.

He flinched, eyes bugged out, looking like he was about to run.

"We have to talk." Before he could flee, she grabbed

the sleeve of his uniform jacket and pulled him to a padded bench around the corner.

The bruise on his cheek had turned an amazing purplish-gray, spreading around his eye in a crescent. Otherwise, he didn't seem too badly hurt. He favored his shoulder, but he could still move it. It could have been so much worse. Her big fear was that he would be knocked unconscious while invisible and not rematerialize. Just stay invisible forever, and she'd be the only person who could find him, zeroing in on him with her power and tripping over his body.

"I'm surprised you even came to school today," she said.

"I could only stay away so long."

"But you're okay, right? What are you doing here?" She nodded toward the nurse's office.

He looked changed. "As soon as I showed up, one of the teachers dragged me here. They kept asking questions about trouble at home."

"They think you're being *abused*?"

"Look at my face."

"Yeah. It's pretty bad." She resisted an urge to brush a flop of brown hair off his forehead. Weirdly, the bruise made him look simultaneously tough and vulnerable.

"I told her I walked into a door," he said.

"You couldn't think of a better excuse than that?"

He huffed. "I wasn't thinking. It's not important. I know what I did wrong. You're right, I have to figure out how to phase out when people are hitting me. I'll do better next time."

How about avoiding getting hit at all? "That's what we need to talk about. You need to back off."

"It didn't go perfect but I did okay—"

"You have to back off," Anna said. "My mother knows it was you."

He stared. "What? That's impossible, how could she?"

"I don't know, but she does. It's her thing, she's a control freak."

"But how does she know about *me*?"

"She keeps tabs on everybody."

"So it's not enough that she's president of the richest company there is, she has to spy on everybody?"

Flustered, Anna waved him off. "I don't know, she's paranoid. That's not the point right now. You need to cool it because she's watching."

He thought for a minute, so grim and serious she almost laughed. "I can't back off now. It'll go better next time, I know it will. I need more practice."

"Crime'll still be there in a month or two. You need more practice where someone isn't trying to kill you."

"But that's just it, how am I going to get practice using my powers when there's danger if I'm not really in danger?"

"That's a stupid argument," she said. "I worry about you, Teddy."

"Well. Thanks for worrying." Even with the giant bruise, his gee-whiz smile lit up his face. It was hard staying mad at him.

"Any time."

The warning chime sounded, a bell tone that was meant to be soothing but managed to be annoying as it echoed through the halls, because it meant they had five minutes to get to class. Anna didn't much want to go to class at the best of times.

She hooked her arm around Teddy's and hauled him away from the nurse's office. "We'll talk about it later."

"What if I go out with Teia or Lew? Or Sam? We can watch each other's backs—"

"So you can get in twice as much trouble?"

He brightened. "You could go with me."

"I'd be useless."

"No, you wouldn't. You're not useless," he said, but the words were rote and they both knew she was right. He added, "Maybe you shouldn't worry so much."

Her mother's words from yesterday's after-school conference echoed. Math quiz, she wished. "Somebody's got to worry, the rest of you sure aren't."

They arrived at the second floor, north wing corridor, and history. Her first class. Teddy had chemistry. What he really needed were some physics lessons—pressure, velocity, force of impact.

"Are you saying that you want me to quit?" he said.

"No, it's not that. I just . . . you could have been killed."

"I could get killed crossing the street—"

"That's another stupid argument."

"We have to keep going. We've started this. It's the right thing to do, isn't it?"

That all depended on whom you talked to. Which sounded like something her mother would say.

"Yeah," she said. "We have to keep going." They didn't have a choice. They'd already come this far.

Tom picked Bethy up from middle school first, then Anna, who didn't have anything after school today. She could have lied about it and taken the bus home, like she usually did when soccer was on or she had a group project. But she didn't want to push her luck. Dad might be able to tell she was lying. Or not. That was the trouble, he hardly ever let on what he knew or didn't. He'd just let her keep digging whatever hole she started on until she hit bedrock. And he'd just stand there, his eyebrow raised, not saying anything.

The car waited because she was late, between picking up books from her cubby and talking to friends on the way out. Tom never gave her a hard time about lingering. Bethy was in the back of the car, math book open, doing her homework. Anna shoved the book over as she slid onto the seat. "Drive on, Jeeves," she called to the front seat.

"Afternoon, ma'am," Tom said, his smile amused. He was a silver-haired man who'd been working for her mother for eons. Anna couldn't imagine that, working for the same person forever. Getting old doing the same job. She didn't know what she wanted to do with her life, but it wasn't that. She didn't want to run West Corp, either. Her mother had taken over right where her father, the previous president of West Corp—*and* the famous Captain Olympus—left off. Like they were some kind of clones or something. Anna was afraid to ask if everyone expected her to do the same. She'd rather they give it all to Bethy.

Throwing her an annoyed pout, Bethy gathered up her books and papers as the car pulled away from the curb.

"You flunk your quiz?" Anna asked.

"No. A minus. Mom was right, how did she know?"

"You love math, it's your favorite, you'll never flunk a math quiz."

"But I was worried."

She could tell Bethy that everything would be perfect for the rest of her life and she'd still worry. "You're weird, you know that?"

Bethy should have said, "No, you are," after that, but she didn't. Instead, she hugged her book bag to her chest and watched her sister, staring hard until Anna squirmed.

"What?" Anna said. The plea hung through a long pause.

"If you got powers, would you tell me?" Bethy asked.

She could answer with a straight face because she'd been dealing with the question her whole life. Her grandparents, her father—all superhuman, and sometimes superhumans passed on their powers.

The trick was not to respond any differently from all

the other times. People were always watching her; she just had to act normal, always.

"Yes, I would." Except she wouldn't, because she hadn't, because if Bethy knew, their father would be twice as likely to find out, so Bethy couldn't know about any of it. Anna had to keep it all to herself.

"Really?"

"Why are you asking me this?"

"Because if I got powers, I'd tell you."

"Do you have powers? Are you getting powers?"

"No. But I was just thinking about what I would do if I did."

"Having powers isn't all it's cracked up to be, you know."

"Be nice to figure that out for myself."

"Mom's right. You worry too much."

"Runs in the family," Bethy said.

Because they had a lot to worry about, in the end.

THREE

The large conference room at City Hall was filled with the worst sort of business sharks, lobbyists, developers, profiteers, and robber barons. Gathered here in the name of progressive urban development, of course. But they all had blood in their gazes and were licking their chops, figuratively.

And Celia was here among them. What did that say about her?

City government had been trying for twenty years to institute major urban redevelopment. The idea fell out of favor when a previous mayor who advocated revitalization turned supervillain on them, so Commerce City was long overdue for such a plan. Finally, though, the wheels were moving—in part thanks to Celia West's advocacy.

The city had asked for comprehensive bids to be submitted to a planning committee. This committee would decide the tone and direction of Commerce City for the next generation. Of course, Celia had gotten West Corp involved. Along with every other construction and development company in the city wanting a piece of the pie.

A variety of consortiums and contractors had just delivered their spiels to the mayor, members of the city council, and the planning committee, which included police, fire, and safety officers. Police Captain Mark Paulson was among them. She'd asked him to join the committee specifically. Wasn't normally his sort of thing—bureaucratic stuffiness took him off the street, where he could do real good, he was always saying. But they needed to take the long view. The work they did now would have repercussions for decades, including in the area of law enforcement. And she wanted at least one ally in the room.

The second-to-last presentation was wrapping up. Two men in suits—she thought of them as trained monkeys, doing their little dance—stood by the wall screen where they'd flashed their maps and drawn their lines and squares where their company would build freeways, outlet malls, and tract housing, if they had their way. The thing that gave them those confident smiles? The fact that everyone in their audience, whose approval they needed to move forward, was also a potential investor. Conflict of interest didn't exist in these people's world. They kept looking at Celia in particular like she was a bag of money waiting to burst open.

"Very impressive, gentlemen," Mayor Edleston, who didn't know any better, said as he nodded appreciatively. "Any questions? Any information the committee can add about what this would take in terms of permitting, legislation?" He looked to the side of the room where the people who actually got things done sat.

Celia said, "Maybe we should go ahead and move on to the final presentation."

A silence fell, thick as snow and heavy as lead. She loved when that happened. Everyone stared at her, and her audience was suddenly entirely captive.

Today, she'd started out tired and sore, but she'd powered through it and brought out all the poise and resolve she could muster. She stood, running her hand along the edge of a file folder. She knew without looking that her dark gray dress suit didn't have a wrinkle in it, and her short red hair and makeup were perfectly arranged. Good grooming was power. One of the little things that determined whether people would listen to you.

"We've seen a lot of big, ambitious plans. Lots of free-ways, lots of suburbia. Looks great on paper, doesn't it? But you can track this pattern in a dozen other cities: You build a freeway system that drains resources from the city center, you end up with an empty shell and all the problems that come with it. I want to see economic development as much as the next person, but not at the expense of the city itself. I propose that we can have an economic boom, a vibrant Commerce City, without the sprawl."

First monkey said, "But the development our plan promotes *will* benefit the city—"

"The whole city, or your little cadre of investors?" she replied.

"*You're* an investor—"

"That's right. But you're advocating an either-or situation, and I want both."

The second monkey had returned to his seat with the other developers. He muttered to a colleague in a way that made it clear he was only pretending to whisper, "Bitch."

Mayor Edleston shifted uncomfortably, rubbing a hand across his chin. The suits from the other development firms cleared their throats and stared at their hands. First monkey grumbled at the tabletop.

She could buy them all, and they knew it. They hated it. She was enjoying herself immensely.

"If you'll indulge me," she said, "West Corp has put together a plan that benefits both Commerce City's investors and citizens, and I'd love to show it to you." She held up a flash drive. No one even had time to go for coffee before she started in.

The city council's IT guy plugged the drive into the video system, and a second later the wall screen displayed her graphics, dominated by the West Corp logo, the latest redesign of which included elements from the earliest logos, the crescent symbol forming the arc of a bow ready to fire a star into the heavens. The retro look of it had gone over well. The trick was, she'd been in here consulting with the IT guy half an hour before the meeting started. She knew her file worked, and it was the only file on the drive. No chance for screwups. Really, it took so little effort to appear entirely in control, entirely powerful, it was surprising so few people managed it. The IT guy handed her the display's remote.

She walked up to the wall screen, displacing the remaining monkey. "I advocate an approach that utilizes Commerce City's downtown resources rather than abandons them. Make downtown a destination, an attraction in itself. Block off Preston Street here and here to create a pedestrian mall. Buildings on these blocks here are already slated for demolition. Replace them with high-end residential lofts. West Corp is already investing in low-income housing a few blocks out, here and here. There's your workforce. Increase the number of teachers at the city's public schools. Create an art district by refurbishing the Old Opera House, link it to the City Art Museum. Build light rail lines that travel in from north and east, here, with a major stop at the university, allowing industry and manufacturing interests to take advantage of cheap real estate on the city's outskirts. Most of what we need to implement this plan is already in place. Ultimately, focusing on renewal rather than transplanting will be cheaper, promise a greater return on investment for more people, and improve the city's morale. And you can't put a price tag on that."

Some people accused her of playing the altruist as a front. A trick to make her and West Corp more popular with the general public. The accusation told her a lot about the people making it.

After the meeting, every member of the city council and half the planning committee came to shake her hand

and congratulate her on the magnificent proposal. Most of them assured her that she had their support and that her plan was all but approved. Of course it was, she thought. She wouldn't have taken it this far if she hadn't secured the majority of her support in advance.

Most of the players lingered after the official meeting ended. Meetings like this were theater that let you see the results of dealing. The real business went on before and after. Celia stuck around, not because she had anything she wanted to get done but because she wanted to size people up and listen to the gossip.

One of the out-of-town investors, a fifty-something man with a permanent thin smile, had cornered Mark. Celia wondered if he needed rescuing, then got close enough to hear what they were talking about.

"Commerce City is famous for its superhuman vigilantes. How do they factor into the planning committee's discussions?" His name was Danton Majors, and he'd made a fortune on real estate speculation. Self-made billionaire before forty, that kind of guy. He'd thrown his company, Delta Ventures, into the melee with a plan very similar to the others, one that depended on developing new real estate and promoting it to the city on the basis of potential property tax revenue, rather than emphasizing the well-being of the people actually living here. Meanwhile, the investment-seeking monkeys were trying to woo him just as hard as they were trying to woo her.

Majors probably looked down on Celia for inheriting her money. Probably assumed she hadn't worked a day in her life.

"They don't, really," Mark said, holding his own. "They do a lot of good, but they're unpredictable. We can't make them part of law enforcement policy, or any other city policy, really. Not unless they want to go through the police academy like every other cop." He smiled at his joke; Majors didn't.

"But that must make it impossible to implement long-term strategies," Majors said.

"We've had superhuman vigilantes in Commerce City for almost sixty years. We've managed to do okay. We try to work with them as much as possible. Citizens generally appreciate them, and any trouble we have can usually be handled within existing code and policies. You know about our Compensation Fund for Extraordinary Damages? What damages from vigilante activities private insurance won't cover, that does."

One of the developer suits—call him Third Monkey—butted in, wearing a grin. "You know, just last year some kid jumped me outside a bar on Ninth and tried to mug me. Block Buster Junior stopped him. Bounced right out of nowhere, knocked the guy off his feet, and next thing I know he's putting my wallet back in my hand. Like it was nothing. *Amazing.*"

Block Buster Junior usually teamed up with Senior, his father. Edward Crane, also junior and senior, though nobody else in the room knew that. Senior had been slowing down and appeared on the streets less frequently of late.

"Bruce here can do you one better," Chen from one of the law firms said. "You remember the elementary school fire twenty-five years or so ago?" Many in the room nodded, recalling the spectacular story. Bruce, the guy he was elbowing, another hot-shot lawyer, blushed and shook his head, but Chen kept pushing.

"There were like ten kids stuck on the roof," Chen said. "The Olympiad saved them, right? All four of them, tag teaming the way they did in the old days. Tell 'em, Bruce."

"I was one of the kids," Bruce said reluctantly. "Captain Olympus hauled me out of the fire himself."

He got a lot of admiring oohs and ahhs, pats on the back, requests for storytelling. Mark glanced at Celia, a sympathetic smile emphasizing the creases around his eyes.

The mayor was the one who blew her cover. "Ms. West here knows all about the Olympiad, don't you?" He beamed like he was showing off a golf trophy.

The others looked at her expectantly. Celia set her expression in stone. Edleston went on, blithely. "Warren and Suzanne West are her parents. She's married to Dr. Mentis." Warren and Suzanne, Captain Olympus and Spark, along with Dr. Mentis and the Bullet. The Olympiad. She'd long ago stopped trying to remind people that she and Arthur had never actually married. She had too many other battles to fight to waste her breath.

Most of them already knew who she was and remembered her past, at least in its broadest strokes. But a couple of them—the younger ones—didn't. They knew only the stories, not that she was a part of them. The out-of-towner—he narrowed his gaze, intrigued. *That* Celia West. She'd been facing that expression her whole life.

"What was that even *like*?" said a junior exec who'd been fetching coffee.

Celia's answer to that question had changed in the almost twenty years since the Olympiad was active. Since her father died. "It was an adventure," she said and left things at that.

She could count on Edleston to keep sticking his foot in it. "It's just not like it was in the old days," he said, sighing and shaking his head, a perfect expression of nostalgia. "The Olympiad zipping around, big battles against the Destructor raging all over the place. That was something else."

"I can't say I miss those days at all," Celia said.

The mayor shrugged. "I have to admit, I worry sometimes—what happens if someone like the Destructor comes along? Not just a high-powered bank robber, but someone who, I don't know, wants to take over, do some real damage? We have our vigilantes, but could they really stand up to something like the Destructor?"

"You want a team again," Danton Majors said. "Like the Olympiad."

"Well, sure. That'd be something, wouldn't it?" He might have been looking forward to the next football game between crosstown rivals.

Memories were short, Celia thought. To actually want those days back again was psychotic. "If someone like the Destructor ever did come along," she said, "I think we'd manage somehow."

Fortunately, the conversation moved on to more relevant topics, business cards were exchanged, people started drifting off. Before she could make her own escape, Majors called to her.

"I hope you don't think this is too forward of me, but I would like to shake your hand." He held his out, not giving her a chance to refuse. "I've heard so many stories about your parents. About the Olympiad. You were there through all of it, weren't you?"

"Only most of it," she said, wearing her polite mask. "Really, it was a long time ago. The torch has passed on."

"You're settling for other kinds of influence, I suppose," Majors said, glancing to take in the room and its players.

She shrugged with false innocence. "I'm just carrying on the family business."

"Your plan seems to have struck a chord. It's pretty radical, I take it." He nodded at the wall screen, where her urban renewal images were still on display. She'd planned that, too.

"Only if people weren't paying attention."

"I only have one question," he said. "What do *you* get out of it?"

One rarely heard the question asked so bluntly. The last thing most people ever said was exactly what they were thinking. Motivations in particular had to be squirreled away if they didn't conform to standard moral values. Of course Celia had an angle. Everyone assumed it, even if they didn't know what it was.

Which meant that Majors might or might not believe her answer when she said, "I get to live in a nice city."

Mark walked with her to the building's lobby. "My father always wanted me to go into politics. Looks like he finally got his wish." Mark's father had been the infamous Mayor Anthony Paulson, who in addition to serving two terms as mayor, was the city's last great supervillain, who'd attempted to literally blast the city into submission so he could then mold it to his will. Those plans must have looked so good on paper. Celia thought it just as well Mark hadn't followed in the man's footsteps.

"I'm sorry to put you through this," she said. "But it really helps having a friendly face in the crowd. Not to mention you have this air of respectability. You're the only one in the room who doesn't have imaginary fangs sticking out of his mouth."

"Thanks. I think. I just hope we can get something going soon. We needed a redevelopment plan ten years ago."

"How's it looking out there?"

"Edleston may be clueless, but he's a little bit right—without a powerful team of superhumans like the Olympiad on the streets, criminals are bolder. I know we've still got vigilantes working, but they can't protect the whole city. And the younger generation of crooks doesn't remember what it was like. Hell's Alley, the harbor district—they're getting worse. It feels like trying to hold back the tide with sandbags."

She knew the argument: superhuman vigilantes as deterrent. But she also knew a team that wasn't dominant could be worse than no team at all—see Teddy Donaldson's outing.

It was too early to tell if the kids would grow up to be any kind of deterrent.

"You have time to grab lunch?" Mark asked.

"No, I have to get back," she answered. "Get through the afternoon's pile of emergencies."

"Greasing those wheels?"

"More like fleeing the avalanche, some days."

He'd aged more than his almost fifty years warranted, his hair had gone salt and pepper, furrows lining the corners of his eyes. He worked too hard, even after an early near-miss heart attack scare slowed him down. He took the desk job, finally. He still worked too many hours, but at least he wasn't trying to chase down muggers anymore. He'd even found himself a serious girlfriend, a court clerk he'd met during a trial related to one of his cases. Celia and Arthur had been to dinner with them a couple of times.

But no kids. He'd had a vasectomy and ended relationships over the issue. He just couldn't be sure, he'd always explained. How could he ever be sure what his genes would pass on? She thought he was being overly cautious, but she couldn't blame him. His father may have been the Rogue Mayor, but his grandfather had been the Destructor himself. No matter how good a man Mark was, the shadows of his predecessors stood over him. She often wondered if he thought he had to make up for them. He probably looked into the mirror every day and wondered how much he looked like former mayor and archcriminal Anthony Paulson, or mad scientist and master villain Simon Sito. More alike than he wanted, probably.

Celia and Mark had dated, back in the day. Not for long, just a few months, which meant they hadn't accumulated so much baggage between them that they couldn't be friends after enough time and space had passed. He was one of the few people in her life who knew the secrets. Most of them, at least.

"Car picking you up?"

"No, taking cabs today," Celia said.

"Still keeping touch with the common folk?"

She rolled her eyes at him. "I've got Tom riding herd on the kids this week."

He laughed. "Poor girls! I hope it's nothing serious."

"They're teenagers. They're *acting* like teenagers. I don't know why I thought I'd somehow avoid this phase."

A twinge in her neck made her rub the muscle of her shoulder, and she sighed. She wanted to go home and take a nap. Not that she had time for a nap, but she might not have a choice.

"You okay?" Mark asked.

"Tired. That's all."

"Not like you haven't been busy or anything, arranging the fate of the city."

"You make it sound sinister."

"Well, if you put it like that, maybe."

It wasn't a very good joke. "I'll talk to you later, Mark."

"Take care, Celia." He waved her off and returned to the bowels of City Hall.

FOUR

Anna had planned for the night when she would have to sneak out of West Plaza without anyone finding out.

Teddy and the others convinced her that they needed to practice more if they were really going to do this. They'd practiced some already—they put together a "study group" with the five of them, made excuses to their parents, hid themselves in Teddy's backyard or other unobserved corners around school where they could test their powers without drawing attention or doing damage. But those sessions had always been in daylight, and they'd always, by necessity, been small. Unambitious. The others were getting restless. So now they were going big: gathering at City Park in the middle of the night, in costume, to finally let loose. Anna was sure they were all secretly hoping for the appearance of a swarm of muggers they could take down.

What all this meant was Anna finally had to try out her plan to get out of the building.

West Plaza had more security and surveillance than any other building in Commerce City, and that included the jail and the criminal wing of Elroy Asylum. Anna figured most of it was left over from the old days when her grandparents were the city's greatest superheroes, and the plaza was the headquarters of the Olympiad.

But the Olympiad had disbanded years ago, before Anna was born. As far as she knew, her parents had dismantled most of the equipment from then—but they'd kept the building's security up-to-date. Why, Anna couldn't say. She'd know it if they were doing some kind of vigilante gig and needed all that tech. They weren't, because they were always exactly where they said they were going to be, and that usually meant at work during the day and home at night. More likely, her mother was just that paranoid. That meant she watched the elevators, the entrances, the lobby, the corridors, and could track everyone coming and going not just from the penthouse but from the entire building. Which made sneaking out something of a challenge.

The building had dozens of standard, publicly marked exits, including emergency stairs—also under surveillance. Not that she could walk down West Plaza's hundred flights and still be good for anything by the time she reached the bottom. For weeks she'd studied building plans, blueprints, and superhero fan websites like Rooftop Watch that speculated about how the Olympiad used West Plaza to hide its headquarters. She'd worked up harebrained schemes to smuggle herself out in boxes, or to bribe the security staff that worked the front desk. She hadn't implemented any of them because they were pretty much all crazy. Best thing would be to use the study group excuse again and tell her parents she was going to the library, but she couldn't very well say she was going to go study with friends at midnight.

She refused to tell them what she was really doing. She didn't want them to know she had powers, and her mother was already too close to the truth with her guess—it *had* to have been a guess—about Teddy. Her mother, father, grandmother, everybody would try to pin some kind of legacy on her, and Anna didn't want that.

Besides, how disappointed would they be when they found out how little she could actually do with her so-called power?

Eventually, she'd discovered one of the Olympiad's old secret elevator chutes. It didn't lead to the penthouse, which might have been why her mother missed it. Instead, it ran along one of the staircases in the middle of the building and let out in the basement. It might have been a contingency, a way to traverse the building if the penthouse and headquarters had been compromised. It wasn't sealed up like the command room and other Olympiad elevators, and it didn't seem to have any cameras watching it. No alarm triggers.

At first, she'd been terrified to try it. The mechanism controlling the car was probably fried after going unused for so long. But no—it wasn't electrical. Another contingency, if power to the building was ever cut off. It ran on a kind of spring-loaded clockwork, with an automatic mechanical safety break. It couldn't fail. She experimented with it before climbing into the narrow, two-person car herself. Riveted steel, undecorated, with no-slip rubber matting on the floor. The rubber had dried out over time and was hard, cracked. She pressed the lever, pointed it down, and the car slid smoothly on its rails to the basement and a hidden door. One that wasn't covered by security cameras.

She still brought her cell phone, just in case she had to call for a rescue. But she didn't. She got out of the building just after midnight. Her phone didn't ring, and no one came after her. Mom and Dad were in their bedroom, probably asleep. Their presences glowed in her awareness, tugging at that sixth sense that was her power. If Mom had been in her office, Anna might not have risked sneaking out. But no one knew she'd left; she was safe. The others were already at the park, so she had to rush. She took the last bus to travel the few blocks to City Park; Sam had a car and could take everyone back home.

The bus stopped at the corner, and the driver looked

at her funny when she got off. Girl in the park at midnight—yeah, what did he think she was going to do? Tugging her knit cap more firmly over her ears and wrapping her coat around her, she made her way along a jogging trail to the center of the park.

City Park was supposed to be dangerous at night, people had been telling her that her whole life. That was half the reason they wanted to practice here in the first place, not just because it was wide open and unpopulated, but because they had a chance of actually *seeing* crime. Maybe they could stop it. Or *try* to stop it, rather.

Teddy and Lew were already at it. Lew had a paintball gun, and Teddy, in full costume, or what currently passed as his full costume—sweats, T-shirt, a bandana with eyeholes cut into it over the top half of his face—was letting Lew hit him, paint spattering in flower patterns all over him. Then going invisible. The hits looked like they hurt. Lew wore a blue cloth mask tied around his eyes, making him look more like a pirate than a superhuman vigilante.

Wearing a matching blue mask, Teia was sitting, along with Sam, on a bench under a maple tree, watching, looking bored. Anna joined them, and they scooted over to make room for her. Teia was a shadow under the tree, dark skin and dark clothes. Sam had his arms crossed and he smirked. A tanned white guy, he wore a bandana mask like Teddy and a red leather jacket as his costume. A pretty slick look, she had to admit. He was only sixteen, but he was the strongest of the bunch, the only one with any kind of training, even if that meant tae kwon do classes that he stopped taking when he was thirteen. He had muscled shoulders and an athletic, physical presence. He fidgeted a lot. Sometimes he'd snap his fingers absently and throw sparks off his skin.

They were badass, which seemed to be the point for them, mostly. To her, this all still felt like playing house.

None of this felt real. That was why Teddy went out the other night, to finally try to do this for real. They'd talked about it long enough. And she understood how they all felt, she really did. But they weren't ready.

"It's sort of entertaining," she observed finally.

"If you like watching grass grow," Teia said. She called out, "Hey Teddy, the whole point is if you're invisible, you won't get hit."

Anna said, "Use the code names, someone might hear us. There's no point in wearing masks if we don't use the code names."

Teia—Lady Snow, rather—rolled her eyes. "Fine. Hey, Ghost—how about you try *not* getting hit?"

Teddy paused, huffing for breath. "But I need to learn to stay invisible. To fight through the pain." He pumped a fist.

Smack, another of Lew's paintballs slammed into him. Teddy's face twisted as he cringed, right before he went invisible, and reappeared twenty feet over a couple seconds later.

Anna shook her head. Guy was a freaking masochist. "If the school nurse flipped out at your last set of bruises, she's going to love this."

Sam called out, "I thought you were supposed to freaking phase out before you get hit."

"I'm *trying,* it just happens too fast! You guys are so smart, why don't you get out here and try not to get hit!"

If the paintballs were too fast for him to let them pass through his phased-out body, bullets would definitely be too fast.

"Ghost, you'd better run!" Lew raised the paintball gun again. The sadist to go with the masochist, evidently. They had about half an hour before the cops showed up, Anna guessed. When Teddy tried hiding behind a tree, Lew held up a hand, and a fierce gust of tightly focused wind shoved him back in the open. Lew called himself

Stormbringer. This time, Teddy turned invisible, and Lew's next paintball shot missed.

"You are *not* getting into my car with all that mess on you," Sam, code name Blaster, stated.

"Don't worry, I'll change," Teddy called between shots.

The two of them seemed to be making this way more difficult than it really needed to be.

"He's making me dizzy," Anna said, watching Teddy flicker in and out of visibility.

"I keep telling you, it's either this or go patrolling for real," Teia said. They bent their heads together in a conference.

"We're not ready," Anna declared.

Teia didn't argue about that. "So how did your grandparents get started? How much did they practice before they started?"

"I'm not really sure. The biographies kind of gloss over that part."

"You don't talk to your grandma about it at all?" Teia said, disbelieving. She shouldn't have been surprised. Teia had spent enough time with Anna's family, she knew that *nobody* talked about it. Suzanne West had gotten rid of her skin-suit uniform twenty years ago and never looked back. These days, she used her power of heat and flame mostly to cook.

"It's not that easy, okay? The minute I start talking about it, they'll know something's up, and I'll either have to tell them what we've been doing or figure out how to lie about it to my dad."

"Ugh. Yeah, that would be a problem."

They all understood the need for secrecy, and not just because of tradition. If nothing else, they needed to keep their parents from grounding them until graduation.

The next time Teddy turned visible, Sam cracked his knuckles and flung an arm toward him, pointing with flat fingers. Searing red lights shot out from the gesture, snapping through the air, leaving a trail of steam behind. The laser bolts hit Teddy, popping into his back, knocking him over. Sam had used low-intensity beams this time. They'd sting a little, not burn through, though Sam could do that, too, if he wanted. During one of the small-scale practices, Sam had burned through a steel garbage can in an alley. It had taken awhile, but he'd done it.

"*That's* what I'm talking about," Sam said, grinning. Sam could be a bully sometimes.

Teddy cried out in shock and fell, and though he stumbled back to his feet quickly enough, he'd lost his focus and remained visible. He turned on Sam. "Hey! What the hell?"

Sam laughed. "I'm just helping out. Doesn't do any good when you *know* Lew's going to hit you. You need the element of surprise."

"Code names," Anna muttered futilely.

A determined frown settled on Teddy's features, and he clenched his hands at his sides. Anna knew what came next, and sure enough, he vanished, and the scratching of running footsteps on the gravel path followed. Sam stood and ran, but that didn't stop invisible Teddy from tackling him. From the outside, it looked as if Sam spasmed, leaping a few inches and then smashing into the ground. He writhed, hitting and punching, yelling. A few red bolts flashed from his hands, scattering wildly. Anna, Teia, and Lew scurried behind the tree trunk for shelter.

Sam managed to grab Teddy's hand the next time Teddy threw a punch, which was the major drawback for an invisible guy trying to fight hand to hand. Anna kept trying to convince him of that, and he kept not listening. The two were locked together now, trying to hit each other one-handed.

Anna moved out from behind the tree and cupped her

hands around her mouth. "Ghost, now's when you're supposed to phase out!"

There came a grunt of effort, and suddenly Sam was batting at air, his quarry slipped out of his grasp. He sat up and stared at his hands. "Okay, that was weird."

He fell over, shoved aside by the figure of Teddy, who was once against flashing in and out of visibility like the image on a broken TV. Sam hollered and fired another bolt, which slammed into a tree trunk and left it smoking. Just what they needed, to set the whole park on fire.

"Would you guys stop it!" she shouted, but it didn't help. They kept wrestling, Sam lunging back at Teddy, who wasn't invisible and who forgot to phase out again. Maybe because he was amazed it had worked. It was almost funny. They crashed to the ground, landing punches on each other.

Thunder cracked, and the temperature dropped enough to make Anna hug herself and shiver. Frost gathered on grass, and on Sam's hair and clothing. Sam stopped fighting, and footsteps shuffled away from him as Teddy backed off.

"Teia!" Sam called, jumping up, rubbing his arms. "Lady Snow!"

Teia knelt, hand on the ground, where a fan of frost now grew. Smiling, she blew across her fingers, raising a cluster of ice crystals that dispersed in a fog. Lew laughed. The thunder had been Lew's—Stormbringer's. The Arctic Twins, Anna called them sometimes, but they didn't approve. Anna wondered if both their powers were weather related because they were twins, and she wondered if anyone else in their family had weather-related powers. They insisted their parents didn't have any powers at all, and they were probably right. Their father had died when they were nine. Anna remembered him as a big, amiable man. Their mother didn't seem like the su-perheroing type.

Anna's mother probably knew for sure.

"You guys need to grow up," Teia said.

"You need to take this seriously," Teddy's disembodied voice answered.

Teia said, "How much more practice do we need? Ted-dy's gone out already and did fine. We need to *do* some-thing."

"He didn't do fine, he got the crap beat out of him," Anna said.

"Only half beat," Teddy said defensively. "Any fight you can walk away from . . ."

Anna grumbled.

"It's simple," Teia said. "We go out, find a way to prove ourselves, and do it. The crime rate in this city is terrible, and everyone keeps saying we need a new superhero team, and here we are."

Lew hefted the paintball gun like it meant something. "And if we're really smart, we call the papers first so they can cover the story."

"That's your worst idea yet," Anna said. But Teia would side with her brother, along with Sam. Stalemate.

Teia said, "Anna, the five of us together? We're power-ful. Even more powerful than the Block Busters. We can *do* this." Everyone agreed that the Block Busters hardly counted as a crime-fighting team because they hardly went out together anymore.

But Anna wasn't powerful. If she was honest, she was scared. She couldn't defend herself, she couldn't stop anyone. Most of the time she couldn't prove that she had a power at all. And they all knew it.

"Then why don't you go do it?" Anna said, tired. She hugged herself, trying to melt away the last of Teia's frost, but her arms were still covered in goosebumps.

"She's just chicken," Sam sneered.

Teia was the one who jumped in with, "Sam, shut up, you don't know anything about it. She's not afraid. She just wants us to do this *her* way." She turned to Anna, eyebrow lifted. "Right?"

"I'm just saying we have to be careful," she said, knowing she was losing this fight.

Teia's thin mask across her eyes didn't do much to hide her identity, and if Anna were that pretty she wouldn't either. She was sixteen, striking, and she knew how to stand—hands on hips, shoulders back—to look particularly heroic. "I say we announce ourselves, stage some events, get some publicity—"

Anna said, "You can't do that. My mother is watching us. She ID'd Teddy off one security tape. We have to be sure we can stay secret—"

"Why?" Teia said.

Anna had taken it for granted and resented having to explain it yet again. "Because that's how they get you. It's how they got to my mother, back in the day." The argument felt stale, she'd said it so many times. As soon as her grandparents' secret identity had been revealed— that Captain Olympus and Spark were actually socialites Warren and Suzanne West—Celia became a target. She'd been kidnapped a dozen times after that. Even the Destructor had kidnapped her, leading to the whole sordid mess that happened after that. No, you had to keep the secret so they couldn't find you.

Teia disagreed. She crossed her arms and glared.

Anna soldiered on. "You don't go vigilante for the publicity, you do it because it's the right thing to do. Because you can help people, save lives—"

"*And* for the publicity," Lew added, a roguish glint in his eyes.

She just couldn't win, could she?

Teddy pointed. "You should listen to Anna, she knows what she's talking about better than anyone."

"Because of her famous grandparents?" Sam shot back. "Because of her dad? They haven't done anything in forever. Maybe if you could knock down walls I'd be more inclined to listen to you."

The bad arguments tended to come back to that. The others had flashy abilities, powers you could see, that could actually do something. Powers that looked good on camera. Hers, not so much. When she tried to explain to them how useful her power really was—who was going to be the one to track them down if they ever got in trouble, after all?—she sounded lame and whiney.

And in the end, Teia was right. All of Anna's credibility rested on her family name, and what did that really mean in the end? She couldn't defend herself.

"I'm right," Anna said. "Give it time, you'll see that I'm right."

"And I say we won't know until we get out there and *do* something," Teia replied, pointing into the vague darkness of the city.

They had arrayed themselves—Teia, Lew, and Sam on one side, Teddy and Anna on the other. They'd all settled on their places in the argument, and nobody was going to change anyone else's mind.

"So much for teamwork," Anna muttered and walked away.

"Anna—" Teddy called after her.

"See, that's what I'm talking about," she said, turning on him. "We can't even remember to call each other by our code names. How are we supposed to keep our identities secret?"

"I'm sorry, I forgot—Rose, wait a minute."

Her code name was Compass Rose. It had seemed so clever a few months ago when she came up with it. "Just give me a minute," she said and kept walking. Teddy didn't follow.

She needed to think—by herself, before anyone could say anything more awful.

What she really needed to do was figure out if this was all worth it. Of course it was worth it, she told herself, as she always told herself. Otherwise their powers were nothing more than circus tricks. The powers had been more than that to her grandparents.

She wandered to the fountain, almost by habit. It was the park's main gathering point. This late, the park was quiet. The sky overhead seemed heavy, and the trees surrounding the fountain's wide plaza were still. The setting was right for having a long serious think, but she wasn't sure that was a good thing.

She'd planned on spending a few minutes sitting here at the fountain, with its graceful, stylized lily spouts, shut off and quiet for the night, the water in the marble pool still, until the argument had been forgotten and they were ready to go home. But someone was already there.

The man crouched on the rim of the fountain, perched like a cat who'd casually leapt there and might casually leap off again at any moment. He wore a dark green skin suit that showed off a lean body with well-defined muscles. His rigid helmet-type mask hid his appearance and made guessing his age difficult. He was older than she was, but he didn't seem *old*.

"Who are you?" she asked, trying to sound suave and confident rather than worried. In truth, she felt a touch of panic. They'd expected to find muggers in the park, not a strange vigilante.

The guy didn't seem at all worried. In fact, he donned the hint of a smile. "I'm Eliot."

Like this was some kind of normal introduction and they weren't both wearing masks.

"That's it? No superhero name?"

"Not yet." His expression turned chagrined. "Having trouble deciding on one."

"Have you been watching us? Following us?" Wouldn't it figure, all they'd done was practice and someone had already found them out.

"I saw the flash and came to check it out. That's all. Don't worry."

Blaster's bolt, the flames on the tree. So much for being subtle. She gave a sigh and couldn't find the motivation to stay angry. The guy was just being polite.

"It's kind of embarrassing. We don't know what the hell we're doing."

"I'm sure you'll figure it out."

This guy seemed to have it down pat. His uniform was slick. "So. You new in town or just getting started?"

"I'm—"

"Hey, Rose, what are you—" Teddy came trotting up from the jogging trail and stopped to stare at the man on the fountain. "Whoa. Who's that?"

The man twitched but remained in place. Nervous, despite his calm manner. He almost ran, but didn't.

"It's okay, we're just having a talk," Anna said.

"Yeah. Okay. But Sa—Blaster's ready to take off. We gotta go."

"Give me a sec."

He regarded her, uncertain.

"I'll be fine. I'll scream if I'm not. Then you can practice rescuing me, right?"

Her confidence was possibly not well founded, but Teddy backed away and left her alone with the guy. She was sure he hadn't gone far.

"Rose?" the man asked. "That's not your real name, is it?"

"I'm Compass Rose," she said. She felt ridiculous, but she stood tall, refusing to let it show.

"Your superhero name."

"That's right."

"What's your power, then? Perfect sense of direction?"

She blushed, because it was hard to explain, and compared to people like Teddy or Sam, hers wasn't a real power anyway. "I find people. I know where they are."

"That's handy."

"Sometimes." Her sour expression told otherwise. Her power worked only on people she knew well, friends and family. But she didn't have to tell him that.

A car horn honked half a block over, where Sam had parked. "I have to go. See you around?"

"Probably."

"Okay—" She'd been about to say good-bye when he jumped, straight up, muscles in his thighs rippling as they launched him a hundred or more feet into the air. He didn't fly but sailed over an arc that would carry him to the other side of the park.

Hell of a power.

"He's gonna get pissed off when the blogs start calling him Frogman," she murmured.

She'd been fourteen years old when her power awakened. The books and biographies about superhumans and their powers said they often manifested at puberty. It had for her grandmother and father. Anna had started to assume she wouldn't get powers at all, like her mother. But she woke up one morning, and her brain ached. Aspirin didn't help. It was like her entire mind cramped—she'd had her first period the year before, and this felt like that, only in her head instead of her gut. Then she seemed to *fill up*. Her mind expanded, taking on an extra sense. Because of who she was, who her family was, she'd known exactly what was happening. Her awakening power was probably mental, like her father's. Was she developing telepathy? Telekinesis? Clairvoyance?

But no, after a couple of months of testing, trying, and

thinking way too hard, the cramps settled, the extra sense lodging firmly in her hindbrain. Her mind felt full, but the information was limited. Shortly after the cramps faded, she came home from school, started for her mother's office like she always did after school, and realized before she got there that Mom wasn't there. She was in a meeting at the West Corp offices ten floors down. It felt like a light in her mind, bright as a flashlight turned on in a dark room. And her father was in his office, and her grandmother was in the lobby, coming home from a lunch outing. Without calling, without checking, she just *knew*. Their presences were glowing spots in her mind. She was a human radar. A homing device.

She didn't tell anyone. She didn't want to have to explain it, and she didn't want to hear what they'd have to say about it. Time passed, she grew firmly into adolescence, and her family stopped watching for what power she'd develop. She began to move furtively through the world, because she didn't want anyone to guess.

Her power—any power—had to be good for something, she'd thought then. She still thought. Otherwise, why have power at all? She just had to figure out how to use hers.

And then her best friend, Teia, came to her with a secret, and Anna began to hope.

Teddy and Sam had another argument about getting paint all over the inside of his car, until Teddy finally stripped to his boxers and stuffed his outfit and Lew's paintball gun into a couple of grocery bags and put them in the trunk. Teddy sat in the front seat, arms crossed, pretending he wasn't shivering. Blushing red the whole time, with Anna trying not to stare at the curve of his bare shoulders. The three of them piled into the backseat, practically in each other's laps. She thought about offering to sit in Teddy's lap to warm him up, but that would embarrass them both, and they'd all had enough embarrassment for one night.

Fortunately the drive wasn't too long.

"Who was that guy?" Teddy finally said. They'd all seen the stranger make that epic leap out of the park.

"I don't know."

"Was he checking us out?" Teia asked.

"Probably," Anna said.

"You think he goes to Elmwood?" she asked.

"No, he's older than that. Maybe he goes to the university."

"So much for being careful," Teddy grumbled.

"He wouldn't have stuck around to talk to me if he was planning on giving us away," Anna said.

Sam looked at her in the rearview mirror. "You sure he's a good guy?"

"I don't think he's a bad guy."

"I don't like it," Teddy said. "Guy's sneaky."

"Maybe you should give him a break until we know more."

"You think he's hot, don't you," Lew said, grinning.

Teia turned to her, disrupting their precarious seating arrangement. "Is he? Hot, I mean?"

"I don't know, he was wearing a mask. Don't worry, if he blows our cover, I can track him down and blow his."

Teddy craned around to look in the back. "Can you do that?"

"Sure," she said, but she didn't know if she could. She'd never purposefully looked for someone she'd met only once. She hadn't even seen his face. But he'd told her his name. It was a start.

"Well, no worries, then," Sam said.

The route took them past West Plaza first.

Anna told him, "Sam, don't go to the front of the building, pull around back."

They said *good-bye*s and *see you at schools,* Teia leaned over to give her a hug, and she clambered out while a reorganization went on around her. From the sidewalk, she watched Sam's sedan drive away. Teddy waved at her through the window.

The secret elevator took about twice as long to work its way back up to the penthouse than it did to glide down. Thank you, gravity. On the way up, the thing creaked, and Anna could feel each tooth of each gear catch stiffly in its sprocket as the old mechanism cranked on. She was sure she'd get stuck, but she didn't, and finally she was in the stairwell, through the door to the real elevator, then up to the penthouse, and back home.

The only complication: Her hindbrain sense located her father in the kitchen, not the bedroom. He was waiting up for her, and the only way to sneak into the penthouse was to walk right past him. Her first option: hide somewhere. Don't go home at all. He couldn't wait up forever, and as soon as he gave up, she could sneak in and pretend like nothing had happened. Except that her father wouldn't give up, and he already knew she was here, dithering. He could feel it.

Second option: walk in and face him. To do anything else would delay the inevitable. Fine, then.

She let herself in. The place was dark except for the faint circles from a couple of night-lights in the kitchen and hallway. Enough to find her way to her bedroom, and she didn't make a sound on the carpet. But the moment she crossed the kitchen, the lights came on. Her father was standing next to the light switch. She wasn't surprised.

"You're out rather late," he said, his English accent coming through strong. He did that for effect, when he wanted to intimidate. He wore a button-up shirt tucked into his trousers. He'd dressed for the occasion. Smiling wryly, he leaned against the wall.

Her heart pounded, but she forced her mind to stillness. Don't think of anything, or if she couldn't go blank, think of the beige carpet or green grass, anything but what was actually at the front of her mind. Shove it far back, bury it, and maybe he couldn't see it. She certainly couldn't let her thoughts run wild, flailing, where he could read them on the surface without even trying. She'd had a lot of practice at this but couldn't guess how successful she was. Arthur Mentis, the Olympiad's telepath, never let on what he did or didn't know.

She had to assume he knew everything. But just in case he didn't . . .

She hated it. She could never stop paying attention around him, which often made her want to avoid him. Which wasn't fair. He was her dad, she didn't want to avoid him. But she didn't want to tell him anything, either.

Nobody else in the world had this problem.

"Hi," she said. "Um. Can I go to bed now? I'm kind of tired."

"I imagine you are. Aren't you supposed to be grounded?"

"Um." He waited. "Yeah."

"I'm sure you had a very good reason for being out and about in the middle of the night."

"Um . . ." She tried to think about school, homework, the library. Maybe he'd think she'd been out studying. That was a good reason, right? As if he'd actually believe she was studying. There was no point in saying anything when he'd know she was lying, so she kept her mouth shut.

"Can you at least tell me how you managed to sneak out of the building without alerting security?"

"Why do you even bother asking? You already know."

"As a courtesy."

She swallowed. "I don't want to talk about it."

"Fair enough."

God, he just stared at her, as if he could split her open by looking. And if she stood there long enough, with him hovering over her, she might spill it all. She inched away from him, down the hallway, hoping he'd just let her go.

He said, "Anna. There's no shame in asking for help. Or advice. Or for anything at all, really. We're here for you."

She choked up a little on that but fiercely shut down the emotion, not thinking or feeling anything at all. "I know. I'm okay. Really."

"I know you are, sweetheart. But nothing will stop us from worrying."

"Good night, Dad."

"All right. Sleep well."

She scurried down the hall and to her bedroom, relieved. That could have gone so much worse. At least he hadn't gotten her mother involved.

FIVE

Arthur came back to bed around three in the morning. Celia was waiting up for him.

"Well?" she asked, as he closed the door and began unbuttoning his shirt in the glow of the lamp on the nightstand.

"That girl has so much on her mind I can hardly make sense of it all. Poor thing."

"But she's okay, she's not hurt or in trouble?" She had reconciled herself to not learning the details. But she wanted reassurance. A basic, simple yes or no. Was it so hard?

"She's fine, for now. But she's determined to have this secret life of hers." Tension in his mouth, around his eyes, showed through his habitual calm. His anxiety made her even more anxious.

Celia rubbed her face. She was exhausted, but there was no way she could sleep while worrying about Anna.

"If you tell me she's okay, not doing drugs or working at a strip club or anything, I'll trust you. But I really wish you'd pry, just this once."

"It wouldn't be just once, that's the problem." He finished undressing, switched off the light, and climbed into bed with her. His skin was chilled, and she shivered at his touch. They hunkered under the covers together to warm up, and he wrapped his arms around her. Only then did Celia start to relax. "She found one of the old Olympiad escape elevators and got it working. That's how she got out of the building. May I recommend *not* sealing it up, at least not right away?"

"Because if we know where she is we can keep an eye on her. Yes, I know. At least let me put a camera in there."

"If I may be so rude as to point it out, this was what you wanted: You wanted the children to find each other and help each other learn to use their powers. If they're taking the effort farther than you're comfortable with, you can't complain."

"I just wish she'd *talk* to us. She's never shown any sign of having powers—what could she possibly be doing?"

"You should ask yourself if you really want to know," he said, chuckling. "I'm sure it would appall us."

"I always hoped she wouldn't have powers. That she'd have a nice, boring life."

"I don't think she wants a boring life, love. At least she hasn't roped Bethy into things. At least not yet."

Bethy was the sensible one, except she worried too much. Maybe superpowers made people crazy. Celia wouldn't know. "Can you tell me that everything's going to be all right?"

"Everything's going to be all right," he said dutifully, with that sinister, studious look in his eyes. Even Arthur had this weird, mad look to him sometimes, when he knew something that the rest of the world didn't.

"You're lying."

"You didn't even have to be telepathic to know that," he said, kissing her forehead.

The next day, Celia had her weekly lunch date with Analise Baker. No matter how busy she got, she couldn't miss this.

Their preferred spot was a downtown diner. As usual, Analise had gotten there first and claimed a table in back. She stood, arms open, to greet Celia with a hug. The brown-skinned woman was tall and had filled out some in her middle age, but the extra roundness made her seem even more statuesque and impressive.

She hugged the woman hard, and Analise laughed. They'd been friends for half their lives. Celia didn't have many friends from her early days. Burned too many bridges back then. But Analise was still around.

"What's the news?" Analise asked, after they ordered their salads.

Celia could feel the war-weary, startled look in her eyes. "I have teenage daughters, how about you?"

"Twins, Celia. You will never one-up me." Analise pointed with her fork. "But tell me the dirt anyway."

Celia tore a corner off her paper napkin and mangled it while the wheels in her mind turned. The impulse to keep secrets was strong. But few people would understand like the woman sitting across the table would.

"I think Anna has powers, but she won't talk about it. She won't tell anyone."

Analise was quiet a moment, her expression still, like she hadn't heard. Finally she said, "She setting pillows on fire or what?"

If only it were that obvious. Then she could sit Anna down and wheedle it out of her. Turned out this was worse than the birds-and-bees talk. That had been easy compared to simultaneously wanting to treat Anna like an adult while learning all her secrets. Celia shook her head. "I think she takes after Arthur. Some kind of mental power, something nobody would know about unless she said something. I just don't know how to get her to talk."

"You ought to bug the girls' restroom at Elmwood if you want to find out their secrets."

Celia had considered it but ran into Arthur's perpetual problem: How much did she really want to know? "This too shall pass, right? Arthur won't pry, and he's right not to, but anything he's learned by accident he won't talk about until Anna talks. That's the right call, too, I'm sure. He says she's fine, but . . ."

Analise sat back in the booth and smiled. "But it's totally outside your control, and that drives you nuts."

This was why she and Analise had been having lunch almost every week for two decades. "Bingo."

"If it's any consolation, I'm sure my kids are up to something, too. Creeping around like spies, not saying a word they don't have to."

"Powers?" Celia questioned, even though she already knew the answer.

"Probably. But it's the same problem you have with Anna—if they've got powers, why won't they just tell me?"

Celia picked at the lettuce on her plate and smiled. "Because they don't know who you are—were—and they don't think you'll understand. Because they have to protect their secret identities if they're going to go fight crime."

Analise looked at her as if the concept had never occurred to her, which had to be a supreme case of cognitive dissonance. Then she slumped. "Oh, God, I hope not."

Back in the day, Analise had been Typhoon. She hadn't worn her costume or used her powers since she'd accidentally killed a cop with a flood of water through the streets downtown. Guilt had shut her down. Celia constantly wanted to ask if she'd tried using her powers since then, if she ever hoped that she would get them back. But Celia didn't have the courage to open that old wound.

"I'd hoped whatever it was that got me would pass them over. Like it did you, you know? I figured you were proof that I couldn't pass my powers on to my kids."

"Yeah, I know."

"I just—" Analise leaned her elbow on the table, her brow furrowed. She worked hard to appear calm and in control, but this worried her. "They'd better not do anything to lose their scholarships. I don't know how they managed to swing them in the first place, but they'd better not screw it up. It's too big a chance for them."

They wouldn't lose their scholarships to Elmwood Academy, not unless they did something to get kicked out of the school entirely. Celia had given them their scholarships anonymously, through a charity that assisted the children of firefighters who'd been killed in the line of duty, as Analise's husband had been.

"They'll be fine," Celia said. "They're good kids." Because that was what you said to your best friend about her offspring.

Analise shook the thought away. "Whatever's going to happen is going to happen, whether we like it or not."

The conversation turned to other topics, *normal* topics, like jobs, politics, school schedules, and the tragedy of aging.

Analise seemed happy, Celia reflected. But as she often did, her expression held a sadness. A resignation. Such mundane domesticity was not where the original trajectory of her life had aimed her. As a young woman, she'd never planned on being the widowed mother of twins.

Once again, Celia was on the verge of asking. Pushing her water glass forward, casually suggesting that Analise try to spill it with only her mind.

"You are thinking deep thoughts, my friend," the woman said finally.

Celia smiled. "Oh, not so much. Just the usual."

"You might think about taking a vacation," Analise said. "We haven't all gone to the beach house since the kids started middle school, and you're looking tired."

"I can't look any more tired than I normally do."

"Yeah, you do, actually."

Great. Just what she needed, to start looking like crap

as well as feeling like crap. "I'll see what I can do. I keep thinking maybe once the kids are out of school."

"That's years away. Go on vacation and take them with you. You used to be able to manage a trip every summer."

"I'll think about it."

They could all make the trip together. Sit around stewing about why their kids wouldn't talk to them, and didn't that sound like fun? Still, it was nice to know she wasn't the only one who worried.

Didn't a vacation sound lovely? Someday soon, she promised herself.

The city planning committee initiative, and her determination to make sure West Corp's bid was the one the committee picked, was the culmination of some five years of work, of reviewing civil engineering surveys, ordering a dozen or so studies of population and community patterns, making countless projections of all possible plans and outcomes to find the one that didn't just work, that didn't just make money, but that made Commerce City *better*. This drive, this loyalty to the city, wasn't entirely hers, Celia knew that. She worked for this plan for the same reason her parents had donned skin suits and battled villains for most of her childhood: It was in the blood. The powers written into their DNA had to be used for the protection of the city. She didn't have powers, but ultimately she had that need. She didn't argue with it.

The city had a process for getting things done, and she was adept at operating in its bureaucracies to make her plans work. She wasn't worried that the West Corp proposal would lose out. But the arrival of Danton Majors was a variable she hadn't expected. The most prominent outside participant in this dance, of unknown reach and resources, he made her nervous, and she wanted to know more.

She searched online databases and news services for every reference she could find on Danton Majors. A native of Delta, comparable to Commerce City in population and resources, but inland. Proud citizen, et cetera. The articles she found were mostly shiny puff pieces in financial publications, extolling his genius and virtues. She read between the lines, decided he'd had a couple of lucky breaks but had parlayed that luck into a substantial business. Publicly, he did what self-made men usually did with their money: attended society functions, patronized the right charities. He was married—twenty-two years, impressive—had two college-age kids, though his family stayed out of the public eye. The man was careful with his image.

She'd have to dig somewhere else to find any dirt on him, so she called a contact at the *Commerce Eye*. Over the years, the onetime tabloid rag had turned respectable by scooping its rival, the *Banner,* on a string of big stories. In the meantime, the *Banner* had gone stodgy and eventually folded.

"Hello, Mary? It's Celia West. I need a favor."

She could almost hear the reporter sputtering on the other end of the line. Celia had done her a few favors over the last couple of years—an exclusive interview, some on-the-record quotes about West Corp, and even a statement for a memorial retrospective about her father. Mary Danforth owed her big-time but probably never thought Celia would actually call her on it.

Mary managed to recover some kind of enthusiastic demeanor. "Certainly, Celia, whatever I can do to help."

"Have you ever heard of a guy named Danton Majors? From Delta, rich real estate tycoon, he's in town for that city planning meeting. You have anything unofficial on him?"

She hesitated. "You know, that's funny."

"What's funny?"

"Well . . ." The reporter didn't want to tell her.

"Out with it, Mary. It's no big deal. If he's going to bid on the development initiative, I just want to know more about him."

"The thing is, I spoke with Majors a day or so ago. He was asking me for information about you."

That wasn't a shock. Guy was smart, covered his bases. "What did you tell him?"

"That's just it. I started to tell him all about West Corp—nothing serious, you know, just all the public record stuff. I mean, that's all I really know."

"But?"

"He wanted to know about the Olympiad and whether or not you had powers."

"I don't have powers, everyone knows that."

"Yeah, but . . . he seemed to think that maybe you'd hidden it. I told him that was silly. You've publicly distanced yourself from superhuman vigilantes your whole life. And you know what he said?"

"That the very fact I've distanced myself suggests I'm hiding something."

"Uh, yeah, that's pretty much it. Celia, I have to tell you, and my instincts are pretty good on this sort of thing—I started wondering if he's got his sights on you. From a business perspective, I mean."

"Wouldn't be the first time that's happened. Thanks a lot, Mary. I owe you one."

"Then how about giving me an early look at your annual report for last year?"

"We'll talk. Later." She said farewell and hung up before Mary could do any more cajoling.

The message light on her phone was flashing, and she picked up the line. "Celia, it's Mark. I'm sending you a file. Let me know what you think."

She checked the encrypted e-mail account she and Mark had set up for this sort of thing.

This new video came from a traffic camera. In color this time, a little better quality, but still no sound. Didn't matter, because there wasn't much to the clip anyway. The scene showed a deserted intersection, half an hour after midnight. She double-checked the location—near City Park. She knew the place.

A figure darted into the frame—straight down into the frame. A flyer, then? No—he descended at speed, landed in the middle of the intersection, absorbing the shock of impact in his knees, ending in a crouch. Straightening, he looked around, then gathered himself, pulling his arms close, bunching his legs. He launched himself into an epic leap that took him once again out of the frame of the camera, straight up. Not a flyer but a jumper. Celia was impressed in spite of herself.

She isolated a frame of film that gave the best view of his figure and features. He had a confidence in his movements that pinned him as just a bit older than teenager. He was lean and muscular and had a determined set to his angular jaw, the thin frown that jutted out under his helmetlike mask. He had a good-looking outfit, a green skin suit that showed off his physique, as was tradition, and that slick helmet. He'd put some thought into this, even if he hadn't gotten a whole lot of publicity out of it. Yet.

But something about him wasn't right. She took out her list of the Leyden Lab employees, the points of origin for them all. Studied the names, though by this time she had most of them memorized. She knew them all, and that was what bothered her. This new guy wasn't the right age. Justin Raylen's and Ed Crane Jr.'s kids were elementary school age; next oldest came the slew of them currently in middle and high school. The few descendants who hit in between that younger generation and her own hadn't shown any sign of powers. Everyone older than Arthur was retired.

This guy didn't match anyone on her list.

Which was impossible, or should have been impossible. She'd spent hundreds of hours and almost twenty years tracking down every single descendant of every single person who had been present in Leyden Laboratories when Simon Sito's experiment failed. Every single person who had even a hint of potential. She'd pulled strings and broken laws to get access to adoption records, to track down secret affairs and illegitimate children. Every time a new superhero appeared, she'd been able to trace them back to one of these families, and she'd learned the secret identity of every superhuman who'd ever gone vigilante in Commerce City. She *knew*.

Except for this guy.

Her hands felt cold as she picked up the phone handset and called the precinct. Once she got past the gate keepers, Mark answered. "Captain Paulson."

"Hi, Mark, it's Celia. I just watched that clip you sent over."

"And?" He sounded so eager.

She shook her head, an unconscious show of confusion. "And I don't know who he is."

SIX

Anna and Bethy had been friends with Teia and Lew Fletcher since forever, because their mothers had been friends since forever. They'd spent a lot of time on the same playgrounds, and the two families had even taken a few beach vacations together when they were little. Anna hadn't been aware of a lot of the dynamic when she was younger, but now she realized that her family, the rich family, had paid for the beach house, and there'd been a lot of mostly good-natured arguments between the adults about pulling their weight and being too generous to the point of charity. At the time, all she cared about was the fun they had. Teia and Lew's mom had taught them all how to swim, which was great, but she spent a lot of the vacations sitting on the beach looking out at the water, kind of wistful and sad. Teia said something bad had happened to her mother in the far-gone past, something that she never talked about, and Anna wondered if it had something to do with the ocean. Or if it was just the hypnotic waves sweeping in and out that could make anyone melancholy.

Then Teia and Lew's father died. They'd taken one more beach vacation after that, which hadn't been the same at all, because they kept tiptoeing around the empty space where Morgan Fletcher should have been. After that came middle school, and they all got too busy, or that was what they all kept saying.

Lew had been the first of them to discover his powers.

He might have had them since he was born, but who would notice if a brief thundershower happened every time a baby was cranky? It would be coincidence and slide by without comment. But in sixth grade, when a major storm causing flash flooding happened in exactly the Fletchers' neighborhood—and only there—on the day of a test that Lew hadn't studied for, he realized it wasn't a coincidence. It was him. He told his sister because he told her everything, and Teia told Anna, because Anna's family was filled with superhumans and she would know what to do about it. The only advice Anna could think of to give: Keep it secret. Practice controlling it, but keep it secret. Avoid attention and publicity. Attention had gotten them, especially her mother, in trouble.

As if determined to keep her twin from showing her up, Teia learned to freeze with a touch soon after. She described it as a "popping" sensation—one day, she just knew she could do it, like a lock had broken and released her power. From then on, her sodas were always cold.

After that, Anna began to suspect that supers were everywhere, she just had to know what to look for. That was how she caught Teddy disappearing when their English teacher asked for volunteers to read parts out of *Romeo and Juliet*. He always sat in the back, slouching in his seat and hiding behind the people around him as much as he could. He didn't want to be noticed, obviously, but not because he was shy. It was because, sometimes, he *really* didn't want to be noticed. At first he freaked that Anna wanted to talk to him at all—his eyes bugged out, looking back and forth for a place to escape. Clearly, he wanted to go invisible but couldn't while she was looking right at him. But she explained: He wasn't alone. He relaxed, as if the rods that had been holding him upright vanished. Later, Teddy figured out he could do more than turn invisible. The next step: turning insubstantial. He'd wanted to impress Teia and Anna with the new ability but didn't think too far ahead when he passed through walls to follow them into the girls' bathroom. They hustled him out quickly and gave him a lecture on being subtle.

Anna found Sam zapping flies in the courtyard during class. Like Teddy, he seemed relieved rather than angry that someone had discovered his secret. Happy that he wasn't alone in the world with his power and wondering what came next.

That was their club. They'd found each other, and while they didn't always get along, their desire for secrecy kept them together. Out of the whole world, they were the only ones who understood each other and what it meant to have powers.

After school, Anna went to the kitchen, where she knew she'd find her grandmother involved in some food-related project. Mom kept threatening to hire a cook—it wasn't like the family couldn't afford a cook, for goodness sake. But Grandma argued every time. She liked to cook, let her cook. Even Mom backed down from that.

"Grandma, can I talk to you?"

Suzanne looked over her shoulder. "Sure! You mind hanging out while I make cookies?"

Mind a chance to grab some cookie dough before it went into the oven? Oh hell no. Suzanne wouldn't even complain when Anna sat on the counter, out of the way of the mixer and cookie sheets.

"Gingersnaps sound good to you?" her grandmother asked.

Of course they did. Anna barely fit on the edge of the counter anymore, without running into the cabinets overhead. But the seat gave her a sense of nostalgia. It was habit, sitting on the counter while waiting to test the cookie dough. And sometimes, when her parents weren't around, Anna didn't mind feeling like a kid.

Still slim in her jeans and sweater, her grandmother always seemed to be moving, bustling, promoting her charities, working in the kitchen. Suzanne's roan hair, red fading to gray, was braided in a tail down her back. She certainly didn't look like someone who could warm up a pot of soup by touching it or shoot fire bolts out of her hands. Or like someone who would run around after dark in a skin suit, fighting crime.

Anna had a hard time thinking of her grandmother as the superhuman crime fighter Spark, but she'd seen the pictures of a young, svelte woman in a black suit, brilliant red hair showering across her shoulders and down her back, launching jets of fire from her hands.

She'd put away the suit after Captain Olympus was killed. That period was a bit murky in the family lore. No one talked about it much. They talked about Warren, they talked about the Olympiad. They still got together with Uncle Robbie, who'd been the Bullet back in the day but had also eventually retired when arthritis began affecting his hips. But no one ever talked about how it had all ended, and Anna had been hesitant to ask. The dark cloud lingered in the distance, and she didn't want to be the one to drag it close.

"I thought you said you wanted to talk," Suzanne said with a smile.

"I was just thinking," Anna said. Figuring out how to start, really. She took a deep breath and dived in. "What was it like, with the Olympiad?"

Suzanne raised a brow, cracked eggs into a bowl. "What do you mean, 'what was it like'?"

What *did* she mean? "How'd you guys get started? How did you know you were doing the right thing? How did you not screw up and get yourselves hurt?"

Anna felt her cheeks burning; she wasn't fooling anyone, was she? She kept her expression still—mild curiosity, that was all she'd reveal.

But Suzanne didn't seem at all suspicious. She just shrugged and rattled on. "Oh, I don't know. Going out, using our powers—it always just seemed like the right thing to do. Warren and I met in high school and started then. Robbie came along, then your dad about ten years after that. We were always stronger together than apart. We didn't really think about getting hurt—you know about Warren, we didn't much worry about him getting hurt. *Nothing* hurt him."

Until the end. Suzanne didn't say that.

"We started small—street crime, accidents, the usual thing you always read about in the news. The whole thing got really big when we didn't have a choice. When the Destructor showed up, somebody had to do something. There we were."

The Destructor had been the archnemesis of the Olympiad, had been involved in countless battles with her grandparents and father, and was the only person known to be immune to Dr. Mentis's telepathy. He'd kidnapped her mother when she was a teenager, and she'd subsequently teamed up with him as a henchman during a particularly outrageous bout of teenage rebellion. Anna had never worked up the courage to ask Celia about it, what she'd been thinking at the time, how she'd gone from victim to villain, however briefly.

Maybe that was the problem. They didn't have a Destructor to face off against. Not that most people would consider that a problem . . . But if they had a target to focus their energies on, maybe they'd stop bickering about whether or not they should publicize themselves in the *Commerce Eye*.

Anna asked, before she realized the words were out of her mouth, "Why'd you quit?" She hadn't meant to get that personal. The biographies and reports always said the same thing, that Suzanne had been broken-hearted by the death of her beloved husband. Who wouldn't retire after that? But Anna had never heard Suzanne answer the question.

She didn't speak right away. She might have been concentrating on the spoon she was wielding, the bowl, the dough taking shape inside it. Or it might have been a bad question. Anna began to regret asking it.

"Warren and I were a team," she said finally, sadly. "With him gone, I didn't see the point in going on." Using a teaspoon, she scooped a piece of the dough and handed it to Anna. "How is that?"

Anna could hardly taste the dough, but she ate it and smiled. "It's great."

Suzanne returned her focus to the cookies. "There've been enough books and articles written about the Olympiad, you could probably find out everything you wanted to know from them."

Anna said, "It's not the same as hearing it from you. It's family history. Besides, you don't give interviews. Why not?"

"Because it's just like you said. It's family history and none of their business." She set down her spatula and put a flour-dusted hand on her hip. "Any reason you want to know all this?"

Shaking her head in what she hoped was an innocent manner, Anna said, "Just curious." There she went, blushing again. "Hey, what's for dinner?"

"I've got some shrimp for stir-fry. I'll get started just as soon as your parents get back, whenever that is. They didn't tell me, and I don't have any idea where they've gone off to."

"Mom's on her way back from a meeting at City Hall, and Dad's in his office."

"He'll probably come up when she gets back, then.

He can always tell the minute she's back in the building. Did Celia call you to let you know?"

"Yeah," Anna said, flailing a moment. Time to change the subject again, without looking like she was changing the subject. "You know how she is, always has to check up on us."

"She just worries."

"Or she's a pathological control freak." That came out a little stronger than she meant, and she tried to smile it away.

"That, too," Suzanne said sunnily. "Just remember it's because she loves you."

Anna wondered sometimes. More often, she felt like a cog in Celia's plans that had fallen out of place and didn't particularly want to fit back in.

After dinner, she fled to her room, making excuses about needing to study. Instead, she turned out all the lights, sat on the floor below the window that looked out over the city's west side, and closed her eyes.

Bethy was in her room, actually studying instead of just using it as an excuse to be antisocial like Anna did. Her grandmother and father were in the kitchen, cleaning up. Her mother was in the living room, lying on the sofa, resting. Anna pushed her awareness outward.

Uncle Robbie's condo was a couple of blocks away, and he was at home. Teia and Lew, also at home along with their mother. Sam was at his family's apartment. Everyone safe at home, as she expected. There was Teddy, at his family's east end brownstone. She lingered at the spark that was his presence in her awareness; she could tell where he was but not what he was doing. He was stationary, which meant he could be doing anything from sleeping to watching TV to reading to showering. Not for the first time, she felt a deep envy for her father's telepathy. He never had any questions about anyone, did he? She thought it would be worth finding out things you didn't want to know, to learn the things you did. She thought about giving Teddy a call, or sending a text, or something, then decided against it. She'd see him at school tomorrow.

Their presences glared in her mind because she'd searched for them so often. They were always simply *there*, the moment she looked for them. Spotlights shining up from her mental map of the city, each with its own hue and shape, depending on whom it belonged to.

It was a comfort, knowing where everyone was, knowing they were safe, and that they would be there for her the minute she called. She didn't know how other people got along without such reassurance. That was what cell phones were for, she supposed. But she never lost her charge.

She could find her family and closest friends without thinking of it; to find others—acquaintances, people on the fringes of her life rather than in the center—she had to work at it. If she needed to, she could find police Captain Mark Paulson, another good friend of her mother's. Her teachers, people who worked at West Plaza whom she saw nearly every day but didn't know well. She'd been able to track down some of the city's superpowered vigilantes—the Block Busters, Earth Mother, Breezeway— when she needed to. Mostly to avoid them, when she and the others were out practicing.

But she had one specific person she wanted to find tonight. Since she'd met him only the one time, she didn't know if she could. But she wanted to try.

She held a picture of the green-suited super in her mind. His costume, his voice, the slope of his chin. The way he perched on the fountain, the way he moved. Where she'd seen him last, where he might have gone next after making that epic leap.

She didn't have any trouble ignoring most of the lights

and presences she encountered on her search. If she wasn't looking for them, they faded to the background. It was like searching for friends in a crowd: you knew what defining traits to look for, if they were tall or short or redheaded or always wore a certain leather jacket. You scanned the crowd, and those details snagged your attention. Same thing.

A spark flared in her mind. East, on the university campus. A young man, fit and agile, with a sharp gaze and calm demeanor. It was him. She'd found him.

The secret Olympiad elevator hadn't been shut down or closed off after her talk with her father. Which meant he didn't know about it. Or he didn't care if she used it, which meant letting her have access to it was part of her parents' plans, and they were watching her anyway, despite how hard she worked to avoid the building's surveillance. She was an interesting rat in their maze. Which meant she shouldn't use it anymore if she didn't want them tracking her. But what choice did she have?

She could go crazy thinking of it.

Once outside, she made her way two blocks over to the main east-west bus line, the one that stopped right on the university campus, where she disembarked and walked on. Her target, the mysterious superhuman, drew her forward. Now that she'd focused on him, his presence grew brighter. She could follow the map in her mind right to his location. He was stationary, she thought. In a room—not the dorms but in one of the buildings near the auditorium. Maybe he was a student. As she closed in on him, her heart pounded. She felt strong, all-knowing. Times like this, her power thrilled her. She could do *anything*.

Here she was, doing something exciting and powerful. If only the others could see her.

He was close. The knowledge of his location was just there, like knowing where the corner store was, or the placement of the sofa in your own living room. The paved bike path she followed curved around a grassy lawn, past a big square cinder-block building. Even this late at night, a few students were out, keeping to the well-lit paths, walking back to the dorms from the library or coffee shops. The assumption in the family was that Anna would be a student here in a couple of years. Anna couldn't picture it. She knew her way around because she'd grown up in the city, but the university still felt like another world.

When she passed the cinder-block building, the spark brightened—there, he was inside there. It was the university gym. A student at the front desk asked to see her ID. Startled, she patted her pockets, shook her jacket, and muttered, "Shit, I forgot it. Look, my friend Eliot's here, I just need to talk to him a second and I'll come right back out."

"Eliot Majors?"

"Yeah," Anna said, bemused.

"Okay, go on in, he's in the weight room," the guy said and went back to slouching over his textbook.

Late at night, the glaring fluorescent lights seemed incongruous. They made the place seem too bright, when her body felt more like going to bed. But around her, university students seemed to be at peak energy. She rounded a corner, walked past a gym where a group was playing volleyball, and followed signs to a weight room at the end of the hall.

The room was small, with whitewashed walls and hardwood floors. A variety of machines and benches sat in the middle, racks of round weights were lined up along the walls, and posters demonstrated correct positions and safety rules. Only one person was here, a young man sitting on a bench and doing curls with what looked like an awful lot of weights. It was him. Recognition flashed in his eyes when he looked at her. If not for him noticing her, she might have doubted herself—all she'd ever seen of him was his mouth and chin under his mask.

He wore a T-shirt, sweatpants, and sneakers. Without the mask, he had an angular face with broad cheekbones and a short, dark buzz cut. When he didn't say anything, kept curling with his mouth shut and jaw set, she thought he was going to ignore her, pretending they hadn't met.

But he paused and set the weights on the floor. "How'd you find me?"

"I told you last night, that's what I do," she said. "Wasn't sure I'd be able to, since we only met that once. But I wanted to try."

He was definitely college age, she thought, now that she could study him without the mask and costume. Older than she was. Too cool to go to prom with her, at any rate. Not that she wanted to go to prom with him . . .

"Okay, you found me, you know who I am, now what?"

"I don't know who you are. Not really. You're just a guy with a superpower. I was curious." Really, she didn't know what she'd expected. That he'd at least want to talk. That he'd be curious about her and the others. That he'd see what they all had in common. That he'd see it the way she did.

"I'm sorry, I'm sure you mean well, but I'm not going to get all open and sharing just because you managed to find me. I don't want to be part of your team."

She couldn't blame him for that, given how the team was shaping up, or rather how it wasn't. "That wasn't what I was going to ask."

"You just wanted to see if you could find me."

She looked away, fully aware that he was basically right, and that she hadn't thought at all about what she was going to say if she actually found him. She should have just peeked around the corner, confirmed it was him, and left. She scuffed her feet. "So. Working out. That's a good idea."

"You might try it, if you're going to be fighting crime and all." He smirked at her, and she felt even more dumb.

And still, she didn't turn around and walk out. "I also wanted to tell you . . . to ask . . . you know, if you ever need . . . I don't know. Help or something." She blushed, because the thought sounded stupid once she said it out loud.

He didn't need her help, and they both knew it. His tone was amused when he said, "I'll let you know. You should probably get on home." He retrieved the weights and started the curls again.

"Yeah, right," she muttered, turning and walking out. The guy at the front desk waved at her when she left.

The cool air outside soothed her mortified and blushing cheeks. Walking fast helped, too. She felt like an idiot. He probably thought she was an idiot. She wondered why she even cared.

Because he was powerful. Because they could use his help. And he was cute. Maybe not hot, but definitely cute.

She huffed, disgusted with herself. If she could at all help it, she was going to avoid him from here out. And since she had his full name now, and his presence firmly lodged in her mind, she'd always know where he was and she could avoid him easily.

SEVEN

Celia hadn't been able to sleep, again. She dragged herself to her desk in the morning and wanted nothing more than to lay her head on the surface and sleep some more. Her head was throbbing and that crick in her neck hadn't gone away. Four aspirin hadn't done the trick.

Arthur came into her office, hefting a rolled-up newspaper. "You'll want to see this."

It couldn't be good. She took a deep breath and braced herself. "What do I want to see?"

He straightened the paper and set it in front of her. It seemed to hit the desk with a *thunk* that rattled her head; she had to squint to read. It was the *Commerce Eye*, harkening back to its histrionic roots with a headline blazing in inch-high letters: "Commerce City's Newest Crime-Fighting Team Makes Its Mark!"

Celia should not have been surprised when, like some powerful exothermic reaction, the subjects of her experiment spun out of control on their own trajectories. It was the natural order of things. A better person—someone who knew what they were doing—would be pleased that the kids seemed to be not just learning to use their powers, but forming the kind of team that had made her own parents so effective. Instead, she felt nascent ulcers blooming in her gut.

The whole thing happened by chance. Analise had had her twins a year after Anna was born, then Bethy came along, so naturally they scheduled playdates. At one time

Celia would have stabbed herself over the idea of doing something so predictably maternal as playdates. But it was a great excuse to dump the kids on the playground while she and Analise sat on a park bench and caught up over coffee. It was also a great excuse to watch Teia and Lew without seeming like she was scrutinizing them for the odd case of superstrength or telekinesis. Analise had superpowers, after all. Never mind that she hadn't used them in twenty years, she still had them, theoretically. If her children had powers at all, they'd likely manifest them at puberty rather than have them from birth. Of the nearly two dozen supers Commerce City had produced, only six had manifested powers at birth. Her father had been one of those.

Arthur and Mark Paulson were the only other people who knew about the list in her safe. According to that list, a whole cluster of Leyden descendants had been born around the same time. Celia's kids, Analise's kids, the Stowe grandchildren, Donaldson's grandson, a couple of others from the Masters line—cousins of Barry Quinn, aka Plasma, who had been institutionalized for schizophrenia, so Celia kept an especially close eye on them. Before this generation, supers had been scattered, appearing alone or in pairs. But this was different. It seemed like the most efficient plan in the world to secretly grant them all scholarships to Elmwood, to get them all in one place where she could better watch them. With a good education in a safe, stable environment, they would be better able to manage their powers if they had them, yes? That was what she told herself. It certainly couldn't hurt, and maybe some good would come of it.

But once they were all together, she couldn't stop tweaking: subtle suggestions to the school guidance counselor, anonymous hacks into the computer database, and she'd gotten the kids of the same grades into the same homerooms, the same gym periods, the same intramural sports programs, the same lunch hours. Nothing overt, simply increasing the odds that they would spend time together. Find each other.

And it had worked.

Her parents had met at Elmwood Academy. They'd discovered each other, shared their abilities, learned how to use them. Taught each other. For good or ill, the Olympiad had been born at Elmwood. Maybe, for good or ill, it would happen again. Celia wanted to see, and she'd turned the school into her petri dish without anyone knowing.

Arthur would stop her, she kept thinking. If she ever went too far, Arthur would tell her. He hadn't yet, so she kept watching, and waiting.

Finally, here it was, and she could stop waiting.

The *Eye*'s story even had a picture, a major coup for a newspaper covering new vigilantes, who usually kept to the shadows and loathed publicity. Not these guys. In the photo, three of them stood in the middle of a downtown street, hands on hips and chins lifted proudly. They were in shadows—the picture had been taken without a flash, which made them seem like ghosts—masked and shrouded in costumes so their identities weren't apparent. But they were definitely posing, and they were obviously a team, all in black shirts and jeans and jaunty masks made with bandanas with cut-out eyeholes. The first formal superhero team in twenty years was what it looked like.

She was absolutely sure that when she studied those figures, she'd find Anna under one of the masks. But she didn't. In fact, she had a pretty good idea who these kids were. She continued on to the story.

The fire at the south side tenement block would have been a tragic disaster, if not for the arrival of the three superhuman heroes—

Celia looked up from the page. "They went after a burning building their first time out? Very traditional."

"Indeed. Keep reading." Arthur seemed to be enjoying this. He wouldn't have been if Anna had been one of the trio. But then, he probably would have known about it ahead of time. And he wouldn't have told Celia. Was it too late to lock Anna in her room for the rest of her life?

The article was breezy and admiring. *Our young crime fighters,* it called the trio, arrived shortly after the firefighters. While the firefighters were busy attaching hoses to water supplies, raising ladders, and whatever else firefighters did at the scene of burning buildings, the heroes had gotten to work: One had caused a rainstorm that soaked the fire, another had frozen the building to keep the fire from spreading, and the third had had some kind of explosive power that broke down walls and allowed people to escape. The fire department mostly stood around watching. Of course, someone called the newspaper, and the reporter and photographer arrived to snap pictures of the team before a backdrop of smoking brick façade. No one had died, no one had been hurt. They'd been smart, staying out of the building, stopping the fire first and not trying to rescue people directly from the blaze.

But she wished they hadn't done it at all. They weren't ready, not yet.

"Just trying to help," said one of the intrepid heroes, before the team disappeared into the night.

These stories never changed, not once in her whole life.

"Lady Snow, Stormbringer, and Blaster," Celia read off the names the vigilantes had given themselves.

"Teia and Lewis Fletcher and Sam Stowe, aren't they?"

Sam Stowe was sixteen, one of the many grandchildren of Gerald Stowe. The Stowe family had produced more superhumans than any of the others from the laboratory accident—his oldest grandson was Justin Raylen, aka Breezeway, and his second daughter, Margaret Lee, had a career as the vigilante Earth Mother before retiring to have kids. Margaret's son Cody was ten now. She wondered if any of the Stowes had ever sat down and figured out just how many cousins donned masks and fought crime. Probably not, that was what the masks were *for*. But Raylen had gone public years ago; Margaret Lee and other Stowes with powers had to be wondering. At some point, someone else had to make the genetic connections that Celia was keeping secret in her files.

And then there were the other two in the photo. Out fighting fires at age sixteen, just like their dead father. They might have waited specifically for a fire to come along, so they could swoop in for a rescue in some kind of tribute to him. They must have thought they were following in his footsteps, not their mother's. God.

Celia sat back and sighed. "I need to call Analise."

"Probably," Arthur said. "If she doesn't call you first."

She studied the picture further, looking for other figures hiding in the shadows. Theodore Donaldson, maybe. Anna, who was sneaking out at night to do God knew what. She closed her eyes, squeezed the bridge of her nose, futilely willing the headache to go away.

Arthur sat on the edge of her desk. "Celia, are you all right?"

"I just . . . it's just shocking to see the picture. They're so young." Ridiculously young.

"I thought this was what you wanted."

"I wanted them to meet each other, to practice with each other so they wouldn't feel lost, so they wouldn't grow up alone, like you and Robbie and Analise and my parents did until you all met each other."

"You hoped they would work together."

A superhero team, even better than the Olympiad had been. "Yes, eventually. Not before they've even graduated."

"But the experiment is out of your control now. Alas." He was laughing at her, quietly, at least. Nothing overt, just a wry smile and a flash in his eye.

She leaned back in the chair. Was she getting a migraine? Was this what a migraine felt like? When she finally opened her eyes again, Arthur wasn't smiling. That worried tension in his mouth had returned.

"Are you sure you're all right?"

"I've been working too hard. I need a vacation."

"So we'll take one."

Easier said than done. As soon as the development plan went through the committee. She kept saying that, didn't she?

"Celia—"

Her cell phone rang. Her personal phone, with Analise's name on the caller ID. Too early to be facing this call. She hadn't worked out what she was going to say. Arthur merely gazed innocently at the ceiling; he wasn't going to be any help.

Carefully, like handling dynamite, she answered the call. "Celia?"

She tried to judge Analise's mood by her voice—stressed, certainly. Sharp, edged with anger. And panic. Celia could guess her emotional state because she'd been living in that state herself the last week or so.

"Hi, Analise," she said, sighing.

"Have you seen the *Eye* this morning? Are those my kids? Tell me those are not my kids."

She spoke slowly, trying to give so very little away. "Yes, I've seen the *Eye*. I don't know if they're your kids, they're wearing masks."

"Don't give me that bullshit, the masks don't mean anything to you."

Celia first met Analise precisely because she'd recognized the woman in her civilian guise, without Typhoon's mask. "Really, you'd know better than I would—have they been sneaking out at odd hours?" Like my kid has . . .

"I don't know, they're being . . . sneaky!"

"Analise, do you want to go get lunch? We should have lunch."

"No, I don't think we should, because I need to yell, and I'm not going to yell at you in a restaurant."

I should have told her sooner, Celia realized. Right from the start, I should have told her. We should have been doing this together. "Have you asked them? Show them the paper and see what they say—"

"I did, and you know what they said? 'Mom, that's crazy.' In unison, like they'd been practicing. But I'm not asking them right now, I'm asking you."

"Analise—"

"Back in my day I was the only black superhero in Commerce City, and now two black kids show up in costumes fighting crime and you're going to tell me they're *not* mine?"

"Fine. You're right. It's Teia and Lew."

A long pause. Analise probably hadn't expected her to admit it. Celia wanted to crawl under the desk. Arthur stood by, being very quiet, looking sympathetic.

"You knew," Analise said finally. During the pause, she'd obviously figured it out. "You knew they had powers, that they were planning something like this, this whole time."

"I didn't know they were planning something, honest, I only thought . . . I guess I hoped that if any of them did have powers, they'd be there for each other. Help each other."

"They—this isn't just about my kids, is it? My kids, your kids—that other kid in the picture. And who else? And they were only ever going to help each other if . . . The scholarships. That was you, wasn't it? So you could put them right where you wanted them. Putting together your own little Olympiad."

"No, that isn't—"

"And you couldn't tell me? Why couldn't you tell me?"

Keeping it secret seemed like a good idea at the time was a very lame excuse. "Analise, I'm—"

"I can't talk to you right now," she said, flustered, and the phone clicked off.

Celia tossed the gadget onto the desk and glared. The gnawing hole in her stomach seemed to be getting bigger. She probably could have handled that better. Starting about five years ago, when she put together this crazy scheme.

"That didn't go particularly well," Arthur observed helpfully. As if she needed it spelled out.

"It'll be okay. She's been pissed off at me before. This is exactly how she reacted when she found out about me joining the Destructor. It'll pass." Eventually . . . Celia would call her later this afternoon, after she had time to settle down. After Celia figured out what she was going to do next.

Arthur's own worry grew strong enough to be evident, pressing out past his usual carefully maintained mental shields. All of it was directed at her.

"What?" Celia asked.

"Get your things together. We're going for a ride."

"I don't have time for a ride—"

"Yes, you do. I'm clearing your schedule for the rest of the day, and I'm taking you to a doctor."

"*What?*"

He repeated, offhand, "I'm clearing your schedule and

we're going to the doctor. Tom will have the car outside in a minute."

"But he's supposed to be dropping off the girls—"

"Soren can drop off the girls today. Tom is driving us to the doctor."

"Arthur—"

"Celia, you're not well."

"I'm *fine*—"

"You don't believe that. You're worried. You're ignoring it, but you're worried."

She'd never been able to hide from him. "I'm just tired," she said, but even she could hear the lie in it.

"You've been 'just tired' before. This isn't it. When was the last time you went swimming?"

Celia's favorite sport and workout of choice was swimming. She'd even had a current pool installed in the penthouse so she could duck in for a few laps whenever she wanted. In her early teens, it had been the only thing she was good at, and she still enjoyed it out of a sense of nostalgia if nothing else.

She couldn't remember the last time she'd used the pool. Weeks—no, months. Maybe longer. Well, that explained a lot. But even now, the thought of swimming made her tired rather than inspired. She blinked up at Arthur, defeated.

"Please come." He held out his hand, and her further arguments faded. She took his hand because he'd asked, because he was himself, and she trusted him.

Analise married a firefighter, which Celia always thought was perfect. They'd met at the rec center where Analise taught swimming. Morgan was teaching a first aid class. They'd hit it off, his fire to her water; they were opposites and a perfect match. He was methodical, she had a temper. He could always make her smile—it was a game, even, her trying hard not to laugh and him poking at her until she did. And he was a hero, without having a single superpower. He was living, walking proof that the powers weren't everything and that maybe she was better off without them. At least she could keep telling herself that, and in the meantime live vicariously through Morgan's exploits. He was tall, six-three, with a great physique, dark skin, and close-cropped hair. Movie star handsome but down-to-earth, and his eyes lit up when Analise walked into a room.

They had a small ceremony with a justice of the peace at City Hall. Just a few friends, no fuss, and they all went out to dinner after. Partway through the evening, Arthur graciously took baby Anna home—at six months, she was too wiggly and her attention span too short to last the whole evening so Celia could keep celebrating with her friend. Somewhere in between all the drinking and dancing, Celia ended up sitting in a booth with Analise, just the two of them slumped together shoulder to shoulder, and they talked.

"Have you told him about Typhoon?" Celia asked, her voice low.

"No," she said.

"Are you going to?"

"Why bother? She's gone now, long gone. No need to talk about her."

"What if he figures it out?"

Analise turned a lazy, tipsy smile to Celia. "Cross that bridge when I get to it. It's not important anymore." She kept telling herself that.

Celia wondered what had happened to the scrapbook Analise used to keep, clippings of all the news stories praising Typhoon's exploits. Maybe she still had it, well hidden. Maybe, more likely, she'd thrown it out when her power became blocked.

Ten years later, when Teia and Lew were nine, Morgan was killed fighting a fire. The unit had been trying to keep a convenience store fire from spreading to neighboring buildings, and a hidden propane tank exploded and caught him in a wall of flying debris. He'd died instantly. After, Celia did everything she could to keep Analise in one piece; it hadn't been easy. Arthur and Suzanne and the girls invited Teia and Lew to the penthouse for sleepovers, while Celia sat on Analise's sofa, holding her friend while she cried and cried. Everything had been perfect there, for a little while, and now it wasn't, and would it ever be again? Well, maybe not. But things got better. You moved on because you had to, because you had kids and they needed to see you strong. Celia didn't talk much. Just held Analise, as best she could.

"Typhoon could have saved him," Analise sobbed the first night after the accident, curled up, barely responding to Celia's grip on her. "She should have been there, she could have saved him."

Except that was wrong, because Celia had read the medical examiner's initial report, and the fire hadn't killed Morgan, the explosion had. All Typhoon's rainstorms, all her floods and waves, however quickly she might have put out the fire if she had been there, Analise still couldn't have guaranteed saving him from the blast. But Celia didn't try to tell her that.

The what-ifs went on forever, and your rational brain might try to shut them down, but your heart kept dwelling on the future that might have happened if you'd been a little faster, if you'd gotten free more quickly, if you'd sabotaged Mayor Paulson's apocalyptic weapon just five minutes sooner, so it had exploded and killed you before Captain Olympus arrived and shielded you, at the cost of his own life . . .

Analise collected Morgan's pension, gathered herself

enough to comfort her children, put them all through counseling, and somehow mended the pieces of their lives enough to keep going. Their father was a hero, no one could argue that, and Celia knew that the knowledge actually helped. A little.

EIGHT

Two weeks left on Anna's punitive school escort. Soren, West Corp's backup driver, dropped her and Bethy off that day. He was younger and more intent on the job than the amiable Tom, so he didn't smile at them over the backseat and actually scowled when Anna jumped out of the car on her own without waiting for him to come around and open it for her. Whatever. He'd learn. She left the car without saying good-bye to Bethy, slamming the door on the way out.

She was sure her face was burning. Her red hair and pale skin—she couldn't hide a damn thing, couldn't stop the blood from rushing and telling everyone that she was embarrassed. Pissed off. Furious, really. Everything, all at once.

She was going to kill them. If she had Sam's laser beams, she would kill them. But all she could do was find them the minute she got to school. That was something: They could never, ever hide from her.

Teia and Lew were right out front, off to the side of the steps. Thank God Sam wasn't with them, but only because he wasn't at school yet. The three of them standing together, they might as well have worn their costumes and waved a flag announcing their superhero identities. They might still do that, because wasn't that their whole point?

They should have told her what they were doing. They should have *talked* to her.

The siblings leaned on the brick wall, side by side, waving at friends entering the building, looking pleased with themselves. Especially when they spotted Anna marching up the sidewalk. A double image of smug, arms crossed, beaming at her.

She couldn't even talk at first and just stood there, glaring at them.

"Hey, Anna," Teia said. Smugger than smug. Ultrasmug.

"What did you think you were doing?" Anna demanded. It was a stupid question, an unreasonable question. It didn't matter what Teia thought she was doing, it was already done, and Teia might not even know it. "You went out late, didn't you? Like three a.m. late so you knew I'd be asleep and not figure out you were running around."

"And you thought you were the brains of the operation, didn't you?" Teia said.

Lew laughed. "Just chill out. Nobody got hurt, we saved some lives, and people love us. They're talking about us. It's great!"

Anna hadn't had a chance to gossip with anyone, but looking around, catching a phrase of conversation here and there—yeah, people were talking. New supers in Commerce City. Wasn't it exciting? A couple of girls at the foot of the stairs were bent over a smartphone, wondering aloud if the boys were cute under their masks.

Teia was grinning like an idiot. Who did she think she was fooling?

Anna stepped forward, lowered her voice. "It's too much publicity, you'll get screwed over before you even get started."

"You worry too much. This is exactly what we wanted—for people to pay attention."

"You've painted a giant target on your chest. All three of you."

Teia dramatically rolled her eyes. "That just means

we're doing something right. While you're sitting on your ass."

Anna leaned in close, looking for a big stick to poke with. "I notice you went for a fire. Very dramatic. Is it because of your dad, is that why you want to be a hero so badly?"

Teia's expression darkened in a way Anna had never seen before. She almost took it back, but Teia said, "It's got nothing to do with him."

Anna started to apologize for the low blow, when Lew waved at someone over her shoulder. She didn't have to turn around to know that Teddy and Sam were walking up the sidewalk. The gang was all here. Sam sauntered on over to join his conspirators.

"I guess you saw the news this morning," he said. If possible, he was more smug than the other two put together. There they were, just like the picture in the paper, and Anna wondered if anyone else noticed.

No. The girls were still hunched over their phone, giggling at the picture online. Nobody else saw it because they didn't expect to see it. The biggest component of any superhero costume was context.

"It's a mistake," she said, no matter how lame it sounded. "You'll see."

"Anna." Teddy grabbed hold of her sleeve and pulled. "Let's go for a walk."

She wanted to say something else to Teia. This wasn't over. She wasn't just angry, she realized—she felt betrayed. They were supposed to be in this together. She'd always thought of them, the whole group of them, as a team. Friends. Were they still? But she couldn't think of anything to say, so she followed Teddy and scowled at everything.

"They're going to get themselves killed," Anna muttered. "Why can't they just listen to me? Can't they see I might actually know what I'm talking about?"

"Maybe they want to get themselves killed. Go out in a blaze of glory," Teddy said, and Anna looked at him sharply.

"That's stupid. It's a stupid idea."

Teddy shrugged. "I have to admit, if that happened to me everyone would stop asking me what I'm doing after graduation. It'd save a lot of trouble. And I'd get the blaze of glory."

She stopped. They were almost at the corner of the building, at a stand of shrubbery. Beyond that was lawn, then the wrought-iron fence that separated the school grounds from the road and the city. Part of her wanted to just keep walking. It would feel good but wouldn't solve anything.

"Please tell me you're not going to go team up with them." That you're not going to stab me in the back, too . . .

Teddy slumped against the stone wall. "No. They didn't tell me what they were doing, either. I wouldn't team up with them now. It's not just about getting themselves killed, they're likely to get everybody else killed, too. They've got all the firepower, and I don't want to get in their way."

"They should have told us," Anna groused. "We're supposed to be a team, why didn't they tell us?"

"Because you'd argue about it, and they didn't tell me because they knew I'd tell you." He shrugged, like it was that easy. He still had the lingering shading of a bruise around his eye from his previous encounter.

"Well, thanks for that. I think."

He chuckled, and the knot in Anna's gut eased a bit. Maybe she did worry too much. Maybe she was making a big deal out of nothing.

"I just wish I knew which of us was right," she said.

"You both are, probably. Here's the thing: I figure I've got powers for a reason. I don't just want to sit on my ass pretending I don't. I want to use them. And you're right, there has to be a better way. I think that's what they're trying to figure out. What we all are."

"It's different for you," Anna said. She picked a leaf off a lilac bush, tore it apart. "I know you have to get out and use your powers. You can't keep them shut off all the time. But the thing about me is—my power never shuts off. I can't ever *not* use it." Bethy was at the middle school now, walking down the hall with a gaggle of friends. Mom and Dad were together in her office, talking presumably, which made Anna feel somehow warm and protected even when they were across town. Her grandmother had a charity board meeting at one of the fancy hotel restaurants downtown. She knew exactly where her family was, knew how to find them. She couldn't get away, and she would never be alone.

"But don't you want to *do* something with it?" Teddy said. "Not just have it *sitting* there?"

Right. That was the whole question. They could be heroes, if they could just figure out how. "We have to show Teia she's wrong," Anna said. "Getting on the front page of the papers isn't the way to do the most good."

Teddy said, "So, what? Does that mean you're finally ready to go out and do something, as long as we avoid publicity?"

She took a deep breath and said, "Yes."

They looked at each other, then back along the building to the stairs, to their rivals. A warning bell rang, summoning them inside. They'd have to talk about it later, but already Anna felt better. Like she had a plan.

Teddy said, "So when do we show them how it's done?"

"Tonight."

He grinned. He'd been waiting for her to say the word.

Back in front of the school, just a few minutes before the final bell was due to ring, a car pulled up to the drop-off zone. A latecomer, except that Anna recognized the car and the driver who stormed out, leaving the motor running: Ms. Baker, Teia and Lew's mom. She came around to the sidewalk, hands on hips, glowering in an expression of fury.

"Teia, Lew, get over here!"

They did so, because how could they argue with that? Warily, Anna and Teddy approached the twins.

"Mom, school's starting in a minute," Teia said. Her brow was furrowed, confused.

"You're not going to school today. Get in the car."

That should have been great, but something was wrong. Teia hung back, glancing at Anna.

"What's up with her?" Anna asked.

"I don't know. Okay, wait, I do know. She was all in a fit this morning and asked if that was us in the picture, and of course we told her no. But you don't think she suspects, do you?"

The words "I told you so" were on the tip of Anna's tongue, and she bit them back. "Even if she did, what has that got to do with school?"

"Teia, into the car, now!"

"I'll call you later," Teia said, running to climb into the car after her brother.

Teia and Lew didn't come back to school for the rest of the day.

Teia called that afternoon, and Anna hid out in her bedroom to talk so no one would overhear.

"What happened?"

"Mom's completely freaked out but she won't say why," Teia explained. "Something about Elmwood not being what it's cracked up to be, how we'd be better off in public school—"

"But she was so excited when you got the scholarships," Anna said.

"I know, and I don't want to go to a different school!

All my friends are at Elmwood! I'm thinking this isn't about the picture in the paper—she found out something about Elmwood."

"If this was about Elmwood, *my* mother would be freaking out."

"Then I don't know what it is. All we can do is play dumb until she cools down."

She was right—her only other option was to tell their mother that they had powers. Who knew what would happen then? Celia and Arthur could handle their kids having powers. They expected it. But Ms. Baker?

"Maybe you should cool it with going out. Lay low for a while."

"Hell, no," Teia said, vehement. "She's not going to stop us."

"Maybe . . . what would she do if you just told her you have superpowers?"

"She would lock us up forever," Teia stated. "After what happened to Dad. You weren't totally wrong, we couldn't help but think about him. But it felt . . . good. It felt right. But yeah, Mom would *freak*. She couldn't actually stop us from going out. But she'd never talk to us again."

That sounded about right, from Anna's experiences with Ms. Baker. Not an optimal outcome.

Teia went on, "If Dad were still here, I'd tell him. He'd understand. Convince Mom, you know?" More than sad, even, she sounded regretful, imagining that other life where he was still alive.

"Yeah, I know. What are you going to do?"

"Keep doing what we've been doing. Can't stop now."

"If you could just be careful for the next week or so—"

"*You* be careful. *You* stay home twiddling your thumbs. That's what your real power is, isn't it?"

"I'm only trying to help—"

"I gotta go. Mom wants to have a family night. Bye."
She'd already clicked off before Anna could reply.

Anna knew how to go out and fight crime without
drawing attention because of her grandparents. Or
she thought she did. The others wore the masks as much
because they looked cool as to hide their identity. They
didn't understand how important hiding their identity
really was. Things had pretty much fallen apart for the
Olympiad when their identities had been revealed.

Teddy's observation about them having all the firepower had clarified an issue for Anna: It was easy for
Teia and the others to be brazen and forward with their
powers, to look for publicity and appear in pictures on
the front page of the paper all high and mighty and badass. Their powers were offensive. They could actually
do crap. All she and Teddy could do was duck and stay
out of the way. How were they supposed to look badass
in a picture that way? They couldn't. But that wasn't the
point. The point was to help people, stop bad guys, protect the city. The best heroes didn't need publicity. Publicity was a by-product, not the point. Finally, she figured
out how to prove that.

At dinner that night, her parents were distracted. Even
Grandma noticed and bustled around the kitchen and
chatted more than usual. Anna had planned all kinds of
excuses about staying up late studying and not to worry
if they saw her bedroom light on, she had to write an
essay for tomorrow, and so on. But nobody even asked
her how her day went. She stayed quiet and tried not to
act too weird. Bethy kept looking at her, like she knew
Anna was hiding something, and Anna almost yelled at
her for it. But she kept her mouth shut, hunkered in on
herself, and studied the lasagna on her plate.

Even if Bethy had powers, Anna wouldn't have taken her little sister along. She didn't think Bethy was getting powers. She wouldn't be able to shut up about it if she were.

Late, after everyone else had gone to bed, Anna put on black pants and boots, a black long-sleeved T-shirt, and found a stocking cap and mask to hide her hair and face. Didn't look like much when she stood in front of the mirror to check herself out. She looked like a bank robber. Strands of red hair kept slipping out from under the hat. Like that wasn't a tip-off. Oh, well, it would have to do.

She pulled off the hat and mask and shoved them in her backpack with the rest of her gear.

She and Teddy didn't plan to meet at City Park. That was the old meeting place, and it had become too obvious. Too tainted. Teia and the others were at home, so Anna wouldn't run into them. But it was as if the park was their place; Anna and Teddy had to find a new spot now. Fine. They could do this on their own. As an alternative, they went to Pee Wee's, the popular all-night coffee shop near the university campus. They wouldn't stand out there—they'd look just like any other pair of kids studying.

The glass-fronted café had dim lighting and stainless-steel fixtures, hip and retro, a menu written on a chalkboard and baristas with interesting facial piercings. The music was something new and aggressively independent, and Anna didn't want to look like a freak for asking who the band was. She pretended she already knew, like she'd heard it before.

The place was cool, too cool for her, and she tried to act like she belonged as she walked in, shoulders back and expression blasé. The bus ride had taken longer than she expected, and Teddy was already there when she arrived. Also dressed all in black, he sat hunched over a coffee while his foot tapped a rapid beat, and he looked sidelong at the rest of the room. She slid into the booth across from him, furtive, wishing she could disappear, like Teddy.

Right. Not only did they not look like they belonged here, when they sat together they looked like a couple of hapless emo Goth types getting ready to mug children.

This wasn't going to work.

"This isn't going to work," Teddy said.

"We can still call it off."

He didn't say anything, which she guessed meant he didn't want to call it off. She ordered coffee and brought it back to the table so they could both sit there looking sullen and conspiratorial. Nothing suspicious about that at all. Maybe people would think they were in a band.

She drew a packet of computer-printed pages from her backpack. Her voice was hushed. "We can't win in a straight-up fight, not like the others can, so I figure we have to go at this backward. We can't be fighters, but we can be spies, right?" Teddy didn't seem happy. Well, it wasn't her fault they'd been born with stupid defensive powers and couldn't blast lasers like Sam. She pressed on. "We can find out things that no one else can. Then we can call in the cavalry. Anonymous tip to the cops. The goal is to stop bad guys, that's how we do it."

Teddy snorted. "So we just wander the city looking for . . . for what, random secrets to jump out at us?"

"No." She spread out the pages she'd gathered. News articles for the most part, some police blotter reports. She'd zeroed in on one set of stories in particular. Jonathan Scarzen was head of a nascent drug cartel putting down roots in Commerce City, but the DA didn't have enough proof to bring charges, and the police couldn't make an arrest. As far as public records went, Scarzen was an upstanding businessman working in imports. But the drugs were coming in somehow. The police were looking for a witness or for evidence linking Scarzen's import business with the new influx of heroin.

"We can do it," Anna insisted. "We can get the evidence."

Teddy nodded thoughtfully. "I sneak into the warehouse or whatever, search the place, bring a camera to record, and bingo. Is that what you're thinking?"

This was why she liked Teddy, he always knew what she was talking about. "Exactly."

"But we don't know where his warehouse is. The cops don't know, that's the whole point," Teddy said.

"I can find it," she said. "I've been looking for it, and I think I know where to find it."

"Anna—" Teddy's tone was more than a little skeptical. "You don't actually know this guy, do you? Don't you have to know someone to be able to find them?"

"I've been practicing. Just because you guys can't see it when I do—"

"I've never doubted your powers, Anna."

Yeah, but she did. She had to prove she could know someone just by reading enough websites about him. If she was going to be anything more than a walking GPS locator for her family and friends, she had to stretch. She had to be able to do more.

Scarzen was thirty-two years old, of Cuban and Italian ancestry. He'd been arrested four times, spent a few years in prison for auto theft in his early twenties, and since then had managed to evade authorities while building influence among the criminal element in Commerce City. According to his mug shots, he had a snake tattoo on his neck, and descriptions said he had more tattoos on his arms. Not just gang signs but also personal imagery. She needed to know as many details about him as she could. Any listed addresses were probably not accurate, but he had a few places where he had been seen. Police usually knew where to find him. The trouble with Scarzen was the cops didn't have any solid evidence to use against him in court, thereby justifying an arrest. He seemed like an ideal candidate for their first mission. Assuming she could find him, and the evidence.

Like some kind of fortune teller, she pressed her hands to the articles, the printed mug shots, the police commentary, and focused. She thought about where he might be, imagined the spots on the map where he'd been seen before, and concentrated on that needle in her mind, waiting for it to press against her awareness. People she'd known her whole life were easy to find. But what about someone she knew only by reputation?

Teddy waited patiently, quietly.

She didn't think she had her eyes closed, but she no longer saw the coffee shop. Instead, she saw a brick building with a fire escape climbing up the side like an exoskeleton. The building was low compared to others in the neighborhood, and older. Some of the windows were boarded up. In Hell's Alley, of course. Not the best part of town. She was pretty sure she knew where it was. To the needlelike instinct in the back of her mind, it *glowed*.

"I think I've got it," she said, breathless.

If they were going to keep doing this, this taking the bus thing had to stop. Sam was the one with the car—the others didn't have this problem. Anna was going to have to talk her parents into letting her learn how to drive. And they'd ask "Why?" and she'd have to come up with an excuse. Maybe she could say she was volunteering somewhere.

And her father would know she was lying. After tonight, she might not be able to stand in the same room with him ever again.

She'd worry about that later.

The bus driver raised an eyebrow at them when they

got off at their chosen stop—a few blocks from their target but still in a crappy part of town. Two kids, dressed in black, in Hell's Alley. No, nothing suspicious here. Anna's heart was racing, and her face flushed. She tried to ignore it. Had to concentrate on the task at hand. She put her hand on the mug shot photo of Scarzen, folded up and stuffed in her pocket. Turned that image and the information over and over again in her mind.

The bus's diesel engine growled as it pulled away, and off they went. She led Teddy around a corner. Once off the main street, she retrieved her mask from her bag; Teddy had his shoved in a pocket. They suited up.

That made Anna's heart race even faster, but with something other than trepidation this time. Suddenly, they looked like they were on a mission.

Not many streetlights worked in this part of town. No people around, either, and the few storefronts that weren't boarded up were locked with grates and dark. How could a place be scarier when it was utterly deserted?

"This is so cool," Teddy whispered. The invisible boy—Ghost, she reminded herself—walked decisively. In fact, he wore a thin smile under his mask, like he was enjoying this. Even after getting beat up last time, he was happy to be out again.

He actually looked like a superhuman vigilante—chin up, alert, confident. She wasn't sure what she looked like. The scruffy sidekick? She should be so lucky. Anna was a little freaked out, truth be told. But they'd be fine. They'd watch each other's backs. She had her cell phone with her.

When they crossed the next street and turned onto another block, she stopped, startled, because the building they approached made her feel a stabbing moment of familiarity, like she'd been here before, even though she never had. That needle in the back of her mind was singing. He was here, right now, in that building. It was the right shape, had the skeletal fire escape, and seemed to nestle among the buildings around it.

She grabbed Teddy and pulled him into a nearby alley. "That's it, that's the one."

"Okay," Teddy said, with a world's worth of confidence. Like he was absolutely sure he knew what he was doing. Maybe that was the trick of it, you had to act like you knew what you were doing. "Let's go over it again. I get in, stay invisible, and take pictures of the drugs or weapons, right?"

Anna said, "And a picture of Scarzen, if you can. It's best if you can get them all in the same shot." They had decided that Anna would stay outside, rather than have Teddy unlock a door to let her inside. If Teddy were discovered, he could turn invisible and phase out of the building before anyone caught him. Anna would be stuck. As much as she hated staying out of the real work, she had to defer to logic. She'd stay hidden and wait for Teddy to get back.

Teddy tested the camera on his phone, taking a couple of shots of the brick wall. "I'm set."

"Make sure the flash is off," she reminded him.

"Got it. And the ringer." He put the phone in a pocket and cracked his fingers. "Awesome."

This could work. This could actually work. "I really want to go with you."

"We talked about this . . ."

"It's just I feel useless."

Surprising how much expression she could read in just his mouth and jaw, under the mask. He was determined, confident, and his lips pressed in a sympathetic line. "You need to stay out here and call for help if something goes wrong." Trying to make her feel better by giving her a job, even a silly job that a real superhero shouldn't need. He gave her arm a brief touch that was probably meant to be comforting.

All she could think was: Even on Team Defense, she was the useless one. Great.

"This shouldn't take long," Teddy said breezily and offered a grin.

He left her standing on the sidewalk, arms crossed, trying to look unassuming and not horribly out of place as she leaned against a brick wall. The night was pleasantly cool, but Anna still shivered. Behind her, something rattled, made a screech—a cat, trotting the other way, vanishing into shadows. It happened so fast she didn't have time to be startled. She waited, trying to figure out how she could go into a situation like this without being totally useless. If she could track not just one person, but everyone within a certain area, she could warn people. If she could do that, she'd be great at surveillance, at knowing when the bad guys were around, when the cops were—but the only person in that building she could sense right now was Teddy. He'd made his way inside and was moving upward on a staircase. She knew Scarzen was there, somewhere. But not what floor he was on, or in what room. Her power could only make the generalization.

Maybe if she had a gun—but that defeated the purpose of being a superhero. Superheroes weren't supposed to need guns. She didn't know the first thing about getting hold of a gun, much less using one. No guns, then.

What had her father done when he was with the Olympiad? He couldn't run faster than the eye could see to get out of trouble like the Bullet, he didn't have the sheer raw firepower of her grandparents, Captain Olympus and Spark. Oh, yeah, he didn't just read minds, he could control them. He pried information from them, intimidated them with his reputation, and incapacitated them by forcing them to sleep.

He insisted that he'd never used that particular aspect

of his power on his daughters. Mostly, Anna believed him.

Mom and Dad were at home, in bed. Bethy was in the living room—she'd probably snuck out to watch TV. Anna would have to dodge her when she got home. Her power had never felt so inadequate. It was a parlor trick, that was all.

Her sixth sense followed Teddy's progress as he reached the third floor, where he stopped for a long time. Minutes dragged.

She wanted nothing more than to run over there and find out what was happening. She'd call, but they'd turned their phones to silent as a precaution. At least they figured that much out. They weren't entirely stupid, or so she kept telling herself.

More minutes passed, and Teddy hadn't moved. He might have had a good escape plan—turn invisible and phase out was pretty darned good—but even the best escape plan could go wrong. What they hadn't worked out was a signal for when she should call for help if something really did go wrong. How would she ever know? It would be terrible if on their first outing as a superhero team they had to call for help. Wouldn't Teia love that? Oh, but if this worked, Teia wouldn't be able to say a thing.

She started pacing until her knees felt wobbly, then she crouched and hugged herself. And waited.

If things went *really* wrong, she'd probably hear gunshots. So she started listening for the sound of gunshots from the squat building.

After what seemed like half the night, Teddy started moving again. The light of his presence moved back down the stairs. Quickly. She went to the corner across the street from the building to wait for him.

A dark figure phasing through the door, he emerged

from solid metal. It was always disconcerting seeing him do that. You blinked a few times and looked again, sure that there'd been a gap in the wall that you didn't see, or that the door that was there had opened without you noticing. But no, he ran through solid matter without stopping. He arrived at her corner, and they ducked into a doorway, out of sight.

"Well?" she asked.

"Got it, let's go," Teddy said, bodiless. He pressed his hand to her back, urging her on.

The buses had stopped running, but they'd planned for that and she'd brought along cash. They shoved their masks into their bags and had to walk eight blocks to find any cabs. Even then, it took three tries to flag one down, this late and with them dressed like cut-rate ninjas.

The driver studied them in his rearview mirror. "Don't you kids have school tomorrow? It's a little late."

"Just go to Seventy-second and Pine," Teddy muttered.

On the drive, he showed her the pictures he'd shot. They were good. They'd nail the guy.

They stopped a few blocks from Teddy's house. That would have been stupid, going straight home. After dropping him off, Anna had the cab take her to a hotel a couple of blocks from West Plaza. She had to hope that was good enough to throw people off. Her calculations were good and she'd collected enough of her allowance to pay the driver. Twenty minutes later, she was at West Plaza taking the secret elevator up.

Finally, she could breathe. She hadn't realized she'd spent all night feeling like she was being strangled until she got home, and the air seemed clearer.

But they'd done it. They'd really, really done it. They'd show everyone. And Dad wasn't even waiting up for her. Victory.

Nothing in any of the superhero biographies or memoirs talked about how you were supposed to get any sleep, fighting crime at night and pretending that everything was normal during the day. This was even worse than the nights they all went out to practice. She hadn't burned herself out on adrenaline those nights. She hadn't spent those nights with her heart beating in her throat.

Getting out of bed and getting ready for school the next morning was a complete nightmare. Especially since the work from the night before wasn't over.

Her parents were distracted when she asked them if Tom could take her to school early that day. She had a test to study for, she lied and didn't care if her father knew. But he didn't even blink. Bethy howled over having to leave early, but Mom and Dad didn't seem bothered by the change in routine. They told Bethy she'd just have to study in the library an extra few minutes before school started. Bethy stared bullets at Anna. If anyone was going to guess what was going on and blow the whole thing open, it would be Bethy.

She wondered if Bethy had learned to read minds and had sense enough not to tell anyone. That gave Anna a chill, which she had no choice but to ignore.

At school, she waited for the town car to pull out of sight. Then she ran. There was an Internet café a few blocks away. A lot of the kids went there for caffeine jolts before school, so Anna wasn't out of place. This was part of the plan, and she had work to do.

Anna had already taken the photos from Teddy's camera and stripped identifying information off them, except for the location marker. The pictures were great—he had gotten one with Scarzen standing right behind a pile of money and weapons, and another showing a pile of bagged white powder. They ought to work. She mailed them to the "tips" address on the police department's website, using an anonymous and she hoped untraceable web address with no identifying info.

They'd done this as anonymously as they could. Now all they could do was wait to see if their tip did any good. Unlike fighting fires, they didn't get the instant gratification of knowing they'd helped someone or seeing news of their exploits in the paper. It was frustrating. But they had to be patient. They just had to.

I t happened faster than they thought it would. The very next morning, Teddy called her cell phone, breathless and nearly incomprehensible. She wasn't even out of bed yet.

"Anna! Anna, have you seen the news? You have to look at the news, I sent you the link, check your messages, right now!"

"Teddy, it's five in the morning." She was still catching up on sleep from the night of their raid. Didn't Teddy sleep at all?

"Anna. Check your messages." He was suddenly very serious.

She did. Teddy had sent her an e-mail with a link that led to a news story. "Breaking," the headline announced. She squinted, read on.

Notorious drug dealer Jonathan Scarzen has been arrested on charges based on evidence delivered in an anonymous tip.

Anna clapped her hand over her mouth to keep from screaming. "It worked!" she finally managed to squeal.

"Told you you had to look."

If he'd been there that minute, she would have hugged him.

W hat she wanted more than anything was to go to school and rub Teia's face in their success. But Teia still hadn't returned to school, third day in a row. This became apparent on the car ride over, and Anna grew more anxious, until Bethy asked, "What's wrong, you have a test today or something?"

"Yeah, that's it," Anna muttered.

She'd printed out the article about the arrest and the anonymous tip. She wanted to frame it, but she couldn't, so she kept it folded up in the pocket of her uniform blazer. She kept hoping to sense Teia's approach, hoping that her mother had changed her mind about pulling the twins from Elmwood.

But no, Teia was at home. Again. Anna ducked behind the corner of the building and called her.

"Where are you?" she said when Teia answered.

"You know exactly where I am," she shot back.

"I thought your mom would change her mind and let you come back."

"Not a chance. She's definitely taking us out of Elmwood. We're home until she can get us enrolled somewhere else."

"She can't do that, can she? Not in the middle of the school year."

"I keep trying to talk to her and she just tells me I don't know what I'm talking about. Elmwood is suddenly evil. I mean, we all know it's evil, but not like that, you know?"

"I'm really sorry, Teia. Maybe my mom could talk to her."

"I don't think anyone should talk to her, the mood she's in."

This proves I'm right about publicity being a bad thing . . . She didn't say that because that would just twist the knife, and she wasn't *that* petty. Only sort of petty.

Anna continued, casual-like, "I don't suppose you checked out the news this morning? Look up the *Eye,* on the front page."

A few minutes passed while Teia found the website. Anna waited, smug, sure Teia would be impressed.

"Wow," she said finally, as amazed as Anna could hope for. "Pretty cool."

"See?" Anna pointed out. "No publicity, no exposure. Fight crime and stay secret, no problem."

"That was you and Teddy who sent in that anonymous tip? Really?" Teia said.

"Yeah," Anna said, trying to keep the grin off her face.

"Prove it."

The breath went out of her, just for a moment. Anna didn't cough, sputter, tear up, or shout, even though she could have done all of those things. She had never wanted to punch anyone before, but she did, right then. Not because Teia was being mean, even though she was. But because Teia was right.

Anna hung up on her.

NINE

When Anna came home and told Celia that Teia and Lew hadn't been at school the last couple of days and were likely withdrawing from Elmwood, Celia wasn't surprised. It was what she'd have done, finding out her children had this shadow life that her best friend had been manipulating behind the scenes.

What she had to do now was figure out a way to change Analise's mind. To recruit her to the cause.

She called Mark. He'd left her three messages about the latest vigilante news story. She hadn't gotten back to him because she'd been distracted with Analise, the doctor's appointment, a burgeoning hypochondria spurred by the doctor's appointment, and so on. The vacation was sounding better and better. Surely the city wouldn't crumble to pieces if she left it alone for a week. *After* the development plan was settled.

"Finally. I've been trying to get hold of you all day," he said, flustered, and she worried about his heart.

"I know, I'm sorry, I've had a lot on my plate."

"Well, I've got another one for you. We arrested Jonathan Scarzen based on an anonymous tip. Good information, the DA thinks she's got a case, we're moving forward."

She had to remind herself who that was, what it meant. Crime lord who'd kept himself very underground. Right. "That's great, isn't it?"

"I'm pretty sure the tip came from a team of vigilantes.

A *different* team of vigilantes than the kids at the fire."

Oh. Oh, dear. "How do you know?"

"We got a call from a cabby about some suspicious activity in the area. He picked up a fare, a couple of kids dressed in black. He thought they might have been cat burglars or something. The timing puts them a few blocks away from where we arrested Scarzen. Frankly, I don't know whether to be amused that they're taking cabs around town because they can't fly or pissed off that they're putting themselves in so much danger."

Teddy Donaldson was one of them, she'd bet. He hadn't been part of the first group, Teia and company. "What are their descriptions?" Celia asked.

"I don't think I'm going to tell you," Mark said, sounding entirely too gleeful. "You've been holding out on me, now I'm holding out on you."

She did not have time for this. "I'm just trying to keep you from pulling up to these kids' houses and arresting them on some trumped-up curfew charge or whatever the hell you're planning."

"Celia, it's for their own good. They're running around Hell's Alley in the middle of the night, they're going to get hurt."

He was right, of course. It was the same reason Analise was so angry about it. He kept on, "I've got two brand-new superhero teams hitting the streets now, and neither of them knows what the hell they're doing. They're kids playing with dynamite, and it has to stop before one of them gets killed. You know who they are, you have to stop them."

"You know how I can tell you don't have teenage kids?" Celia asked.

"I get teen delinquents in here every damn day. Don't tell me I don't know what I'm talking about," he said, sharp as a razor.

She'd cut too close. Mark didn't have kids of his own, not because he didn't want them but because he'd made a responsible choice not to inflict his genes on the next generation. Guy ought to get a medal, not her sarcasm. Backing up, she tried again. "It's not a matter of making them stop. You've been dealing with supers as long as I have. It's a compulsion with them."

Mark understood the compulsion, because along with the powers came a need—a need to protect, to act, to control. It was why he'd become a cop when he could have been anything he wanted. Sometimes the Leyden descendants were born without powers, but still they felt the compulsion.

When she was younger, people used to ask Celia why she didn't just leave Commerce City if she wanted to get away from her parents' shadow. She could never adequately explain why she had to stay. It was *her* city, she always said, vaguely, earnestly. She couldn't leave.

Maybe Arthur was right. She was trying to do too much. Maybe it was time to delegate. Mark was already half on her side. He might be able to help her get Analise on their side, too.

"Mark, I want you to meet someone. Can you pick me up and go on an errand with me?"

She was grateful when he agreed.

Celia was even more grateful that Analise didn't slam the door in her face when she and Mark showed up. It was early evening, when Analise was home from her job managing the downtown rec center.

"I'll tell you everything, I swear," Celia said, before hello even, and Analise paused. She and Mark must have looked very serious, standing there together, both of them still in their business suits from their workday.

Analise glanced over her shoulder to the staircase and, by extension, the kids' bedrooms above them. "All right, but let's go somewhere the kids can't eavesdrop."

A block from the town house, a small park occupied an empty lot between cross streets. After dark, the place was empty, and they gathered on a secluded bench.

Celia started, "Analise, I don't know if you remember Mark Paulson—"

"We met briefly," Mark said. "I don't know if you remember, that stint Celia pulled in the hospital after the bus crash."

Celia had forgotten that they'd both been in her room when everyone came to visit at once. Not that she'd been thinking too straight then, drugged up and suffering from a concussion.   •

"How can I forget the cute detective you ditched for the freaky telepath? I remember," Analise said.

They both blushed at that one, how could they not? Didn't help that Mark was still awfully cute. But with his serious calm and salt-and-pepper hair he also resembled his father, onetime mayor and Commerce City's last serious supervillain. Kind of weird.

"Um. Yeah. Mark, Lady Snow and Stormbringer are her kids. I thought she should be in on the conversation about what to do about them."

Analise's gaze burned fierce. "You are *not* going to arrest them—"

"No, not at all," Mark said. "This is entirely off the record. This . . . this all has to be off the record." He looked to Celia to explain. She gathered herself and did so, carefully.

"There's a genetic component to superhuman powers. It has to do with an accident that happened at a laboratory run by Simon Sito, the Destructor, that was funded by my grandfather and where your father worked. They were both there during the accident, along with a dozen workers. The powers originate there, and they're passed down from parent to child. Not always." She and Mark exchanged a glance there, because they'd never been entirely sure how much of their makeup came from that accident—they didn't have powers, but they both had a love for and loyalty to the city that was almost superhuman. Was that part of the Leyden Labs inheritance, or a coincidence? "But sometimes, yes. I found this out by accident, but I've been tracking the lineages ever since. With our kids hitting puberty, along with about a dozen others, I wanted to get the potential inheritors into one place, so they'd be safer. So we could watch them."

Analise glared at Celia. Wondering how much she'd told Mark, no doubt—or if Mark had guessed. It wasn't hard, once you put all the pieces down on the same surface.

Mark made a peace offering. "Since we're sharing secrets, I'll tell you mine: Simon Sito, the Destructor, was my grandfather. I didn't inherit anything, but I could have. That's why I'm working with Celia, to try to prevent another Destructor from happening to the city."

Celia expected shock, even horror from Analise, processing that information. But it was old history now. Abstract, irrelevant. Then, her friend's brow furrowed as she decided if her own history was old enough to reveal.

But Analise shook her head. "As much as I'd like to go public some days, there's still a warrant out, and no statute of limitations. I can't say anything." It was as much an offering as Analise could give, and it was enough.

"I understand," Mark said.

Somehow, moving on after that became easier. They all knew where they stood now, even if the words hadn't been spoken.

"I've been thinking," Celia continued. "We know we're not going to stop them from trying to be heroes. The powers come with the need to use them. Our choices are to lock them in their rooms until they're eighty, and have them bust out anyway and do something crazy. Or we give them an outlet, and we supervise them." Like keeping the secret elevator open. At least they would know where their kids were.

She looked at Mark. "I can give you my files—but only you. None of this gets recorded. And you have to keep the police off their backs. Watch them, supervise them, keep them out of serious trouble—hell, give them missions if you want. But keep it secret. Give them the freedom to figure this out on their own. It's not like they'd actually listen to us. Analise, you know what they're going through. Let them go back to Elmwood and be with their friends. They can help each other."

Analise sat on the park bench, a little apart. She closed her eyes, put her face in her hands—thinking. And if she said no, absolutely not, and kept the kids out of Elmwood and told Celia and Mark to stay the hell away, would Celia stay away? No, she realized, she probably wouldn't.

"Single parenthood's been hard enough," she said finally. "And now you slam this on me?"

"This is supposed to help them, Analise. To help *you*. It'll be better, with more of us looking out for them."

"You're not doing this to try to manipulate them into creating a second Olympiad."

"That's an unintended side effect. Honest." She wasn't sure Analise or Mark believed that one, the way they were looking at her.

Analise said, "I just want to keep my kids safe. Whatever it takes."

"Me, too," Celia said. "And I have some ideas about how to do that."

For a stretch of time in her teens and early twenties, Celia had been the object of about a dozen kidnappings. Her parents' secret identities had been revealed, the Olympiad's cover blown, and she became the ultimate target for villains and supervillains who thought they could attack the heroes by holding her hostage. The scheme never worked, and the Olympiad rescued her every time. She'd never been seriously hurt, and only a little traumatized. Okay, maybe a lot traumatized.

Now, sitting in a nondescript, inoffensive doctor's office waiting to hear the results of a barrage of tests felt a little like being kidnapped. Time had slowed, her future had become fuzzy. But she couldn't see her captors, and she had no bindings to struggle against. To ground her. She felt like she was floating, and her heart raced. She had been kidnapped in a sense, hadn't she? It was enough to make her nostalgic.

But this time, she couldn't look her captor in the eye, there'd be no pompous monologue about his nefarious plans. And the Olympiad wasn't on the way to save her.

She took Arthur's hand, held it a little more tightly than she meant to.

The checkup three days ago hadn't gone the way Celia expected. She expected the doctor to tell her she had a cold or some other virus. Mono, maybe. That she needed to rest, take a vacation like Arthur said. She'd have her temperature and blood pressure taken, her heart would race a little, the doctor would tsk at her and send her home with anti-anxiety medication.

No, be honest: That was what Celia had hoped would happen. She had hoped very hard for something simple and nondisruptive. Something she could laugh about in a week, while teasing Arthur for being overprotective.

But then the clinic had called. "We have your results. We'd like you to come in to discuss them," they'd said, which meant bad news. Not just bad, but the worst. They wanted to see you only when it was bad. She hadn't been able to focus, so Arthur had had to call the town car and guide her down the elevator and to the garage.

Arthur didn't say a word the whole time. Just kept

hold of her and grimly took charge of the situation until they were sitting in the clinic waiting room. Waiting. Anyone else would have muttered vague, untrue reassurances the whole time, but not him. He knew exactly what she was thinking and that there was nothing he could say to comfort her. He was there, and that was enough.

If he was angry, upset, or scared, he couldn't show it. He controlled his emotions because they'd impact the people around him, and she'd long since gotten used to him reacting like a stone to the most chaotic situations. But just this once, she wanted to know what he was feeling. The tension in his face had become constant.

A receptionist called them in and locked them away in the quiet of a doctor's office. Not an exam room but an unassuming office with a plain desk and uncomfortable padded chairs. Diplomas on the wall, family pictures on the bookshelves.

When the door opened, Celia flinched, and Arthur squeezed her hand.

Dr. Valdez approached, full of pleasantries, shaking their hands before setting down a manila folder, then sitting behind her desk like it was a shield. Celia didn't hear a word of it, and when Valdez stopped moving and she finally got a good look at her, the doctor's smile seemed stricken.

"As you might have gathered from my call, the results of the blood work weren't normal. In fact, it's rather more serious than was initially expected, which is why you were asked to come in."

That switch to business passive voice grated on Celia's nerves. The woman really didn't want to talk about this, and Celia was trying to figure out how to interrupt the awkward introduction to get to the actual diagnosis when Arthur did it for her.

"Leukemia," he said. "It's leukemia."

Having a word made it somehow less nerve-racking. Celia could breathe again. She couldn't think, but she could breathe.

The doctor appeared to deflate, unable even to fake a smile. "Yes. I'm sorry."

Celia kept repeating the word to herself. It was bad, okay. But how bad? And how had it happened in the first place? It wasn't like catching a cold, was it?

"Do you know what could have caused it?" Arthur said, voicing her question before she could formulate it herself.

"We're not really sure. A variety of causes have been shown to have an impact in some cases. Particularly if you've ever been exposed to powerful radiation—"

A wave of vertigo shook her and she clung to the arm of the chair. A flashback, a visceral smell of a secret laboratory in the process of burning, and her father coming to save her . . . The Psychostasis Device exploded, and he'd hunched over her, shielding her from a massive burst of radiation. "You're safe," he'd whispered, his dying words.

The feeling was so strong she wanted to run. Instead, she put her hand over her mouth to stifle laughter. Oh, God.

The radiation from the psychostasis ray that her father had died to protect her from. He'd died thinking he'd saved her, that she was safe, but she wasn't, the radiation had just taken twenty years to kill her.

She swallowed back the scream that came next. Calmed herself.

"Celia," Arthur whispered. His expression was taut, scared. His fear pressed out, against her mind. She squeezed his hand back. She was okay. She was going to be okay. She decided, right there, that she had to be.

—*The girls, how am I going to tell the girls about this?*—

—*Wait.*— Arthur urged calm without speaking.

She took a breath and settled. Looked straight across the desk to the doctor. "What do I do?"

The treatment plans were extensive and arduous. Her case would go through a panel review in the next few days, and the panel would likely recommend chemotherapy, which ought to be started as soon as possible. The doctor encouraged her to do as much research as she could in the meantime.

Oh, would she. She would *kill* that research. She'd started her career in forensic accounting; nothing would escape her hunt for information.

"How am I going to tell my mother?" she said abruptly as the car pulled onto the ramp that sloped down to West Plaza's parking garage. "I don't know how to tell my mother." She didn't want to tell anyone. She wanted to pretend this wasn't happening, but she wasn't that good an actress. "I don't want to tell the girls. Not yet, not till I know what I'm doing next."

"I'm not sure that's a good idea."

"Is that the telepath or the psychiatrist talking?"

"It's the man you've been living with for twenty years and the father of your children talking," he said. "We're already keeping so many secrets." He actually sounded sad. Tired, maybe.

She leaned against him, snuggled under the crook of his arm, and let the warmth of his mind as well as his body envelop her. He could whisper *hush* directly into her panicking hindbrain. She'd never tried to keep secrets from him.

"We'll wait until this city development deal is finalized. It should just be a couple of weeks, then I'll tell. I've got sharks circling for me, and I don't want them finding out about this. I can install equipment for treatment in

West Plaza. No one will ever see me at the hospital, and I'll tell people when *I* want them to know. I can do this."

"*We,* Celia. We can do this. It's going to involve all of us sooner or later."

One day at a time. She had her plans, they were all in order, it would all work out. She just had to keep telling herself that.

Arthur held her hand in a gesture that seemed desperate.

Her mother was gone from the penthouse when they returned, so that was one decision Celia could put off until later. Suzanne had left a note about shopping at the Asian market on the north side for dinner ideas, and reminded her that she'd invited Robbie over for dinner and she hoped they could all be there because it had been quite awhile since they'd all gotten together, what with the girls being so busy with school, and so on.

It was like she was still in high school herself. Only back then, the notes Suzanne left were just as likely to be about some mysterious unnamed "errand," which always meant that the Olympiad was off thwarting plots, and if she got hungry there was lasagna that she could put in the oven.

Celia stared at the note a long time until her eyes brimmed with tears, which she scrubbed away a moment later. She didn't have time for that.

Sitting at her desk in her office seemed remarkably futile. She had the work she'd abandoned, the day's task list, and the mental acuity needed to perform a simple task like open her e-mail folder seemed monstrously difficult. Arthur took one of the chairs and sat, legs stretched out.

"Are you going to be all right?"

She wondered sometimes why he bothered asking.

She didn't have to say anything, but the silence was harsh, so she did. "I thought work would distract me. I don't want to tell them, Arthur. I just don't. I can already see the looks on their faces, and with Robbie coming over tonight . . ." The weight of all their stares, all their pity. Their fear for her. She just couldn't.

"You may be right, for now," he said. "We can at least enjoy tonight."

She was surprised he agreed, and she stared at him for any nuance in his expression. He radiated only calm, with no indication of how hard he had to work for that calm.

"I love you," she said.

That night, the kids roared home from school like a whirlwind. She didn't need to check the cameras because it seemed she heard them all the way from the ground floor. They stormed into the penthouse, Bethy going on about two friends at school fighting over something ridiculous, and Anna grumbling at her about how there were more important things to worry about and could she please grow up, then Bethy insisting she was grown up, and Anna declaring she was going to take a nap and could everyone please leave her alone. They used to play together, Celia thought wistfully. They still had tubs of dolls and blocks in their bedrooms that they hadn't touched in years.

From her office, Celia heard Suzanne call from the kitchen, "Don't forget, we're having company for dinner, so you can't skip, okay?" Mumbled acknowledgments followed.

If Celia could just forget that she was sick, she'd be able to get through the next few hours without a problem.

She wrapped up her research, carefully purged her web browser of all medical links, and locked file folders in the safe. By the time she'd finished, washed up and changed into jeans and a blouse, and returned to the living room to crack open a bottle of wine, building security announced that Robbie Denton had arrived and was on his way up. She was at the front door to meet him when he emerged from the private elevator.

Once upon a time, Robbie Denton could run faster than the eye could see. As the Bullet, he had joined the Olympiad and battled crime and defeated supervillains. He was legendary.

Now he walked with a cane, held discreetly at his side to prop up a weak leg. Arthritis in the hips, the degeneration of joints that had worked many times harder than they'd been designed to. When he finally retired a good eight or so years ago, he revealed that he'd been in pain for a long time. He'd been slowing down, hoping no one would notice, until he finally stopped. He'd had hip replacement surgery. There'd been complications—his mutated physiology rejected the implants. Further surgeries kept him on his feet and out of a wheelchair but hadn't given him back his speed.

He was terribly good-natured about it, Celia thought. He smiled and made jokes about the rest of him holding up just fine, and how he was lucky to have survived long enough to have these problems. Which made her think about her father, who'd had so much of his identity wrapped up in his powers that he probably wouldn't have survived losing them. At least not easily.

Celia let Robbie fold her into a squeezing one-armed hug while he leaned on his cane.

"How you doing, kid?"

She would always be the kid to Robbie, even though she had two kids of her own now. Her smile turned stricken, but she moved on quickly, hoping he didn't notice the hesitation. "I'm fine. Busy, tired, the usual, but fine." And she would be, as long as she kept declaring it.

"Your mom in the kitchen? Is that stir-fry?" Robbie took a long breath through his nose.

"Yup." They could hear the sizzling all the way in the foyer, not to mention smell the spices and vegetables. If they went to look in on her, they'd find her, wok in hand, pan spitting hot, stove cold. Still using her powers to do something as simple as cook a meal. She hadn't burned herself out, so to speak. Powers were so unpredictable, so chaotic. Celia didn't like to think what would happen if Arthur ever lost his powers—or lost control of them.

She quickly tucked that thought away because Arthur came in then from the elevator. He'd retreated to his own office to wrap up the week's paperwork—pretty much at the exact moment Celia decided she'd be okay on her own, with her computer and a project. He'd probably been listening—sensing, scanning, however he did it—and knew that Robbie had arrived. The two men shook hands. Standing next to his former teammate, Arthur looked older. Not old—he was ten years younger than the rest of the Olympiad. But the sheen in his hair had begun to go silver, noticeable next to Robbie's icy gray.

They were all so much older.

The kids came out a moment later, and Robbie gushed over them. He was their Uncle Robbie, and even Anna smiled for him. They trekked to the dining room adjoining the kitchen, and the evening rolled along nicely after that. The kids set the table. Everyone asked Suzanne if she needed help, but the cook shooed them away.

Sitting at the table next to Arthur, across from her children, Celia regarded the pleasant chaos of her life, which suddenly seemed fragile.

The food arrived, stir-fried pork with an amazing array of vegetables and perfectly seasoned noodles, and everyone oohed and ahhed, then debated the merits of chopsticks, the skills required to use them, and commenced eating.

Conversation started innocuously enough with the perennial topic of school, and Bethy went off for five minutes about math and thinking about trying out for the school play and the stupidity of book reports because it was all just opinion anyway, and she finally took another bite of food, which slowed her down. Anna stared at her plate, industriously paying attention to her bites and not much else. She didn't even roll her eyes at Bethy's monologue, like usual. Teia and Lew were back in school, she reported. They didn't know why they'd been taken out in the first place. Their mother was having a midlife crisis or something, was Teia's opinion.

Everyone else reported on the state of their lives. Celia made what she hoped was an unassuming comment about too many meetings, hoping to avoid an interrogation. She did, and talk moved on.

Then Robbie said, "How about the news lately? That new super team? Looks like we might finally have that second Olympiad we've been waiting for."

Suzanne lamented, "Oh, yes, that photo. They all look so young. We were never that young, were we?"

Robbie snorted. "Everybody looks young to me these days."

They're Anna's age, Celia thought, clamping her jaw shut so she wouldn't speak. They're Anna's *friends*. Children. What would he say if it were Anna under one of those masks? She glanced at her elder daughter, who was staring at her plate, but her fork was still.

Celia's father, Warren West, the legendary Captain Olympus, had wanted more than anything for Celia to follow in his footsteps and become a superpowered hero. He hadn't gotten that. What would he think of his granddaughter following in his footsteps? Celia couldn't even guess. She was *so young*.

Arthur, eternally serene, said, "The real test will be if they stick around, or if they quit after a year when they realize how tough the job is."

"They do seem to be more enamored of the publicity than is really good for them, don't they?" Suzanne said.

"I don't know," Robbie said, spearing noodles with a fork. "There's something about these guys. I think they may be in it for the long haul. They have some real hard-core powers. They aren't going to sit on the sidelines. And you know that anonymous tip that took down Scarzen? I think that might have been them, too."

Celia realized the awful, ironic truth: In his retirement, since he was no longer able to live the vigilante lifestyle himself, Robbie had become a superhero groupie.

She said, as gently as she could manage, "What you really want is to sit them down and dispense advice, isn't it?"

"If I thought they'd actually listen to an old man like me. But no, the books are out there, let them read up on me if they want advice. It's all on paper."

"You think they can do it?" Anna asked, after her long and pointed silence. "I mean, do you really think they can be like the Olympiad?"

"I really think they're crazy," Robbie said. "But then again, *we* were crazy." He chuckled like it was a good thing. "I'm looking forward to seeing what they do, that's for sure."

"It'll certainly be interesting," Suzanne added.

"Can we talk about something else?" Anna said. "This . . . it's just sensationalism."

"Sometimes I think that's the point," Robbie replied.

"Anna's mad because she wishes she had superpowers," Bethy observed.

"No, *you're* the one who wants powers," Anna shot back, more a reflexive argument than one that made sense.

"Girls," Celia said in a warning tone that was rapidly losing its effectiveness. Soon, they'd stop listening to her entirely, and wouldn't that be a fun day?

"It's not even about the powers, isn't that what you're always saying?" Anna looked straight at Celia, a challenge or a warning. "It's about doing good whether or not you have powers. Right?"

"Exactly," Celia said, but without confidence, worried where this was going to go next.

Robbie shrugged. "It's still the superpowers that make Commerce City what it is. It's part of your family heritage."

"See?" Bethy proclaimed.

Celia glared at Robbie, with a curl to her lip. "I don't know. *Not* having them is a pretty big part of their heritage, too."

"Can we *please* talk about something else?" Anna pleaded. She propped her head on her hand and was looking a bit green.

"God, you're so touchy," Bethy shot back, and Anna rounded on her.

"Girls," Arthur said softly, and wonder of wonders, they shut up. Celia was pretty sure he wasn't even using his powers on them. But when he looked at them, like he was looking *through* them, they were very aware that he was likely seeing more than they wanted him to. It would shut anyone up.

They focused quietly on their plates.

"I have dessert," Suzanne said brightly, making her way to the kitchen. The old defense mechanism, not a bit rusty.

"I'm not really hungry. Thanks for dinner, Grandma," Anna said, then shoved away from the table to stomp off, not looking back.

Celia was relieved that no one called after her. That left them all a little bit of dignity, at least. Anna was in a mood, pleading with her wouldn't change it. She remembered what it was like, wanting nothing more than to be left alone. She wondered if the others remembered.

The fruit and sherbet tasted as wonderful as expected, but they were all distracted, and conversation stumbled. Bethy finished only half of hers before fleeing, claiming a mountain of homework. Then, oddly, Celia felt like the kid at the table. The evening ended quickly after that. Robbie said enthusiastic thank-yous and made farewells. Arthur walked with him to the elevators, leaving Celia to help her mother clear up.

Suzanne, who usually bustled through the kitchen cleaning up after meals, was slow to start. She sat straight in her chair, in her place at the head of the table, gazing over the remains of the meal. Mostly successful, despite the moodiness of teenage girls. But tonight, Suzanne seemed sad.

"Mom?"

"I miss your father," she said.

Celia started crying. She couldn't help it. All day long, all the reasons she'd had to cry and hadn't, not once. She was saving it up, she told herself. She'd cry later. But then her mother said exactly what she'd been thinking and it all came out, tears streaming, her swallowing her own breaths to try to keep from making noise.

"Oh, honey, shh." And just like that Suzanne came to her and held her tight, and Celia clung back. She almost told her mother everything. But she just cried until they pulled apart, and Suzanne smoothed back her hair and kissed her forehead, and they cleared away the dishes. Everything back to normal.

TEN

When Robbie insisted that Teia and her bunch had been the ones to tip off the cops about the drug dealer, Anna nearly screamed. Everything after that, she deserved a medal for self-restraint. Turned out she did care about publicity. Or at least recognition. Who knew? But she kept her mouth shut. She could lead the secret double life of a superhero vigilante, just watch her.

She practiced. She looked for Mayor Edleston after watching videos of his speeches and reading articles about him from the last campaign. Found him, but only when he was where she expected him to be—City Hall or the mayor's mansion, for example. She attempted to track down various celebrities and found she could really do it only when she knew what part of the city they were going to be in anyway. She tried to hunt them down after only looking at a picture, but that didn't work—she actually had to know something about them, which meant trolling celebrity gossip websites. It was a frustrating handicap. And she gave herself a headache.

She'd started searching missing children websites and reports. She hadn't yet gotten enough information to be able to find them. But she kept trying, because if she could save just one kid she'd at least feel useful. Most of the stories just made her sad.

The next day, superteen trio made the news again, stopping a gang fight outside a convenience store late the previous night. Five guys with knives and lead pipes about to pound each other into goo, and they'd been stunned and frozen in place—obviously the calling cards of Lady Snow and Blaster. The official police statement repeated well-worn phrases about not condoning vigilante justice, even as they took the gang members into custody. The tabloids and hero groupie websites were rapturous: "Commerce City's New Ice-Cold Supers Are Red-Hot!" The accompanying pictures were stills from black-and-white security footage, and the darling among those showed Stormbringer and Blaster high-fiving while Lady Snow looked on proudly, hands on hips. Anna could have gagged.

The trio had gotten a name, too: the Trinity. The Super Attention Whores would have worked just as well.

Anna wasn't ready to give up, but she and Teddy needed another plan. Another mission. So what if they didn't get credit. They did this because it needed to be done, not because they wanted attention. They just had to keep going until people realized that there was another, subtler, more mysterious team at work in the city.

At school that day, Anna avoided Teia. The car pulled along the drive, and Anna knew Teia and the others were hanging out by the front steps like usual, probably grinning and ready to brag. Anna wasn't up for it, so she asked Tom to continue on to the middle school. She would walk back.

"I need the exercise," she explained. A really lame excuse, but she didn't care.

"I'll just nag you for five more minutes," Bethy said. "Who are you avoiding?"

"I'm not avoiding anyone."

"Liar."

Tom looked at them both in the rearview mirror. He never yelled at them when they fought, like Mom and

Dad and Grandma did. Which meant they actually fought less in the car than anywhere else.

"I don't want to talk about it," Anna said finally. Amazingly, Bethy didn't respond. At the middle school, they both piled out of the car and Anna started the trek back to the other side of the campus.

"Anna," Bethy said, and Anna hesitated. "Is something wrong?"

"No," Anna said and kept going.

Her power was absolutely useful for avoiding people, and she made it all the way to first period without seeing anyone she'd have to talk to for more than a hello. She waited until lunch to track down Teddy, dragging him off to a table way in the back of the lunchroom to talk. From the far side of the room, Teia might have looked at her and laughed at one point. Whatever. For years, they'd eaten lunch together. They were supposed to be a team. Their separation now was an ache that Anna tried to ignore.

"We have to do something else," Anna said. "A follow up. We have to build up some momentum." Like the Terrible Trio, she thought. Not that this was a competition or anything.

"I've got some ideas," Teddy said, eager. "This spy thing, it's working, I think. I mean, it will work. It's a good idea. It worked with Scarzen, we can make it work again, if we have good intel." He nodded sagely, obviously pleased with his use of the vocabulary. "We study police reports, right? The most wanted lists, things like that. We could go after some of those guys. Maybe not catch them—we're not really good at catching people, I'm guessing. But even if all we do is collect evidence for the cops, it'll help."

"It's not enough," Anna said. "We can't just keep

sneaking into buildings and hope we grab the right thing, then hope the police actually do something with it. You know that Scarzen is out on bail already? Everything we went through and he's not even in jail. You'd probably be better off joining the Threesome of Doom."

"But I want to work with you," he said, stretching his hand on the table, like he stopped himself from reaching out to her. "But we have to do *more*." Because that was the whole point, to do something with the powers they had. "You want to feel like we're really doing something— let's try a patrol tonight. A real patrol. Just to see what happens."

"So you can get beat up again?"

"I've gotten better," he said, frowning. "Let's try, just once."

He was so eager, she couldn't say no. That floppy hair, that innocent smile. So straight and tall he might have been a figure on a recruiting poster. I want *you*. "You're such a Boy Scout," she said. He blushed.

They made a plan to meet that night. Just to see.

Anna had math class with Sam in the afternoon. She wasn't prepared to face his sneer and whatever so-called witty insults he came up with. So she moved to the front of the class while he went to the back, bent her head, and frowned in anticipation. Ten minutes into class, she glanced back to see him with his head down on his desk, asleep. The glamorous life of the costumed superhero— there it was, right there. She was absolutely gleeful, in a petty, vengeful way, that he was so tired. But she also felt sorry for him. Just a little.

The teacher hadn't noticed yet, mostly because he was facing the chalkboard, writing and explaining. Quietly, Anna tore a page from her notebook, crumpled it up, took aim, and threw. Didn't quite make it—the projectile bounced on his desk instead of hitting him directly. But he started awake anyway, blinking sleepily.

She noticed the shadows under his reddened eyes. He looked around, saw the paper and her staring back at him. Figured it out, pressed his lips into a chagrined pout. She turned back to the front before the teacher noticed.

They met at the fountain in City Park and made plans from there.

Teia and the others—Anna refused to call them the Trinity, whatever the newspapers said—were also out and about that night. They were in the harbor district, though, and Anna made sure they would all stay carefully out of each other's way. She wondered how Sam was coping, how many ultra-energy drinks he'd downed in order to be able to function tonight.

She'd had a cup of coffee from the shop around the corner from West Plaza.

Midnight at the fountain, they masked up and started a circuit that tracked around the park's perimeter and pushed into neighboring cross streets. At the wilder corners of the park, it was easy to imagine that the place turned into a forest at night, oak and maple trees sending skeletal canopies across bike paths, surrounding buildings giving the impression that they were trapped in a canyon, traveling toward an unseen exit point. The chill on Anna's skin came from more than the winter air. Her breath fogged.

They didn't speak. They both looked around as if searching, but Anna didn't see anything but rocks, trees, lawn, benches, skate park, duck pond. Only what was supposed to be there. When shrubbery rustled, it was always an animal, not a hideous criminal who'd decided the lilac bushes were a great hideout. Her mind wandered. She should probably be in better shape for this. If they were going to be spending a lot of time running around the city on foot, they probably ought to work out in the meantime. And keep up with school, and continue pretending that absolutely nothing was out of the ordinary. Right.

They circled back around to the fountain after a couple of hours. Nothing had happened, not even on the bad side of the park. Not a single crime in progress or any nefarious goings-on. All they saw were some harmless street people and a stray dog. Teddy suggested that maybe they could catch the dog and leave it at an animal shelter where it could get help, but when they tried to go after it, it ran out of sight. They couldn't even heroically save a stray dog.

They had a scare at one point. When they reached the west edge of the park, a police car turned the corner and cruised right along the sidewalk where they walked. They froze, and the car's spotlight turned on and swung over them.

The cop definitely spotted them. The light hesitated for a second, and they stood like idiots, staring back at it. But the light passed on, and Anna was able to see into the car well enough to spot the cop talking into his radio. The next thing he'd do was come after them, tell them to stop, question them, maybe even arrest them. Well, arrest *her,* since Teddy could use his powers to escape. But the cop didn't stop the car and continued down the street and out of sight.

Anna's knees went to jelly and she almost had to sit down.

"That was close," Teddy said, heaving a nervous breath. "Do you think he saw us?"

Yeah, Anna knew they'd been spotted. But they weren't important enough to do anything about. Figured.

Walking patrol didn't provide any more opportunities for immediate action than searching crime-ridden neighborhoods for evidence did.

"Maybe that wasn't such a great idea after all," Teddy

said, finally breaking the silence. His voice seemed loud. "I'm sorry."

"Well, it wasn't a total waste. It proved I need to take up running or something to get in shape. Is it too late to join the Elmwood track team?"

"Maybe we can try again tomorrow," Teddy said.

"Maybe."

The routine of getting home was well practiced. She took the late bus, got off to walk the last couple of blocks. Before reaching home, though, she stopped, her gaze gone suddenly fuzzy. A presence intruded on her awareness. Someone familiar but not family. She hadn't been looking for him, he wasn't a part of her everyday awareness, so she noticed only when he got close. Right before he sailed out of the sky, almost on top of her, and fell to a three-point landing a few yards away. She didn't flinch.

"Eliot," she said. He was wearing his mask and costume tonight. "Were you following me?" She flushed, all her embarrassment at their last encounter rushing back.

"I spotted you at the park, sure." Didn't seem at all apologetic. She'd been so focused on Teia and the others, and looking for bad guys, she hadn't thought to look for him. All he had to do was track the bus from the air. If he'd followed her all the way home, that would have been a disaster.

"Why not show yourself there? Why follow me?"

"Don't get so worked up there, kid."

He was making fun of her. She marched off, determined to be angry.

"Hey, Rose—wait a minute. I'm sorry. I wanted to talk to you. Just you, not your friend."

In spite of herself, she felt a bit of a flutter at that. Maybe he wasn't making fun of her. No, either way, she was being stupid. But she stopped and waited for him to catch up. "Okay."

"We can talk on the way to wherever you're going—um, where are you going?" He looked around to the skyscrapers and office developments of the downtown business district. Not someplace she'd be expected to stroll around in the middle of the night. The glowing blue logo at the top of West Plaza glared like a beacon, the crescent shape like a half-lidded eye surveying her, judging her.

She pointed in a random direction opposite West Plaza. Some bars and all-night food stands lined the street a few blocks away; that ought to distract him. They walked.

Eliot said, "You know Commerce City better than I do, since I'm not from here—"

"Where are you from?"

He hesitated, not wanting to give up information any more than she did, and she was about to tell him it didn't matter, but he said, "Delta. Ever been there?"

"No. Is it cool?"

"About the same—big city, with all the big city stuff. Commerce City is always better if you like superhumans."

"Or worse if you don't."

He smiled. "Yeah, I guess so. Anyway, I've been going out. Like you guys, not really doing anything but just looking around. And I've been hearing rumors. Commerce City hasn't had a real supervillain since the Destructor. Is that right?"

Anna said, "It depends on what counts as a supervillain. There was Steelyard, the carjacker. He didn't have powers, he was just the ringleader of all the grand larceny in town for a couple of years, and the Block Busters took care of him. Techhunter shows up every now and then, but nobody knows if he really has powers. I don't know if he's a real supervillain; he's pretty small scale, robberies and pranks and stuff. He's never tried to take over the city or anything, and no one's been able to find him to go after him." Every few years saw a new master criminal looking to take over the title of Commerce

City's grand archvillain, but none of them had risen to the level of fame and terror the Destructor generated. Her own family's history with the Destructor was the stuff of legend. When Anna read the old news stories, they felt like fairy tales. She did the research on the old heroes at the school library, so no one in her family would see the books or look up her browser history.

Most commentators claimed that for whatever reason, the city's golden age of superpowered heroes and villains had long since passed. Everything after that would necessarily blaze less brightly. All the city had now were petty criminals and clueless kids playing dress-up.

"So if I told you I was hearing rumors about a new supervillain on the rise, you'd be surprised."

"A little, maybe. I mean, anyone can call themselves a supervillain but they'd need to prove it."

"This one's subtle, apparently. Works behind the scenes, gets others to do the real dirty work. Has a long term strategy. Taking-over-the-city stuff, but doing it without anyone noticing."

"Subtle, huh? Like what, bribing politicians, buying up property?" Because that was how she'd do it. Maybe run for office. It wouldn't even be illegal.

"Yeah, along with powers like mind control."

She gave him a look, her brow furrowed. "Really?"

"The thing about mind control, you wouldn't even know it was happening, would you?"

She couldn't tell him that she was very familiar with how mind control worked. "You think there's a villain mind-controlling the whole city to do his bidding?" The thing was, it wasn't entirely outside the realm of possibility. The implications were frightening, so she wasn't willing to latch on to the idea just yet.

They were approaching a noisy part of downtown, and she guided Eliot down another block. They were both still dressed up and would attract too much attention.

"People—the people I'm hearing the rumors from—are calling him the Executive."

She raised an eyebrow. "Is that supposed to be scary?"

"Ominous, I think. You have to admit, if you think about how much someone can do behind the scenes, it is pretty scary."

"I haven't heard anything about it. You want us to keep our eyes open for anything suspicious? Anything out of the ordinary that might suggest a mind-controlling supervillain?"

"We're probably not ever going to catch someone like that directly, but we should be able to find the effects of his power."

"I guess you needed help after all, didn't you?" She grinned at him, feeling smug.

He spread his arms in a shrug. "And I let you know, just like I said I would."

"Now it's gotta work both ways. If you find out anything about this Executive, you'll let me know?"

"Then I need to know where I can reach you."

A cute guy was asking for her phone number. She didn't even care that he wasn't talking to *her,* but Compass Rose. Or that she couldn't really give it to him. The mystery just made it all more interesting, didn't it?

She wrote down her e-mail address, the anonymous one she'd used to send the pictures to the cops. Then he waved good-bye, stepped back, and launched himself skyward. He landed agilely on an art deco overhang of a building, and a second leap carried him out of sight.

To hear Eliot talk, this villain, the Executive, was less than a rumor. More like an idea he just came up with. If Commerce City really did have a nascent villain, surely she'd have heard about it. Rooftop Watch or one of the other superhero fan blogs would have mentioned it.

Shockingly, when she went searching, Rooftop Watch

did have a few hits. The site didn't use the name Executive, but there was speculation. A hint here, a bit of gossip there, nothing more than that. No confirmed sightings, no verified activity. Just conspiracy theories thrown into the ether. Anna read them all.

The Executive was a shadowy figure, of course. So shadowy nobody knew anything about him—or her. In fact, this supposed villain was mostly a convergence of patterns: city government made unexpected decisions that coincided with certain political scandals, that removed a specific person from office, that allowed passage of a new set of legislation, and suddenly the whole future path of the city changed.

The Executive was a villain for the conspiracy minded. The so-called clues involved shady real estate deals, buildings downtown that might or might not have been built to code, which meant they might or might not harbor deadly secrets—West Plaza was the prime example of how a seemingly ordinary building could be fitted with hangars and bunkers and fantastical gear. The Franklin Building, Horizon Tower, even City Hall was suggested as having a secret subbasement containing the evidence collected from past supervillains—a tempting target for new villains, perhaps? Were they secret supervillain lairs? And how would one tell? It was all woolgathering. Nobody could ever point to an individual behind the conspiracy, though some people tried—the mayor, the DA, and even the owner of the Commerce City Chargers baseball team, who had apparently benefited from a change of zoning laws that allowed a new stadium to be built. But commentators figured there must be someone or a cabal of someones acting as the secret masters of the city. Of course, and this was more likely, it could all just be coincidence.

Anna thought of something her mother said sometimes, with a grin and a knowing look, suggesting a joke no one else got: There's no such thing as coincidence in a world with superhumans. The website featured occasional posts from various contributors suggesting that this news item or other indicated another piece of evidence as to the possible existence of the Executive. The recent series of city planning meetings was a popular topic of discussion. If someone like the Executive existed, certainly the planning committee would attract his attention and serve as a tempting target for interference. Someone had even done a chart of all the people who attended the meetings and which of them might be the Executive. Anna's mother was on the list, but without any accompanying notes or evidence. Too prominent, the commentators agreed. She couldn't possibly be a shadowy, behind-the-scenes manipulator simply because she was too well known, as the daughter of the Olympiad who had so publicly rejected that part of her life.

Then again, she had that youthful association with the Destructor. Most commentators dismissed that as old news.

It was all very vague. Anna could try to track down some kind of evidence of who the Executive was and what he was really doing. But there wasn't even enough information to start an investigation. She'd just have to do what Eliot suggested: keep her eyes open for any evidence that might present itself.

That same night, the Trinity stopped an actual, honest-to-God bank robbery. The MO was standard by now: The police arrived to find the robbers immobilized and unconscious, chilled by ice or knocked out by blasts, and the supers lingered just long enough to make sure that blurry photos were acquired. Anna was sure Teia was calling the *Eye* to tell them where to be. Teia was also probably keeping a scrapbook and practicing lines to use on Anna to rub her face in it.

Even if she and Teddy had stumbled across a bank robbery during their patrol, what could they have done about it? Nothing. That day at school, she avoided everybody, Teia, Lew, Sam, even Teddy. She didn't want to talk about it, so she hid out until the bell rang and everyone else had gone to class. Being five minutes late was a small price to pay.

Maybe Eliot would e-mail her. Maybe.

The second time they went out on patrol—Teddy insisted on giving the patrol another try because he said it made him feel like a real superhero even if they didn't actually accomplish anything—he brought his paintball gun, fully loaded.

She'd been furious. "What, we can't actually stop bad guys so you want to just piss them off?"

"I just want to try something," he'd insisted. At this rate, they were going to end up in jail for being public nuisances. She couldn't talk him out of it, so there they were, in the run-down tenement neighborhoods south of downtown, Anna skulking and Teddy striding confidently, holding the paintball gun across his chest like he was in some war movie. The guy *really* wanted to be an action hero, and it seemed tragic that his powers were so unassuming.

He was still more powerful than she was. She wondered if she could expand her awareness to, maybe, concepts. Like she could think about "crime" or "mugging" and be able to locate something like that happening nearby. She gave herself a headache trying, but she could only ever find people, and only ones she'd already spent a lot of time thinking about. Like Eliot.

She needed to stop thinking about Eliot.

The city at night was becoming increasingly familiar, and even comfortable. The regularly spaced yellow halos of streetlamps illuminating near-empty streets, walls of shadowed buildings blocking out the sky made the whole place seem like a kind of oversized playground. As long as you knew where you were, knew where you were going, and paid attention to what was going on in between, the city at night couldn't hurt you.

She was pretty sure they weren't going to find anything just by walking around. The Trinity had all the luck on that score. So she was surprised when they heard an incongruous wrenching, metal on metal, and an associated string of cursing.

They slowed at the end of the block and peered around the building's corner. Up ahead, two guys with a crowbar and bolt cutters were breaking into the steel overhead door at a loading dock. Anna didn't know what was in the building; in this part of town, it was just as likely to be abandoned. Still, the guys were breaking and entering. This was exactly the kind of situation the Trinity would eat up. She sighed. Teia and the others were out and about, but not here.

"Here," Teddy said, handing her a cell phone. She didn't recognize it—it wasn't his usual phone but a cheap pay-as-you-go model, the kind you could get at convenience stores.

"What's this?" she whispered.

"Call nine-one-one."

That plan was better than nothing. They might be little more than a neighborhood watch at this point, but at least it was something.

"And stay out of sight," he said, before vanishing.

She stopped herself from calling out to him, gritted her teeth, and called the cops.

"Nine-one-one dispatch, what is your emergency?"

"Um, yeah, I'm at the corner of Vineland and Fifty-third, and there's a couple of guys breaking into a building here. They've got crowbars and stuff and they're wrenching the door open."

The *thunk* of the paint gun firing sounded up ahead, right in front of the loading dock door. No sign of Teddy. Point-blank range, and they didn't see him. He fired four or five shots, and all of them hit. The guys writhed and shouted, but when they turned to look for their assailant, they saw nothing. Anna saw nothing. Teddy fired another two shots, which hit, and the guys doubled over at the impact, straight in their guts. Had to hurt.

"Ma'am? Are you still there?" the dispatcher asked.

"Um, yeah. These guys? One's white, one's black. They're dressed in black coats and stocking caps. And, um . . . they're splattered with yellow paint. Really bright yellow paint."

"Did you say paint?"

"Yeah. Like from a paintball gun."

"I'm sending a patrol car to that location now. Are you in any danger?"

"No, I'm fine. I . . . I have to get going, bye." She switched off the phone.

Unable to figure out who was attacking them with paintballs, the hoodlums ran. The problem was, they ran right toward her and would be on her in seconds. She turned and charged for the nearest likely hiding place—the stairwell down to a garden-level doorway. They probably wouldn't take well to having a witness and were still hefting the crowbar and bolt cutters.

Hunched down on the concrete steps, she listened to their footsteps pound away. Much closer than she expected, a police siren howled. A patrol car, right in the neighborhood. One of the crooks cursed, and this was all going to get very exciting in a couple of minutes.

The actual pursuit and arrest happened a couple of blocks away, so Anna didn't get to see it. If the guys were still holding their array of tools, they were sure to be taken in and charged. She imagined the stray yellow paint spatters would tell the cops exactly what door they'd been attacking.

She wanted to get out of the area entirely, but she didn't feel like leaving her hiding space until she was absolutely sure she wouldn't be spotted. Teddy had it easy.

Finally, a voice hissed above her. "Hey, you can come out now."

As she tromped up the stairs, Teddy flashed into visibility. It was like switching on a TV.

He was grinning. "Wasn't that cool?"

She handed the phone back to him. "You could have told me you had a plan."

"I wanted it to be a surprise."

She rolled her eyes.

"So now we have a system," he insisted.

"That isn't a system, it's—" She threw up her hands and glared, because she couldn't think of what that was. "We still need the cops to do all the work, you know?"

"You're no fun."

"I'm sorry I'm no fun." She walked off. She was tired, frustrated, and she wanted to go home.

"Anna—I mean, Rose! Wait up!"

"I'll talk to you later," she said and caught her own bus home.

ELEVEN

Celia's schedule was full. She liked it that way, now more than ever.

Second and third opinions on the leukemia diagnosis were acquired, confirming the first diagnosis. She and Arthur spent an afternoon poring over treatment options and survival statistics. The prognosis was generally good. If the chemotherapy worked, she'd probably be fine. If it didn't, treatment options remained, but her odds decreased. It felt like rolling dice. Nothing to do then but roll and get it over with. Arthur made discreet phone calls and they arranged for her to receive treatments in one of the penthouse's unused guest rooms. She hired a nurse and paid very well for her secrecy. Celia would receive her first round of chemotherapy by infusion on Friday afternoon, have the weekend to deal with side effects, and do everything she could to be back on her feet by Monday. No one would ever know, not until she was good and ready to let them know.

In the meantime, she had a company to run.

At the next city planning meeting, the committee would vote on which contract to award: West Corp's downtown development project or one of the sprawling suburban expansion plans, including the one backed by Danton Majors's company.

The meeting itself looked much like the previous one—same people, same room, same bitter coffee smell, same political subtexts. The vote didn't cause much tension because the outcome was predictable. She'd worked hard for this, on behalf of the company and the city, and the committee wouldn't award the contract to an outsider with a misguided agenda. This vote was just a formality, Celia hoped.

When she entered the room, she noticed Danton Majors right off. It might have been her imagination, but he seemed to be watching for her. His face was turned to the doorway, and his dark eyes lit up when she entered. He gave her a moment to exchange pleasantries with the deputy mayor's assistant and chair of the city planning committee before he strolled over to have his own words with her.

"Mr. Majors," she said. "One might think you've decided to move permanently to Commerce City."

"I confess, I'm tempted," he answered, his smile charming, his gaze predatory. "I had no idea there were so many opportunities here."

"Oh, yes. Endless opportunities."

"Ready for round two, then?"

"Is that what you're calling it?" She tried to look thoughtful without laughing.

Mark was here again as part of the committee and gave her an encouraging smile across the room. Her heart sank at the sight of him. He was another person she'd have to tell about her illness, another person who would kick her ass for keeping it secret. She put on a good face and returned the smile. A good face: That was the whole point of keeping the secret.

She made a decision then, sudden and abrupt, which was unlike her. But right now, she felt like she was drowning and had to do something. Arthur was right. She couldn't keep the secret for long. The committee vote was the important thing, the business could run itself after that. After the vote, she could hand the whole project over to her managers, tell everyone she had cancer, and focus on taking care of herself. Just a few more hours.

The chairman of the committee consulted with Mayor Edleston, who then made his way to the podium and called the meeting to order. The shuffling of papers and file folders rained throughout the room, which amused Celia because everyone also had laptops and netbooks open.

As the mayor began his opening remarks, a very young man, probably fresh out of law school, came into the room, fidgeting and seeming out of place despite his nice suit and fashionable haircut. Intern, she pegged him. He glanced around, swallowed, and found the courage to approach the planning committee chair, sitting at the head of a long table at the side of the room. He handed the chair one of several manila envelopes he carried, they whispered a moment, and the chair looked across the room to Celia. The guy blanched, then came toward her, holding another slim envelope like a shield. The mayor hesitated, trickled out a few more words of his opening remarks, then fell silent. Everyone watched her like she was on stage.

"Thank you," she said, accepting the package. She drew out the contents in what she hoped was a confident manner, without fuss. It was a clipped stack of papers. She read the cover page, flipped to the page behind it, flipped back. The format was familiar, she knew what it said, but she couldn't quite seem to take it in. The words made sense, but their meaning didn't. Her brow furrowed, and she attempted to strategize on the fly.

"Mrs. West?" Majors asked. "Is something wrong?"

Leave it to him to poke at her. She made a noncommittal hum and tried to wave him off. She'd just been served papers, and she couldn't think of why. The language was dense legalese, she needed to parse it, and wasn't at all inclined to discuss it with a rival like Majors. Though the man seemed suspiciously pleased, like he already knew what the packet said.

It was the committee chair who said, "West Corp is being sued."

Might as well have said her cat had died, the way everyone looked at her with shock and pity. She scowled back. The plaintiff was a small contracting company, Superior Construction. She'd heard of them, barely, but they'd dropped out of the city development talks early on. Too big a pond for them to play in. Now, they were suing West Corp for monopolistic practices that excluded fair trade and competition. The company had also applied for an injunction against any further planning committee activities until West Corp's role in the proceedings and the true extent of the company's monopoly on city development could be determined.

While the meaning of the pages sank in, the committee chair, city attorney, and mayor huddled together in a conference. She wished they hadn't been clever enough to move away from the podium's microphone, so she could hear what they were saying.

Danton Majors sat with his hands steepled, resting on his chin, examining the scene like a chess player, revealing no emotion but studious interest.

Celia couldn't say a word until she got her own lawyers on the case. And figured out what Superior Construction was really trying to do. This smelled fishy.

The mayor, looking a bit green around the gills—the results of the planning committee's work was supposed to be his big triumph this term, with his reelection bid coming up next year—returned to the podium microphone, clearing his throat. "In light of this new development, we have decided that it is in the city's best interest to postpone the planning committee's vote on pending projects until the matter can be investigated and details brought to light. Thank you all for understanding. We'll be in touch with your various offices when we know more."

Someone wanted to sabotage West Corp's plans. That was all this was. Celia was certain she could get the whole lawsuit thrown out, but in the meantime the vote would be delayed, and anything could happen in the interim. First thing, get the suit dismissed, then she'd figure out who was behind it, and why. So much for her vacation. So much for letting go of the project, letting go of the secret . . . She could see the worst-case scenario play out if her medical news went public now: Superior Construction would accuse her of making a play for sympathy, demand to see her records, her right to privacy be damned, and there'd be yet another court fight over the whole thing. The best solution: maintain status quo for as long as possible. Keep pretending that all was well. Don't give them the least little crack to dig their claws into.

Everyone came up to her wanting to talk. She shoved the summons into her attaché case, smiled nicely at them all, and didn't budge from the standard line: "I'm sorry, I can't comment until I've discussed this with West Corp's lawyers. I'm sure you understand."

Mark was on hand to deftly block the bulk of the crowd from her path.

"You okay?" he asked.

"Annoyed," she said, smiling confidently for anyone who might be watching. "It'll be fine. Someone threw red tape in front of us, I just have to cut through it."

"Anything I can do?"

"Better not, someone will accuse you of a conflict of interest for just standing here. But thanks."

The *good luck* expression he gave still seemed worried, but she waved him off.

Celia gathered her things, personally thanked the mayor

for delaying the vote, said a few unassuming words to the rest of the committee, and avoided talking to anyone she didn't absolutely have to. Danton Majors was the last in the line waiting to ambush her on the way out. She couldn't dodge.

"An unexpected round two, I take it," he said. His smile was maybe meant to be sympathetic. Or smug. Or both.

She smugged back. "I'm sorry, I can't comment until I've spoken with West Corp's lawyers."

"Ah. Of course. Well then, until round three, Mrs. West."

Mrs. West was her mother, not her. She saved her ire for a more important argument and left the room.

Reporters were waiting in the lobby. Tipped off by Superior Construction, no doubt. Maybe this was all a stupid publicity stunt. She wouldn't put that kind of thing past anyone.

She spent a stunned moment standing frozen in the elevator after the door opened, confronted by a crowd of photographers snapping pictures and reporters holding out recorders. Maybe only five or six of them, but the group seemed immense when they were all standing in front of her. Shades of days gone by, when they'd shout questions about her joining the Destructor and expect her to say something coherent.

Then she smiled and said, "I'm sorry, I can't comment until I've spoken with West Corp's lawyers." Marched straight through the middle of them to the car waiting outside, where Tom ran interference, blocking the way while she escaped into the back.

She never understood it, but she'd come to appreciate it over the years. Warren West's grave had started as a simple granite block at the edge of the family plot, where his own parents were buried. A square gray head-stone read:

WARREN WEST
CAPTAIN OLYMPUS
HUSBAND, FATHER, HERO

Green lawn covered the space and sloped down a hill to the rest of the cemetery, rows and rows of headstones dating back a hundred years. But his grave had acquired additions: a couple of extra blocks announcing "in honor of"; tributes from the city and other organizations; a statue of a heroic, stylized figure standing tall and look-ing skyward—not exactly Captain Olympus but certainly meant to recall him. After twenty years, the grave site had become a shrine. It was always covered with flowers.

Usually when Celia went to visit, she did so early in the morning to make sure she didn't have to share the space with any of the hundreds—maybe even thousands—of Captain Olympus's admirers trooping through to pay their respects. She stopped by a couple of times a year. Sometimes on his birthday, sometimes on the anniver-sary of his death. Sometimes, like this afternoon, just be-cause. A couple was already there, standing before the headstone, snapping pictures. Celia waited some distance away until they were finished before approaching and settling on the lawn, legs folded to the side.

"Hey, Dad." She didn't like to think about how much easier he was to talk to now than he had been when he was alive. He was in a box, six feet under, rotted. She didn't like to think of that, either. "I've got a lot of stuff going on right now. I know I always say that. But this time . . . I don't know. I want to walk away from it all. Grab Arthur and the kids and just go. But I can't. I keep wondering if you ever felt like that. Like throwing out the suit and just being you. I know you'd never say it out loud. Maybe I should ask Arthur if you ever thought it.

"The kids . . . well, they're teenagers, they just have to get through it. I can't make it any easier for them, but God, I wish I could. Anna—you know what I keep thinking? That Anna would talk to you. She won't talk to any of us, not even Mom. But maybe, if you were still here, she could talk to you. It wouldn't even bother me, because then at least she'd have someone. Isn't it crazy? That I just keep thinking how much easier this would all be if you were here? And I know that isn't right, because you weren't really like that, you never made anything easier, you would just keep telling me that I was doing everything wrong, and that I don't know what I'm doing or what I'm talking about—"

She shook her head, wiping her eyes before tears could fall. Gazed at the heroic statue with the smooth features that wasn't even supposed to look like her father and realized that that was what her memories of him had turned into: a featureless palette upon which she could map any emotion, assumption, supposition she wanted.

"That's not fair, I know. I'm sorry. I just . . . you'd love the girls, Dad. I wish you could have met them. And I miss you. I miss what we all might have turned into. And . . . I have leukemia. Because of the radiation from Paulson's device. I'm sick and I don't know what to do."

Her father didn't say anything.

She pursed her lips, sighed. Got up from the grass, brushed herself off, and walked away.

Almost her whole life, people came up to her—at business meetings, symphony galas, museum fund-raisers, everywhere—and grabbed her hand, squeezing it with an emotional desperation, the look in their eyes sharp as needles, and thanked her. "Your father saved my life. I can't thank him, so please, let me thank you. He saved my life." They'd been on a school bus that caught fire, they'd been held hostage at the baseball stadium when the Destructor sealed it in his electrified force field, they'd fallen from a crashing airplane, and Captain Olympus had been there to catch them, to save them.

She would offer a sincere smile and tell them that she understood.

Once, exactly once in the last twenty years, at the ribbon cutting of a new hospital that West Corp had built, a woman with a teenage daughter approached Celia and thanked *her*. Not her parents, her. "You probably don't remember us, it's been so long and it was such a mess. But that day the bus was hijacked, and you stopped it from going into the river—we were there. I'm the one with the baby. This is my baby." She put her hand on the girl's shoulder, gripping her like a prize.

Of course Celia remembered, and just the mention of the baby brought the scene back: the overheated bus, the baby screaming loud enough to rattle glass, the horrific moment when they all believed they were going to die, the bus launched into the harbor by a homicidal driver. Celia had stopped him. Killed him, actually, but no one seemed to mind that part. The faint scar on her forehead from her own injuries twinged at the memory.

The girl, a skinny thing who hadn't grown into herself yet, smiled awkwardly and looked both embarrassed and awestruck. "You saved us," the mother said, tearfully. "You saved us."

Celia had hugged them both. The girl was just a few years older than Anna, and she was alive because of Celia. For a moment, she understood her father a little better.

When she got back to her office, she found a message waiting from Director Benitez at Elmwood. Please call back, no details. This was almost certainly about Anna. Celia checked the time—the kids should be getting home from school soon. Steeling herself, she called the director.

"Hello, Ms. West? Thank you so much for returning my call. I wanted to talk to you about Anna."

"Yes, I expected that you would," Celia said. "What's the problem now?"

"She fell asleep in two different class periods today. If it had only happened once, I wouldn't worry, I know how teens are. But this really isn't like her. Ms. West, I'm sorry for asking this—but is everything all right at home?"

No, it wasn't. Of course it wasn't. Might not ever be again. But she couldn't say that to this woman. "I appreciate your concern, Ms. Benetiz, really I do. I'll talk to her, I promise."

Celia could hear frustration in the director's reply. "Yes, I'm sure you will, but there's only so much a simple talk can do, if the underlying issues aren't resolved."

"What do you suggest then, Ms. Benitez?"

"Have you considered counseling for Anna? She comes from a high-profile family, and I'm afraid she may be finding ways to act out in response to that."

Oh, honey, you haven't *seen* acting out. More polite, she said, "You may be right. I'll definitely consider it and speak with her father about it. Thank you very much for calling." She hoped the dismissal was obvious, and sure enough, the director signed off, and Celia sighed.

She didn't want to deal with this. Her daughter was falling asleep in class, neglecting her studies, and Celia somehow couldn't care all that much. Anna was a good kid. Falling asleep in class was not a moral failing. She wasn't getting enough sleep, obviously. Because she was running around all night hiding the fact she had superpowers. Mark called her—two kids matching Anna's and Teddy's descriptions had been seen wearing masks and wandering City Park. No, not wandering, Celia had told him. Walking patrol, like good little superheroes.

Mark hadn't done anything about it, thank goodness. The cops were keeping tabs, letting the kids practice, that was the whole point.

What the hell kind of superpowers Anna had that she needed to practice using—that was Celia's real concern, her most pressing question. If only Anna would just *tell* her. Which was really rich, considering what Celia was hiding.

This had gotten very complicated.

Her parents never kept secrets from her. They might have been vague on a lot of the points of what exactly their superheroing involved, but they never tried to hide the Olympiad from her, and their secret identities were never secret to her.

But this was different. Celia kept telling herself, this was different. It was personal, and painful, and she didn't want the pain to spill over to her mother, her daughters. This wasn't like a kidnapping; nobody could swoop in to rescue her.

Celia picked out a bottle of wine, got a corkscrew and a couple of glasses, and went in search of her mother. She found Suzanne in the living room, stretched out on the sofa in yoga pants and a T-shirt, reading a book and absently twirling a strand of gray-roan hair around a finger. She looked so comfortable, and Celia would have loved to join her. Take the time to read a book, God, what a concept.

"Mom, you have a minute?"

Suzanne folded the book closed and sat up. "Yes, of course. What is it?"

How had Celia ever thought that Suzanne was a terrible mother? "Want a drink? I could use a drink."

Suzanne agreed, and Celia set to work uncorking the bottle and pouring.

"Well, cheers," Suzanne said, raising her glass. She

sipped and waited. Celia sat in the armchair opposite and pondered. She wasn't even sure what she wanted to talk about, she only knew that she wanted to talk, and the blank wall of her father's grave wasn't enough. So here she was. Her brain was full and she didn't know where to start.

"How did you do it?" she finally blurted. "How did you put up with me, when I was being so awful?"

Suzanne took another calm sip and smiled affectionately. "Funny, I'm usually asking myself how you put up with us. We didn't exactly provide an ideal home life for you."

Celia couldn't count how many times her parents left in the middle of dinner, or skipped some school function, or missed Christmas, to don their skin-suit uniforms and jet off on an adventure. Celia came second.

"At least you had a good excuse," Celia said, which was not something she'd have been able to say when she was seventeen.

Suzanne gave a noncommittal shrug. "Maybe, maybe not. I really don't remember how we put up with it. We mostly didn't, if I recall. I'm just glad we managed to get through it and survive. Mostly." A sad smile for the absent figure in their lives, an acknowledgment of the great gaping hole Warren West, Captain Olympus, had left behind.

Celia had reconciled with her father there at the end. She hadn't had a chance to enjoy the reconciliation. He'd died in her arms after saving her life, and she held on to that.

Celia said, "I'm worried that Anna's not doing well and I don't know what to do about it."

"This is the moment when I'm supposed to feel a sense of sweet revenge." Suzanne did seem rather pleased, and Celia didn't blame her for it.

"I'm sorry. For the record, for all records, I'm sorry."

"Water under the bridge. We all made mistakes." She took another sip, considered. "You know, your father couldn't see past his nose sometimes, but he was always there when he needed to be. *Always.*" Emphatic, it was a statement on her own life. A declaration that Celia wouldn't argue, however much she might have wanted to.

"Celia, you and Anna and Bethy will all be fine," Suzanne declared.

The door to the penthouse foyer slammed open and shut again, and teenage footsteps, like a herd of antelope, pounded in.

". . . I don't *care.* If she asks I'm telling her, I'm not going to lie to cover your ass." That was Bethy. Bethy swearing. The word sounded odd in her young voice. They were both growing up. At least Celia's parents only ever had to deal with her. But she had two of them. Double the revenge for her own teenage sins.

Suzanne arched a brow at Celia, asking if she knew what that was about, and Celia only sighed, because she suspected she did.

"Hey, girls," she called to the foyer, and the footsteps stopped. A moment of quiet, and she could imagine them standing there, looking at each other, trying to figure out why Mom wasn't in the right place for the afternoon routine. "How was school?" Celia added as a prompt. She rejected the very notion of asking, "Tell me *what*?"

Side by side, a matched set in their uniforms, wide-eyed and uncertain, the two of them came cautiously into the living room, hesitating like they didn't know what to expect. Mom and Grandma, drinking in the afternoon like a couple of degenerate lushes. It must have been shocking.

Girls—they were young women. Anna at least was full grown. They'd long since lost their baby fat and had the lean frames they'd inherited from their athletic grandparents. They were both wearing bras, sneaking on mascara before school, and in a few short years they'd both fly the coop. Celia almost burst into tears.

"So," she said. "How was school?"

"Fine," they both said, in unison. It was kind of cute.

"The ride home was good?"

"Yeah," Bethy said. Anna was chewing her lip, looking at the ceiling, the floor, the far window, everywhere but at her mother.

"And school was boring like it always is?"

Bethy looked at Anna, waiting for a cue. When Anna didn't give her one, she mumbled, "Yeah."

It would be funny if Celia weren't so twisted up with worry. She decided not to bring up the director's call. Celia could see how puffy and shadowed Anna's eyes were. Arguing about it wasn't going to change anything, since Anna would just deny everything.

Maybe she'd make Arthur talk to her. It would serve him right.

"I really have a lot of homework, so I'm going to get to it, if that's okay," Anna said finally, pointing a thumb over her shoulder.

"Okay," Celia said. "I'm glad you're home—" she called after them, but they'd already fled.

She slumped against the back of the chair. The wine in her glass had somehow vanished. On the sofa, Suzanne looked like she was trying not to laugh. Celia glared.

"Oh, honey, you're doing fine," her mother said. "Really, you're all doing fine."

Time would tell, she supposed. A few more years, and maybe neither one of them would turn out to be a bank robber, or a henchman for the next master criminal to come along. Wouldn't that be swell?

Suzanne announced that it was time to start dinner, and the house settled into its early evening routine. Celia retreated to her office to go over a few last things and the next day's list.

An urgent e-mail flashed on her screen—from the assistant in the legal department. The initial report she'd asked for on Superior Construction was already done. And why shouldn't it be, that's why it was called an initial report. She opened the file and started reading.

Summary: The lawyers believed they could get the lawsuit dismissed as baseless easily enough, but they thought it would be worthwhile to look into countersuing for bringing a frivolous suit. And this was why Celia hired lawyers. She definitely wanted to consider a countersuit.

But what was interesting was the summary of the company itself. She had expected to discover that it was a subsidiary of a subsidiary, and that tracing the holding companies back far enough would reveal which of her crosstown development rivals was throwing up roadblocks. But the report wasn't that complicated. Superior Construction was only a few years old, and it didn't have much real history at all. It had never been awarded a contract with the city—it was unclear that it had ever made bids on any projects, which the lawyers found encouraging because proving West Corp hadn't damaged their business would be that much easier. But the details still nagged at Celia; she couldn't help but think this was all smoke and mirrors. Most telling: The company had a CEO and board listed. But the ultimate ownership? Hidden behind the law firm that had drawn up the incorporation papers. Which meant the whole thing was a front that apparently existed for the sole purpose of making Celia's life difficult. And she had a pretty good idea who might be behind it.

But suspecting that Danton Majors had thrown up a fake company to derail West Corp and proving it were two different matters.

Before dinner, she drifted to Anna's room, stepping softly and listening carefully, not eavesdropping so much as feeling like she was edging toward a minefield. She didn't know *what* was going to happen.

Steeling herself, she knocked softly on the door frame. "Anna?"

Celia expected to hear shuffling as Anna stopped whatever she was doing to arrange herself in front of her homework instead. But she only heard music playing softly from her computer.

"Yeah?"

"Mind if I peek in?"

"Sure, go ahead," Anna said, and Celia cracked open the door.

Anna was lying across her bed in front of an open book. History text, looked like. So the kid really was doing homework; Celia never doubted. The girl looked up, blinking expectantly. She'd changed out of her school uniform and into grubby jeans and a T-shirt. Her red hair was loose, flopping around her face, and she chewed absently on a fingernail. She looked comfortable. Like a normal teenager. The sight filled Celia's heart to bursting.

"Everything okay?" Celia asked. "You've seemed a little preoccupied lately." Understatement. Celia was fishing. But barging in here informing her that her father knew very well she was sneaking out wouldn't make her any more chatty.

"Fine. Mostly fine, I guess. Stressed out at school and the usual. But okay."

"Good," Celia said, mentally flailing because she didn't want the conversation to end there, but she couldn't think of anything else to say. "That's good. You know, if you need help, if there's anything I can help with . . ." More flailing. Celia could wrap the city's wealthiest and most powerful around her finger, but she couldn't talk to a teenager.

Anna's brow furrowed. "Is something wrong?"

It shouldn't be so difficult to say out loud, but it was. Wasn't going to get any easier, but Celia brushed past the moment anyway. She was protecting Anna, she rationalized. No need to dump any more problems on the kid. "There's a lot going on right now. It's getting hard to juggle."

Was that a smile flashing on Anna's lips? It might have been. "Yeah."

"I've been thinking about the beach house a lot," Celia said. "We should take a trip out that way. Maybe for spring break." The planning committee nonsense would be all wrapped up by then. She'd be just about done with treatment. Maybe by then she could drop some of those balls she was juggling.

"Yeah, that'd be cool," Anna said, and sounded like she meant it.

"All right, then. I'll put it on the calendar."

"Okay. Cool."

With that, Celia quit while she was ahead, left her daughter alone, and retreated. For one brief, brilliant moment, she and Anna had been on the same page, and Celia took that warm feeling and held on to it tightly.

TWELVE

Director Benitez must have called Mom about her falling asleep in class—she certainly threatened to—but Anna couldn't figure out why Celia didn't confront her about it. Instead, Mom had shown up at her door with that weird, probing conversation. Not that Anna was complaining. But it was becoming clear that *everyone* around here was acting wonky, and Anna was afraid it was her fault. She was the one throwing the family off, and she didn't know how to stop it.

She splashed cold water on her face to try to keep it from looking so worn and trod very quietly for the rest of the evening, hoping no one would notice her. Dinner was tense. Not even Bethy talked but kept looking at everyone as if waiting for them all to explode. Anna wasn't going to be the one to light that fuse.

And Dad just kept *watching* her. She repeated her favorite insipid pop song to herself over and over again, filling her mind with it, so he couldn't possibly see what was really there. His wry smile when he finally looked away was downright insulting, like he knew her tricks and saw right through them. He was just waiting for her to crack, and she wouldn't. She refused.

She and Teddy didn't have an outing planned that night, and Anna had the luxury of a long, splendid sleep.

The morning brought the news that the case against Scarzen had been dismissed and the guy walked. The defense lawyer argued that the evidence was obtained illegally. The DA argued that the anonymous tip gave probable cause that allowed the police to search the premises. Defense came back to say that because no one knew how the original tip was obtained, it could not be admissible, and therefore the subsequent police search was illegal. And the judge threw it out.

"The judge is crooked, want to bet?" Teddy said at school. "Scarzen must have paid him off."

Anna thought he might be onto something. Everyone knew he was guilty, so how had he been let go on a technicality? Anna looked it up. There'd been other cases where evidence obtained by anonymous tips, or even provided covertly by superhuman vigilantes, had decided cases, so why throw such evidence out now? Crooked judge. Made perfect sense, because if the justice system were infallible, the city wouldn't need superheroes.

They made a plan to spy on the judge that night. They figured there must be some evidence of a payoff, which meant bank statements or deposit stubs. Probably made as anonymously as possible. Maybe they only had to point out that the deposit was there and let the authorities take over. Teddy could go insubstantial, reach into any safes the guy had, and pull out any records. Paper was light enough he ought to be able to make it go insubstantial, like he did with his clothing.

"We can't send it to the cops," Teddy decided. "It's not like they'll thank us for helping after the last time."

Anna asked, "Well, then, assuming we get the evidence, who do we give it to?"

"How about the *Commerce Eye*?" Teddy said. And why not?

She researched the judge, Roland, found his house— a very nice brownstone in the Upper Hill neighborhood. They would stand out, walking around in all black, so they'd have to keep to backstreets to get there. She studied his pictures, his schedule, whatever she could glean from websites and news stories. Fortunately, with the news about the case being dismissed there was quite a lot out there. He didn't have much in his history suggesting he'd been bought by the drug lord. He was considered fair, if a bit of a hard-liner. Maybe they were wrong about him, and Scarzen really had been let go for a good reason. Maybe they were just looking for trouble. But that wasn't what her instincts said. And one thing all the superhero memoirs said—and even her mother when she was talking about a business deal—was that you should listen to your instincts. If something didn't feel right, it meant something was probably wrong.

Unless you were a paranoid schizophrenic like Plasma. But never mind.

If they didn't find anything at Judge Roland's house, then no harm, no foul. But if they did, they were justified.

They were getting better at this. Anna hesitated to call them "good" just yet. But they didn't have to spend as much time on logistics, and they no longer fumbled putting on their masks.

They made excuses about studying at the library for a group project and took the bus. With her power, Anna had a bead on the judge, who was due to be out of the house for a legal society dinner, along with his wife. He was a social guy and went out most nights, they didn't have any live-in staff and their kids were grown and out of the house, so the place would be empty. It would also likely have an alarm—so they wouldn't go in through the door. Teddy would climb the fire escape behind the building and phase through the back wall.

Anna played a more active role this time, as lookout rather than just navigator. They had exactly until the Rolands returned home from their dinner, and Anna would have to say when that was. Teddy would set his phone to vibrate, and she'd call him to give a warning.

They arrived earlier than they expected and had to wait in the clean-swept alley behind the brownstones for the Rolands to leave. They seemed to take forever, and she and Teddy huddled in the shadow next to a Dumpster.

She explained for the millionth time the kind of thing he needed to look for: bank statements, hidden safes, weird-looking deposit slips, anything that didn't look like it belonged. Take pictures of everything, put it all back the way he found it.

"How am I supposed to know what's weird looking?" he argued in a whisper.

"I don't know," she argued back. "Haven't you ever seen a bank statement or balance sheet? They just look a certain way."

"Easy for you to say, your mom's a financial genius. My parents are a librarian and a mechanic, I've never seen a bank statement in my life."

She sighed. "You're looking for numbers with a lot of zeros after them."

"Okay, fine. Are they gone yet?"

They were lingering by the front door, and she couldn't tell why, only that they weren't moving. "No."

They sat side by side on the concrete pavement. The ground was cold, and the air had a crystalline feel to it, like it was about to snow. She thought of Teia, but Lady Snow and the Trinity weren't out tonight. They were at home, where they were catching up on sleep like sane people. She and Teia hadn't talked in days. Anna kept waiting for her friend to call, but she never did, and Anna didn't want to be the one to back down.

She wrapped her coat tighter around her and hugged her knees. Teddy started tapping his foot. The alley was quiet, which should have been a relief. No one was going to find them back here. But she'd be happier once they had what they came for and moved on.

When she shivered, Teddy looked at her a moment, then said, "Here," and stretched his arm over her shoulders.

Her first thought was to shrug him away, but his arm settled against her, and it was warm. She just had to scoot an inch or two to be sitting right against him, so she did. His arm tightened around her, just a little. Her heart pounded, she was blushing, and then she felt *a lot* warmer. She couldn't really look at him. He didn't move, as if he worried that even twitching a muscle would make her flinch away. But she'd stopped shivering, so she huddled with him and didn't say a word.

After five or so minutes, Teddy whispered, "Um, Anna, can I ask you something?"

She forgot to chastise him for using her real name. "Yeah?"

"I know it's early to be thinking about, a few months out yet, but I was wondering, if you wanted to go to prom this spring, would you maybe want to go with me?"

For some reason, in that moment, she thought about Eliot and immediately felt guilty for it. "Um . . ." she stammered and tried to come up with a response, because she hadn't thought much about prom—except when she'd met Eliot in the gym, and she didn't really want to think about that right now. It was still months away, like Teddy said. And she honestly hadn't thought about Teddy. Not until he put his arm around her, anyway, and now they were sitting here and she was having trouble focusing—

Judge Roland and his wife were gone, out of the house. "Hey, they're gone, it's time!"

She shoved him to his feet. He looked stricken, staying rooted for a moment like he really was going to wait for an answer, but she gave him a push, and he nodded, vanishing before he'd gone two steps toward the brownstone.

She was alone in the alley, but she heard his footsteps slapping ahead into silence.

She waited, again. The air felt much colder without Teddy's arm around her. She had to think about that, what it meant, and what her answer was going to be. They were trying to fight crime, she didn't want to think about fancy gowns and awkward school dances.

She imagined how disappointed he'd look if she told him no, and she didn't want that either. God, why'd he have to bring that up tonight? Couldn't he have waited until daylight when both of them were dressed like normal people? No, he had to wait until he was dressed as Ghost, because then he had all the courage.

Tracking his progress, she followed him up the fire escape to the third floor, where Judge Roland had his home office. Teddy phased through the wall, which meant he didn't trigger the burglar alarm, which was wired to the doors and windows. Anna held her phone closer, in case he needed her.

She'd about decided he didn't need her help at all when her phone vibrated, and she clicked it on. "Rose, hey Rose."

"Yeah," she pressed the button and answered.

"There's a safe in here, I reached in and managed to phase a bunch of papers out, but I don't know what I'm looking at."

"Anything that looks like a bank deposit slip, anything that shows a lot of round numbers in a column. Lots of zeros," she reminded him.

"It all has lots of zeros," he said, plaintive.

She sighed. "Then just take pictures of it all. You remembered to put on your gloves, right?"

"Of course I did."

She checked in with Judge Roland—still out and not anywhere near the town house. They were safe, with time to spare. Teddy was rushing down the fire escape, still invisible, and she mentally tracked his progress.

"Boo!" his voice burst, right next to her.

Unflinching, she glared at the place he was standing. "I can sense where you are, you know."

He flashed visible and looked crestfallen. "One of these days I'm going sneak up on you."

"Right," she said. "Let's get out of here before somebody spots us."

They took off their jackets and masks, shoved them into their packs, transforming them back into normal teenagers who probably shouldn't have been out this late but who probably wouldn't get called on it. Five blocks away, they found a bus, and from there went to the Internet café they'd used before. Open twenty-four hours—Anna had checked. She gratefully ordered a coffee and gripped it tight to warm up her hands.

They found a booth in back of the café and made sure not to talk too loud. She scrolled through the pictures on Teddy's phone, e-mailed them to herself, and used one of the Internet kiosks to print out the most likely looking documents of the bunch. The images were mostly not *too* blurry.

From a distance, the pages that Teddy arranged on the table looked like homework. Anna took a glance around the café, which was doing a pretty brisk business for ten o'clock at night. The patrons were diverse, from the punk-looking guys at the counter to the scattered nondescript blue-collar types getting off one shift or another. A pair of uniformed cops occupied a booth at the far end of the shop, and Anna's heartbeat sped up. But they weren't paying any attention to her, and she quickly turned away.

Did this ever get less stressful? Her grandmother never

struck her as someone who'd spent a significant amount of her life stressed out—so how did you be a superhero without freaking out every time you saw a cop? Yet another thing to work on.

Teddy unhappily shook his head at the spread of pages. "I have no idea if this is going to do us any good. Wow, does that much money even exist?" He pointed at the number on what must have been a retirement account statement.

Anna turned the sheet around and looked at it. The amount wasn't that big—well, not West Corp big. Anna had a rough idea what her mother's company was worth, and this was a drop in that bucket. But she didn't say that. She bit her lip and didn't say a word about how much her family was worth. Teddy was at Elmwood on a scholarship.

Compared to the average, Judge Roland made a good living, a good annual salary as a judge for the city court. She'd looked up how much he ought to be making so she'd be able to compare, and the first few bank statements and the retirement account Teddy had commented on—for a city pension fund—lined up with that. Nothing looked unusual.

Until she got to a second set of statements. Foreign bank transfers and accompanying records. Roland might have had a good explanation for having this; she didn't know enough to be able to tell. But did one guy, even a high-ranking city judge, really ever make three six-figure money transfers in the space of two weeks? All after the date of Scarzen's arrest?

"I think this is it." She showed Teddy, who studied the page with a blank look. She couldn't tell if he understood. "Trust me, this is it."

"How do you even know this stuff?" Teddy said.

"I don't know. Osmosis or something." Every school day, her whole life, she'd go to her mother's office and give her report. Used to be, she'd spend more than a scant few seconds there, trying to detach from the situation as quickly as she could. Used to be, her mother would have her work spread everywhere, printouts with arcane lists of numbers, highlighted with colors or marked with bold, and Anna would ask, "What's that?" And Celia never said, "It's nothing, never mind." Celia always told her, showing her what the pages were and what they did. She never learned what a balance sheet was, she always just knew. She and Bethy both, but Bethy was the one who'd probably follow in Celia's footsteps and take over the business.

Anna never thought she'd actually *need* to know what a financial statement was. But suddenly she did, and she knew these looked squirrelly. Mom would know what the oddness meant. The judge had never been investigated—he'd never needed to be. He was smart enough to pay his taxes and not flaunt the windfall that exceeded his income. But a large amount of money was tucked away, waiting for retirement in another country.

She put the suspicious pages on top of the stack, shoved the whole thing into an envelope, and left the coffee shop for the *Eye*'s offices. Before handing it off to Teddy, Anna included a note in the package signed in large, anonymous block letters: "Espionage."

Teddy looked at it. "That's it? That's our team name? They'll think it's one person, not a team."

"Better to throw them off our track, right?" she said, grinning.

He said, "I kind of like it."

The *Eye*'s main office was open twenty-four hours, reporters and staff working late, but after concentrating herself into a headache, Anna was able to tell Teddy where the people were and which parts of the building he had to avoid. The editor in chief was gone for the night. Her office was empty. Teddy entered through a back wall and left the package there, then retreated along darkened hallways to the back alley where Anna was waiting for him.

"I think we're getting better at this," Teddy said brightly as they walked back to the bus routes they'd take home.

"That'll depend on what happens tomorrow," she said, unconvinced. Hopeful, but not sure that the *Eye* would believe the evidence they'd handed over.

"So. Um. You have a chance to think about what I asked?"

On the contrary, she had purposefully ignored the question. She pursed her lips and considered. "Can you maybe ask me again when we aren't running around all sleep deprived and wearing ski masks? When we're not being Ghost and Compass Rose, I mean."

"Yeah sure, okay, I can do that," he said. But he had that crestfallen expression she'd been trying to avoid.

They split up and headed for home after monosyllabic farewells.

Anna woke up early to check the *Eye* website, Rooftop Watch, and other superhero groupie sites. She figured what was most likely: The *Eye* wouldn't publish anything about Judge Roland's corruption without doing some checking. So there wouldn't be anything. But that wasn't what happened.

"Who Is Espionage?"

That was the headline and lead story, accompanied by a photo of the note she'd written. It was a shock to see her note as front-page news. But a kinda cool shock. The scoop about the judge was there in a side article, along with various comments about the judge not responding to repeated phone calls and the word "alleged" in front of everything. The *Eye* also printed a bunch of additional information, stuff she and Teddy hadn't delivered—so the paper had been keeping its own file on Roland for years and already had a stack of allegations. They published the new scoop because it gave them the concrete proof they needed to go public.

But the story the *Eye* was most interested in was Commerce City's newest and most mysterious hero. The article was filled with speculation and quotes from police and professional superhero watchers, academics, and psychologists. The article drew the line between this and the original evidence collected against Scarzen and suggested that maybe it was a personal vendetta. One of the commentators got close to the mark, speculating that Espionage's power must have been geared toward "clandestine activities"—a phrase Teddy would probably latch on to. Invisibility, teleportation, and mind control were all suggested.

Nobody suggested that Espionage could be more than one person. Anna couldn't have come up with a better disguise than that in a million years.

But there was no sign that anything was going to happen to Judge Roland. Roland reported a theft from his house to the police, but the police investigated and couldn't find any sign of a break-in, no busted locks, not so much as a fingerprint, and Roland wouldn't give an inventory of exactly what had been taken. He claimed only that items in his safe had clearly been tampered with. Roland's lawyer threatened a libel suit, but the *Eye* countered with the evidence it had in hand, and the police promised to launch an investigation, and the story faded to sidebars and afterthoughts.

No instant gratification was forthcoming. But the *Eye* managed to find something to say about Espionage every day for a week. So they were famous, sort of. And once again, the attempt to do good hadn't worked out like it was supposed to. Maybe she just ought to learn kung fu and start punching people out directly. Somehow, that didn't appeal.

"We have to go patrolling again. Tonight," Teddy insisted, during lunch. "Keep up the momentum."

They were sitting in one corner, and Anna kept glancing at Teia, Lew, Sam, and a couple of other people who were sitting in another corner, laughing about something or other while eating sandwiches and pizza. Probably not superpowered stuff, because of the civilians there. And she was thinking of their nonpowered classmates as civilians. She was going insane.

"I don't know. I'm really tired," she said, picking at her food.

"You want to let them keep having all the fun?" His gaze darted to the corner where the sometime Trinity was having an ordinary high-school lunch.

"Teddy, that's not the point, how many times do I have to say it."

"We can do more, Anna, I know we can. But we have to get out there."

He hadn't asked her about prom again. He'd completely forgotten about it, or he really didn't have the guts to look her in the eye and tell her he liked her. She thought about asking him about it—reminding him. But a perverse part of her didn't want to give him the satisfaction. She didn't want to seem that needy. It all felt so ridiculous.

"If that's how you feel, why don't you just go do it on your own?" she said.

"Because we're a team." Like it was obvious. His expression was clean, stark, not a lick of deception there. Her heart melted a bit. "Look, we head back to Hell's Alley and I bring my paint gun like last time, since that actually worked out pretty well . . ." He rambled on for a little while with an even more ambitious version of the paintball-tagging scenario, while she thoughtfully chewed her sandwich. They made plans about where and when to meet, and whether they should think about putting together some better-looking outfits. Since they weren't likely to get their pictures taken anywhere, Anna didn't know why it mattered. But it did, so there.

If they were going to go on patrol, she thought, they needed more than a paint gun. They needed to be intimidating. They needed more power.

They finished eating and gathered up their things to leave for next period.

"So . . ." she said carefully, testing. "I wondered if it would be okay if I invited someone else along."

"Who?"

"You remember the guy from the park that one time? The jumper?"

Teddy froze, like he needed a minute to process what she'd said. "Frogger? That guy? Don't tell me you've been talking to him."

"Yeah, so what if I have?"

"It's just . . . we don't know anything about him. Are you sure he's a good guy?"

She knew exactly where Teddy was coming from on that one, but she breezed past it. "I think he can help us. We can really use someone powerful. Some muscle." And boy, did Eliot have muscle. He *still* hadn't e-mailed her, though.

"And you trust him?"

"I trust him enough," she said, which was a terribly evasive answer.

"Well, I don't. Sign up Toad Man? No way."

"Jealous?"

He glared. "What? Why would I be jealous."

"You know, you were supposed to ask me again if I want to go to prom with you. You know, when we're not wearing masks in a back alley at midnight." That sounded a lot kinkier than it really was. Her life probably looked a lot more exciting from the outside.

"Okay, um." He winced, scratching the back of his head. "Yeah. So. Um. Do you . . . I mean, I guess you've had time to think about it and all. So, will you maybe go to prom with me?"

She thought about Eliot, and let that thought go. "Yeah. Okay."

"Um. Okay. Cool." He actually looked startled.

What were they supposed to do now? Hug? Shake hands? Make out? Um . . .

The chimes for next period rang, and they both made nervous, grateful chuckles.

"I'll see you tonight, then," he said, waving awkwardly and backing away.

"Yeah, see you." Her waving was just as awkward.

She started to walk to her own next class, mostly because she felt Teia coming up behind her and wanted to get away. But Teia grabbed her arm.

"Anna, can I talk to you?" Teia said.

"I'm really busy right now." She sighed, letting more frustration edge into her voice than she meant.

"This is important," she said, sounding just as frustrated and increasing her pace to keep up with Anna's retreat.

"We're late for class."

"Two seconds. Please."

At that, Anna let Teia pull her into a corner. "I read the top news on the *Eye* this morning. Nice work."

Anna supposed that if you actually knew her and Teddy, the identity of the most mysterious superhero ever was pretty obvious. What she couldn't tell was if Teia was being sarcastic. A sneering observation of how little they were really able to do. She didn't want to engage.

"You going to blow our cover?" she said, not able to sound entirely neutral.

"Nope. Code of honor. You haven't blown ours, right?"

Was that what it was? Honor was what drove Teia to make headlines? No, they were all just making it up as they went along.

"But that's not what I want to ask you about. When you guys have been out, have you noticed a lot of cops around? Maybe not a lot of cops. But maybe a patrol car driving by, or they just happen to show up right after you bag a bad guy. And I mean *right* after."

Not that she and Teddy bagged all that many bad guys, but she didn't have to say that. "I don't know. Except now that you mention it . . ." She'd noticed the cops mostly to avoid them and felt grateful every time a patrol car passed by without stopping. Which happened almost every time she'd been out doing the vigilante thing, hadn't it? She looked at Teia. "It's a coincidence, it has to be. Commerce City has a lot of cops."

"I'm telling you, every damn time we nail somebody, the cops are right there with handcuffs as soon as we call, like they were ready for it. It's been the same for you, hasn't it?"

"I don't know . . ."

"I think the cops are on to us. I think they're *watching* us."

"That doesn't make any sense. They'd have to know . . ." They'd have to know when the Trinity and Espionage were out on patrol, and to know that, the cops would have to know who they all were.

"I know that look, you know something."

"No, I don't." Yes, she did. Her mother knew everything and had recruited the cops to babysit them all. The only reason they hadn't been arrested yet was because Celia West told them not to.

"Anna—"

"I have to get to class."

"Anna! Don't walk off on me like that—"

Anna was too angry—not at Teia, not at all—to do anything but walk away.

THIRTEEN

Mark Paulson's drawling snark greeted Celia when she answered the phone. "And who *is* Espionage?"

"Hello, Mark, how are you today?"

The hardest thing was trying to sound chipper when she felt like shit. She was in bed in her and Arthur's own room pretending to have the flu after her first chemo treatment. She thought she'd have a grace period before it knocked her out. Not a chance. She felt the burn of the chemical in her veins. She wanted to sleep until it went away. But Mark called, and she couldn't ignore him.

"Ready to hear what I have to say?"

She wasn't. She knew what he was going to say, but she could pretend it wasn't true. Right up until he said the words. "Yeah, go ahead," she said with a sigh.

"My people spotted them in a coffee shop. Theodore Donaldson and Anna West-Mentis. They looked like they were doing homework. Then the *Eye* produces this secret evidence the very next day. They're Espionage, aren't they?"

Celia almost admired the elegance of the secret identity, of the clever use of a passive power like Teddy Donaldson's. She still hadn't been able to figure out exactly what Anna was doing. Maybe she just wanted to be a vigilante, powers or no. Wouldn't have been the first time that had happened in Commerce City.

"Teddy can turn invisible and walk through walls. Of course they are."

A pause, and then the real question. "What can Anna do?"

"I don't know."

"You're her mother."

"Which means I'm going to be the last person to find out." She stopped, counted to ten, and rubbed the ache from her head. "We're having some family drama over Anna at the moment. I appreciate you keeping an eye on her."

"Sorry to hear it," but he didn't sound sorry. "Celia, I know you want to let the kids stretch their wings, but I'm worried. Them going after a guy like Roland—that's awfully big quarry. My instincts say they're right, that he's rotten as month-old fish. But they can't prove it with petty larceny and hope. I know I can't completely stop vigilante activity—this is Commerce City, it's the local sport. When they stop robberies or rescue kittens from trees, that's one thing. But this is something else entirely. Breaking and entering, no warrants—we can't use any of this evidence in court because of the way Espionage is getting it. We need to steer these kids in another direction."

"Put yourself in their shoes: Your superpower is turning invisible, you're not going to be taking down any gangbangers with that, so what do you do?"

"Breaking into a judge's house and going through his things is not the answer."

"Even if the judge is corrupt?"

"We can't legally prove it," Mark grumbled.

Spoken like a true servant of the criminal justice system, but Celia didn't poke him with that because Mark was a good cop, and he was putting himself out there by even talking to her about this. Especially because he was right—she didn't want Anna ending up in jail for breaking and entering. So, how to point them in a productive, noncriminal direction? She'd have to think about that.

"Have you heard from Analise lately?"

"She calls me when her kids leave the house. They're going out about three times a week, and we're usually able to find them when they do. They haven't gotten into too much trouble. Yet."

"Oh, give them time."

"I'm afraid they're enjoying all this a little too much."

Celia had to smile at that. Ah, to be young and super-powered in Commerce City. "Wait until finals week, that'll slow them down."

He chuckled. "Whatever you say. And Celia—get some rest, you sound like you might be coming down with something."

Down and hitting bottom. "I might be. Thanks for the concern."

Celia wouldn't be able to keep doing these lunches. Her appetite was failing, so she sipped water and nibbled at her salad and hoped Analise didn't notice she was off. Not that Analise would notice, because she was picking at her own salad and looking pensive. They'd hardly chatted at all, and nothing about their usual topics. The weight sitting over them was too heavy to ignore.

"You okay?" Celia finally prompted, which was terribly ironic, she thought.

"It's killing me," her friend said, setting down her fork. "I can't stand it. I stay up all night worrying about them, and then having to pretend like nothing's wrong, that I don't know what's going on. All I can do is tell Mark they're out there and hope he can look after them."

The kids had a route they used to sneak out, to the roof of their building and then down the fire escape the next building over. Analise knew about it but didn't try to stop them, just like Anna and the escape elevator. When Mark knew that the Trinity was active, he sent a patrol to watch them. Then Mark called back when the kids were on the way home. They didn't always have a confrontation or adventure—sometimes they patrolled and nothing came of it. But he always let Analise and Celia know what had happened, so they no longer had to be surprised by the morning news. Yes, it was nerve-racking, but less so than it might have been.

"I've been out there," Analise continued. "I know how bad it can get, but when I think about Teia and Lew in the middle of that . . ."

"How old were you when you started?" Celia asked.

"Seventeen," Analise said.

"Did your parents ever figure it out?"

"My dad was dead by then, and Mom . . . she wasn't around much. Not physically, not emotionally. Half the reason I started going out was to get away from that. To prove to myself I wasn't like that."

"It worked, I'm thinking."

"I've tried to be a better mother to my kids, I've tried to do right by them—"

"You have. They're good kids. They're doing good. You knew if they had powers they were going to go out sooner or later."

"I wish it had been later. I'll be wishing that when they're thirty. Assuming they last that long."

"They will," Celia said, quickly, reassuringly. "I mean, look at the Block Busters, how long have they been at this?"

"Any sign of a Block Buster the Third coming along?"

She smiled. "I've got my eye on him." Junior had two small children, a girl and a boy. No signs of powers yet.

"That's the way to do it, go out as a team and keep your eye on the kids."

It wasn't just fear for her kids tying Analise up in knots. She had a large dose of regret in there, too. A sense of failure. So much history contained in the lines of worry on her face. Her kids were out there alone because she couldn't help them, and she felt like she'd failed them, Celia realized.

Celia decided to risk it. She pushed her glass of water across the table, to put it in front of Analise, who stared at it like it might bite her.

"Have you even tried?" Celia asked.

Analise pushed the glass away. "It's like a muscle. If you don't use it, it goes away."

Celia didn't believe that. "What would happen if you told them who you were?"

"I don't think they'd believe me. I can't even prove it anymore. You think I should tell them?"

"I think if you did, they might open up to you." And she should probably take her own damn advice, shouldn't she?

"No, I think they're having too much fun playing secret superhero. And I'm just their mother. What about Anna and Bethy? They tell you anything?"

"Not a word. Not that I can blame them."

Analise grinned. "They probably know you're keeping plenty of secrets up your own sleeve, Celia West."

Celia's smile was thin.

FOURTEEN

Anna spent way too much time on Rooftop Watch searching through shadowy cell phone pictures of purported superhuman sightings looking for news of Espionage—and the competition. Scattered among the usual posts were dozens of claims from people who'd seen the ghost of Captain Olympus pulling a small child from the street before said child got creamed by a car. Or alternatively that the ghost of Captain Olympus had been guiding the hand of the normal person who really grabbed the kid from the street. A whole miniature cult of people believed that her grandfather had been transformed into some divinely anointed guardian angel. She showed one of the articles to her mother once. Celia had smirked at it and observed that yes, she had seen the stories. When Anna asked her what she thought of it, Celia wouldn't answer directly. "Doesn't matter what I think. Never did," she'd said.

Anna wished she could have known him. She'd read so much about him. Her grandmother only ever said that she missed him, Dad said he was complicated, and Mom never said anything at all. None of them said anything about what Warren West had actually been like. Even the published biographies—all of them unauthorized—talked about Warren West like he was the disguise and Captain Olympus had been the real person.

She ended up skipping over the ghost of Captain

Olympus–as-guardian-angel stories because they all sounded the same and had the air of folklore. Once you cut through the fluff, Rooftop Watch really was the best place to get the most recent news on what the city's superheroes were doing.

The Trinity got written up in the blog four times this week. Espionage, only once. This made Anna furious, because it didn't seem fair. They weren't any stronger than her and Teddy, they were just flashier. They froze car thieves in ice, blasted vandals with lasers, and Lew saved a window washer who'd fallen from a building by launching a gust of wind under him until he landed safely. Even Anna had to be impressed at that one. Espionage mostly seemed to be good at voyeurism and running away.

She and Teddy went out on another patrol, like they'd planned.

Teddy was already there when she arrived. He'd been there awhile—early. In the end, he'd go out on his own if she refused to go with him. She was glad she could be here to watch his back, even if that amounted to little more than calling 9-1-1 if he got in over his head.

"Hey," he said, when she turned the corner and jogged toward him. He was carrying the paintball gun again. "Ready for this?"

For a moment, she didn't know how to answer that. "Yeah," she said with a sigh.

He'd made adjustments to his outfit, which was looking more sleek, more official—he'd made himself a form-fitted skin-suit mask, black with a smoke-gray stripe across the eyes, and a smoky black shirt and gloves to go with his jeans. Ghostlike. She was still in a rough jacket and ski mask. When she thought about trying to put together something sleeker, her mind went blank. What would she use as a trademark? A skin suit covered in

pink roses? Because that would strike fear into absolutely no one.

She craned her neck, searching the rooftops even though
she knew Eliot wasn't around. He was back on campus.
She'd have invited him along, but he still hadn't e-mailed
her, so she didn't have a way to get in touch with him
except to go find him. Never mind.

"What is it?" Teddy said.

"Nothing. Just thinking."

His lips tightened as he caught her gazing roofward.
"You're looking for the Human Pogo Stick—is he around,
is that it?"

"No—" Eliot wasn't, but another familiar presence
was. She tilted her head, tried to focus. Three familiar
figures were moving this way, exactly where she didn't
expect or want to see them. Anna hissed a curse under
her breath. "It's the Trinity. Lady Snow and the others—
they're here."

"What? This isn't their territory, they always go to the
harbor."

"I know."

"What are we going to do?"

"Ignore them," Anna said, but she knew that wouldn't
be so simple. The trio wasn't wandering but rather moving on a purposeful trajectory as if chasing someone.
They'd found prey and were on the hunt.

The trio emerged from a cross street ahead, confident
shadows on a street where most of the lights were knocked
out. Sam was in the lead, Teia and Lew behind, looking
over their shoulders, keeping watch. The temperature
dropped, a breeze picked up—Lew carrying a microstorm
with him. They'd gotten pretty good, she had to admit.

Anna stepped forward into their line of sight and
crossed her arms. She was pleased when Teddy fell into
place next to her, also arms crossed.

Sam spotted them first and, obviously startled, pulled into a fighting pose—feet spread, knees bent, arms raised, hands pointed. The others came up beside him and braced in their own poses, with whatever gestures they needed to use their powers. A lick of wind ruffled the hair that peeked out from under Anna's mask. She was the only one of the bunch who wasn't surprised or put off balance by the encounter.

"Lady Snow. Stormbringer. Blaster. Hello," she said calmly.

Fortunately, none of the Trinity let loose with their powers; even Lew's breeze faded away, once he realized who they were.

Teia put her hands on her hips. "Anna, what are you—"

"Compass Rose," Anna shot back. "And what are *you* doing here? Don't you guys usually patrol the harbor?"

Lew laughed, Teia shook her head, and Anna wondered what she was missing. He said, "We've cleaned up the harbor. All the crooks have moved on because they know we're watching the place. Pretty cool, huh?"

Sam blew on his fingers like they were the barrel of a gun, and Anna rolled her eyes.

"There's crime all over the city, why'd you come here?" Anna said. "This is our territory."

Sam looked around dramatically. "I don't see your flag planted anywhere." He turned to the others. "That car's going to be coming up this way any second, we don't have time to fuck around."

"What's going on?" Anna asked.

When Sam pointed at her, a shiver of fear twisted her gut—he wouldn't really blast her, would he? "We're busy, you kids step back and watch the real supers work."

Teia shook her head at that. "There's a car full of gangbangers tearing up the neighborhood. We came this way to try to cut them off."

Exactly the kind of thing they could do with their

powers. Anna and Teddy, not so much. She was inclined to walk off, leave them to it, and find easier pickings. No matter how degrading that would be.

Teddy stepped forward angrily. "We'll take care of it, this is our territory."

"How are we supposed to know that? We don't know what you do, you never make it into the news," Teia said.

Did she have to keep rubbing their faces in it?

Lew pointed at the gun. "Paintball? That's what you guys are reduced to?"

"Cut it out, it works," Anna said. At least, it worked that one time.

"Tag and bag," Teddy said, like it actually meant something, and hefted the gun like *it* actually meant something.

"Look," Anna said, wanting to get away before she said something stupid, or rather *more* stupid. "There's plenty of trouble for all of us. We're wasting time standing here arguing—"

The slide and wail of a police siren echoed down the canyon of tenement buildings. They all perked up like hunting dogs.

"We didn't call the cops," Lew said. "What are the cops doing here, poaching our catch?"

Teia turned to Anna. "This is exactly what I was talking about. We don't even have to call the cops to clean up our bad guys because they're always already there!"

"Guys, incoming!" Sam yelled.

The siren was getting closer. A car's tires squealed against the asphalt, turning a corner at high speed.

"Let's go," Lew said and took off running in the direction of the presumptive car chase. Teia and Sam followed right behind.

Anna and Teddy looked at each other. Teddy shrugged. "I wouldn't mind seeing what they do next."

"We might want to back up a little," Anna said. They pressed back against the brick wall.

Another siren joined the first. The Trinity was strung out along the block when the squealing tires rounded even closer than before, and a battered SUV swung onto their street. The pair of men visible in the cab—the vehicle's headlights were off—must have been trying to lose the cops in the grid of empty streets. But it wasn't working; the sirens were getting louder. And now the SUV raced right toward them.

What happened next might have been choreographed, an elegant display of what everyone who didn't actually have superpowers thought it must be like to have them. Teia—Lady Snow—acted first, jumping into the street. Anna almost screamed at her to get out of the way of the rocketing SUV. But Teia had a plan. Kneeling, she put her hand on the ground and a sheet of ice thick enough to skate on expanded away from her, covering the street to the next sidewalk and for a block in either direction, right before the SUV careened onto it.

Stormbringer moved in. A blast of wind came from nowhere—no, it came from straight down, sliding along the side of the building behind them, hitting the ground, slamming into the street. Anna dropped to the ground to avoid getting smashed by it; they all did.

The SUV spun out. The wind shoved it, and the frictionless ice carried it to the far side of the street, where it jumped the curb, tipped sideways, and slammed into a brick façade, with the crunching of steel and a shattering of glass.

The crash didn't stop the two guys from climbing out of the wreckage, brandishing guns. The team backed off, letting the men—typical hoodlum types in leather jackets, worn jeans, dressed up in too much attitude—scramble out of the car and step onto the ice. They held guns at the ready, and Anna figured it was already too late to run.

Blaster's turn to step forward, arms outstretched.

Both hands emitted a series of short blasts, pops of light streaming out. Each stream hit one of the guys, who fell back, sliding on the ice, slamming against the wreckage of their car. They were down.

The Trinity really was a team. They really could do anything.

Anna felt a little more useless than usual.

The two men were alive, struggling as they tried to pick themselves up off the ice, falling again, groaning in pain. Lady Snow leaned on the ground again, and another layer of ice grew across the first, thickening until sheets of it expanded and reached up for the men, encasing limbs, locking them in place. Their guns were long gone, shot out of their hands by Blaster's lasers.

Three police cars roared up, two patrol cars and an unmarked sedan. They screeched to a stop at the edge of the ice slick.

"Guys, cops," Lew called unnecessarily, but it drew the attention of the others.

"They ought to thank us," Sam muttered. "Got their guys all tied up for them."

For once, Teia didn't seem inclined to pose for any cameras. "I'm thinking maybe we shouldn't stick around for pictures this time."

A pair of officers from one of the cars was circling around the ice patch to the wreckage of the SUV, shouting orders at the hoodlums to freeze, which should have been hilarious, but no one was laughing. The guys had started to break out of their ice shells, which ended up being quite thin, but they didn't struggle when the officers picked a path to them, handcuffs in hand. They were wearing cleats on their shoes, Anna noticed. Like they'd planned for it, like they'd dealt with Lady Snow's ice slicks before.

A spotlight from the second car switched on, blasting their side of the street with light.

"Guys, scatter," Teia hissed, and the Trinity ran down the street, away from the cops. They'd had practiced running from cops just as much as they'd practiced everything else. Splitting up, each turned a different corner, in a different direction. To catch them, the police would need manpower and a concerted plan. What they had was two guys cautiously approaching as if hoping to catch a wild animal. Instead of giving chase, they cursed and stopped.

"Anna . . ." Teddy started, then vanished. Turned invisible and ran. She sensed him retreating.

"Wait a minute—" But he was long gone.

She made the mistake of turning to look straight into the light when she launched her own attempt at escape. Temporarily blinded, hands shielding her face, she ran up the block, but she was well behind the others. In lieu of other targets, the cops went after her. They were calling at her to stop, but they weren't threatening to shoot, so she kept running.

She hadn't noticed that the unmarked sedan had left the scene, circled the block, and now sat parked at the end of the sidewalk. She pulled up, trapped by the cops behind her, the car in front of her, and the ice on the street. She gave a wordless, frustrated scream. Teddy and the rest had all just left her here. The jerks. The assholes.

The plainclothes cop leaning against the hood of the car ahead of her was Paulson, captain of the downtown precinct. She knew it before she even saw him. Thank goodness she was wearing her mask. It had been a year or so since he'd been to the house for dinner, since he'd seen her. Probably, he wouldn't recognize her. Except he already knew, because he was working with her mother, just like everyone else in Commerce City with any kind of authority.

She'd unconsciously raised her hands, looking back and forth between Paulson and the two uniformed officers, waiting to see who would leap at her first. Neither of them did, but she still stood there, arms up, trying to catch her breath.

"Put your hands on your head," Paulson called, approaching her with a set of handcuffs.

He was really going to arrest her. She was dizzy, her muscles went loose, and she thought she was going to pass out. This was one of the things she'd always been afraid of, *this* was why they weren't ready to go out yet. Somehow, she didn't fall over and stayed upright while Paulson turned her so she was facing the wall and took hold of her wrists, bringing them back to clamp the steel of the cuffs over them. This was ridiculous. This was a nightmare.

"So which one are you?" Paulson said. "Trinity or Espionage?"

She didn't dare say anything. If he was working with her mother, he already knew everything. He'd take her to the police station, take off her mask, and figure it out then anyway. She had some vague notion that she ought to keep quiet until she could call a lawyer. Her mother knew lots of lawyers.

God, her mother. What was she going to say about this?

"Taking the Fifth, is it?"

Again, nothing. Paulson looked past her, to the other cops. "You two, go help Brown and Martino with those slimeballs. I've got this."

The two uniformed cops returned to their cars without argument, because of course she didn't look like any kind of a threat and hadn't displayed anything in the way of real superpowers. Paulson took hold of her arm and steered her toward the sedan. Her feet scuffed on the sidewalk; her muscles tingled with anxiety.

"Not going to say a word, are you?"

She didn't even shake her head. She was wilting, head

bowed, back curved—and stopped herself. She was Compass Rose, and maybe her friends ditched her, but if she wanted to be a superhero maybe she should start acting like it, even in handcuffs standing next to a cop car. How would one of the old-school heroes stand in this situation? Not necessarily Captain Olympus, who'd bust out of any situation before he could get close to getting arrested, of course. But one of the others, like the Hawk, who hadn't had powers but was clever and strong on his own. Or maybe her father, Dr. Mentis. She'd seen pictures of him when he was younger. He never wore a skin-suit uniform like the others but always appeared in a plain suit and trench coat. Everyday clothes. Maybe she ought to do something like that, fool people by appearing perfectly normal. But everyone knew he had power, and he always seemed like he was studying the people around him, looking right through them.

Rolling her shoulders, she tried to stand like she imagined they would, back straight, chin up, gaze cold, glaring at Paulson. Maybe pretending to be strong was enough.

Paulson sighed then, scratching his head and wincing like he had a problem he didn't know what to do with. "Get in," he said, opening the back door and guiding her inside, hand on the back of her head. She couldn't even come up with a snappy one-liner to throw at him.

He closed the door on her and walked off to confer with the other officers. She perched on the seat, trying not to squish her cuffed hands, and sighed. This was bad. It was a disaster. But it looked like she would survive it without imploding. She just had to wait for it all to be over. The minutes dragged.

Finally, he hiked back to the car, and she perked up, donning her gritty persona. The glaring one.

He opened the back door and leaned on it, opposite hand on his hip, just studying her. He seemed tired.

"What exactly is it you kids think you're doing? Besides messing up entire blocks of already broken-down neighborhoods?"

On reflection, that was a really good question. "Save the world" seemed a bit grandiose. "Petty competition between rivals" was probably closer to the mark, but also not quite right.

She leaned back to catch his gaze and said, "Are you working with Celia West to track us down?"

Paulson hesitated, appearing to think for a long time, looking out at the street, then the sky, then her. "We're keeping an eye on you, to keep you from getting hurt. That's all."

The shame and dread from the arrest faded, shoved aside by anger and a vague embarrassment. Here was confirmation. All this time, they thought they were being clever, sneaking around, successfully hiding their identities, and if not doing good, at least doing *something*. But Mom knew everything and was letting them do it. Indulging them.

She slumped back against the seat, not caring about her squished hands, and let out a deflated breath.

Paulson added, "I'm playing along, but I'm not happy about it. You all should be safe at home, not running around pretending like you're some kind of junior Olympiad. And I've told that to Celia."

"Then why do you go along with her?"

He said, "Just in case I'm wrong and she's right."

Gently, he took her arm and helped her back out of the car. Unlocked the cuffs and let her hands fall to her sides.

"You're not arresting me?"

"No. Not this time. But you kids—you people need to be more careful, okay? Just . . . be careful."

When she met his gaze this time, he seemed worried. Maybe even scared. A whole other story lay behind the one she thought she was in, Anna realized. Her father would know. Her father so desperately wanted her to talk to him. Maybe she should. If she told him her secret, maybe he would explain everything, like opening a book. Reading secrets in someone's mind must not have been anything like hearing someone say the words.

Captain Paulson left her standing on the sidewalk, got back in the car, drove off. Just like that.

By then, the patrol cars had packed up their suspects and driven off, leaving her alone in the dark, looking around, waiting for something else to happen, but nothing did. They'd put up a portable plastic barricade and strung yellow police tape around the wreck of the SUV. The sound of water trickled along the gutters as the ice slick melted.

She jogged up a few blocks until she reached the main block where the late bus still ran, where she pulled off her mask and acted like a normal person until she got home. She kept thinking Teddy would circle back around to try to find her. But no, their trajectories carried them in straight lines, away. She could have called Teddy, she supposed, but she didn't feel like waiting for him.

An hour or so after the whole thing went down, Teddy texted her: "UOK?"

She texted back "FU" and switched her phone off.

She was done with this whole vigilante crap.

On the ride to school the next morning, Bethy stared at Anna the whole time. Studying her, until Anna finally rounded on her. "What?"

"You look like one of the kids in the antidrug commercials."

Was it the shadows under her eyes? The gauntness because she hadn't been eating well? Or the surly glare?

When Anna didn't say anything, Bethy went on. "Is that what it is? You don't have superpowers, you're doing drugs?"

Anna managed to keep from snarling in reply. "I am *not* doing drugs."

"Then it's superpowers."

Anna didn't say anything, and Bethy narrowed her gaze, as if all she had to do was stare at Anna long enough and the truth would emerge.

"What am I thinking?" Bethy asked.

"What? I don't know. Probably that I'm a jerk and a terrible human being."

She frowned as if disappointed. "No, that's not it. I was thinking of the Pythagorean theorem. Just checking to see if you've got Dad's telepathy."

"I didn't get Dad's telepathy."

"Well, yeah, I can see that now. But what did you get?"

Again, Anna couldn't think of what to say. She was slightly in awe and slightly scared of her little sister. Bethy's lips turned up in a victorious smile.

"There's nothing," Anna said preemptively. "Absolutely nothing."

"Yeah, right." Bethy turned away, disgusted.

Tom was driving, and Anna caught him glancing at them in the rearview mirror. She wanted to yell at him, too, to mind his own business and stop looking like he felt sorry for her. But staying angry was taking too much energy as it was.

Teddy texted a dozen more times and tried calling; she ignored him. She didn't want to see Teddy, or even Teia, though Teia would be interested to hear about her conversation with Paulson. The cops really were babysitting them.

Her power meant that even though she could tell Teddy was ranging the halls looking for her, she could stay out of his way. Teia and the others were parked at their usual spot on the front stairs, and Anna decided to share her discovery.

"You were right," Anna said. "The cops are keeping an eye on us."

Teia didn't look at all surprised. "How? How did they know where to find us?"

"My mother knows everything. My dad probably told her. I don't know exactly how, but she's a crazy control freak and she couldn't let this alone."

"Then why? I mean, why not just arrest us? And how did they know where to find us? You don't think your mom told my mom, did she?"

Anna's frustration got the better of her. "I'm sure she did. It's obvious, it's like training wheels, they think we're too young and stupid to do this on our own, and they're probably right. We're not real superheroes, we never were, this is all just some kids' game in the park."

Teia was a wall, no reaction except a twist of her lips. Anna wasn't even sure the other girl heard her.

"Does that mean you're quitting?" Teia asked finally. Like this was a game, like there could even be a winner.

"There's nothing to quit!" Anna said. "I never did anything!"

She wanted Teia to admit she was right, but Teia would never do that. She just glared, another person feeling sorry for Anna.

Then Teddy was coming out the front door, and Anna stomped around the corner and to a side entrance so she wouldn't have to look at him. So much for prom. So much for everything.

FIFTEEN

Celia read the screaming headline on the Rooftop Watch website: "Five-Hero Smashup in Hell's Alley!" with a subheader: "Trinity and Espionage Team Up?" The only picture the site had been able to get showed the aftermath, a soaking-wet street and a smashed SUV, reminiscent of the old days when Typhoon patrolled regularly. An "unnamed police source" revealed details, naming who'd been involved in stopping the high-speed car chase. Whether by chance or design, all of Commerce City's newest heroes had come together, then scattered before police could stop them for questioning, or before any reporters could get pictures or interviews. All in all, a classic superhuman outing.

Mark called as she finished reading all the articles she could find on the incident. "Have you checked the news yet or do I get to be the one to tell you?" he said.

"Just reading it now. Pretty spectacular. What really happened?"

"Pretty much exactly as you read it." He paused, and his tone changed, the overworked cop giving way to chagrined friend. "I sort of pretended to arrest Anna."

Celia raised a brow and was grateful Mark couldn't see her expression. "Oh?"

"I just wanted to talk to one of them. Show them that this isn't a game, that they shouldn't be screwing around."

Oh, poor Anna, she must have been twisted up in knots. When he said "pretended," how far did he get?

Handcuffs? Driving her to the station? Celia had seen the girls briefly at breakfast, and she hadn't noticed Anna being any more surly or upset than usual. The kid was burying it all down deep.

"Did it work?" Celia asked carefully, in lieu of yelling at Mark for scaring her daughter.

"Well, she's onto us. She knows you know who they are and that you're keeping track of them."

Power or no, Anna was good at putting pieces together. Smart kid, and Celia was proud. "Mark—thank you. For looking out for her. For all of us."

"It's like you've always told me, we superhumans have to stick together. Take care, Celia. You sound tired."

If all she did was look and sound tired, she was doing well, because she felt terrible.

Another week and another treatment passed. It was harder than Celia thought it would be. Mostly because she'd been so sure she could get through it without much trouble with sheer willpower, and that wasn't how it ended up going. After the second treatment she threw up everything she'd eaten that day and slept for twelve hours straight. She didn't want to eat. She couldn't focus to read. She dreaded the next treatment. And the next, and the next . . .

Claiming a sudden cold or flu would work only a couple of times without raising more suspicions—or proving the very reality she was trying to deny, that she was very ill. During just the second round, other people than Mark tsked her sympathetically over the phone and asked if this was maybe serious and should she see a doctor. *That's what got me into this,* she wanted to mutter at them.

She needed more time, just another week or so, before she came clean.

She planned a "business trip" that would allow her

to vanish for a few days. She arranged fake itineraries and ticket stubs, just in case someone, namely Majors, checked. Meanwhile, she could hide, be sick, recover, and no one would know.

"And how many weeks is *this* going to go on?" Arthur questioned, looking over her fake itinerary. Celia decided she could recycle the itinerary several times over, "traveling" as part of an ongoing project that would fall through at the last minute. She could account for six weeks doing this, almost the whole round of chemotherapy. She began to entertain a hope that she wouldn't have to tell anyone at all, get cured and let it all fall behind her. A silly dream. She was only making things worse.

"Just a few," she told him, without confidence.

When she started leaving chunks of hair on her pillow, she shaved her head entirely and took to wearing the custom wig she'd had specially made to match her own hair. She penciled in her vanishing eyebrows.

"I'm worried about you," Arthur said. And she could feel it. The emotion was strong enough to slip past his barriers.

"I know. You're very tolerant."

"You're lying to the people who love you most."

"It's temporary. Just till the lawsuit gets cleared up."

He didn't say anything. He didn't even seem to be thinking anything. He stood at the window of her sickroom, her temporary prison, gazing out to a constrained version of the panorama available in the living room. The view here offered a mere slice of the city, not half of it, like the other one did.

"Next week," she insisted. "The preliminary hearing on the lawsuit will happen, we'll get it dismissed, the planning committee will finally vote, and then I'll be able to take off as much time as I need. I'll tell everyone then."

"And explain to them why you've been lying to them for the last month?"

He made it sound terrible. Because it was terrible. "Yes," she said.

"We'll have this conversation again next week," he said.

She nodded. She'd be ready, one way or another.

Celia had contrived to bring the young would-be superheroes together. Now the problem was: Where to point them? Preferably someplace that wasn't in the middle of a car chase and wreck, and that wasn't breaking and entering. Something quiet, involving surveillance and reporting. She had an idea about that.

On the plus side, Celia had direct access to so-called Espionage. On the downside, she had to feed Anna the appropriate information without looking like she was doing it on purpose, or Anna would never take the bait. She left her office because she was feeling lonely and restless and wanted to be close to her mother, to be in the presence of the old comforting sounds of cooking and conversation, and to meet the girls when they came home, before she locked herself away on her so-called business trip. That was the excuse, a side benefit of the plan.

In the meantime, it wouldn't seem strange at all if Celia just happened to spread some work on the table, to leave a folder or two with some pages suggesting some directions of inquiry. Directions that someone who could walk through walls might be particularly suited to follow up on, that a mundane corporate legal team could not.

After crunching numbers, she and her staff discovered that Superior Construction wouldn't gain anything by stopping West Corp from winning the city planning contract—because it was a shell company that didn't have any assets invested in any development contracts. Which meant it had other reasons for stopping West Corp. Which again pointed to Danton Majors, but her lawyers still couldn't draw that line directly. Why would

Majors want to stymie West Corp? A multitude of possibilities existed, from simply publicly embarrassing the company to potentially crippling its future investment plans. West Corp was much more diversified than that, of course, and any one part of its operations failing wouldn't cripple the company. Which made Celia think this was all a red herring. Distracting her from what? She needed to watch the magician's other hand.

The law office that fronted the ownership of the company was the brick wall she kept coming up against, so that was the information she left casually lying out on the kitchen table. These were the strings controlling Superior Construction's actions. Espionage might be able to follow the strings back to learn who —and why.

SIXTEEN

"Something fishy's going on here but I can't figure out what," Celia said.

Anna came home to find her parents sitting at the dining table outside the kitchen. Suzanne was fixing dinner. Smelled like Mexican, warm and spicy. She was sautéing chunks of beef in a skillet at the stove—which was off, as usual. All the heat was coming from her hand, her power, and the meat sizzled and popped in its juices. It was something Anna had watched Grandma do her whole life, but now, suddenly, she saw it from an outsider's perspective. And it was *weird*, the way she held the skillet flat on one hand while stirring with the other. Everybody's grandma cooked, yeah, but not like *that*. And no other kid had to sing songs to herself all the time to keep her father from knowing what she was thinking.

What a messed-up family. And nobody even saw it.

Paperwork, file folders, and spreadsheets were fanned over the table, and Celia was bent over them, chewing on the end of a pencil. Arthur sat next to her, leaning back, hands resting folded on his lean chest, looking amused. He always looked amused. It was his mask, so that he never had to let on if he was horrified by what he read in the minds around him.

"Smells good," Anna said to Suzanne.

"Thank you, Anna. Can you give me a hand? Get out the cheese and lettuce from the fridge?"

Anna dropped her bag by the wall and went to help.

"And how was school?" Arthur asked.

"Fine."

"Of course it was," he said wryly.

"What's that supposed to mean?"

He shrugged. "It always is, and why not?"

She blushed. He knew something, he *always* knew something.

Her mother huffed at them both. She looked tired, Anna thought, and remembered their conversation from a week or so back. She was busy, of course she was busy. But there seemed to be more going on. Her short red hair, same bloody color as Anna's, was disheveled, as if she'd been running her hands through it, and her face was pale and puffy. Suddenly, her mother didn't look right at all. Just tired, she'd say if Anna asked what was wrong.

"What's fishy?" Anna asked instead.

"Hmm?"

"You said something was fishy."

"Oh, West Corp's getting sued."

Anna stopped and stared. "What?"

Celia shook her head. "Don't worry, we get sued all the time. Usually it gets cleared up before ever going to court. But this suit was brought very publicly and very frivolously. I just have to figure out what the ulterior motive is."

Suzanne directed Anna to chop lettuce and shred cheese for burrito toppings, and she did so, slowly, listening with interest to her mother's arcane explanation. "Why sue?" she asked.

"Oh, lots of reasons. They assume West Corp has deep pockets, they want to embarrass the company, they want to embarrass *me,* they want to delay the planning committee vote, they want to distract us from something else entirely. All of the above."

"How do you find out? How do you stop them?"

"Hmm, developing an interest in corporate politics?"

Heaven forbid. "Just asking."

"We look to see if there's anything suspicious in the public record, if there's anything obvious they've done that attention would need distracting from. If they have any plans brewing that would be served by throwing roadblocks in front of West Corp. Trouble is, there's not much on this company at all. Like they exist on paper and nowhere else. So I may have to turn to gossip and find out if anyone's heard anything."

Anna's mind had started turning over a plan. She remembered what Eliot had said about someone trying to take over the city, not through terror and violence but through business and politics—the Executive. Maybe this thread was part of that web. Blocking West Corp certainly sounded like someone trying to influence the city's workings. All Anna had to do was follow that thread. Maybe Espionage could take that on. Except that she still wasn't talking to Teddy for ditching her in the face of danger. And she'd given up the whole vigilante thing because she was hopeless at it.

But this was personal. And if she didn't want to talk to Teddy, maybe Eliot would help her.

"Enough business," Suzanne announced. "Food's up."

While Arthur helped Suzanne with the food, Anna contrived to help Celia clear off the table and got a look at some of the pages, including the name of the company that was suing West Corp: Superior Construction, with an address in a downtown skyscraper.

Suzanne called for Bethy, who ran in and launched into a bunch of chatter about homework, and Anna finally realized that Bethy didn't talk so much about her homework and math quizzes because she was worried, but because she *actually liked math*. Definitely taking after their mother. Anna almost felt better, knowing that at least one of them would be able to take over the business.

"You guys remember I'm leaving on that trip tomorrow, right?" Celia said. "Don't destroy the place while I'm gone."

Anna smirked, because the instruction was perfunctory, the kind of thing she'd said when they were nine. She was trying to be funny.

"What's the trip for?" Bethy asked.

"I'm checking out a real estate development in Clarkeville for investment potential. Never trust the brochures, you know. It'll only be for a couple of days."

"Well, have fun. Take pictures," Bethy said cheerfully.

"Will do."

Everything was normal, nothing to worry about. Her father wasn't looking up from his food.

"Be careful and hurry home," Suzanne said.

"I always do," Celia replied.

That night, Anna grabbed her backpack full of gear and went looking for Eliot. He'd never bothered e-mailing her, which pissed her off, and it was time to call him on it. While riding the late bus to the campus, she followed his progress on her mental map from the gym to Pee Wee's and hoped he would stay there long enough for her to catch up with him. He did. She swung open the front door, stomping in out of the cold—and Eliot was sitting in a booth with a girl. A cool college girl with dyed purple hair and a ring in her nose. They had books and papers spread over the table, and they were smiling at each other. Study date or something.

Anna felt like throwing up right there, she was so mortified. Eliot hadn't e-mailed her because why would he? Why would he find her, a lowly high-school kid, even the least bit interesting? Worst of all, he looked up and caught her eye right before she turned around and stomped back out.

She was across the street and halfway to the bus stop when she heard him shouting.

"Hey! Hey, Rose, wait up a second." His footsteps pounded.

She slowed, then stopped. Reluctantly. It would have been more dignified to keep on walking. She didn't need him.

"Rose." When she didn't turn, he stepped around until he faced her. He and his smug college boy expression. "I didn't expect to see you."

"Why didn't you e-mail me?" she asked.

He shrugged. "I didn't have anything to e-mail about."

That wasn't the point . . . She stopped short of stamping her foot in frustration, which would have made her feel like she was about six years old. That was something Bethy would do. "Well, I've got something, and how was I supposed to tell you about it?"

"Seems like you're doing just fine," he said.

She maneuvered around him. "You're busy. This can wait."

"No, seriously, we're just brushing up for a chemistry test, it's not important. What have you got?"

She didn't have anything, now that she thought about actually trying to explain it. "It may be nothing. But you know about the planning committee? The downtown development project?"

"Yeah," he said. "It's been in the news."

"There's some weird stuff going on behind the scenes—one company trying to block another from having any influence. It reminded me of what you said about the Executive, and I thought this might be something he'd try."

"What's your proof?"

"We have to go find the proof, but I can't do it on my own. There's a company, Superior Construction. It's a front, and we need to find out who's really running it. Actual evidence. The trail stops at a law firm. I want to find out who hired the lawyers to front the company."

"Corporate espionage."

"Yeah, kind of." "Espionage" made her wonder if she ought to call Teddy and get his help as well—this was exactly his thing. But no, she decided, that would take too much time. Eliot was here, ready to help, better to get it done now. She pulled a page from her pocket. "Here's the name and address of the firm, McClosky and Patterson. They're in one of the downtown offices. I couldn't find much about them online, just a plain business page."

"Horizon Tower—I know that building," Eliot said. "Lots of good ledges. I can get us right to their floor. You think if we find out who hired them, we'll find the Executive?"

"It's just an idea."

"No, I like it. It won't even take long, just a quick look through filing cabinets."

"And hope the place doesn't have good alarms."

His grin turned sly. "We'll worry about that when we get there. Let me just go tell Becca that something came up."

Punk jacket and a nose ring and her name was *Becca*? Anna waited, watching her breath fog, telling herself over and over that this was a good idea. It was almost a date, even.

No it wasn't.

He returned quickly, backpack over his shoulder.

Anna asked, "Do you need to go get your suit?"

"Already in the bag."

Anna suddenly didn't feel so weird, if she wasn't the only one doing that. "You want to take the bus?"

They set off side by side, walking along the street by the quad.

"Is that how you do your superheroing? You take the bus?"

"Hey, it works," she shot back.

"Why don't we take my car?"

"Can you get around without the traffic cameras ID-ing your plates?"

"Believe it or not, I've been doing this at least as long as you have."

"Probably longer," she muttered, and Eliot did her the courtesy of not responding to that. He steered her around the block to a student parking lot. She searched the rows, guessing which one was his—one of the beaters or one of the fancy, obviously parent-bought-and-gifted models? One of the latter, it turned out: a two-seater coup half-way to being an out-and-out sports car, all silver and streamlined. It had local plates.

"Nice," she observed. So, he was rich, or came from a rich family.

"Thanks," he said, his tone mirroring hers. Which meant he knew exactly what the car said about him.

If he'd grown up in Commerce City instead of Delta, he probably would have gone to Elmwood. They'd have grown up together, a couple of rich kids in their rich kid world. She probably would have avoided him. He un-locked the car and gestured her to the passenger seat. Leather interior, natch.

He guided the car out of the parking lot and onto one of the westbound arteries. If she thought hard about it, she'd acknowledge that she'd just gotten into a strange man's car and she hadn't told anyone where she was going. Horror movies started this way. No superhero code of honor was going to save her if he turned out to be a psychopath. She couldn't say why she was pretty sure he wasn't a psychopath.

"How long have you been doing this?" she asked fi-nally. "How'd you get powers?"

"Born with them, near as I can figure," he said. "I didn't get struck by lightning or anything. They didn't show up until I was about fourteen. I've mostly kept secret about them. You and your friends are the only other superhumans I've met."

He turned off the main boulevard after a few blocks. The side streets weren't so busy, and surveillance coverage wasn't so pervasive. "What about you?" he asked.

"Me, too. I mean, my power didn't show up until a few years ago. I had to experiment with it for a long time. I've really only started using it in the last year." She didn't say a word about inheriting her powers, that she was part of the famous West family, that her father was the world's most powerful telepath. "You haven't told anyone? Siblings, parents, anything?"

His smile turned pained. "No. I don't think they'd understand. My mother isn't around much—she's a concert pianist and travels a lot. My father—he's kind of a control freak. If he knew what I could do, he'd find a way to monetize it, never mind how I felt. It's kind of a cliché, isn't it? Big wheel corporate tycoon, never had time for his kids who now resent him. I ought to be grateful. If he kept better tabs on me I wouldn't be able to do this."

"Oh, you'd find a way."

"Speaking from experience?"

"Yeah."

"I take it you haven't told anyone, either. Outside of your friends, I mean."

It would have been easy to tell him everything—so nice, to be talking to someone who understood. If she revealed enough clues he'd figure it out on his own. She'd have to tread carefully.

"No, I haven't told my family. I don't even know why. My mom's kind of the same, corporate control freak. She'd be way too interested. Same with my dad. But I think . . . I'm sure they know something's up. I mean, this is Commerce City, if your kid is sneaking out in the middle of the night, she might just have superpowers. But at this point I don't know what to tell them, so I just keep quiet."

Away from campus, the buildings climbed higher, becoming a forest of glass and concrete. The sky above was a hazy patchwork.

She asked, "Did you want to come to Commerce City for college because of its superheroes?"

"Sure. You guys have the tradition. I was hoping to meet some of them. You, I mean. And, well, here we are."

She wondered what her parents would say if she told them she wanted to go to college in Delta and get away from Commerce City. She wondered if she would still be able to pinpoint their locations from that far away.

"This looks good." He found an alley leading to a loading dock a block away from their target. It was even legal parking, since the No Parking signs were business hours only. "Ready to suit up?" he asked.

"Yeah."

He had a cover for the car, which would camouflage it. The thing did stand out, but under the dark canvas it seemed more like part of the scenery. He wore the leggings of his skin suit under his jeans, which meant he was pretty hard-core—always ready to leap to the rescue. He had to switch shirts, and she tried not to stare at his muscular chest. The guy did work out, after all. Probably knew all kinds of martial arts. She should have done karate instead of soccer.

She should also maybe think about getting a real uniform, if she was going to keep doing this. The dark coat and ski mask looked silly next to him.

"You come up with a name yet?" Anna asked.

"What do you think of Leapfrog?"

"Kind of lame," she said.

"Yeah, then no."

"You have to get your picture in the paper if you want someone to come up with a cool name for you." Though that didn't always work out. A few years ago, a vigilante with superspeed showed up busting crime in torn jeans, a T-shirt, and a cloth mask. The papers called him Blue Collar because of the clothes, never mind what his powers were. They'd be likely to call Eliot Greenie, assuming the pictures they got were in color.

Keeping to shadows, they made their way to Horizon Tower, the fifty-story skyscraper housing the law firm. The building was fifteen or so years old, and not one of West Corp's projects, so Anna didn't know as much about it as she would have if her mother was keeping tabs on it. The fake-bronze framing around the mirrored glass lining the exterior was already looking dated, part of a style that was hip and cutting edge at one time but had been quickly abandoned for more classic designs. Eliot was right, though—the upper floors were tiered, offering him lots of good landing and launch points. She sighed. Looked like she'd be spending another night hanging out in doorways and stairwells.

The sound of a car engine traveled up the street, and Anna grabbed Eliot's sleeve and pulled him flat against the concrete wall around the building's base. A white police sedan slid up the street and kept going. Didn't see them, and probably wouldn't see Eliot's car under the cover.

Eliot looked up, studying the façade. No lights showed through any of the windows, and from the back they couldn't see if anyone was keeping watch on the lobby. West Plaza had a guard at the front desk twenty-four hours a day. "Can you tell if any security guards are wandering around?" he asked.

"No. I can only find specific people, not people in general."

"Oh. Too bad."

Whatever.

He walked to the end of the alley, craned his neck

back, and pointed. "That one. That ledge will get us to the right floor. If we can't get in without triggering an alarm, we can leave fast enough." And the car was a block away, so they'd have time to get away before anyone found it.

"You have a phone? Maybe I can call you and sound some kind of alarm if I see something out here."

"Don't you want to come?"

"How am I supposed to get inside?"

He looked at her, looked at the roof ledge, and back at her. "I'll take you."

"You can do that?"

"As long as you won't get scared."

Her heart flipped over a couple of times. "I won't."

"Then hold on tight."

His arm wrapped around her middle, and he pulled her close, so their bodies lined up right next to each other and she couldn't help but put her arms around his neck. She could smell him, feel his muscles moving under her grip. He was solid, and she had an urge to wrap not just arms around him, but also her legs, and dig her fingers into his shoulders, and clench her toes. He was so warm, and she could just curl up. She had to work really, really hard to seem completely cool and normal. Professional. Just a fellow superhero doing the superhero thing. No matter how much her insides had turned into complete goo. When his grip on her tightened, tucking in right under her ribs, she thought her brain might melt.

His knees bent, he reached up with his free hand, and launched.

It felt like a roller coaster or an elevator in free fall, wind zipping past her face, whipping at the locks of hair that had escaped from her hat, chilling her hands. The ground was gone, and her legs dangled. She yelped rather than screamed—didn't have time or breath for a scream.

Her muscles clenched even tighter, securing herself to Eliot. She was trying to hold tight to a rocket. Her eyes watered, tears streaming. She didn't even think about looking to where they were going. The world was a blur, scrolling past too quickly, and she held her breath, waiting for the landing.

It came in seconds, though she swore she had time to think in slow exquisite detail through the whole flight. But it was a jump, not flight, and as the arc of Eliot's trajectory started downward, she opened her eyes just in time to see the upper-story patio he'd been aiming toward. The open space had tall railings along the edge to keep people from getting ideas. Eliot easily cleared the railing, and his bent knees took the brunt of the impact. Anna's own knees went out, and she folded in a heap on the granite tiles, her fingers still wound tight in Eliot's skin-suit jacket.

So this was what it was like having a real superpower. She took a minute to get her breath back; she'd had the wind knocked out of her.

"Hey, we're here," he said, chuckling. Leaning against him to brace herself, she got her feet under her, straightened, and absently smoothed out the wrinkles she put in his suit.

"You must carry a lot of girls around." She said it as a joke, but not really. More like a hint. A question, which she hoped he would deny. When he didn't, she tried not to be disappointed.

The patio had tables and lounge chairs designed for fashionable corporate lunches and cocktail parties. This time of night, the place was empty, the table umbrellas all packed away.

"Should we try the door?" he said, moving toward the glass entrance at the back of the patio.

Anna was turning over all kinds of plans about how

they were going to get in—she didn't know anything about picking locks except what she'd seen in movies, and breaking the glass would probably be a bad idea.

But the door wasn't locked. Eliot swung it right open.

"Wow," she said. "Wasn't expecting that."

"You'd be amazed how many places don't lock doors on the upper floors. They figure, who's going to break in on the thirtieth floor?"

"But this is Commerce City. People fly around here," she said.

"Superheroes fly—and what superhero is going to engage in breaking and entering?"

"Us?"

Smirking, he held the door open and gestured her inside.

She waited for the alarms to blare, but nothing did, and she figured Eliot was right: The ground floor was alarmed and guarded, but anything this high? Not so much. Another reason the building, or at least this floor, wasn't so well guarded: The floor was nearly empty. The doorway led to a hallway and a row of prime window offices, but beyond a partition was a typical open-plan space, only with no partitions, desks, chairs, anything. A few power cords dangled from offset ceiling tiles. An emergency light cast a faint glow from a door on the opposite wall. She wondered how many floors were empty and how much of the building was leased. That said something about the law firm; if they needed the cheap office space they could get in a mostly empty building rather than leasing posher, more prestigious space farther uptown, where West Plaza was located. At least, that was what her mother would say about it.

"The lawyers are on the next floor down. Emergency stairs are this way, I think."

"You seem to know a lot about this building," Anna said.

"I just pick things up, you know? Like I said, it's got good ledges."

"I guess the Leaping Wonder would know about ledges," she said.

"I have *got* to come up with a decent name."

He went toward the emergency light, and she followed, scanning for clues about what business might have been here in the past and what had happened to it. Not much of anything had been left behind—a few pieces of nondescript office furniture, a few extension cords pushed up against a wall. The place smelled of musty carpet and long disuse.

The next floor down wasn't quite as desolate, but it wasn't filled, either. A pair of hallways branched from the stairwell door and contained rows of office doors and windows. A few accounting offices, an architectural firm, all with stodgy names and minimal public faces. The lawyers were at the end of the hall.

Eliot had a set of lockpicks, it turned out, and he knew more about picking locks than what you saw in the movies.

"You came prepared," Anna observed.

"It just seemed like a good thing to have if I was going to be running around at night." He inserted a pair of narrow probes into the keyhole of the office door and wiggled them until the lock popped and the door swung in.

"So, you a vigilante hero or a cat burglar?"

"Trying to be a hero," he said. "But I have some pretty wide boundaries."

She wasn't one to talk, considering all her heroing so far had involved breaking and entering. She didn't have time to work through the philosophical implications.

Inside, she turned on the light with a gloved hand. The front receptionist space had a desk and a few chairs. No artwork, no magazines on a coffee table. Just the desk, chairs, and bare walls. She went through to the back office, which also had a desk and a few of chairs. At least the desk had a computer on it, and one of the walls had bookshelves containing an official-looking law library, all perfectly lined up. A diploma for a law degree from the university hung on the back wall. The name on it was Evan McClosky. Patterson's degree didn't seem to be hanging anywhere.

The office was sparse; it seemed wrong. Celia's office in the penthouse was clean and spare, but it still looked lived in and used. Usually, a jacket was slung over a chair or a pen lay out of place. The shelves had books on them. This place didn't look lived in.

Eliot rubbed his hands together and looked around. "Okay, where to dig for these files of yours?"

Anna looked for another door: a closet, access to another room, anything. But no, the place just had the two rooms, and the rooms weren't enough.

"There aren't any filing cabinets," she murmured. As far as she could tell, except for the law books, there wasn't a scrap of paper in the whole place.

"They must have everything on computer, and we'll never get through the encryption," Eliot said.

"No," Anna said. "I don't care how high tech a company is, there's always a paper trail. People sign things, people turn in receipts, they make copies, they get forms and notices from the city."

"You the business expert or something?"

She didn't say anything, because she would have to talk about West Corp and what it was like growing up in the middle of the city's largest privately held business. "It's just common sense."

"I suppose I can try hacking into their computer, just in case there's something there."

"No, you can't," she said and held up the monitor

cable—which wasn't plugged into anything. There was no CPU, just the monitor and keyboard for show. "This is a fake law firm."

"That looks like a real diploma to me," Eliot said, pointing at the wall.

"The guy's probably a real lawyer, but the firm isn't really doing any business."

"So we're dealing with a fake company fronted by a fake law firm? Now what?"

"Makes me want to hide out and see what really goes on here." She pulled out her cell phone and started taking pictures. Not that it would do any good, but it might mean . . . something. She could send the pictures to her mother—anonymously, of course—and see if it meant anything to her.

In the meantime, Eliot opened and closed desk drawers. Pens and other office detritus slid on particle board, but for the most part the drawers seemed empty. Then he came to the locked drawer.

"What's in there?"

"Let's find out," he said and got out the lockpicks. This one took even less time than the front door. Anna moved to look over Eliot's shoulder.

The drawer was deep, but all that lay in the bottom was a file folder. Slim, not much in it. Eliot took it out and set it on the desk's surface, and Anna flipped it open and scanned the scant handful of pages within.

"Anything good?" Eliot asked after a moment.

She couldn't tell right away. The business jargon made her eyes blur at first, until she made the effort to focus. She had to look them over a couple of times.

"They're invoices. But they're going the wrong way. They ought to be charging Superior Construction, not paying them." But she wasn't reading these wrong— Superior Construction hadn't paid the law firm to file their paperwork and front the company. The law firm was paying Superior Construction, apparently for the mere effort of existing—but why?

The last couple of pages in the file were direct deposit receipts, the payments going in, made by a company called Delta Exploratory Investments. Those were pretty big numbers in those deposits—six figures. Not just-doing-business big. Payoff? Bribery?

She showed the page to Eliot. "You ever hear of them? Could this have something to do with the Executive?"

He hesitated and pursed his lips before shaking his head. "Doesn't ring a bell."

This was important. She didn't know how, but her only task this trip was finding the next piece, not solving the whole puzzle. After glancing around the minimalist office again, she growled. "There's no copy machine—what office doesn't have a copy machine?" Finally, she took pictures of the documents and hoped the images came out good enough to be useful.

"You get what you needed?"

"I think so." She tucked her phone away. "Let's go. Make sure everything's locked."

They locked all the doors, turned out the lights, scanned the rooms one more time to make sure everything was in place—not hard, considering how little was there. The offices were just real enough to make a casual visitor believe it was a real business. No more effort than that had been put into the place.

Now that they were on the way out, Anna's sense of urgency grew. They'd stayed too long already, someone would find them out. Eliot kept his cool, though, casually striding up the stairs and across the empty floor until they arrived back on the patio. The night sky opened up, and the edge of the patio loomed.

The thought of Eliot jumping off the building and diving straight down to the street below made Anna's knees lock up. Eliot had already climbed halfway up the patio railing.

"You coming?"

She didn't have a choice, but she couldn't get her legs to move. "I'm not sure I can do this." Closing her eyes, she crept forward, her steps slow, until she reached the railing—and made the mistake of looking through the bars and down the side of the skyscraper. Gasping, she took a step back.

Eliot said, "You can't be a superhero if you're afraid of heights."

"I'm not a superhero, I'm just a freak with a parlor trick," she replied.

He laughed. "We all are. It's how you use the trick that matters. Trust me, it'll be okay."

He even looked like a superhero, standing above her, legs straddling the railing, with the haze-lit city skyline as a backdrop, his smile blazing under his mask and helmet. *I wonder if I should ask him to prom . . .* Maybe if she asked him to kiss her. For luck, right?

With that distracting thought, she took a deep breath and grasped the hand he reached out to her. Instead of looking down again, she stayed focused on the plastic shell of his mask. His grip around her middle was tight, and she tried not to cling to him too hard.

"Hold on," he said and then dropped. Just stepped off the ledge. Anna squeezed her eyes shut and clamped her jaw to keep from screaming.

He bounced once, and in spite of herself she looked—he'd pushed off from the side of the building, changing direction and slowing down. They swooped toward the building across the street, and Eliot shoved off from that one as well, aiming them downward, until he landed with a controlled jolt. At the last moment, he lifted her up in both arms, holding her completely off the ground. She was pretty sure she would have smashed into the pavement otherwise. He straightened from his shock-absorbing crouch and set her on her feet.

"See? I told you it'd be okay."

"That was . . . that was really cool. Thanks." Her smile at him felt ridiculous, silly, but she couldn't help it. She really wished her heart would stop flipping over like that.

And then she stood on her toes and kissed him, just briefly, on the cheek. For luck, after the fact. It might have been the most impulsive thing she'd ever done in her life, and she instantly regretted it. In a novel or movie, he'd kiss her back, of course. Get a steamy look in his eyes and sweep her off her feet with those strong arms. Instead, he looked back at her with a kind of bafflement. Her cheeks burned.

"I'm sorry . . . I just . . . I'm happy to be alive, I guess . . ."

His grin was crooked. "You're pretty cute, Rose," he said, in the same way he'd describe a kitten dressed up in doll clothes.

The end of the night was a letdown. Marching off in a huff would have made her feel even more childish than she already did, but her feet dragged on the way back to his car, and once they were driving, she didn't want to take her mask off. First time for that. But the mask hid the blushing. Eventually she did, and he was already back in his mundane clothes, and they were just two normal people out for a drive again. The world somehow seemed plainer.

"Can I drive you home?"

"Back to campus is fine, I still have time to catch the last bus." She almost apologized again for kissing him, but if he wasn't going to say anything, neither was she.

"You don't want to give anything away, do you?" he asked.

"Not really, no."

By the time Eliot pulled back into the student parking

lot, it was later than she thought—she'd be cutting it close for the bus, so she didn't have much time to stand around and chat. Thank God.

She grabbed her bag and climbed from the car. "Thanks for your help."

"Let me know what else you find out, okay?" he said.

She almost said no, that she had just about vowed to never speak to him again, but—

"I'll e-mail you, I promise," he said.

Nodding, she turned and jogged to the bus stop a couple of blocks away. Caught it just as it was pulling away, yelled at the driver to stop, and he actually did. Which was good, because if she'd missed the bus she'd have been tempted to go back and ask Eliot for a ride home. Never mind that she still wasn't ready to give that much of her identity away. What was left of her dignity wouldn't have survived.

The next morning before leaving on her trip, her mother dutifully hugged them, told them to be good, and sent them off to school. She seemed awfully sappy about the whole thing, in a way she hadn't since they were little. She was supposed to catch her flight while they were at school.

But she didn't go anywhere.

When they got back home, Mom was still there, in one of the penthouse's guest rooms. Obviously hiding out and not gone at all. The compass's pressure in Anna's mind didn't lie. If she'd canceled her trip, she would have just been in her office or bedroom. But she was hiding.

Something really weird was going on.

Dad was at his office on one of the building's lower floors—keeping up the pretense that everything was normal, which meant he was in on the deception. He'd pretty much have to be. Anna waited in the living room for him to come home. She had homework, reading for

English and math worksheets and all the usual crap, but she couldn't focus on any of it. She sat in an armchair and looked out the vast living room window to the cityscape beyond. West Plaza was still, after some forty years, one of the tallest buildings in Commerce City, and from this vantage the whole city spread out like a 3-D map. The tangle of downtown architecture, the silver line of the harbor marking out the edges. From here, she should have felt above the chaos. Instead, she imagined it rising up to swallow her.

The presences she'd cataloged in her own psyche were growing. She could find her family, Uncle Robbie, and all her friends laid out like glowing spots on that map. Eliot was at the university; she was thinking about him a lot more than she probably ought to be. She couldn't really help it. His presence was a warm, comforting glow. A fuzzy blanket in her mind. The thought embarrassed her. Even Ms. Baker, Mayor Edleston, Judge Roland, and Captain Paulson had begun to intrude on her awareness. Once she found people, imprinted on them, they never really left her.

She wondered: If one of the people she knew so well that she always knew where they were, if one of them died, what would happen? Would she feel it? Would she still be able to find them? She was scared to find out. She'd had such an easy life, she realized, that no one she cared about had ever died.

The thought gave her a chill, and she pulled her knees to her chest and hugged herself.

She knew when her father left his office and mentally followed him to the elevator, where he keyed himself to the penthouse and rode up to the private top floor. When the elevator doors slipped open and he strode through the foyer, she was waiting.

He wasn't at all surprised to see her there, of course. Nothing she did would ever surprise him, and the thought made her suddenly angry. They regarded each other a moment, and for once she didn't try to cloud her mind with thoughts of music or flat colors. Let him see her confusion. Let him try to calm her down.

"Where's Mom?" she said.

Not a flicker of emotion from him. Not surprise, not chagrin from lying, not anything. Like he was some kind of mutant statue. Anna wondered how far she'd have to push him to get a reaction from him.

"She told you, she's traveling."

"No, she isn't. She hasn't gone anywhere."

Her father raised an eyebrow, tilted his head. "How do you know?"

Oh, yes, how indeed . . . "I just know. Why are you guys lying, that's what I want to know."

"Anna, is there something you'd like to talk about?" So inhumanly calm. Though the lines around his eyes seemed more creased than usual.

If she kept pestering him, she'd never have to answer questions about herself. "Just tell me why you and Mom are lying."

"I can't tell you. I'm sorry."

And that was that. She didn't have anywhere left to push. She could stomp off to her room in a rage, but that would mean he'd won. She glared. "I wish I could read minds, like you."

"Or perhaps not."

She marched across the living room. "How about I go ask her why she's lying to us—"

Arthur planted a hand on her shoulder, and emotion trembled through him—frustration, determination . . . fear. A tightly wadded-up ball of panic that flashed in his eyes and faded, but not before it pounded into her own psyche, and she couldn't tell then if he was transmitting his own fear too strongly to control, or if her own fear was boiling over.

This is what he's holding back all the time, she realized. He had to constantly lock himself behind that cool expression . . . the price for being able to read minds.

She swallowed the lump in her throat and stilled her racing heart.

"Please don't do that," he said. The emotion had lasted for only a flash; he was back to stone now. "She'll tell you everything when she's ready, I promise, but for now"—he pursed his lips, his hand tightened—"please wait."

She didn't know what she was going to do. Two paths opened up, one in which she confronted her supposedly absent mother, one where she didn't, and neither option looked right. What she did know: Confronting her mother meant revealing her power. How did you follow your gut when it was telling you two different things?

Out of a sense of directionless rebellion she said, "You going to stop me?"

He could. He had the power to control minds, and if he controlled hers, would she even know it? But he drew his hand away from her.

She strode off—but not to go to her mother, and Arthur would have known what she would do as soon as she made the decision. Instead, she stormed to her room, slammed the door, and stayed there the rest of the night. She didn't speak, because she knew he'd see it all written plain in her mind, and he wouldn't be able to fix it any more than she could.

SEVENTEEN

"Anna knows," Arthur said.

Late at night, he came to stay with her in the guest room. Nurse her, more like. She was too cranky and in pain to sleep, so she propped up a laptop on pillows next to her, thinking maybe she could get some work done. She couldn't just *lie* there, could she? But she was having trouble focusing on the screen. Reading a single e-mail seemed to take an hour, so she ended up just staring at the device, pretending, too woozy to do anything else.

However angry Anna might be with her on general principle, Espionage came through, using an anonymous e-mail address to send a pack of information on the McClosky and Patterson firm. Now if only Celia could concentrate enough to read. But she was supposed to be delegating, so she forwarded the packet on to her law team. The initial court hearing was in a couple of days; the info had arrived just in time.

Her little nudge had worked, and she resisted feeling guilty about it. She was a terrible mother, just awful. Either that, or she was successfully encouraging her daughter in her current interests. Sure.

She was frustrated and depressed. "One day at a time" had turned into "one hour at a time," and Celia could imagine a point when it would become "one minute at a time," just trying to breathe enough to make it to the next day. She'd recover soon enough. She had to. She refused not to. But for this particular round of treatment, she would just lie here, weakly fuming.

"Anna knows what?" she murmured.

"She knows that you haven't really gone away. That you've been here the whole time." He sat on the edge of the bed, delicately, like he was afraid of disturbing her. She wanted him to hold her but was afraid that his touch would hurt. So he kept back.

"How could she possibly know? What is she doing, hacking into the building's security cameras? Spying on me?" But she stopped, stared a moment, and the pieces fell into place. A roiling sense of discovery. "It's her power, it's mental. Telepathic, like you." Squeezing his hand made her ache, but she did it anyway, because his touch was more important than pain right now. "How long have you known?"

"About three years. It seems to have started then. She's only really been learning how to use it in the last year. It's not precisely telepathy, more like what I'd call psycho-location. She knows where people are."

Celia put her head in her hands. So many pieces falling into place.

Arthur went on. "I've been waiting for her to say something, encouraging her to talk about it. But she's only re-treated, burying it all deeper and deeper. She's gotten very good at blocking me. If I didn't know her so well already I wouldn't be able to read her at all."

"You sound proud of her," Celia said.

"I am. She . . . I think she wants to see if she can do this on her own. She wants to live up to some kind of ideal she's invented for herself. Sounds like someone else I know, eh?"

"This is my fault, isn't it? I'm a terrible mother." She snuggled closer to Arthur, and he took the cue, putting his arms around her, holding her. The pain faded.

"No, you aren't," he said dutifully. "Celia, she's going

to continue asking what's going on. I don't know what to tell her. I can only put her off for so long. It's not really fair to her, when I keep asking her to share her secrets. Suzanne is worried, but she's very sensitive about giving you space. No one wants to pressure you, but the fear is there."

She thought for a long time. Thinking had become difficult. "My parents never kept secrets from me. I always knew who they were and what they were doing."

"Yes."

"I'll tell her. I'll tell everyone. Let me get through the court hearing. Let me get well again, and I'll tell."

"I love you, Celia."

"I don't deserve you, Arthur." The guilt crept into her voice because she was too weak to hold it back.

He touched her face, tipped her head back, kissed her lightly, knowing exactly how much pressure he could use before she started hurting. His love washed through her like a drug, one that burned fiercely but left strength behind it instead of weakness. She could change the world with him standing beside her. All his love said that yes, she did deserve it. Somehow.

When Anna was about six and Bethy was three, Anna fell. Celia had been carrying Bethy and, arms full of squirming little girl, didn't see exactly what happened, but they'd been descending the stairs outside the Natural History Museum on a summer outing, and Anna was running too fast. Celia called to her to slow down, but Anna didn't listen. Celia hadn't really expected her to, but the calling out had been an instinct. You did it because at least then you'd tried. The alternative was keeping the kids on leashes, and while Arthur joked about her being controlling, she wasn't that bad, she hoped.

So Anna fell, probably tripped, and just for a moment, she flew. For that split second, Celia would swear she saw her daughter suspended in air, weightless as no person ever could be, sailing in defiance of gravity, and her heart lodged in her throat, not because her daughter had tripped, but because this was it, the thing that would change their lives, the power she'd been searching for and hoping she wouldn't find.

But no, Anna hadn't really flown. Her momentum had simply carried her down the rest of the stairs and onto the sidewalk below, and Celia's perception of time had slowed during that fraction of a second. Postcrash, the kid had screamed like a banshee, bystanders came running and gave Celia that look that people always gave the mothers of screaming children, the this-must-be-your-fault look, until it became clear that it was just an accident, one of those things that happen to little kids. By that time Bethy was screaming because Anna was screaming, and Celia managed to ignore them both long enough to call the car and rush to the hospital.

Broken arm. Anna had stuck her hand out, cracking the bone on impact, and that was another power Celia could check off the list—Anna didn't have her grandfather's invulnerability to injury. But for the first time, Celia wished both her children had that superpower, suddenly envying her own grandmother for never having to worry about the young Warren West breaking himself in a fall.

Anna was very proud of the purple cast she had to wear for the next five weeks. Celia decided that maybe she wouldn't worry so much about whether the kids had powers. They would fall, they would fly, they would run as fast as they could, they'd have good days and bad.

When the girls hit puberty, the watching started again, but the anomalies Anna displayed had more to do with being a teenager than being superhuman. And after all was said and done, the power she ended up with had no external manifestation. It was undetectable.

Celia couldn't win this game.

After just a couple of days of being sequestered on her "trip," Celia returned to her office Monday morning and swore she found a layer of dust on her desk, and her computer was cold. Everything she'd worked for, everything she'd done to keep West Corp alive and growing after her father's death was slipping away.

This was an exaggeration. But her strength had become precious. She felt that the least shock would destroy her, and her life's work seemed fragile. She'd look away, and it would vanish.

She had an hour or so to review the information for the case before heading to court. The evidence Anna had been able to dig up was . . . interesting. Blurry pictures of check stubs and invoices that on their own didn't mean anything, but when lined up revealed a financial smokescreen. It proved McClosky and Patterson was a front, but Celia'd already suspected that. The data also offered a new name, the next step on the trail: Delta Exploratory Investments was a holding company, one she'd actually heard of, and one whose line of ownership was much easier to track because it wasn't just a front. She dug into her own notes, the thick file folder full of research about the other companies making bids on the city development project, and there it was: Delta Exploratory was the company through which Delta Ventures, Danton Majors's company, had made its own bid. This gave her a straight line between the lawsuit and Majors. Her lawyers had built a powerful case for their defense. They weren't just hopeful, they were smug.

Maybe Anna really had been paying attention all those afternoons she'd spent in Celia's office, just hanging out. She'd brought them exactly what they needed. God, she wanted to hug the kid right now.

A phone call to Mark confirmed that a patrol had spotted two of the young new supers out and about a couple of nights ago—descriptions matched Anna and the stranger, the jumper whom none of them could identify. Him, and not Teddy? And how the hell did Anna know this guy? It made her question her assessment that he must have been a stranger. It made her worry about Anna more, not less.

If she trusted Anna this far, she had to trust her daughter's instincts about this as well. But it wasn't easy.

Out in the kitchen, the girls had finished breakfast and were gathering their things to head to school. The usual, perfectly normal weekday morning chaos of the house. Celia paused, just to listen—Suzanne clearing away juice and cereal, the girls arguing back and forth about who put whose uniform sweater where, and where their books were. Bethy was already at the elevator. Anna was moving more slowly, lingering by the kitchen table, rearranging books in her bag. The school uniform made her look younger, and Celia had to remind herself that she was almost an adult. Almost full grown.

"Hi," Celia said. Then just stood, watching.

Anna looked at her sidelong. "Hey, Mom."

Whew, deep breath, stay calm. "If you have time after school today—do you think we could have a talk?"

Her daughter froze, just for a moment. And what must she be thinking? She seemed to shake herself back to the moment. "Yeah, I can do that."

"Good," Celia said. Her relief was physical, the tension of weeks draining away. "Looking forward to it."

Anna flashed a nervous smile. "That hearing about the lawsuit's today, right? How do you think it's going to go?"

"I think it's going to be just fine. I expect the whole suit to get thrown out. We got some last-minute information that really pushed our case over the top." Thank you. After school today, she'd be able to just say thanks.

"Good. That's good," Anna said, totally straightforward. She'd learned her poker face from her father, after all. "Well, good luck with it all."

"Thanks. I'll be glad when it's over."

"Don't forget," Anna said, "you promised a vacation when you're done with all this lawsuit stuff. I'm holding you to it."

"I haven't forgotten."

"Anna, we're going to be late!" Bethy shouted from the next room.

"I'll see you this afternoon," Anna said, waving as she peeled into the foyer to the elevators.

Anna was going to be just fine. Maybe Celia wasn't a terrible mother after all.

"Vacation," Suzanne said, wandering in from the kitchen. "I like the sound of that."

Celia smiled. "Yeah, so do I."

"Is everything okay?" her mother asked, gaze narrowed.

"No," Celia said, before she could edit herself. It just popped out. Then she realized that saying no was a relief. No, everything was not okay. She'd said it, it was out there. Good. "I have to be at court in an hour, and you know how I feel about court appearances."

"And who can blame you?" Suzanne said, putting on a cheerful face. "I'm sure it'll be fine."

Celia sighed. She'd made it this far, she could get through today as well. Onward.

For a long time, Celia had hated courtrooms.

She still had bad dreams—hard to call them nightmares, when they were vague and nerve-racking rather than terrifying—about the trial of Simon Sito, the Destructor, where she'd been called as a witness and her brief foray into juvenile delinquency as one of the defendant's hench-idiots had been exposed to the world. The revelation destroyed her budding relationship with Mark

Paulson, damaged her friendship with Analise, and cemented her reputation in the city as the completely useless bag of flesh who'd failed her amazing parents, the Olympiad. Yet oddly enough, her testimony started to repair her relationship with her parents. They stood by her during those rough weeks. Arthur stood by her.

Courtrooms were fraught. On one hand, they were a symbol of bureaucratic tediousness. On the other, they destroyed—and repaired—lives. On the whole, she preferred that her confrontation with Danton Majors was going to take place in the formal, controlled atmosphere of a courtroom rather than come to a head in the kind of showdown that her parents would have faced back in the day, bolts of fire and laser beams blasting destruction across the sky. Courtrooms were always better battlefields, and she'd come to embrace them. Even though they still gave her hives. They smelled like paper and cheap floor polish.

Midmorning, Celia led her team into this particular courtroom like a general at the head of her army. Motions and countersuits, all lined up. She was high on painkillers and caffeine, but no one needed to know that. If this went as planned, she wouldn't have to say a word. Just sit there looking serene and in control. Bored, even, if she could manage it. Without actually looking sleepy, which she might not be able to manage. Security wouldn't let her bring one more cup of coffee into the courtroom, alas.

Danton Majors was in the gallery, seemingly out of innocent curiosity, but she thought he might look a tiny bit worried. He sat a little too still, and his gaze was a little too focused. He glanced toward her when she came in, and his reply to the bright smile she gave him seemed somewhat pained. One of his aides from the committee meetings had accompanied him, a young man—another monkey in a suit. Protégé, lawyer, secretary? Bodyguard? Or did Majors just like having minions around?

On the plaintiff's side of the courtroom, Superior Construction made a good show of appearing to be legitimate. The central figure, a large man in a light gray suit, was the on-paper owner of the company. The gray-haired shark to his left was McClosky, of McClosky and Patterson. Celia's team had learned that Patterson had retired five years ago, and McClosky maintained the skeleton of the law firm for exactly this sort of purpose—fronting shells, corporate smoke and mirrors. Right now, McClosky only had one client: Delta Ventures.

More men in suits accompanied them, giving every sign of presenting a strong front. Aides, clerks, additional staff, whatever. Records would show they'd been hired in the last month, about the time the initial suit was filed. Nothing in the up-front admissible evidence would show any double-dealing. Which was why Celia's investigation had gone through back channels: payroll tax filings, building permits on record. Walk through the door of Superior, you'd find nothing but bare wooden struts holding up the pretty front.

This was all theater, anyway.

A bailiff called them to attention, and the judge entered. She was a no-nonsense woman who would get through this quickly and without fuss, Celia hoped. She declared the session opened, called opposing attorneys to the bench, gave instructions, papers were exchanged, quiet conversations held. The performance continued.

Her team was the best money could buy, but the secret to a successful business was that you couldn't actually buy the best. You had to earn their loyalty by winning them over. By bestowing your own loyalty, by promising them you'd look after them, protect them, and then making good on the promise. Make it infinitely worth their while to do their very best work for you. Money had very little to do with those considerations in the end. Celia's employees worked hard for her because they loved working for West Corp. They respected her. She worked hard to earn their respect. When her lawyers prepared their arguments and countersuit, they weren't just doing it for her, they did it out of pride in the company. They felt like they had a stake in it all. Of course they worked hard.

Such a small investment of her own respect and loyalty, with such endless rewards. These hired puppets working for Danton Majors didn't stand a chance.

Her frame of mind was solidly in a state of offense and attack, so she had to remind herself that West Corp was the defendant here, and she didn't get to just stand up and reveal all. The case was read, antitrust complaints brought by Superior Construction, monopolistic practices, so on and so forth, suing for seven figures of damages and a stay on any bid made by West Corp or any of its subsidiaries.

The evidence they brought forward was all in the public record: newspaper articles, building licenses, contracting bids, property deals, investments, tax returns. Celia wasn't worried about any of her dealings being pried open and investigated. She ran West Corp as transparently as she could and adhered to all reporting laws for precisely this reason—she wasn't going to be the one sideswiped in court, not over something stupid like a frivolous lawsuit.

One of her lawyers accompanied the team for the sole purpose of countering every single piece of evidence Superior Construction brought. The rest of her team was set to filing the countersuit and proving that Superior wasn't what it said it was.

Her lawyers proceeded in a rapid patter of legalese, drowning the court in an avalanche of orchestrated data. Exhibit after exhibit entered into the record, charts and graphics showing that West Corp adhered to the spirit of the law as well as the letter, and the diversity of construction and contracting firms proved without a doubt that

West Corp had not damaged competition in Commerce City.

Then the countersuit, after a motion to have Superior Construction's suit thrown out as frivolous. The judge didn't react, so this couldn't have been unexpected. Good.

"Your Honor, we can show without a doubt that Superior Construction has not only *not* been damaged by West Corp's business practices, but that Superior Construction, in fact, does not exist in enough of a recognizable corporate form to *be* damaged by normal competitive business practices." This was Liz Bastion, one of West Corp's senior litigators, thirty-five and a badass. Celia had hired her personally out from under another firm and liked her a lot. She wanted the woman on her side precisely so she'd never have to face her down in court like this.

Then came the evidence Espionage—Anna—had provided, cleaned, vetted, and supplemented so that all appeared legal and admissible. Mountains of paperwork followed, tax returns and property records, newspaper articles and testimony from public officials, and a beautiful visual aid, a chart showing organizational structures linking Superior Construction to the shell of a law firm on up to Delta Ventures and Delta Exploratory, and to Danton Majors. They never mentioned Majors by name, because that wasn't the point here. But they didn't have to. On the plaintiff side, McClosky glanced back nervously at Majors, which just about clinched it. They hadn't expected Celia and West Corp to go digging, had they? They thought that legal loopholes and shields would protect their corporate façade.

Or they'd known the edifice wouldn[...] tiny, and in essence the true purpose o[...] simply to embarrass Celia and delay the[...] vote. Which was why her team needed n[...] West Corp, but to crush the suit into obl[...]

"In obvious conclusion," Bastion declaimed, "the plaintiff's suit and claims are not merely frivolous, they are actively meant to damage the defendant and the defendant's reputation. They are a conflict of interest and potentially illegal based on city statutes regarding business licensing and fair business practices, the details of which are outlined in a countersuit that West Corp plans on filing against the defendant. We'd like to enter a copy of the preliminary filing into the records as Exhibit BB. In light of these considerations, the defense moves to have the suit brought by Superior Construction against West Corp dismissed entirely because it is frivolous, obstructionist, and a conflict of interest for a plaintiff who is merely seeking to eliminate competition, not engender it. Thank you, Your Honor."

The judge scanned the latest file folder that Bastion delivered to her, her frown growing deeper, her brow more furrowed. When the judge glanced at the plaintiff's side, not with neutral regard but with active annoyance, Celia knew she'd won.

After a moment of thought, the judge announced, "Would both counsels please approach the bench."

After a discussion that ran long enough to be agonizing, the judge straightened. "All right, it's an unusual request, but I'll give you more rope to hang yourself, if that's what you really want."

"Your Honor, I want to state my objection to this for the record," Bastion said, fuming, her jaw taut.

"Your objection is noted and overruled. Counsel, you have the floor," the judge said to the plaintiff.

What was going on? Then Celia found out.

"Your Honor, we'd like to call Celia West to the stand."

Of course. It always came down to *her*. Bastards.

Bastion returned to the defense table. "I'm sorry, I to stop this," she whispered to Celia.

ng a weary smile, Celia shook her head. "Don't

worry. This just proves it isn't about the company at all. It's about me."

She suddenly wished Arthur was here, sitting in the gallery, offering his support by his mere presence.

—*You know I'm always with you, don't you?*—

Her heartbeat steadied, her breathing slowed. —*Thank you.*—

—*Of course, my love.*—

She settled into the witness stand and, hand on Bible, gave her oath in a confident voice.

She couldn't imagine what questions they wanted to ask her. Her own guilty conscience offered up bizarre possibilities: Is it true you've neglected your daughters in favor of furthering your business? Can you tell us how you've lied about your recent medical diagnosis? Aren't your efforts to win the planning committee contract more about stroking your own ego than benefiting the city? Well, she wouldn't say *more*, regarding that one. The considerations were about equal. The rest, she would throw herself on the mercy of the court and hope for forgiveness.

The plaintiffs had hired an experienced trial lawyer, and it was this guy, a Marshal Jones, who questioned her, not McClosky. Alas.

"Ms. West, to what lengths would you go to ensure that West Corp wins this city development contract?"

"I'm not sure I understand the question."

"You've researched your competition, of course. You know the other companies competing for this contract, you know their resources. I simply want to know if you've taken any actions beyond the usual due diligence."

She thought she knew what he was asking, but he was really just feeding her rope, hoping she'd tie it around her own neck, so she played dumb. "I'm still not sure what you mean. Can you give me some examples?"

"Is it conceivable, in your opinion, that your extensive

influence among city officials gives you an unfair advantage and handicaps your competition?"

"No," she said. "I think filing a frivolous lawsuit is what attempting to handicap your competition looks like."

The few observers in the courtroom tittered. The judge frowned, unamused. "Just answer the original question, Ms. West."

"I have no control over my competition, and my competition has as much access to city officials as I do. I'm better off not worrying about them and focusing on my own efforts. So to answer your first question, I'd do everything I legally could to present a solid bid that benefits everyone so the city can't possibly award the contract to anyone else. No need at all for the kind of gamesmanship you're implying."

"You—and West Corp—seem to have what one might call . . . what would one call it?" He turned to his colleagues as if he really was asking for advice and not playacting. "Obsession? With Commerce City and its development."

She chuckled. This was making no sense, but that gave her all the more reason to squash this clown flat so no one would entertain the doubts he was trying to raise.

"Commerce City has been my family's home for generations. West Corp is one of Commerce City's oldest family businesses, and its dedication to making contributions to the city and its growth is well documented. I'm sorry that looks like obsession to you."

"Don't you think it's a bit disingenuous, Ms. West, to call a multimillion-dollar corporate entity a family business?"

"No. Not when it's been helmed by a West for three generations. What else would you call it?"

"A grab for power, Ms. West. Outside of normal political channels. Corporate domineering."

She smirked. "I haven't gone into politics precisely because I'm trying to do some good in the world, Mr. Jones."

That got a laugh, and Jones flushed, finally looking a tiny bit flustered.

"And it's *your* definition of good that must prevail—"

She leaned forward. "I'm just trying to make a living, like everyone else."

The judge interrupted. "Mr. Jones, I think you're finished here. Counsel for the defense, do you have any follow-up questions for the witness?"

"No, Your Honor, I do not," Bastion said.

"Ms. West, you may step down."

"Thank you, Your Honor," she said politely and returned to her place. By Bastion's pleased expression—looking a bit like a cat with a plate of fresh tuna—Celia assumed her responses had been acceptable. She had to work not to slouch in her chair, deflated. Her performance had about tapped her energy reserves. Maybe this wouldn't take too much longer. She could go home, tell everyone she was sick, and sleep for the next two months.

It didn't. The judge spoke: "In light of evidence and testimony presented, I find the suit brought against West Corp by Superior Construction to be baseless. Not just baseless but baseless in the extreme. I encourage counsel for West Corp to proceed with any countersuit it might have prepared, but this initial hearing is over. And to the plaintiff, I have a warning: My statement on this case will be strongly worded, so keep that in mind if you're thinking of appealing, because I predict such an appeal will not go well for you. Case most definitely dismissed." The gavel cracked. Celia sighed.

She gathered the energy to look over her shoulder at Danton Majors—and found him staring back at her, frowning. So he really was out to get her. Not West Corp, not the development contract, but *her,* and she wondered why. Why he wanted to, and why he thought he could.

He'd failed, and here he was, Danton Majors, lying bloodied and defeated on the field of battle, never to recover. Nice image, but nothing that could ever happen in real life.

Her team was shaking hands, congratulating each other. Bastion crossed the aisle to shake hands with Jones, who complied but snarled as he did. Celia settled her purse strap over her shoulder and passed through to the gallery.

"Mr. Majors," she said. "I look forward to seeing you when the planning committee reconvenes to make its vote on the development contract."

"Yes, I imagine you do. Don't get too confident, though."

"Oh? You have a backup plan in case this little dog-and-pony show didn't work?" She couldn't keep a dig out of her voice.

"Ms. West, I really must be going. I've been away from Delta too long. But it's been interesting meeting you."

"I just bet it has."

The rest of her law team returned to West Plaza in taxis. Celia lingered, killing some time, ensuring that Tom would have brought the girls home from school by the time she returned to the Plaza. The end of the lawsuit had lifted a weight off her. Cleared a large part of her mind of worry. She felt light. The planning committee's development contract would take care of itself now, and so would the chemo treatments for that matter.

She took a walk, just a short one, and stopped at a coffee shop near City Hall to indulge and bleed off some anxiety. Enjoy the brief moment of respite in the day. She could stand on the street and watch people go by, and didn't that sound lovely?

She was so rarely alone. At the Plaza she was surrounded by her West Corp employees or her family. She didn't often go into the city unless it was to some event or to meet with officials, colleagues, friends. Tom or another driver ferried her back and forth. Arthur was almost always nearby. It wasn't like the old days, when she lived alone and rode the bus alone and walked alone, and thereby inadvertently created opportunities for those who would harm her. Over the last twenty years, she'd insulated herself with layers of people who watched out for her, and she hadn't meant to do it any more than she had meant to isolate herself during those rough years in her early twenties. It had been a consequence of the life she'd led. Now, the consequence of having a family, of having a stake in her company and her city, meant she was protected. She'd never looked at it that way before. Not until the protection was gone.

She was very occasionally alone when she stopped off for a cup of coffee or a sandwich between meetings, an echo of her early working days when she was just another woman on the street, one of thousands who would run into a café without thinking about it. She liked to think she wasn't so much of the elite that she couldn't buy her own damn coffee.

Fancy hipster coffee in hand, she emerged back on the street and didn't think anything of it. She needed to call Arthur to let him know how the hearing had gone—he already knew, really, but she liked hearing his voice. She had a long list of items she'd been putting off without even meaning to: calls to Analise, to Mark. A talk with her mother, to tell her about the leukemia. The talk she'd promised Anna. Maybe she could even get rid of the scratchy wig and the pretense that she was well. The coffee didn't taste like much since the treatments had affected her sense of taste. But the heat of it was comforting, and she sipped it gratefully.

She walked on to the corner, turned, and felt a sharp stab in her shoulder, like a narrowly focused punch. It seemed oddly familiar, and the wave of déjà vu that passed over her was so strong she paused, brow furrowed, trying to figure out the instinctive dread blooming in her gut even as her free hand pawed around to her back and met the cylinder of a syringe protruding from her suit jacket.

Just like the Destructor all those years ago when he'd kidnapped her and attempted to brainwash her for the sole purpose of striking at her parents. She felt the same astonishment, the same despair that she had somehow walked into a trap.

Suddenly, a man and a woman in dark suits, obvious bodyguard types, were at her sides, holding her arms, keeping her upright. One of them took the coffee cup and purse out of her hands before she dropped them.

"Ms. West, you seem unwell, let us help you," the woman said very calmly. A nondescript black car was waiting at the curb, and the two impassive escorts guided her into the backseat. They wore dark sunglasses, and their expressionless faces made noting their features difficult. They might have been wearing masks.

They stared straight ahead, not at her, and when Celia thought to demand that they tell her who they were and what they thought they were doing, her tongue seemed to swell and fill her mouth. Her whole body had gone numb. Good thing she was sitting down, because the world was tilting sideways.

She had a weird, panicked thought about how the tranquilizer would interact with the cocktail of drugs already in her system. Had they just killed her without meaning to?

What are you going to do to me? She tried to speak but didn't know if she actually said the words. The two kidnappers didn't respond to her. Her whole face was feeling too big for her skin, and she was afraid she was drooling. *Goddamn it,* she could only think, over and over. And then, —*Arthur, help*—

He didn't respond.

"Is she really the one? She doesn't seem like much," said the woman.

"She's the one," her partner answered.

The one what? Celia thought. *Who am I?* Filled with vague fear, she lost consciousness.

EIGHTEEN

Anna got home from school and sprawled on the living room sofa to do her homework. To *try* to do her homework, rather. So. She and Mom were going to Have a Talk. Because Mom knew about Espionage and the Trinity, and Anna knew she knew, and everything else was pretense. Anna strategized the conversation, trying to figure out what she'd say. How she'd explain why she hid her powers. In hindsight, her reasons seemed mostly stupid. She hoped her mother would understand. Of course, if Anna could ask her why she lied about the business trip first, get in a preemptive strike that way . . .

Or maybe they could just have a talk.

Mostly, she stayed in the living room to get away from Bethy, who kept studying her like she was a bug pinned under glass. Anna would have to come clean to her, too. And Grandma. Maybe she could get Dad to tell everyone. She threw her pencil across the room out of frustration.

Dad was in his office, Mom was still at the courthouse, so she opened up her math text and tried to focus. She wasn't entirely successful, but that was mostly algebra's fault. And it seemed like Mom really should have been home by now, so she checked in on her—

Shoved the book away as she stood up and went to the window, as if she could look out over the city, the streets, the tiny little figures walking on the sidewalk far below, the toy cars driving on streets, and pick out which one was her mother. Because her mother was gone. She couldn't find her.

Anna put her hands on her temples, squeezed, as if the problem was with herself, as if she could fix herself by wishing. But no, she could find Bethy, her grandmother, her father, Teddy, Tcia, everybody except Mom, and that wasn't right. It was a giant gaping hole that filled her mind at the expense of every other thought. That mental compass needle spun wildly, its pressure gone.

She didn't know where her mother was. How could she not know?

A sudden bout of dizziness struck, and she sat on the floor, closed her eyes. The whole building seemed to be swaying. The whole world was swaying. She didn't know how to make it stop. She just kept thinking of Mom, every thought and every memory she had, the good feelings and bad, all wrapped up together, and sent it out into the world to find her.

But she was gone. Vanished. Anna couldn't breathe. She didn't know what else to do, so she yelled, "Bethy! Beth! Something's wrong! Beth!" Screaming, almost.

Down the penthouse hallway, a bedroom door slammed open and Bethy came running to the living room. "Geez, Anna, why're you freaking out?"

But she stopped, and her eyes went wide when she saw Anna curled up on the floor, arms around her head, gasping for breath that wouldn't come.

"Anna. Anna, what's wrong?" She sat on the floor, very close, but her hands were clasped together and she wouldn't touch her sister.

"Mom's gone, she's gone," Anna said, choking, trying to catch her hyperventilating breath.

Her father was coming home, riding up the elevator because he'd felt her panic. He'd know what to do.

"She's just out, she had a court thing, didn't she?" Bethy said.

"No, this is different, she's gone, I can't find her. Don't you understand, I can't find her!"

"Did she have another business trip and we just missed it?"

"I'd know where she was. If she was out of town, I'd know it, if she was here, I'd know, if she was at City Hall, I'd know. *But I can't find her.*"

She's dead, came an unbidden thought. The worst thought of all. She didn't know what would happen if someone she loved, someone she could track over the whole world just by thinking of them, died. Would they vanish from awareness—just like this?

Bethy said quietly, "Anna, you're being really scary."

Anna should have told her about her power a long time ago. She couldn't think of how to explain it now.

The door to the foyer opened and their father strode in, looking as shocked as Anna felt. But calm, somehow. Still in control.

"Anna, what's wrong?" he asked, kneeling beside her, placing a hand on her shoulder. The touch weighed on her, anchoring her.

Bethy launched in. "Daddy, she's freaking out, I don't know what's wrong—"

"Shh," Arthur said to her, quietly and firmly. "Anna?"

"I can't find Mom. Mom's gone." She started crying, because the implications were too much for her to bear. Mom couldn't be gone, she just couldn't.

Arthur put his hand to his head, and his gaze turned inward. Anna managed a sigh and scrubbed tears from her face. He was a million times more powerful than she was; he'd find her.

But the seconds ticked on. Then minutes. Arthur stood, went to the window to look out over the city, just as

Anna had. He held hands to both temples now and winced with concentration.

Bethy was staring at Anna. Her expression was neutral. Maybe even calm, like the expressionless calm their father often wore.

"What's your power?" Bethy asked finally. "What can you do?"

"I find people. That's all."

"But you can't find Mom." Anna nodded. She waited for Bethy to yell at her, to be angry at her for keeping the secret. They would have an argument, if things were normal. But Bethy just nodded, decisive. "Dad'll find her."

He was still thinking, concentrating. He muttered, "Celia, bloody hell, where have you gone?"

"Have you called her?" Bethy said. "Have you tried her phone?"

"I'm better than a phone," Arthur murmured, staring out the window as if he could find her by sight.

Anna's gut wrenched. "Dad, she's not . . . she's still alive, isn't she? If she wasn't, I would have felt that. You would have felt it. She wouldn't just disappear, would she? If she, if she was . . ." She couldn't say the word.

He didn't answer.

A terrible future spun out before her. A life flashing before her eyes, but surely not the right one. If Mom was really gone: no more arguments, no more checking up on her, the office desk empty forever, and what would happen to the company, what would happen to Dad, and what was she supposed to do next? She imagined wandering the condo, searching for a mother who would never be there again.

In the meantime, Bethy got out her phone. "*Some* of us aren't telepathic," she muttered, punching speed dial. Then she waited, and waited. "She's not answering." She tried another number. "Hey, Tom? It's Bethy. Were you supposed to pick up Mom at the courthouse like, now? Um, yeah, he's here . . . Dad, Tom wants to talk to you."

Dad took the phone and listened for a moment. "And you can't find her anywhere? All right. No, come on back, I'll take care of it. Thank you." He clicked off the phone and handed it back to Bethy. "He was about to call me. He was supposed to meet her after bringing you home, but she didn't show up."

Her father looked lost, with a stark stare, his muscles gone slack. If that empty spot in her awareness was nerve-racking for her, how much worse for him? Her parents had been inside each other's minds for decades. In a sudden panic—a different one from the first, this one immediate and localized, and one she could do something about—she scrambled to her feet and went to him, holding his arm.

"Dad? Are you okay?"

He took a shuddering breath and nodded. Returning her grip, he shifted so that one arm was around her and the other reached for Bethy, until they were all pressed together in a clumsy embrace.

"Oh, my darling girls," he murmured. "We'll manage. Somehow, we'll manage, I promise." His love and anxiety pounded outward, a wave that almost made Anna sit, knocked down by the power of it.

Bethy said, "Daddy, what's wrong?" That question, still at the front of it all.

When Anna looked up, waiting for his answer, he'd changed. She recognized his new expression from old pictures, from newspaper clippings from the days of the Olympiad: determined, glaring, ice-cold. He was frightening, but somehow the intensity calmed her. He promised they would manage, and so they would.

After giving them both rough squeezes, he left them behind to march down the hallway. "Come. We'll find her."

Anna looked at Bethy, who was looking back, and she expected that Bethy's numb and wondering expression was mirrored on her own face. Together, they rushed after their father.

The penthouse was made up of the open living areas— living room, formal dining room, spacious kitchen and eating area. From that, off a primary hallway, were her mother's office, the master bedroom, a suite that belonged to Suzanne, and down a secondary hallway came a series of guest rooms, bathrooms, a library, and walk-in closets for storage. Bethy and Anna's rooms were here, along with a dozen rooms that Anna didn't look inside more than a couple of times a year. At the very end of this secondary hallway stood a wood door with a keypad lock. They caught up with Arthur here, and he was punching a code into the keypad.

"The combination is your grandfather's birthday," Arthur said. "Do you know what that is?"

Anna's heart was racing. This was the door to the old Olympiad secure command room. Her parents always told her the place had been dismantled and sealed off. That there was nothing behind the door but an empty room. But here they were.

Bethy gave the date. Anna was chagrined that she didn't know it.

"Good," Arthur said. "Let's go in, then."

The lock clicked, and the door slid open, gliding smoothly on its tracks. Operating perfectly, though it supposedly hadn't been used in more than a decade.

The place had a dusty, stale smell to it, like Anna imagined a museum vault or an ancient tomb might smell. An emergency light over the door cast a pale white glow that didn't extend more than a stride out, but Arthur went to a control panel on the wall nearby and pushed buttons. A whirr and a hum sounded as dormant power lines and circuits came back to life. A bank of lights came on, revealing the extent of the room in all its sleek, stainless-steel glory, hard lines and gray shadow. Along the right-hand wall were cabinets and cupboards, presumably containing the gadgets, devices, and artifacts that the Olympiad had used or acquired. On the opposite wall were the computer banks, multiple giant screens above keyboards and control panels, instruments of arcane purpose.

In the middle of the room was a metal conference table surrounded by a half dozen chairs. This was where it all happened, all those years ago.

Bethy went to the table, ran her hand along the surface, and looked back at Anna. "It isn't dusty," she said.

Arthur was at the computer bank, pressing buttons, watching screens flare on, displaying text and status messages.

"Your mother kept it all functional, all upgraded and ready to go. Just in case."

"Just in case of what?" Anna asked.

Arthur glanced over his shoulder at her. "Just in case we needed it."

A ventilation fan started up, and the stale air dissipated. The computer fans were humming, and status lights flashed green. Arthur lifted a phone handset from its cradle.

"Captain Paulson, this is Dr. Mentis. That's right, you heard me. Celia's missing . . . I'm certain." He covered the mouthpiece and said to Anna, "Where did you last sense her? Where's the last location you can confirm?"

This was surreal. This was a dream. It was crazy. A piece of history coming to life, something out of an old story. This wasn't supposed to be happening. She shook her head to try to focus. "The courthouse. About half an hour ago. She should have been on the way home, but when I checked she was just gone."

"Do you have any cameras at the courthouse, Captain? Would you mind sharing the feeds? I've activated the old system. I believe Celia gave you the codes." The smile Arthur wore was thin and predatory. He was on the hunt. "Yes, I do think it's that serious. Let's just find her, then we can learn what's really going on."

"Serious, what do you mean serious?" Bethy said, voice sharp. Anna thought she should comfort her. Put her arm around her sister, like her father had. Be a grown-up for once. She was also pretty sure Bethy would just shove her away. But Bethy looked so scared.

He pressed a few more keys, and the images on the peripheral screens flipped to show street scenes downtown: traffic and security cameras around the courthouse.

"We'll have to back up to about an hour ago and track forward," Arthur murmured. The scenes on the images sped up, people scurrying down the sidewalk like insects, cars zipping in and out of frame, doors to the building swinging open and closed, over and over. They watched, all of them intent on one hoped-for figure, the middle-aged woman with short red hair, wearing the slick business suit. She didn't appear, yet.

Maybe Mom was asleep. But no, Anna could find her when she was sleeping. So maybe unconscious—in an emergency room somewhere? Should they call hospitals?

Dad wouldn't be acting like this if he thought it was that simple.

"Dad," Anna said, tentative. This was thinking out loud, but if she did it out loud maybe she wouldn't scare herself. "Have you ever heard anyone talk about the Executive?"

He turned from the screens. "The Executive? In what sense?"

"It's just rumors. But I've heard a few people talking about a villain—a new archvillain, like the Destructor, but different. This one is manipulating things behind the scenes, working in secret, but through official channels."

"And nobody knows who he is, of course. Shadowy, powerful," he said.

"Right. It's just that I was thinking, if . . . if you were a villain, and you wanted to take over the city using political channels, corporate channels, stuff like that, what would you do?"

"I would target Celia."

"Do you think somebody might have taken her?" Anna winced, because she didn't want it to be true, she wanted the idea to be crazy. But Arthur didn't tell her she was crazy.

"Somebody powerful enough to be able to keep me from looking for her. It's possible."

Bethy was hugging herself, looking up at the screens. Then she lunged forward, pointing. "There! There she is!"

Arthur went to the control panel to stop the footage, rewind it, play it back. He spoke into the handset he'd held aside. "Captain, we've found her, on the corner security camera."

Alone, their mother left the courthouse looking tired but pleased, smiling with a flash in her eyes. The hearing must have gone well. She ducked into the coffee shop on the corner, also something she'd do. They waited; Anna held her breath, like this was some kind of thriller, and the bad guy was about to strike.

Coffee in hand, Celia left the shop and continued down the street and off the screen. Anna almost screamed.

"You've picked her up?" Arthur said to the phone, and the image shifted. The angle from the new camera was high, looking across an intersection. Traffic camera. And there she was, approaching the intersection—until two people in dark coats and sunglasses joined her, walking on either side. They'd ducked out from a doorway, making their approach look natural—just two people who wanted a word with her. But one of them stuck something into her shoulder, through her jacket, and then a car pulled up to the curb. Before Celia could react, they'd guided her into the backseat.

Then she was gone.

"You saw that, Mark?"

Anna wished she could hear Paulson's answer. She had to wait as they made some kind of plan. The next step was obvious: figure out who the people were and identify their car. As nondescript as they all were, there had to be some kind of identifying marks, and some kind of database they could check against. License plate, mug shots, something. They could follow the car, but traffic and security cameras could do only so much once you got out of the downtown area. The police could do this, they had the resources. Now that Paulson knew something was wrong, he could handle it.

But it might be too late. Anna wanted to find Celia *now*.

Bethy was glaring at her. "You couldn't tell me? All this was going on and you couldn't say anything? Not even a little? I kept *asking* if you had powers—"

"It was for your own good," Anna said lamely. "To protect you."

Bethy blew out a disgusted sigh.

"I'm sorry," Anna pleaded. "I was wrong, I'm sorry."

"No you're not," she muttered.

"All right, Captain. Thank you . . . No, I don't think I can promise that, but I will let you know when something happens." Arthur ended the call, dialed up a new one, while Anna and Bethy watched, entranced. "Suzanne, it's Arthur. Would you be able to come home now?" A pause, listening. "Yes, it's trouble. The old kind, I think. Celia appears to have been kidnapped . . . Yes, I know, that's what I thought. All right, then. See you soon." He turned to face his daughters, and Anna couldn't tell if he really was that supremely confident, or if he was just putting on a good face for them. He was keeping his emotions under iron-fast control—he didn't radiate anything. Not self-assurance, not fear. Just a solid, wall-like implacability. "Don't worry, girls. We'll find her. We'll bring her home safely."

"How do you know?" Bethy said, glaring and petulant.

"Because we always do," Arthur said.

NINETEEN

Celia woke up tied to a chair, because of course she did. If she lost consciousness in the course of a kidnapping, she woke up either tied to a chair or strapped to a sleek metal table that was part of some fearsome device of unknown purpose. The chair was always better, because it meant she was dealing with ordinary criminals with ordinary motivations and imaginations and probably not much of those. The metal table and fearsome device meant a mad scientist, someone with ambition and imagination. When the Destructor kidnapped her, she ended up strapped to a metal table under a mysterious device full of copper wires and glass domes, believing that whatever torture he had planned for her was undoubtedly worse than death.

This was a chair. She was upright. The nylon straps binding her wrists and ankles to the arms and legs of chair were tied in knots, improvised. This was a standard kidnapping and nothing to be worried about. Probably.

—*Arthur, you can come looking for me now. Anytime.*—

He didn't respond. That didn't mean anything. He might not be looking for her yet. She'd just keep thinking about him until he did start looking for her. Not hard to do. —*Please, Arthur. I love you.*—

Near as she could tell, her wig was still in place. The itch made it feel like it was still in place, so she'd probably been upright most of the time, the two goons carrying her between them. Her captors hadn't blindfolded her, which meant they assumed she was powerless and that nothing she could observe would hurt them. Fair enough. She was in what looked like the unfurnished floor of an office complex, a wide-open space waiting for the partitions that would create a farm of cubicles. Evenly spaced posts held wiring and outlets, and along one side of the space was a wall of windows. They were high enough up, and she was far enough away from the windows, that all she saw was gray sky through the tinted glass. The décor was aggressively corporate: gray Berber carpeting, off-white walls, fluorescent lighting with an almost imperceptible flicker. The kind of thing you wouldn't notice unless you had to work under it for eight hours a day. A few orphaned desks and office chairs stood here and there. Her own chair was isolated. Air-conditioning hissed through a vent somewhere. She was alone, facing away from any doors.

All she had to do was wait, practicing calm, so when her captors finally showed themselves, she wouldn't flinch. She wouldn't show the least bit of surprise, and certainly not fear. The old skills came back, even though she hadn't done this in twenty years. The old habit, being the unresponsive captive, not giving them the fear they wanted. To keep that power for herself. She could be superior, even tied to a chair, looking up at them, whoever they were.

The question of why they'd kidnapped her would have to come later. That was fine, she could wait. She passed the time by studying the ceiling and seams along the walls, looking for where any secret cameras might be hidden. A small black globe in the corner of the far wall got her bet. A three-sixty fisheye in there could survey the whole room. She stared at it a moment, willing some awareness of her to whoever was watching, then looked away. Shifted to get some feeling back into her muscles and hoped she looked bored.

Her captors left her sitting there for at least an hour after she regained consciousness. She could be bored, or worried, and she refused to show them she was worried. She saved that for Arthur. —*This is getting less fun. I have no idea who these people are. Can you hear me?*—

No answer.

They might have gotten him, too. He might be unconscious, unable to hear her. But no, that was impossible, because no one could sneak up on Arthur, ever. No one ever got the jump on him. He was fine, just fine. Maybe he was distracted, and at that her thoughts spun out of control, because the only thing she could think of that would distract him from looking for her would be if something had happened to the girls. Maybe he was busy looking for the girls because if she could be targeted, so could they. Please, let nothing have happened to Anna and Bethy . . .

Voices approached, and she flinched, startled, exactly like she didn't want to do. But she focused on her approaching captors, and she wasn't worried or scared. She had progressed to a slow-burning fury. She heard low voices, footsteps padding on carpet, a door closing, maybe to an adjoining conference room. They approached from behind, and she suppressed a chill along her spine. They were watching her, studying her, and she had to not care. She'd done this before, she'd be fine. She settled an expression of cold superiority on her features. She would bury them at the first opportunity, oh yes.

Finally, they moved forward, around her chair to stand fanned out before her. There were five of them. The man and woman who had kidnapped her entered first. Two more men, young toughs with a polish that made them at home in the office setting. They'd have been out of place in a back alley brawl, but here they were sharks.

The fifth, standing in the middle of the group, was Danton Majors. His suit jacket and tie were gone, his expensive starched shirt was unbuttoned, revealing the top edge of what looked for all the world like a shimmering black skin suit.

"Danton Majors." A statement. She wasn't at all surprised.

"Celia West," he said, crossing his arms, gazing down on her with a triumphant sneer. "Welcome."

She looked at the straps binding her wrists and snorted. "I can't swing you an invite to the country club, if that's what you're wanting."

The curl on his lips twitched to a frown. "Be amusing as long as you can. I'm here to do business."

She studied his four companions. Their positions in relation to Majors were deferential, to the side and a little behind. The two sharks she recognized as assistant types he'd brought to the planning meetings; they'd fit in to that setting well enough she'd hardly noticed. One of them had been the assistant in the courtroom with him. The other two were equally confident, as if they had no doubt that they were the superior beings, and they all looked at her as if they'd caught difficult prey. They stood with an alert readiness, like sprinters preparing for a race—that stance she knew all too well. They were superpowered.

But they weren't from Commerce City. They were all from Delta, she bet. She didn't know them or their histories. She looked at each of them, amazed.

"All right," she said calmly. "Which one of you is blocking Dr. Mentis?"

They all, except Majors, glanced at the man who'd initially kidnapped her, dark haired and thin faced, lithe and intense in his business suit. So they had a mentalist. Problematic, not impossible. She caught the flicker of uncertainty in their eyes. Not quite fear, but close. Majors had probably told them this would be easy. The mentalist unfolded his arms, frowned.

"Are your powers active or passive?" she continued, regarding the mentalist, poking. "Can you actively influence other people's minds, or just block another mentalist's powers?"

"Enough," Majors said, as Celia expected he would. She could guess the answer on her own—they'd had to physically take her off the street and drug her. This guy couldn't do anything but block. Still, it meant Arthur wouldn't be able to find her. Not right away. Anna wouldn't be able to find her, either, and that meant Anna probably knew she'd been taken. She would tell Arthur. Help was on the way, and Majors and his team wouldn't know that.

This was all going to be okay.

Majors came to stand before her, just a bit too close, so she had to crane her neck back to see him, so she could feel the body heat coming off him. "We need to talk."

She said, "I have an office, and it's a lot more comfortable than this. I'd have been happy to schedule you in."

"Oh no, not like that. This is bigger than that."

"It always is," she muttered.

"You can't be allowed to continue on your current path," he said. Matter of-fact, condescending. The kind of tone that indicated he wasn't used to being argued with. His henchmen arrayed behind him supported his claims.

"What path?"

"West Corp. You're going to sell West Corp to me. You won't be able to use it as your base of power anymore. I'll break up the company, sell off its subsidiaries, and no one can ever use its power and influence again."

This both confused her, and not. What did West Corp have to do with any of this? They'd grabbed her to use as bait in some other scheme, she was being held hostage for some kind of leverage. That was how it always worked.

On the other hand, West Corp was everything, wasn't it? And she *was* West Corp. Something else was going on here, some subtlety that Majors was assuming, that she wasn't picking up on.

"I'm the third generation of my family to run this company, and you think I'm just going to sell it? Are you crazy?"

"And after you sell the company to me, you'll leave Commerce City forever. I don't care where you go, but you can't stay."

She stared. The former suggestion seemed laughable. This one landed in her gut with a punch. Her shock faded to a cold resolve. "I don't think so."

"I'm not giving you a choice, Ms. West. You're too dangerous, and you've manipulated this city's affairs for your own ends for too long. It's time you step aside."

A burst of laughter escaped, and she clamped her jaw shut to quell it before continuing. "I'm *dangerous*? What have I done?"

"I'd heard rumors, but I wasn't sure, so I came to Commerce City to watch. We all did. And now we've seen how you work. Commerce City's judiciary is in your pocket. I don't know why I thought I could have used the courts to expose you. You control City Hall, the police, the newspapers—and no one's the wiser because you put on this respectable public face. No one can see it, not even the superheroes, because you've used your reputation, your identity as the daughter of the Olympiad to reassure people that you're not a threat, oh no, you only have their best interests in mind. It's for the public *good*!"

This astonished her more than anything; she'd hated her parents' superhero identities when she was growing up. She'd hated being the daughter of the Olympiad. It had gotten her into too many situations just like this. She hated being judged by their standards, which she could never hope to reach, plain and powerless as she was.

Identify with them? She'd *fled*. The picture he painted of her—ambitious, manipulative, amoral—was so *weird*. She could only look up at him, confused.

He was on the verge of frothing, angry like he'd been personally insulted. "But we know what's *really* going on. Who you *really* are."

"And who am I?" she said softly, as if afraid to shatter some precious object.

"You're the Executive."

A code name. A secret identity. A superhero name, and with it a power. It was strange, twisted, and marvelous. She wondered what her father would think. He would smile, she decided.

"I see," she said. "I'm the archvillain. And you're here to save the city from me, like the heroes of old. That makes you the good guys, is that what you're saying?" She pointedly looked at the straps binding her arms to the chair.

"I had to convince you how serious I am. In all good conscience I can't let you leave here unless you agree to abandon your activities. If you don't, I'll deliver you to Elroy Asylum. I'll tell them you've snapped, and I can make sure they believe me."

She'd fallen down some kind of rabbit hole into an alternate universe. She was being subjected to some mad scientist's strange mental experiments in nightmare manipulation. It was the only explanation. She could only respond with wonder, and calm, because what good would panic do? Telling him he was insane seemed too obvious a reaction. Too close to the standard hostage playbook. No matter that Arthur couldn't hear her, she thought at him anyway. —*Arthur, I really need help right now. Help.*—

"How do you expect to convince me, Mr. Majors? Or do you have some other fancy nickname I should be calling you? Commander Arrogant? Ego Man?"

One of the henchmen quickly choked off a snigger. She thought it was Shark #2 and gave him a smile.

"You don't have to call me anything, Executive. You have a family—do you care about them?"

Calm, ever calm. "I do."

"I had to ask. I couldn't assume that they're anything more than extra pawns in your game, your personal pet superhumans. If you won't cooperate, we have other ways of pressuring you. Like you said, it's a family business. We'll go after them next."

"Oh, you can try."

"I really don't expect you to agree to my demands on my first request," he said. He'd begun pacing, and his henchmen stepped back to make room. Perversely, this made her want to agree to everything, just to throw him off. Turned out he had a script and wasn't really paying attention to her at all. "If you could see reason, you wouldn't have done any of this to begin with. So I won't insult you by expecting you to see reason now."

"You just keep going, this is getting better and better," she said.

"I can't trust the courts and police here to see what you really are—they all take orders from you. I'm sure most of the superhumans do as well. So all I have are threats."

"How very noble of you," she said, deadpan.

He stopped, glared at her. "You've forced me to this." He seemed agitated, like he'd expected her to be frightened and was frustrated that she wasn't. They always were.

"Yeah, you just keep telling yourself that." She was way too tired for this, and her stomach had started squirming. Vomiting all over their nice empty office would be gross, but it would serve them right. But no, she had to stay well and alert. As well as she could, anyway.

"Sonic, Shark, bring her daughters here. Then we'll have this conversation again."

"Shark?" Celia questioned, raising an eyebrow at him. She'd been calling him that to herself as a joke. "And what do you do, bite people?" Nobody answered.

The mentalist said, "We're not going to hurt them—"

Majors cut him off with a gesture. "Of course not. But we need to have some kind of leverage."

Celia's imagination spun out because she'd had too much experience with men like Majors and their plans. He could find plenty of ways to threaten Celia without physically hurting the girls: take them away, hold them hostage for the rest of their lives, brainwash them, turn them against her. Convince them to convince her. Make *her* hurt them. His mistake: seeing them as pawns. Her girls were better than that.

"I'd rather you kept your hands off them," she said, and was pleased to hear an edge in her voice. A supervillainy edge, even. *You meddle with powers beyond your ken, puny mortal . . .*

Majors smiled like he thought he'd gotten claws into her. "You see? I'll get through to you. Soon enough you'll understand that this is for the best."

He nodded at the others, who moved into action. They began stripping, peeling off jackets, shoving down trousers, and unbuttoning shirts. They all wore skin suits of some sleek, shimmering black material. She guessed the fabric had some kind of reflective, antitracking properties. It might even have been bulletproof. At least that was how she'd have done it. The woman put her hair up with a clip, a couple of the guys put on gloves, they stretched muscles and cracked joints in an obvious show of preparation. When they all lined up with Majors, still mundanely clothed, they looked as badass a team as Celia had ever encountered.

She raised a skeptical eyebrow at them. They made an effort to ignore her, but they had to make the effort.

Majors said, "Mindwall, you'll have to stay so her pet telepath won't find her."

"I'll give you as much protection as I can," Mindwall told the others.

"Don't worry, we'll be back before you know it," the woman said.

"Pet telepath?" Celia said to Majors. "Really?"

He chuckled. "What else should I call him?"

"The father of my children?" she said to the departing team, heading toward the elevators. "You might want to keep that in mind. Just saying."

"Can we gag her?" the remaining shark said.

After thinking a moment, Majors said, "No. I want her to be able to say she's changed her mind."

They settled in to wait. Majors retired to a chair across the space. He sat facing her, his arms crossed, studying her. She wondered what he was discovering. She just looked back, her expression still. Maybe she'd learn something about him, if they kept up the staring contest long enough. Like whether he had superpowers, and if so, what they were. He probably did, to be able to head up a superpowered team like this. Or he might have just been the money, the organizer. So, Delta had superhumans. Majors had to win this battle, or he wouldn't be able to keep that secret for much longer. That was all she really needed to know, that his threat came out of fear. Frankly, she didn't much care about Majors in the long run. She knew his type, and his type made mistakes. He needed her alive, so she was okay for the time being. A solution to this would present itself.

The second shark planted himself in a guard position behind her. Her skin crawled, sensing his presence without being able to see him. He was probably some kind of heavy, with a combat-related power. A kinetic strike or superstrength. She wondered if he had a temper to match. The superstrong ones often did. Like her father, who'd have made short work of Majors.

The mentalist wasn't happy, pacing along the side of the room, just out of sight of the stretch of windows. She couldn't tell if he was frustrated because the group had separated, or because he disagreed with Majors's decisions. Maybe this was a weak point in the group. She didn't have the first clue how to get around his telepathic block. Setting him against Arthur would be placing the irresistible force against the immovable object. Knocking him unconscious would probably do the trick. Simple, really. Too bad she was tied to a chair.

This was not how she wanted to be spending her afternoon.

The second part of any kidnapping was the waiting. The kidnappers made demands, everybody had to wait while the demands were delivered, then wait for a respectable amount of time to pass while negotiations continued. Celia, meantime, waited for rescue, which could happen quickly if the kidnappers weren't that clever. Or she could be here awhile.

The chair was a standard padded task chair, comfortable for what it was, with plenty of lumbar support. But no headrest, nothing to lean on if she tipped her head back. She wanted to lie back and maybe take a nap. Kidnappers always hated it when she was able to sleep during her own kidnapping.

She dozed off anyway, but it wasn't comfortable, and she jerked awake when she started to slump forward and tugged against her bindings. Her nose had started running, and she awkwardly wiped it on her shoulder. No dignity. That was fine, she didn't need dignity to get out of this.

A phone rang. Celia instinctively looked around at her own pockets, but they'd taken her purse and her phone.

The noise came from Majors. He retrieved the device from his pocket. Even halfway across the space, Celia heard a panicked voice on the line. Majors's expression darkened.

"Fine," he said, when the explanation had stopped. "Just get back here. We'll deal with it." He put the phone away and looked over her shoulder, taking in his remaining henchmen. He told them, "There's a problem."

Celia smiled.

TWENTY

Arthur stayed in communication with Captain Paulson as the police attempted to locate the car and identify Celia West's captors. They succeeded at neither. The car dropped off surveillance after a couple of blocks, ducking through blind alleys and into the south part of town that didn't have so many cameras. The features of the two people weren't clear enough—they wore large sunglasses and turned up the collars of their coats—and the facial recognition software, even the advanced version on the Olympiad computer, couldn't identify them.

Suzanne arrived within the hour to find Arthur at the computer, Bethy slouching in a chair at the conference table, and Anna pacing.

Anna had been pacing the whole time, thinking. Focusing. Trying to drill through whatever the bad guys had done to block her ability. That was Arthur's hypothesis, that they had a way to block his telepathy, and the same block affected Anna's power. But she had to be able to do something, and she knew she could find Celia if she could just figure out *how*. She was giving herself a headache.

"Grandma!" Bethy called and ran to the woman, who caught her up in a hug. Suzanne glared at Arthur over Bethy's shoulder.

"I had to include them. It was Anna—" He sighed. "Anna, would you care to explain?"

"Not really," she said. But now everyone was looking

at her, and she didn't have a choice. "I find people. I know where people are."

"That's your power?" her grandmother asked, looking thoughtful. "We'd been wondering. That's . . . all right." Anna realized just how closely her family had been watching, waiting for her to reveal . . . something. If she'd been anything like Captain Olympus, they probably wouldn't have had to wait so long. She'd never have been able to keep it secret.

She probably shouldn't have kept it secret for so long. "It's not very impressive," she said, frowning.

"Don't sell yourself short. You knew instantly that something had happened to Celia," Arthur said, not turning from the computer displays.

"But if they've got somebody who can block mental powers, then I can't do anything, none of us can do anything—"

"We can always do something," Suzanne said. Anna suddenly felt better. They were the Olympiad.

"I'm afraid we're at a bit of a loss here," Arthur said. "Paulson will do what he can, but this came out of the blue, and we're not expecting any ransom demands—"

"No, it didn't," Anna said. "It didn't come out of the blue. Mom was leaving the courthouse after the hearing about the lawsuit. What if . . . she thinks the lawsuit happened because someone wants to stop West Corp from getting the city planning contract. She must have gotten the lawsuit thrown out, and what if those people are working for whoever wants to stop her?" The empty office building. Superior Construction's fake lawyers. If this had anything to do with the lawsuit, the trail would start there. She blushed.

"Yes, Anna?" Arthur prompted gently. "What is it?"

She was thinking out loud but afraid to speak too quickly lest the pieces that were falling into place got jostled. "I think I know where we can go to figure out who took her." She explained about Horizon Tower, about tracking down information for the lawsuit, about the empty law office. Her father politely didn't ask her how she knew so much about all this.

"It's as good a place to start as any," Arthur said with a renewed sense of purpose. He picked up the phone again and talked to Paulson, passing along the information and closing with, "Wait for me, I want to be there when you go in . . . Well, I don't exactly know what good I can do, and I won't know unless I'm there, will I?"

He hung up the phone and started to flee the room before turning back. "Wait here. I'll call as soon as we learn anything."

"But Dad—" Anna called after him, but he was already gone. The real superheroes were on the job. Fine, okay. She returned to pacing.

Suzanne sat with Bethy at the conference table and took her youngest granddaughter's hand. "It'll be all right, I promise you. We've always gotten Celia back in situations like this."

"How many times was Mom kidnapped?" Bethy asked, shocked.

"1 . . . you know, I lost track." Her brow furrowed, revealing bemusement.

Anna's sense of panic was growing. The old Olympiad had always gotten Celia back, but the old Olympiad wasn't around anymore. Just the elegant older woman who hadn't, as far as Anna knew, used her power for anything but making crème brûlée in twenty years, and the telepath, and she knew very well how effective mental powers *weren't* in a straight-up fight, especially if someone was blocking them.

She had to do something, so she got out her phone and pressed buttons. "It's not working, why isn't it working?"

"The room's shielded, outside signals can't get in," Suzanne said.

Anna marched to the door, following her father.

"Anna, who are you calling?" Suzanne asked.

"Everybody."

In the hallway, she sat on the carpet because her legs were shaking. "Come on, come on . . ."

Teddy answered on the first ring. "Anna, oh my God, I'm so sorry, I didn't think you were ever going to talk to me again—"

"Teddy, shut up, I need your help. I need everybody's help."

"What's wrong?"

"Somebody's kidnapped my mom and they have some way of blocking mental powers because I can't find her, my dad can't find her. But I think we know where to start looking."

He paused for a long time. "And you really think we can help? I mean, this is serious."

"Exactly," she said, exasperated. "You wanted to stop screwing around, so this is it. If we can't rescue my mother, what good are we?"

"I'm just saying . . . maybe some of the other supers . . ."

"Fine. You don't want to help, I'll call Teia and Sam—"

"No, of course I want to help. We'll get her back, Anna. You call Teia and Lew, I'll call Sam. We'll meet you at West Plaza, okay?"

"Yeah. Okay. Teddy—thank you."

Suzanne stood by the entrance to the command room, watching Anna, her expression thoughtful. Anna prepared her usual defensive glare.

"Don't tell me that I shouldn't go out, that I'm too young, that I can't handle it—"

"I'm not going to do that. Wait just a minute, though."

Back in the command room, Suzanne went to one of the metallic cabinets along the side wall and opened a drawer. She didn't have to dig around long before drawing out a set of thumb-sized devices and wires—earbud and microphone sets.

"Take this," she said, hooking one of the devices around Anna's ear, settling the bud in place. "It'll keep you in contact with the command computer. We never had to use them much because of Arthur. I hope they still work. Bethy, here, you take one, too. We'll need you to monitor the computer scanner and keep us all in the loop. All right?"

"You want me to help?" Bethy stared at them both. Anna wanted to hug her.

"I won't have to teach you how to use the computer," Suzanne said. "You're your mother's daughter, you know very well it isn't all about the powers."

"Bethy, you're the smart one," Anna said. "Everybody knows it."

She had a look on her face like she didn't believe them.

"Oh, Celia used to look just like that when she was your age." Suzanne chuckled.

Bethy quickly hooked the speaker over her ear and turned to the console.

Back in the hallway, Anna's phone beeped a missed call at her. She hit Reply. "Teia?"

"Teddy just texted and said someone grabbed your mom."

"Yeah, I really need your help, can you come?"

She gave a short growl. "We'll try. We usually sneak out after Mom's asleep, but she's up now and practically sitting in front of the door. But we'll figure out how to get past her."

Anna had a radical proposition. "Maybe if you just told her what's happening—"

"And tell her everything else? I don't know that I'm ready for that."

"What is it?" Suzanne said.

Anna realized she was going to have to tell her grandmother everything. "Okay—Teia and Lew, they're . . . they've got powers, too. We . . . we've all been practicing together, and we have to figure out how to convince their mom to let them go—"

"Anna, let me talk to Teia," Suzanne said, holding her hand out for the phone.

Confused and caught too off guard to argue, Anna said, "Teia, my grandma wants to talk to you." And she handed the phone over.

"Teia? This is Suzanne, is your mother there? May I talk to her? Just tell her Suzanne wants to talk to her." A few moments ticked by, then she said, "Hello, Analise. Yes, this is Suzanne West. How are you? Not great, I'm afraid . . . Celia's missing. That's right. Can you help?"

Anna would have given anything for five minutes of superhearing, to be able to follow both sides of this conversation.

"Frankly, I don't much care about that," Suzanne said, hand on hip. "But will you please let Teia and Lew come over? Anna very much wants their help on this . . . Yes, Anna, too, they're all in on it together . . . I know, but what did you expect? Yes, Arthur and I will be there looking out for them. So will Mark Paulson . . . That's fine, just get over as soon as you can. Thank you."

She clicked off and handed the phone back to Anna.

"What was that about?" Anna said, baffled. Ms. Baker knew about them? About everything? But how . . .

"You kids think you're the only ones keeping secrets. Let's go downstairs and meet your friends."

"What secret is Ms. Baker keeping?"

"Not mine to tell. Bethy, are you going to be okay?"

"Yeah," the younger girl said. "I've tapped into a couple of video feeds around Horizon Tower. I think I can tell you what's going on, at least on the street. I'm trying to see if I can hack into any cameras on the inside."

"Good girl. We'll be back soon. Anna, I assume you have a suit or costume of some kind? Grab it before we leave."

"Okay."

"Grandma, Anna—be careful." Bethy's voice was stark, and Anna pursed her lips.

"Yeah. We will."

On the elevator ride down, Suzanne snapped her fingers a few times. When she did, sparks flashed above her hand, and on the last snap a torchlike flame burst to life and burned for a moment before fading away.

"I'm really out of practice," she admitted. "I may not be much help if this gets rough."

"I'm really glad you're here," Anna said. "Thanks."

"Family tradition. Your grandfather would be loving this."

"Loving that Mom got kidnapped?"

"Maybe not that part. But he always loved showing her kidnappers exactly how he felt about it." Her smile was almost gleeful.

Anna fielded a couple more calls by the time they reached the lobby. Sam was driving Teddy over, and Teia and Lew were on the way—with their mother. Teia wouldn't say how she felt about that. Probably because Ms. Baker was driving the car. Anna didn't have a chance to ask or find out about their side of that conversation. Time enough to discuss that later.

Outside, the day was overcast, and on the sidewalk and wide off-street drive that marked the front of West Plaza the late afternoon rush-hour crowds were walking past like everything was normal, which seemed terribly wrong to Anna. That hole where her mother should have been still gaped. People in suits left the building, moving down the sidewalk, picking up cars from valet parking. Taxis sped by. She tapped her foot and looked at her grandmother, wondering how she could be so relaxed.

She was about to say something when she spotted an odd pair striding around the corner and crossing West Plaza's front drive, right toward them. A man and a woman, they were athletic, muscular like sprinters, and their sleek black skin suits showed off their powerful figures. The woman had black hair clipped up off her neck and sharp, glaring features. The man was thuggish, intense.

"Grandma . . ." Anna murmured, touching Suzanne's arm.

The pair looked, walked, acted like superheroes, but Anna didn't recognize them. They didn't wear masks. Anna and her grandmother seemed to be their targets.

The man kept his gaze on Suzanne while the woman focused on Anna.

"Anna West-Mentis?" she said.

"Who the hell are you?" Anna replied. Then Anna recognized her, mostly from her hair and the shape of her face—the woman from the video who'd snatched her mother.

"God, she's just like her mother," the man muttered.

"I need you to come with me," the woman said, reaching for Anna as if she would just go along with her.

"Excuse me, can I help you with something?" Suzanne said in a falsely pleasant voice, pulling Anna back, stepping deftly in front of her.

The woman glowered at Suzanne. "Please get out of the way."

"Do you know who I am?" Suzanne shot back.

"She said to get out of the way," the man growled, grabbing Suzanne by the arm and yanking.

So no, they didn't know who Suzanne was.

She grabbed him back, clutching the arm he'd wrapped around her to immobilize her—then she glowed. Her form seemed to waver as heat radiated off her skin. The cuffs of her blouse started to smolder. Her captor was sweating, his face reddening and his teeth gritting in pain. Suzanne—Spark—must have been boiling him. Finally, he cried out, and Spark wrenched away from him.

In the meantime, the woman grabbed Anna, who slammed a heel on the woman's instep. Turned out to be harder in practice than in theory—Anna's foot mostly slid off the woman's armored boot. But the woman hissed, and her grip loosened. Anna dropped her weight and yanked herself away.

Teia, Teddy, and the others were close, their cars nearing West Plaza's block. She and Grandma had to hold out only a few more seconds.

"Anna, get over here," Spark commanded, gesturing for Anna to get behind her. The fire starter wasn't wearing her flameproof skin suit, and the sleeves of her blouse smoked and flared as the fibers caught fire from the heat. She stood braced, one arm outstretched, prepared for battle.

Her opponent in black opened her mouth and let loose with . . . it wasn't a scream, it wasn't even sound, but Anna could feel a powerful burst of energy rippling through the air in a focused beam, directly toward them. Some kind of hypersonic projection. Her ears rattled with it. She clapped her hands over her head and doubled over.

Around them, people screamed and car windows shattered. Suzanne hunched over Anna to protect her.

The man, the sonic woman's partner, picked Suzanne up and threw her. Lifted her clear off the ground, swung her, and let go, so that she sailed across the tiled plaza, hit the ground, rolled, and lay still.

Anna screamed. The man came for her next. "We said, we need you to come with us." He reached for her.

She was preparing to run when bolts of energy sizzled

across the drive, slamming into concrete before finding their mark. They hit the thug and bowled him over. One streaked a burned scorch mark across his cheek. Before the sonic blast woman could open her mouth again, Sam's next round knocked her over. The two black-suited villains seemed drunk for a moment, studying their limbs and brushing themselves off as they stood back up, taking defensive positions against the new assailants.

Sam's car had swung into the driveway, jumped halfway up the curb, and both front doors stood open. The engine was still running. Sam hadn't even gotten all the way out but stood reaching over the door, ready to blast another round. He was in full costume—jacket, mask, and all—and would have looked great if he wasn't standing next to his beater sedan. But really, he did look great, like he meant business. He flexed his hands and sent another round of glowing laser blasts, which caused his targets to dodge and scatter.

Anna couldn't see Teddy, but she didn't expect to.

The two unknown supers bent their heads together in conversation, took a brief look at Sam, then fled.

As soon as they turned their backs, Anna raced to her grandmother. Tom was with her, arm around her shoulder, helping her sit up. She was holding her head, and her roan hair was tangled around her shoulders.

"Grandma!" Anna stumbled to the ground next to her.

"God, I haven't taken a hit like that in a long time."

"Are you okay?" Anna said, her voice tinny with panic. She was afraid to touch Suzanne; the sleeves of her blouse were hanging in scorched tatters.

"Ma'am, I'll call an ambulance—"

"No, I'm sure that's not necessary—" But when she tried to stand, she hissed, her face contorting in pain, her body gone rigid. "Oh, dear."

Tom was already talking on his cell phone.

"Grandma?"

"Anna, it's going to be okay," Suzanne said, squeezing her arm. "The rest of you need to get to Horizon Tower to save your mother. We don't know how many super-humans they have or what all they can do—warn Bethy, warn Arthur. Tom will take care of me, you all get going." Her gaze darted up, and Anna realized they were surrounded, not just by Sam and a now-visible Teddy but also by Teia, Lew, and their mother, who must have just arrived.

—Dad? Dad, are you there?—

—I would prefer you staying at West Plaza, out of harm's way.—

—No, everyone's here. They have really powerful supers. We can help.—

—I know you can, sweetheart. I'll see you soon.—

"Dad already knows everything," Anna said.

"Of course he does." Suzanne smiled, but the wince didn't go away.

Sirens sounded in the distance—an arriving ambulance. "They'll be here soon, Grandma."

"I know. You all get going." Absently, she patted Anna's hand.

Teia pulled at Anna's shirt. "Come on, let's go."

Anna gave in to an urge to throw herself at Teia, wrapping her in a fierce hug. She didn't even question if Teia would hug back.

"You made it!"

"You need help, of course I did," Teia said into her shoulder before pulling away. "Now, do you know where we're going?"

She told them, and they piled into the two cars—the Baker family in one, Anna, Teddy, and Sam in the other—just as the ambulance circled into the drive. They'd take care of Grandma, and Anna let that worry go.

"Hey, Anna," a voice said through the bud in her ear.

"Bethy! Did you get all that?"

"I'm watching through the security cameras. Is Grandma really okay?"

"I don't know, she really fell hard."

"I'm also watching those freaky superhumans—they went around the back of the building. They had some kind of heli-car parked there, they've already taken off."

"Back to Horizon Tower?"

"Let me check . . . um . . . yeah. Dad's there with the cops."

"He's not too happy, is he?"

"Whatever," she said in her snippy Bethy voice. Anna had to smile.

"I'll check in soon."

They got stuck in traffic still ten minutes out from the Tower. The enemy superhumans had a head start and plenty of time to prepare. This was going to suck.

"This is so awkward," Teddy muttered, tapping a hand against the passenger side door. "I mean, look at us, we don't look anything like superheroes in this thing."

"You insult my car one more time, you can walk," Sam groused back.

"Anna, the Olympiad didn't have any flyers, how did they get around? Didn't they have some kind of, like, helicopter or supersonic jet or something? What'd they do with them?"

Gave a whole new meaning to asking Mom and Dad to borrow the car, didn't it? Except they wouldn't let her drive *anything*. "I don't really know—they had some armored cars and a jump jet, I think, but I don't know what happened to them. They're probably stored somewhere. I mean, the command room still works.

Dad opened it up so we could use the computers to find Mom."

"Really? Holy cow."

"That reminds me—here." She gave them the extra headsets Suzanne had retrieved from the cupboard. "We'll be able to stay in touch. Bethy's coordinating from the Olympiad mainframe."

"Cool," Teddy murmured, without sufficient gravity or respect for the situation, Anna thought.

"The pipsqueak can do that?" Sam said.

"Yeah. She's the smart one."

They didn't argue with that.

Eventually, after interminable minutes, they reached a police cordon surrounding Horizon Tower. A block in every direction appeared to be shut down with barriers and patrol cars, roof lights flashing. Yellow police tape fluttered, reporters pressed close with cameras and shouted questions, and even a few superhero groupies mingled among the usual onlookers and passersby. A man in a ratty coat held a beat-up sign reading CAPTAIN OLYMPUS: OUR ALIEN SAVIOR WILL RETURN. Anna got a little queasy reading that.

"Great," Sam muttered. "How do we talk them into letting us through?"

Any sane cop would look at them—three teens in a car wearing masks and homemade superhero costumes—and laugh, not let them past a serious cordon.

"My dad and Captain Paulson are just around the corner, we can call them over—"

The nearest officer came over and tapped on the window as Sam slowed. Dutifully, Sam rolled it down.

"You guys the Trinity? The captain said you'd be showing up. Park there, meet Captain Paulson at the front of the building. Got it?"

"Yes, sir," Anna replied.

Sam complied, and Ms. Baker slid their car to the curb behind the sedan. The boys all piled out and ran up the block. Anna hung back to walk with Teia and her mother. The cops just waved them all on through. Dr. Mentis must have talked them into making this easy. Anna started to get excited in spite of herself. This—the crowds, the orders delivered through a scratching bullhorn, the rabid sense of anticipation—must have been what it was like in the old days.

"This is the most fucked-up field trip I've ever chaperoned," Ms. Baker said, shaking her head.

"Mom!" Teia exclaimed.

Her mother rolled her eyes. "Oh, hon, calm down."

Anna sidled close to Teia and said, "Your mom seems to be taking this very calmly."

"Yeah, that's because it turns out my mom was Typhoon. Should have known, right?"

"*What*? Holy shit!"

"Tell me about it."

Anna took a surreptitious glance at Analise Baker. Aka Typhoon? She tried to picture it—plenty of photos of the superhuman existed: an athletic black woman with hair in cornrows tucked back by a sleek blue-green mask that matched her liquidlike skin suit. She'd been one of the premier supers in her day, but she'd vanished from public view when a warrant was issued for her arrest on suspicion of murder, after one of her tidal waves drowned a cop. The debate about whether that drowning was accidental or intentional still raged. The Ms. Baker Anna was walking next to now was . . . old. As old as her own mother, and kind of soft, with short halo-like hair tied back with a red headband. And she didn't have any powers, not that anyone knew about. Did she? Typhoon could telekinetically control water and summon rain—storms, in fact, much like Lew did. And Teia's manipulation of ice was just another form of controlling water, wasn't it? Teia was right, they should have guessed.

"Why didn't you ever go public?" Anna asked, blushing at the rudeness of it.

"Because that was a long time ago and it all happened to another person."

"Well . . . thank you. For coming out now, to help get Mom back."

Analise shook her head and seemed sad, full of regret. "I won't be able to help. I'm here to look out for my kids."

Anna didn't press further. She glanced up in time to see a green-garbed figure sailing overhead, as if leaping from one ledge to Horizon Tower's familiar thirtieth-floor patio. And how had *he* found out about this? She expected to feel an embarrassed flush at the thought of talking to Eliot again. But she didn't have time for that right now.

Arthur and Captain Paulson were waiting at the front of the building. A dozen police cars and a SWAT van fanned out in the street, and the place hummed with the tension of a coming battle. Radios crackled with static and orders, and uniformed men and women arrayed themselves like soldiers before a giant.

"You should have stayed home," Arthur said.

Anna said, "You're going to need help. They have their own superhumans. People nobody knows about, who've never gone public before now."

"And I'm betting they're not on Celia's list," Analise said, crossing her arms.

Anna furrowed her brow. "List, what list?"

"Never mind," Paulson said. "There's a team of supers holed up in there, and I want them out. You guys have any ideas before my people bust in there?"

For the first time, Anna had a chance to study the building. It looked different in daylight, the glass and bronze of it reflecting light and the overcast sky. On the ground floor, solid steel walls were bolted down in front of every available access point, instead of the glass doors, windows, and shop fronts that should have been there. The place was locked down.

"You've noticed the building's modifications," Arthur observed. "A squad of hired security are waiting inside."

"You can sense them?" Anna asked.

"If whatever's blocking our powers is in there, I imagine we'll be able to tell exactly how far the range of it is when we start ascending. I can take out the security contingent, but that won't do us any good if we can't find a way in."

"And I'd like to avoid a firefight," Paulson said. He suddenly seemed old, his hair finally more salt than pepper, his frown sagging. His intense glare focused on the building like it was his enemy.

This was their chance. This was why they had to be there. Anna said, "Teddy . . . I mean Ghost, can you go in and check things out? Maybe figure out how to open those doors?"

"I'll still trip anything like an infrared detector if they're set up for that. But sure, I'll give it a try."

"Radio's on?"

He fiddled with the bud hooked over his ear and nodded. "Yup."

"Good luck."

He smiled, took off running, and vanished on his third stride.

Paulson whistled low. "You never get used to something like that, do you?"

Anna didn't know if the radio would still work while it was invisible. She didn't want to try it until she knew he was in a safe place, so she held her hands over her ears and listened.

A click sounded in her earbud—the channel switching, and Bethy came on. "Anna? I'm trying to dig up information on the building, like some kind of floor plan, but I'm not having any luck. It's like nothing was ever filed on it."

"If you can find anything on how to . . . I don't know, shut down the power maybe? The front of the building has these steel doors we have to open."

Bethy blew out a breath that hissed over the speaker. "I'll try. This computer is crazy powerful—did you know I can hack into classified city records from here?"

"I'm not surprised."

Another click, and Teddy spoke in a whisper. "Rose, there's like thirty guys here. They all have guns, like they're expecting a war or something."

"Then please stay quiet and out of sight!"

"I'm fine. But the controls for the doors—I think they're on an upper floor, with the rest of the bad guys. I think the whole building might be set up with defenses."

Anna glanced at her father. "Did you get that?"

"I did. Captain Paulson, perhaps we can use helicopters to reach the upper stories?"

"My spotters say there's some kind of weaponry on the roof and patios. It'll take time to get past all that, and I don't want to spook these guys too bad."

Arthur said, "Oh, it's too late for that. What we have to do now is show them they can't beat us."

Nearby, Teia was cracking her fingers. "Blaster, you think we can take this?"

For the first time in months, Sam seemed uncertain, his lips pursed and his gaze darting across the dozens of square feet of steel they had to get through. "I don't know. Maybe if we focus everything on one spot. Can steel even freeze?"

"Anything can freeze if you get it cold enough."

Anna whispered into her microphone, "Ghost, I think we're going to try breaking in. You'd better get out of the way."

"Okay. I found some stairs, I'm going to scout ahead and let you know what I find."

Lady Snow and Blaster approached the blast doors.

Teia held her hands apart as if she were lifting a giant beach ball, gathering her power to her like it was something light and airy. Frost began to dust her sleeves, her mask, the tips of her escaping hair. Her breath fogged in a space around her that had become a deep, cold winter. The air shimmered with ice crystals. Bringing her hands together, she crouched in front of the door and slammed her hands to the concrete.

A noise cracked across the street, the sound of falling icicles amplified. A reflective sheen spread out from her, covered the pavement, crawled up the blast door and surrounding wall. The sheet of ice hardened, frosted, and a wall of cold pressed out from the building as even the air froze. Teia seemed immune to the drop in temperature. Anna wondered how cold the doors actually were now; the frost formed streaks across the surface, looping patterns, feathered tendrils, beautiful crystalline shapes.

Teia backed out of the way, and Sam stepped forward. In the background, Paulson shouted at his people to back up and take cover.

"Anna, here," her father said, an anxious edge to his voice as he gestured her behind a nearby patrol car.

Sam brought both hands together in a joined fist and aimed. A doubled force of energy, bronzed rays of light, blasted away from him and hit the doors, which shattered. Shards of frozen steel radiated out in a cloud of water vapor, leaving behind a jagged space where the doors used to be. The guards on the inside probably got the worst of it. Peeled, warped edges of steel folded inward, pointing toward a path of ripped floor and steaming debris.

Arthur strode toward the mess.

"Dad!" Anna waited for the gunfire that would mow him down when the guards stormed through the breach in the wall.

His hand was on his head, and he was glaring. This wasn't Anna's father anymore—this was the Dr. Mentis she'd read about in books. Paulson shouted again at his people to stand back.

A silent minute ticked over. And another. Dr. Mentis turned around. "Captain, I believe the ground floor is clear."

The police captain rolled his eyes before waving a SWAT unit forward. The black-garbed and helmeted group of officers held their guns ready as they streamed forward in a military formation, past a nonchalant Dr. Mentis. They peered carefully through the hole before trickling into the building, leading with their guns.

"What did you do?" Anna asked him.

"I cleared the ground floor," he said simply.

The radio in Paulson's hand crackled on. "Sir," a voice scratched, "we've got something like thirty bodies here. Mercenary unit, I'm guessing. Lots of body armor, automatic weapons."

"Bodies," Paulson said, glaring at Mentis. "Are they dead?"

A brief pause, then, "No . . . it looks like they're asleep."

"The usual trick," Arthur said, putting his hands in the pockets of his trench coat, shrugging.

Anna pressed the headset to her face. "Teddy? Ghost? Can you hear me?" No answer. "Teddy, where are you?"

"I can't really make exceptions when I'm trying to

drop a whole room like that," he said, not sounding the least bit apologetic.

"We have to find him," Anna said.

Ms. Baker stepped forward, staring thoughtfully at the hole her daughter had helped make. A mist hung in the air, vaporized particles still settling out. "Damn," she murmured.

Teia flexed her hands nervously, looking like she wanted to say something. Yearning for approval. Her mother just smiled.

Arthur said, "Analise, if I could suggest that you wait someplace safe—"

"I'm keeping an eye on my kids. I'm not even a telepath and I know what you're thinking—my powers are gone, I'm all washed up. Well, if they're blocking your powers, we're in the same boat, right? Handicapped and useless? I'm staying."

Teia, Lew, and Sam—the Trinity—were already running through the breached blast doors, ignoring Paulson's orders for them to stand down. Arthur followed at a more leisurely pace, with Analise not far behind, a resigned set to her shoulders and crossed arms.

Anna hesitated a moment, overwhelmed. The hole in the blast door suddenly gaped like a mouth, and the darkness inside loomed. Lights glowed within, but they seemed ominous. She felt small next to the towering skyscraper and the ignorance of what lay within. The old stories of her grandparents and Commerce City's other heroes had seemed so . . . epic. This—believing her mother was inside but not knowing for sure, hoping she was still alive and unhurt—it didn't feel epic, it felt desperate. Necessary. Like getting a cavity filled. You hunkered down and did it because you had to, and no one could do it for you.

She reminded herself: She wasn't alone in this—in fact, the whole city seemed to be here to help, because anyone who could hurt Celia could hurt everybody. They had to win. Anna repeated to herself: "I am super-human. I am a West and a Mentis, and this is what I was always meant to do."

She ran to catch up to the others.

TWENTY-ONE

Their plan to snatch the girls had obviously gone horribly, spectacularly—and, Celia hoped, hilariously—wrong. She wished she could have seen it, especially if it involved Sam Stowe's laser blasts. Or maybe an invisible Teddy Donaldson pantsing them both. The possibilities were endless and gorgeous. At any rate, the two henchfiends had been thwarted and were returning home. The girls were safe.

"How can they be on to us already?" said the mentalist in response to Majors's bad news. "There's no way she could have warned the telepath—we were supposed to have hours of lead time before anyone found out."

"The telepath must be stronger than we thought," Majors said thoughtfully. "Even with you blocking, he must have known as soon as we took her." The man looked sidelong at her, reassessing.

No, Celia thought. Anna was the one who realized what had happened immediately. The mental block must have erased Celia from her daughter's awareness, and she raised the alarm. Which meant things around here were going to get noisy in short order. She directed a placid smile at Majors.

"Don't think this means you'll be rescued anytime soon," he shot back at her.

"You believe I'm this powerful archvillain—don't you think I had a plan in place for just this event? My people are coming, Majors."

"Your people are deluded."

She turned to Mindwall, who kept throwing worried glances toward the windows. "And what are yours?" she said.

"This building is a fortress. Unless they can fly—and I know they can't—they'll never get here. I hope you enjoy your stay at Elroy Asylum."

"Hmm, I've been wanting to take a vacation. But I was hoping for a beach."

He was just like every other two-bit hack who'd ever kidnapped her in the old days. Expecting her to be fearful and cowering in the presence of his awesome might, he was instead discomfited by her amusement, by her lack of concern. Instead of ignoring her as he should, he struggled to impress her with his strength. The more he struggled, the more foolish he appeared. They never pinged to this.

His expression turned cruel. "Every elevator shaft is trapped. All the staircases have countermeasures. The exterior of the building has antiaircraft weapons that will target anything larger than a human body. No one reaches this space without my permission. But if you give up now, if you agree to sign over West Corp, I can end it all. This doesn't have to be a battle."

—*Arthur, I wish you could hear me, so I could warn you.*—

"You don't know a damn thing about Commerce City, do you?"

An explosion sounded, a rumble from street level resembling the force of heavy-duty construction. Majors stalked to the window and looked down. The mentalist fidgeted, acting like he wanted to flee. Celia imagined saying "boo" might set him off.

"Should I go check it out?" said the thug, Majors's remaining guard.

"No," Majors commanded, returning from the window.

"Sonic and Shark should be back any second. They can scout it out. Steel, you watch *her*." The thug leered at her.

"Steel? Is that supposed to be the noun or the verb?" His smile vanished.

"Ignore her," Majors commanded. "She's baiting you."

A flash of motion to Celia's left caught her attention. She resisted focusing on that space to avoid drawing Majors's interest. Letting her vision go soft, she kept her head still while looking out the corner of her eye.

A figure crouched at the edge of the wall, lurking just at the doorway. Obvious, not real good at staying out of sight. But the others were too preoccupied to notice, and the mentalist's powers obviously had no active component—he didn't have a clue that the room held an extra person. The newcomer had a mask and a dark green skin suit—the strange super, the one she couldn't ID. Just like the rest of them. She should have known he'd turn up here. At least he wasn't working for Majors.

This rescue was going to get very complicated.

She decided to help Majors stay distracted. Plus, she wanted to see how far she could push him before he really got pissed off. Arthur would say that was her old self-destructive inner teenager talking. Some habits died hard, didn't they?

"What is this really about?" Celia demanded. "Are you pissed off at me taking over a city you don't even live in, or are you just mad you haven't been able to do it yourself?"

Majors paused his pacing, and Celia turned out to be right about him: He was so assured of his own righteousness, he'd be happy to explain himself to her, to demonstrate the justice of his cause.

"You're well known, even in Delta. But I see through you, I see what you're really doing. We're here to save

Commerce City from you—from itself and its own misguided worship of you."

What an astonishing picture of her he painted. Had he actually *read* the *Commerce Eye*?

"So what's your power?" Celia asked. "I'm very curious—you know enough about superhumans to be able to identify them, gather them together. I'm just wondering how you did. How you knew. Where did you all come from? Do you even know how you got your powers?" She directed this last at the mentalist.

"I was born with them," he said. "We all were."

"Mindwall, be quiet," Majors ordered.

"Ah," she said. If a lab accident could create all of Commerce City's superhumans, no doubt a similar series of events could do the same elsewhere. Or a previously unidentified descendant of the Layden Labs experiment had moved to Delta and been *very* prolific. She should be able to follow up and find out. Assuming she got out of this. The possibilities turned circles in her mind.

"Mindwall. It must have been tough, growing up. Knowing you were different but not knowing exactly why. How do you even discover a power like yours? Did you know any telepaths, any other mentalists? By the way, do you know who else could block telepathy? I mean, I don't know if he could actively block, but Dr. Mentis was never able to read his mind. The Destructor, Simon Sito. You're not related to him by any chance, are you?"

Majors rounded on her. "Shut up, or I'll gag you."

"Yeah, we usually get to that point in the kidnapping right about now."

She'd thrown out a connection with the Destructor as a lark, but now she wondered. Not all of Sito's time as Commerce City's most dangerous supervillain was accounted for. Had he spent time in Delta? The mentalist—

Mindwall, really?—was sweating, his face puckered in horror. Odd guy out, she was guessing, just like Dr. Mentis. Nobody ever trusted mental powers.

"Danton? We're back," a woman's voice called from the hallway. The figure in green must have gotten out of the way in time.

The two strode in looking flustered and a bit singed around the edges. Which meant Suzanne had gotten involved, and wouldn't that have been something to see. Celia would have to make a crack about them getting beaten down by the grandma.

The man had a bruise covering his cheek, and his scowl was marred by a split lip. "The building's surrounded by cops."

"I don't care about the cops, how many of their superhumans are here?" The man and woman, Shark and Sonic, glanced at each other, neither one answering. So they didn't know. Danton clenched his hands; he was starting to lose it. "Well, *somebody* blew *something* up down there."

Sonic, eager, bounced in preparation of running. "We'll go see—"

"No. Shark, you go see. Call me when you know something. After that, we let the traps take care of it. When—*if*—they get within range of Mindwall's blocks, then we'll finish them."

"What is the range of Mindwall's blocks?" Celia asked casually. Just to see if they would brag.

They didn't. And the guy in green stayed quiet and out of sight. If all he could do was jump real high, he couldn't really help anyway.

The waiting was the hardest part of being kidnapped. Especially when she knew something was happening and she couldn't do a thing about it, tied to a chair. She sweated under her suit jacket and couldn't scratch. Just fidget to get the kinks out of her muscles and wiggle her fingers and toes to keep them from falling asleep. The moment had the feeling of a chess game, about three moves before checkmate. The pieces all slipping into place and nothing left to do but regret the moves you didn't make.

"You can stop this all right now," Danton Majors said, stepping around to the front of her chair, leaning over her. "I've got the documents ready to go, all you have to do is sign, and you can walk out of here and stop this."

His leaning over her was an obvious dominance posture that was meant to leave her cowering, cringing away from him, ducking her face to avoid him breathing on her. She let him breathe on her and never blinked.

"I don't sign anything without having my lawyers examine it first."

"Your lawyers don't need to examine this."

She clicked her tongue. "It's always the fucking con artists who say that. Blow up the whole building around me if you want, I'm not signing."

Majors's phone beeped, and he answered it, stepping away from Celia. Listened for what seemed a long time. He glanced sidelong at Celia. "Right. You've got a look at the surveillance? Holding the ground floor was a long shot anyway . . . so they're in the stairwell now . . . How many of them? Cops? Okay. And kids? The teenagers—how many of them?" His grin was evil. "Anna West-Mentis is there, too? And Dr. Mentis? All right, then. Just watch, and keep me updated."

He put the phone away. "They won't make it this far. They'll probably be hurt in the process. Badly hurt. You can stop that."

The nausea in her gut choked her. What were Arthur and Anna even doing, walking into a combat zone where their powers wouldn't do any good? They should know better than that. Celia kept her smile smug, her gaze terror-free. "You're the one with your finger on the trigger."

"You've lost, Celia West." He rounded on her, fist clenched. "You've *lost*!"

At this point, not saying anything would enrage him more than any snippy comeback. So she sat there, silent, gazing on him with as much pity as she could muster.

TWENTY-TWO

Anna quickly located Teddy, sprawled out asleep on the bottom step in the emergency stairwell behind the elevators. When Dr. Mentis psychically knocked out everybody on the ground floor, he really knocked out *everybody.*

"He should wake up easily. Just shake him a bit," her father said.

"Teddy, wake up, come on, we don't have time for this." It seemed cruel, but she grabbed his chin and shook, and was about to move on to a good solid slap when he groaned and brushed her away.

"Wassit?" he mumbled.

Lew got to his other side and the two helped him sit up.

"Ow," he said, resting his head in his hands. "What happened?"

"Sorry about the headache," Arthur said, though the faint smile he wore didn't seem very apologetic. "I've never been able to reduce the side effects."

Paulson's men arrested and cleared out the hired thugs. There'd been some argument about what they could be arrested *for;* they hadn't made any attacks, the building was private property so technically they couldn't be subject to any weapons charges. Paulson decided on obstruction of justice with more charges pending and had them all arrested on principle. Mentis examined a couple of them, but all any of them seemed to know was that they'd been hired to protect the building—not by whom, and not why. So that didn't help much. They knew there were further security measures upstairs, but again they didn't know exactly what.

Anna tried getting Bethy on the headset, but the thing had gone dead. On a hunch, she ran back outside. "Bethy?"

"Anna? Are you there? Can you hear me?"

"The radio went dead inside the building, away from the doors. I don't think I'm going to be able to keep in touch with you." She wouldn't be able to keep in touch with anyone else, either.

"So I really am freaking useless," she muttered.

"No, you're not," Anna said. "Go to the hospital and stay with Grandma, she needs you. Take your cell phone, I'll call when I can."

"Have you found Mom yet?"

"No. But soon, I think." The building was so well defended, Mom had to be here.

Bethy swallowed hard, and her voice trembled. "I love you, Anna."

This was no time to be tearing up; Anna scrubbed her eyes. "I love you, too. I'll call you soon." She hoped she'd call her soon.

They gathered around the elevators and looked up at the ceiling, as if they had X-ray vision and could see through solid matter to better plan their next moves.

"May I suggest that we not take the elevators?" Arthur said.

They started climbing the stairs, along with a handful of Paulson's SWAT team. They almost had an army. The stairs were concrete, and steel railings crawled upward around a tall shaft, a tower that felt simultaneously claustrophobic and expansive. The walls felt like they were closing in, but just a few floors up she could lean over the railing, spit, and watch the glob sail downward forever.

"We still don't know where exactly in the building Celia is, do we?" Analise said. They were strung out, curving around to the third landing. Anna didn't know how she felt about Teia and Lew's mom tagging along. But when she thought about *Typhoon* tagging along—well, that was different.

"Anna," her father said, "can you sense her or are you still blocked?"

She paused, leaned against the railing, and focused that inner, unerring compass on her mother. Celia still showed as a blank. More than absent. As an afterthought, she tried to find Eliot—and he'd vanished from her awareness as well. Farther up the building was a psychic bubble keeping her locked out. This must be driving her father bananas.

"Nothing," she said with a sigh. "But I think we should start with the thirtieth floor. That's where we scouted before."

Teddy looked at her. "You scouted here already? When?"

"Over the weekend, we had to get some information—"

"What we?" Understanding dawned, and he scowled. "You went out with the Green Gizzard, didn't you? Why didn't you call me? I could have helped—"

She glared. "Green Gizzard? What does that even *mean*?"

Paulson snorted suppressed laugher. "We've been calling him the Weasel."

Arthur said, "As in 'Pop Goes the'? That's inspired."

Eliot was going to *hate* that. Anna had a feeling this was the name that was going to stick. Well, that was what he got for not coming up with his own.

Arthur said, "Captain, what are we likely to find as we move on?"

"Anything. Everything. I don't know. Automatic firing mechanisms, explosives, trapdoors. Think of the worst the old Olympiad faced and ratchet it up a few notches? This is someone who knows your MO after all, to be blocking your power."

"That's what has me worried. Ghost, how do you feel about scouting on a bit more stealthily?"

"What, me? Yeah, sure." Settling a determined frown on his features, Teddy raced ahead and vanished.

Anna resisted shouting after him to slow down and be careful.

They passed the sixth landing. Anna really ought to start working out. Teia, Lew, and Sam obviously worked out. They were pulling ahead. Anna probably could have chased after them but found herself lingering near her father.

"Kids, slow down!" Analise called as the Trinity climbed farther ahead, passing even the SWAT officer Paulson had put in the lead. "God, to have that kind of energy again."

Arthur held out an arm. "Everyone, stop. Be quiet."

It seemed impossible that the whole crowd of them could be quiet. Anna held her breath, trying to hear what her father obviously listened to, his head tilted, focused.

"It's gas," Analise murmured. Anna heard it then, a hissing, as if several helium tanks were filling balloons at once. The sound came from somewhere above them. Her nose started tickling, which might have been her mind playing tricks. She held her breath, just in case, but that would last only so long.

The stairwell started to fill with a pale orange-tinged fog.

"Is that knockout or poison?" Analise asked.

"Doesn't matter, we've got to move," Paulson stated, pushing his SWAT guy back down the stairs. "Get out of here, get gas masks—"

Above them, Lew leaned over the railing, his hands

outstretched. Somewhere far overhead, a vent grating started rattling. A harsher blowing of air overcame the hissing, and what started as a slight draft quickly swelled to a gale. Anna and the rest of the party hunched over, bracing as the wind carried away dust, debris, scraps of paper all the way from the building's lobby, drawing it spiraling up along the stairs and away. The blast of wind thundered upward for several minutes, carrying the poisonous fog with it. Finally, the wind faded, the air stilled. Teia held on to Lew, who slumped on the railing, drained. But the stairwell was clear, the air fresh. The gas nozzles had stopped hissing, presumably after running empty.

"Wow," Analise murmured. Her smile seemed wistful.

That would be only the first of the traps.

Braced against the railing, Paulson was shaking his radio, not getting a signal. "Damn it. This whole situation is ridiculous. You"—he slapped one of his SWAT guys on the shoulder—"go back downstairs, get the tech guys to shut off power to the whole building. It's probably not even on the grid, so tell them to go into the basement and look for generators. And watch for traps." Paulson sighed, and the wrinkles on his worried brow seemed even deeper. "If I'd known we had a fortress sitting in the middle of the city all this time, I'd have shut it down."

"Save it for later, Captain. Let's keep moving."

"My heart is not going to thank me for this," he muttered.

"If you need to stay—"

"No. I'm fine. Let's go."

About ten floors up, the stairs gave out. One minute Anna stood on solid floor; the next, the floor had dropped, the individual stairs collapsing into a seamless ramp that curved endlessly downward. Letting out a yelp, she rolled a few feet before managing to grab the railing.

The chaos seemed to go on for a long time. Startled shouts echoing, the scraping as one of the SWAT guys, thrown off balance by his gear, tumbled all the way down. Arm wrapped around the railing, clinging, Anna was able to survey the damage. Even the landings had tilted, offering no safe haven on the now impossible stairs. Paulson had slipped down to the next flight before stopping himself; Teia and Lew clung to each other. Analise had already been hanging on the railing and managed to stay upright, bracing now to keep from falling. Arthur had stabilized by pushing up against the wall.

"Is everyone all right?" Arthur called. Which was weird—he should have been able to just know, reaching out to them with his mind. Which meant—

She looked for Teddy and couldn't find him. Even if he'd been far ahead of the rest of them, even invisible, she should have been able to sense him. But she just couldn't tell. She closed her eyes, and the world became a blank, all her friends and family invisible to her. She opened them again quickly, lest the vertigo of it overtake her. "Dad, I think we're within range of that telepathic block."

"Yes, I'd noticed. This is your chance to think all those terrible thoughts you work so hard to hide when I'm around."

She stared. "I don't think horrible thoughts. Much."

His smile was wry. He was close enough to reach out, brush her cheek. "You had some dust on you," he said.

"Dad, are you scared?"

He thought a moment, looking up the endless turning of stairs to their unknown goal. "I'm cautious. The block shows how close we're getting." He must have seen some look of consternation on her face. "If I stopped to think of it, I would be scared, so we can't stop. We must find your mother. We'll be scared later, all right?"

The trek up the stairwell became a mountain climb, stepping carefully and hoping the soles of their shoes gripped, clinging to the railing and hauling themselves up, hand over hand. Anna's father got in front of her, sandwiching her between him and Paulson, as if that would keep her safer. She glanced up once and spotted Teddy in the lead, looking back to catch her gaze. He offered a grim smile before turning to run ahead and flashing to invisibility.

Paulson got rid of his suit jacket, and damp circles of sweat showed at his armpits. Arthur kept his trench coat on, like it was part of his uniform.

The worst trap came on the twenty-fifth floor, so close to their target Anna had already felt the first flash of elation at impending success. Almost there. They'd find Mom, catch the bad guys, and be home in time for dinner. Never mind that the details still hadn't completely clarified.

This time, Sam stopped them, managing to look anxious even under his mask. The brash fighter had turned into a grim campaigner

"Hissing again," Sam said. "You guys hear it?"

"More gas?" Arthur said. "I'm starting to smell it, sulfury . . ."

"Oh, God," Analise said, pure dread in her tone. "That's propane. Something's on fire."

They looked up. A light was coming toward them, yellow flickering to orange, wavering with heat. The sound was like distant jet engines coming on, one by one. With each hiss and flare, a flame shot from a projection on the wall—not part of the girders and bolts in the building's framework as they'd been disguised to appear, but nozzles and ignition systems, shooting out gas, lighting it, filling the stairwell with fireballs.

Waves of heat roiled toward them, and the paint and drywall were scorching, bubbling. The fire was scouring the stairwell.

"Move," Paulson shouted. "Get to that door, get inside."

Teia was already there, both hands around the door-knob, yanking on it, rattling it. "Locked!" she called back.

"Teddy!" Anna shouted. "Teddy, ghost through the door and unlock it!"

Lew shouted back, "He went scouting ahead, I don't think he's here!"

Anna cursed. Well, at least he'd be safe from this. Weirdly, she thought of prom. Wondered if he'd ask any-one else, after she was roasted. So simple a trap in the end. They'd be burned to cinders before even reaching the thirtieth floor. She was too stunned to even be afraid.

The lead SWAT guy pushed past the teens to make his way to the door, drew a pistol to fire a shot at the door-knob, when Paulson yelled, "Do *not* fire that gun in a roomful of propane, Mitchell!"

The guy winced, chagrined, and put his gun away.

Teia said, "Sam, maybe you can blast the door—"

"My lasers have the same problem as the gun!" he said, frustrated. Teia let out a string of curses.

With unnatural calm, Arthur reached up to put a hand on Analise's shoulder. The woman flinched away; her eyes were round with terror.

"Analise, there are water pipes in the walls, yes? Con-nected to the sprinkler system. Are they active, and can you reach them?"

"I should have known," she murmured. "I thought, we're in a fucking building downtown, two miles away from the harbor, Typhoon wouldn't be any damn use here anyway. But no."

Arthur repeated, "Analise—"

The woman squeezed her eyes shut and shook her head in fierce denial, clinging to the railing with both hands.

The steel rail was starting to get hot.

"Hang on!" Teia shouted. "I got this!" She gripped the rail, her arms braced, her whole body tensed with effort.

A trail of leafy frost edged away from her hands, then shot out in speeding, winding patterns of ice around the railing, crawling both up and down. The air grew cold, then it grew colder. The frost reached Anna's hands, but she didn't dare let go. Her breath fogged, and the cold stung her face.

Teia reached up, blasting a sheet of frozen air particles up the center of the stairwell, past the upper landings, toward the oncoming wall of fire. The approaching jets of flame sputtered, and for a moment, Lady Snow had the advantage, sending wave after wave of cold toward the fires, which fought to stay lit, to continue progressing downward like some burning avalanche.

A drizzle began falling down the stairwell, a mist of droplets as Lady Snow's cold met the fire, vaporized, and became rain. The next set of jets lit, and the droplets turned to fog, more frost dripped off the railings, and the heat won out.

Drenched with water, Teia shouted out in frustration. The air was steaming.

Arthur said, commanding, "Analise. Typhoon. You *must* do this."

"I can't!"

"Then we burn."

Anna had never heard her father sound so . . . otherworldly. Cruel, that was it. She had to keep reminding herself, this was Dr. Mentis now. The hero thing, it wasn't just a costume you put on and took off. This was what people meant when they called it a persona.

Growling through set teeth, Analise turned away and braced against the railing, looking eerily like her daughter when she did. Her back tensed, her shoulders bowed and trembled, as if a great weight settled onto them.

Anna had crept closer to Arthur, who somehow found her hand and gripped it.

The rain began to fall in earnest. What had been a mist turned to drops, then sheets.

The sprinkler system must have been shut down—not surprising, considering the booby trap that had been put in place. But the pipes behind the walls still held water, and sprinkler heads still projected into the stairwell, giving the building a semblance of normality.

Analise pushed off from the railing to lean against the opposite wall, clawed her fingers as if she would break through the drywall with her bare hands, tipped back her head, unmindful of the water falling on her.

Suddenly, the sprinkler heads burst, and jets of water sprayed out to compete with the blasts of fire. The stairwell filled with falling water. Not just rain, but a powerful waterfall. Water ran in a river down the sloping ramp. The fires sputtered, struggling to keep the gas jets lit, and finally the flames died.

Analise fell, and Arthur caught her, leaning her against the wall and murmuring in a comforting tone as the sprinklers and pipes ran dry and the rain stopped.

"I thought it was gone," she said, her eyes shut and head bowed.

"No, you only put it away for a time," Mentis said.

He might have used his powers on her, gone into her mind and tweaked whatever mental dam was keeping her from reaching her abilities. Anna thought that was possible—until she remembered that his powers were blocked. If she had stopped using her power because she was afraid it had killed someone, the only thing that could bring it back was saving someone. Saving all of them.

From a flight above, Teia and Lew stared down, amazed. Maybe a little terrified.

Analise held her hand up. Water dripped, pooled in her cupped palm. Brow furrowed, she studied it a moment. The surface of the tiny pool trembled, and the vibrations increased until the water contracted, collected together into a spherical drop, which rose an inch from her hand before splashing back against her skin, scattering.

Sighing, she closed her eyes. Rubbed water from her face, not that it did any good. They were all soaked and dripping. But at least they hadn't cooked. When Analise looked up, Teia was sliding down, skating on the wet stairs while balancing against the railing, and pulled up short before crashing into her mother's arms.

"Why didn't you tell us?" Teia muttered into her mother's shoulder.

"Same reason you didn't tell me, baby," Analise said back. "I didn't even tell Dad." They hugged, and Lew slipped down to join them, and they might have stayed like that all day.

Arthur absently reached out to rest a hand on Anna's shoulder. She didn't know what to say.

"We'll find her," Arthur said. Which was exactly what she'd been thinking.

"I thought you said your powers were blocked."

"And somehow, I knew just what you were thinking anyway."

"Sorry to interrupt. But we have to keep moving," Paulson said, nodding up the stairs.

They hauled themselves up the slope, a task made more difficult by the water running down the concrete. But they made good time, clinging to the railings, because they had no desire to see what the next booby trap involved.

Anna didn't let herself think for a minute that she couldn't do this. She didn't have a choice, and that was that.

"I'm perversely encouraged," Arthur said at one point. "This wouldn't be so difficult if we weren't close."

"We're going to get up there and be totally exhausted and no good for a fight," Paulson muttered.

"Plenty of time to worry about that when we get there," the telepath replied.

"Holy crap, what happened?" Teddy said, his bodiless words echoing ahead of him before he flashed to visibility and pitched up against the railing on the thirtieth floor. He stared down at the dripping walls and the sopping wet mess of them.

"Geez, kid, you have got to stop doing that," Paulson said, holstering the gun he'd drawn from his belt.

"Sorry," Teddy said. "But what happened?"

They all looked at Analise, who shook her head. "I'm a really bad plumber, it turns out."

Teddy looked blank, but Teia giggled.

"Ghost, you've been to the thirtieth floor? What did you find?" Mentis ordered.

Wide-eyed, he nodded quickly. "There's five of 'em. The two who tried to snatch Anna are guarding the doorway. Two more guys in skin suits are watching Ms. West. And a guy in a suit, he looks like he's in charge. Ms. West is there, she's tied to a chair."

"You've seen her, she's okay?" Anna gasped. He'd seen Mom, she was okay, she was close, and they would find her. These last few minutes of waiting before they could rescue her were going to be impossible.

Teddy nodded. "She looks really pissed off." That sounded like Mom.

Arthur said, "What's she bound with, cuffs or straps?"

"Straps. Knots, I think."

"Right. I need you to go back and loosen them—don't untie them entirely, we don't want to show our hand. But enough so she can slip out when the time is right. Then get out of the way and wait for us."

"Got it," he said, entirely too eagerly. Must be nice, being able to turn invisible to avoid danger.

"Can you unlock the door for us?" Sam said.

"No, it's got a code lock on it or something."

"Then can I please blast it?" Sam called over his shoulder.

"Give Ghost a few minutes to get out of the way and get to Celia. Then yes, you can blast it," Mentis said.

Once he blew up the door, a battle would start. After that, there'd be little enough Anna could do, compared to her friends who could do so much. But that didn't matter, because they were all here for the same reason: find Mom, get her out safe. *That* was Anna's task.

Teddy vanished through the door again.

TWENTY-THREE

The minions returned and huddled in conference with Majors—out of Celia's hearing, of course. Alas. Not that she would have been able to do anything with any information she gleaned. She kept glancing at the mentalist, Mindwall, wishing she could interrogate him on the extent of his power. Wishing she could knock him unconscious by sheer force of will. But no, that was Arthur's ability.

Arthur. She relied on him for so much. She'd taken him entirely for granted, and now she had plenty of time to review in painstaking detail all the mistakes she'd made in her adult life. Little mistakes, inconsequential. A missed birthday here. A failure to listen to her children sufficiently well. An obsession with details she might have been better off letting go. Celia had given herself a pass because those mistakes all paled when compared to the drama of her childhood. Except for the latest mistakes: She really should have told everyone about the leukemia. And when she told Arthur that he was right, assuming she got out of this in one piece, he wouldn't even say *I told you so*.

Maybe Majors was right, and she should have let the company go a long time ago. Let the big picture fend for itself while she focused on what was important: Arthur and the girls.

No. Those thoughts were a trap, because while she didn't have powers of her own, she was still her parents' daughter. She had the power to make Commerce City better and an obligation to use it. Dr. Mentis of the Olympiad understood. So did Anna, or she wouldn't have spent all these weeks sneaking out on her adventures.

An explosion sounded, the *whump* of a fireball in a distant corridor, the hiss of gas and burning, and a group of people shouting in panic that seemed to echo through the building's foundations and floor. No . . .

Majors turned back to her, his face drawn into a very serious, very pitying frown. "Remember, you could have stopped this."

"You're a psychopath," she said. "I know your kind."

"You don't know anyone like me," he declared.

She smiled, because she could list the names of all the villains who were just like him, who'd kidnapped her or tried to. Who'd failed, no matter how confidently they'd stood before her and ranted that they were different. The feeling of déjà vu was oppressive.

The sounds continued, changing in ways Celia couldn't interpret. The blast of a blowtorch, shouted denials, then . . . rain? Falling water? Whatever it was, the shouting stopped, which could either be good or bad.

Typhoon . . .

Which was only her mind playing tricks on her. A memory from the old days intruding.

"That's it, right?" Steel, the thug behind her, asked Majors. They'd all gone very quiet, listening. "They're done?"

"We'll wait a few minutes and send Shark in to check. But I've studied all the vigilantes who might have come to help her, and none of them could escape those traps."

Just keep blustering. She desperately hoped he was wrong. Tried to imagine a world where he wasn't, and her rescuers just met disaster. Tried and failed. She could not imagine herself *not* getting rescued, and wasn't that an odd thought? Did Majors know that she'd never not been rescued?

Celia flinched back when she felt a tickling pressure on her left wrist. A tugging at the nylon strap binding her. Then a voice whispered close to her ear. "Ms. West, it's Teddy Donaldson. I'm invisible."

Of course he was. She sat very still and kept a smile of relief off her face. When really, she wanted to laugh. The nylon jerked a few times, seemingly of its own accord—a strange thing to see—until the knot loosened. The boy was clever enough to leave the strap there but tied loosely enough for her to easily slip her hand free. He quickly did the same to the right hand and then her feet, leaving them entirely free of the straps.

"When we give the signal, make a run for it," he whispered.

Now *this* was a rescue. She'd been freed right under Steel's nose and no one was the wiser.

A tiny breath of a draft marked Teddy's passing. Steel looked over, as if he'd caught some motion out of the corner of his eye. But he shrugged it off.

Celia wished she could have talked to Teddy, or that he'd leaned close enough for her to whisper a reply: Take out Mindwall. With the mentalist out of commission, Arthur could likely incapacitate the whole room and they could stroll out of here. If only . . .

She took a deep breath to settle her nerves and waited. Everything was going to be all right, and very soon.

The shadowy figure in green chose that moment to step into the open. The vigilante was tall, impressively fit, his arms and thighs leanly muscled under the skin-suit fabric. He stood in a pose of strength, shoulders back, hands clenched at his sides. His mouth and jaw were visible under the sleek helmet and mask he wore. He was clean shaven and seemed young.

Majors and his people jumped like they'd been hit with a static shock. And Celia found out how Steel got his name when a metallic scraping wrenched from his raised arms, which had become elongated, flattened, and edged with vicious-looking blades. The man's arms had become mutated, living swords, and he held them out and bent, ready to wield.

She didn't want her daughters anywhere near that man and hoped Arthur had the good sense not to bring them. The thought of the man standing guard behind her suddenly became that much more terrifying. All he'd have to do was drive one of his arms through her back . . .

The green-suited super didn't seem the least put off by the display, almost like he expected it. He announced, "Danton Majors, I need you to release Ms. West and surrender immediately."

Majors grunted. "Who the hell are you?"

The young super hesitated, as if trying to figure out what to call himself, but he set his jaw and brushed the question away. "I'm a concerned citizen. You've broken a lot of laws here, Mr. Majors."

"Who are you to decide that?"

The vigilante quirked a smile, tilted his head. "Just let her go."

"No," Majors said. His grin turned ugly, and he glanced over his shoulder. "Steel?"

The superhuman cocked back his bladed arms and ran forward.

Even Celia knew you never ran head-on at a strange superhuman without knowing anything about their powers. Seriously.

The mystery man leapt out of the way. He literally jumped, his power taking him across the room in a single stride. He bounced feetfirst against the wall, landed on the floor nearby in a crouch, and looked back at his opponents. Meanwhile, Steel had stabbed his right arm into the floor where the stranger had been standing, tearing through the carpet. Snarling, he wrenched his arm free. The man went after his quarry again, still running, as if moving fast enough would allow him to catch the jumper. This time, Steel slashed instead of stabbed, but the vigilante deftly sprang out of the way, bouncing across the room like some kind of insect. This time, he landed near Celia.

She didn't suppose he'd at all coordinated with the bunch in the stairwell . . .

"What do you think you're doing?" Majors said, laughing. "You think you're just going to grab her and jump off the roof with her?"

"Sure," the vigilante said. "Why not?"

Her eyes widened in alarm. She'd rather stay tied to the chair for the time being. Maybe she could talk him out of this. Mindwall, she noticed, had edged to the wall, where he crouched in a vain effort to hide. No offensive capabilities, scared to death. Good.

The *whump* and crash of another large explosion rattled through the space, closer this time. A couple of ceiling panels shook loose and fell to the floor.

"What was that?" Steel gasped, unnecessarily.

The woman, Sonic, ran into the open space. "Danton, they've broken through! They're on this floor! They survived!"

"Then stop them!"

What followed sounded like nothing so much as a ray gun, a patter of high-pitched whines searing down the hallway. Blaster's laser bolts. When Sonic and Shark appeared from around the corner, they ducked and dodged like a couple of kids fleeing a snowball fight. It was almost amusing.

"What are you *doing*?" Majors yelled at them. He was losing control of the situation, and he knew it.

"We can't get close, it's the kid with the ray beam—"

"I don't *care*! Sonic: *Knock them down!*"

The two supers turned to hold their ground, Shark crouching and Sonic taking cover behind him. He clapped his hands over his ears, and Majors and the rest of his people did likewise—Steel managed to retract his swords first, alas.

The woman leaned around, cupping her hands around her mouth and letting out a noise that didn't seem like it could ever come from a human. Almost an electronic squeal, Celia felt it in her bones more than heard it with her ears. As the vibrations rumbled up through the floor, her gut turned over, and she grew more nauseated. The steel frame of the skyscraper itself seemed to be vibrating on some fundamental resonate frequency. The whole building was going to turn to powder if this kept up.

Celia debated pulling her hands out of her bindings to cover her ears, to give away that her rescuers were already in the room and she'd been freed. Hell, she could probably just run. And go where?

Things happened very quickly, too quickly for Celia to decide on an action, one way or another. First: The windows shattered. Starting with a ringing sound, ethereal church bells, the glass bowed, cracked, maybe only on this floor, maybe across the entire building. The cracks multiplied into a frosted sheen while Sonic's wailing continued to pound them, until the entire wall of glass burst outward in a shimmering crest of glinting shards. Sheets of glass would be raining down onto the streets below.

The otherworldly screeching stopped as even Sonic looked back, surprised at what she'd done.

The man in green took that moment to leap at her, jumping at an angle, bouncing off the ceiling, aiming his legs in a piledriver kick at her chest. She spun but couldn't dodge; he caught her on the shoulder. Strongman Shark was right there, grabbing the kid and literally drop-kicking him across the room, booting him in the chest. He hit the wall near Celia and rolled to the floor, groaning.

The cavalry arrived then, a whole swarm of them rushing in, spreading out, shouting.

So was this the signal for her to run, or was it something else?

God, the kids looked like a real superhero team: Sam kept blasting, focusing a rain of lasers on Shark to throw him off balance, unable to go on the offensive. Shark bent to the attack as if he leaned into a hailstorm. As for storms, the shattered wall gave Lew access to a blast of wind and driving rain, adding to the confusion. Teia had her hands to the wall, and a sheet of ice grew away from her, toward Sonic, until it curled away from the wall and around the enemy super, creating a column of ice around her, trapping her. Sonic shattered it quickly with a short burst of sound, but by that time the floor had grown icy as well, and when she tried to run, she slipped and fell hard.

The others had flowed into the room by that time: Mark Paulson, amazingly enough, along with a couple of his SWAT guys, guns to their sides in this chaotic environment; Analise—and what the hell was she doing here?—and Celia wondered if her flash on Typhoon really had been her imagination; Arthur, thank God, and just seeing him made Celia smile. The expression on his face wrenched her heart—he was looking at her, but he couldn't see her, not really, not without his power. She hoped he could tell just by looking at the surface of her how happy she was to see him. And then Anna. Anna was here, small and pale, mouth twisted in a worried, panicked frown, her red hair wet and plastered around her face. She'd lost her stocking cap and mask somewhere along the way.

Go away, Celia wanted to scream at her. *Hide, please hide.*

Instead, Anna looked across at the superhuman in green, who was picking himself up off the floor, stretching a no-doubt bruised back and shoulders.

"*Eliot?*" Anna exclaimed, loud enough to echo across the room.

Everyone hesitated, turning to stare at the unknown man. Danton Majors himself, who had taken off his jacket and rolled up his sleeves, maybe in preparation for wading into the fight, stared at the kid with a kind of disbelieving intensity that made the rest of them pause. A tension spiked that hadn't been there even with all the fighting and combat.

"*What?*" Majors said darkly. Poor Anna stood frozen, obviously unsure of what she'd done. Despite the new drama unfolding before her, Celia couldn't look away from her daughter. There'd been a moment when she believed she would never see Anna again, and that moment pulled at her gut like fishhooks.

Majors and the man in green faced each other, and the man in green took off his helmet and mask. He was a good-looking guy, with dark hair and an intense gaze, cute and boyish—and obviously Danton Majors's son. They had the same eyes.

"What—" Majors said, and stopped, too shocked to continue. And what shocked him? Eliot Majors's appearance here, his opposition to Danton, or the basic fact of his possessing superhuman powers? Might have been all three; Celia couldn't tell.

"Didn't expect to see me here, did you, Dad?" He laughed a little, which sounded like relief. "Well, here I am. Superhuman. Just like you always wanted."

Oh, to peel back that history . . . it was like looking into a fun house mirror.

Danton finally shrugged, letting his hands drop. "Why didn't you tell me?" He almost sounded forlorn.

"Because I knew you'd try to turn me into that!" He pointed at the quartet in the matching skin-suit uniforms, Majors's personal superhero team. Delta's finest, no doubt, chosen and cultivated by the entrepreneur to be so.

Celia realized something: Danton Majors had accused her of manipulating the city and its superhumans because that was what he'd done in Delta. He couldn't imagine her doing anything else with her wealth and power and connections. And he figured there was room for only one of him in the world.

"Eliot. You need to stay out of this. You shouldn't be here."

"I was trying to help," the man in green—Eliot—said. And exactly how much had Anna been hanging out with this guy? "I know you came to Commerce City to stop the Executive. I wanted to help. Prove to you a lone hero can do some good without you, without the team. But . . . I think you're wrong, Dad. I think you're wrong about what's been going on and about who here really needs to be stopped. When we started looking for clues about the Executive, we didn't find Celia West. We found you."

Danton bared his teeth. "You don't understand anything, not at all! Get out of the way and let me deal with this!"

A roomful of people was poised to jump, if only they knew which way to go. Steel was twitching toward Eliot—but surely Majors wouldn't want him to attack his own son. Arthur and the others seemed to be choosing their targets.

As enthralling as this was, Celia had had quite enough. It was time to go home. "Danton Majors, you should have gagged me when you had the chance," she said.

"What?"

She yelled, "Take out the skinny guy, he's the mentalist blocking Arthur!"

She pulled her hand out of the strap and pointed at

Mindwall, who still crouched by the wall. His eyes went round, and he jumped and ran. Then everyone ran.

Mindwall didn't get far before tripping on nothing but thin air—and that must have been Teddy, still here, still invisible, still incredibly helpful. Teia and Sam charged toward him, Shark and Sonic charged after *them,* and Steel appeared at Celia's side, a razor-edged arm held across her throat.

"Don't move again," he muttered.

She glanced up, held his gaze. "You are *done.*"

When Majors lunged toward her, planting his hands on the arms of the chair, looming over her, she flinched back, startled. "You did this, didn't you? You turned my own son against me."

"I've never met the guy, but if it helps you sleep better at night, sure."

The only response he could manage was a wordless snarl. He turned to Steel. "I'll watch her. Guard Mindwall. If that block goes, the telepath will kill us all."

Arthur would never do that, but Celia could spend hours explaining that to Majors and he'd never believe her. How he must have wished Mindwall could do more with his powers.

The battle was a mess, pure and simple. The Fletcher twins hitting the room with wind-driven rain and ice wasn't helping, more like turning everything into a soggy frozen mess. Maybe the bad guys would slow down when hypothermia set in. The Commerce City heroes focused their attentions on Mindwall, as Celia had requested, but the Deltas were tripping them up. Paulson and the SWAT guys had guns but no clear targets. Everyone was moving and tangled together. Arthur pulled Anna to the wall, shielding her with his body.

Sam managed to pin down Shark with his blasts, but no more than that. The kid had more in him—he'd blasted down walls, after all. But Celia realized: He was holding to the old Olympiad ideal and avoiding lethal force. He must have thought if he could just keep Shark from doing damage, he wouldn't have to actually hurt him. The teenager was trying very hard not to kill. So freaking admirable, Celia wanted to cry. But she knew Sam was making a mistake. The Delta team didn't seem to have such ideals.

The inevitable moment came when a squeal from Sonic distracted Sam, and the swarm of insectlike laser bolts ceased. Shark took advantage of the lull, and his superstrength made him unstoppable. The others, going after Mindwall and doing battle with Sonic and Steel, couldn't help Sam. The strong man seemed twice as big as the teenager, three times as muscular, and was faster than should have been possible for someone that size. Growling, he grabbed up Sam, put his head in a lock, and wrenched back his arm until the boy cried out. Shark pivoted, swung, and threw, and Sam sailed . . . not toward any walls but toward the shattered windows. He fell through and down, screaming.

Anna screamed with him. Arthur grabbed her, to keep her from running after him.

Eliot ran toward the open wall and leaped.

Lew threw himself to the floor, leaned over the edge past the broken glass, arm reaching. "I can get him, I can catch him!" he yelled, while Teia and Analise both kept hold of him, begging him to come away from the space. Celia held her breath, unable to look away.

Outside, wind howled, debris rocketing into the office. The sky darkened, and black clouds descended until they shrouded the buildings across the street.

The thin tornado that passed by didn't seem any more surreal than the rest of it. Not too big, it could travel down the streets without causing too much damage. Just the right size to buoy a falling boy to safety. Celia prayed.

"Did you get him?" Anna begged. Her voice had gone thin, fearful.

"I don't know," Lew said, gasping. "That guy, Eliot— he's jumping, he hit the building across the street and jumped over. He's got him, I think he's got him!" The excitement darkened. "He looks hurt. They hit the ground, I can't see them."

In the meantime, Paulson leveled a handgun at Majors. "Commerce City PD. Danton Majors, stand down, tell your people to stand down. This is over."

Instead of surrendering, Majors raised a hand, and Steel lunged forward, arm leading like a lance. Paulson couldn't swing around in time. The sword arm impaled him through the middle. The flak vest didn't slow Steel down, and the superhuman grabbed the gun from Paulson's hand as the police captain dropped to his knees, groaning, arm clutched around his middle.

One of the SWAT guys shot at Steel, but he merely flinched back, and the bullet ricocheted into a wall. Snarling, Steel rounded on the cop, who didn't have much choice but to try again. Meanwhile, Shark stood before Analise and her family, threatening merely with his presence, and Sonic focused her attention on Arthur and Anna.

Celia's hands clenched, and her throat closed, too shocked to cry out. This was too high a price to pay for her rescue. Her gaze turned dark as her anger built. She pulled her arms from their loosened straps and shook the ones off her feet as she stood.

"Enough! That's . . . quite . . . enough."

A draft, the tail end of Lew's storm, maybe, flapped through the broken windows, catching stray bits of paper and shaking ceiling tiles. She had everyone's attention now. Majors and his people stared, startled by her freedom. She could see them wondering if she really did have powers, but if they were really paying attention, they'd notice Teddy, visible now, standing near Anna and Arthur. And Analise, standing just like she used to as Typhoon, feet apart, shoulders back, arm bent, ready to call the ocean to her if needed. What had happened to spring the lock that had shut off her powers? Teia and Lew, of course. Typhoon had returned to save them. A family of miracle workers.

They all waited for her to do something. What could she say that would make this all stop, make it all go away?

She took off her wig and let it hang by her thigh. There, that inspired audible gasps of shock. As chilled gooseflesh crawled over her naked scalp, she suppressed a shiver.

"You're wrong about me," she said to Majors. "I know there's nothing I can say that will convince you. But you're wrong. I'm very tired. I'm very . . . sick right now. I want to go home, and I want my family and my city to be safe. That's all. I'm going to ask you very simply, very calmly, to let us go. Take your people and go back to Delta. Leave us alone."

After a long hesitation, Majors offered a wicked smile. "You're very good. You think of everything, don't you? A play for sympathy, is it? Thinking I'll just roll over for you. If the case didn't go your way, would you have done this in the courtroom? Anything to get people to do what you tell them."

Not even the worst of her kidnappers had looked on her with such loathing. To the rest of them she'd always been just a tool, a means to an end. But Danton—to him, she was the source of all evil. How very odd.

"She has leukemia," Arthur said, pleading, desperate. "She's in the middle of chemotherapy. My God, can't you see how ill she is?" His power was blocked; he didn't have to worry about his emotion overpowering the others, so he bared himself and his fear as he begged.

"It's certainly a good act," he said.

"Damn you to hell," her beloved shot back.

"Arthur, it's all right," she soothed him. Celia studied the wig in her hands, a mop of tangled red hair. An ugly thing. A mask, of sorts.

Danton Majors expected to see in her a mastermind, an architect of villainous schemes. To him, she was a criminal genius. She was the Executive. All right, then. That's what he'd get.

She dropped the wig on the floor. Step by step, she crossed to Danton Majors. "You don't know anything about me. About Commerce City. You can't succeed here."

"Stop me," he said, sneering. "Save yourself, if you can."

She'd been watching his people, Steel and Shark, Sonic and Mindwall. All through this exchange they hadn't moved, and their expressions had shifted during that time, falling, their gazes turning inward. To uncertainty. To pity, possibly for her. To horror, maybe? She hoped. Sonic, in particular, kept looking at that wig, as if she knew exactly what it meant, what it cost her to take it off in this setting. Celia hoped she'd read them all right.

"Mindwall?" she said, glancing over her shoulder.

"It . . . it's Edgar. My name's Edgar." His voice shook.

"Do you have control over your blocking powers, or is it autonomous?"

"I can't control it. It's always there."

"Can I ask you to leave, then? Go downstairs, as far away as you need to until the block stops working here."

"Mindwall," Majors said predictably, "don't move."

Celia said, "You can do what you like."

The man walked away, past the whole crowd of them, exhausted and injured, and disappeared into the hallway beyond.

"Edgar!" Sonic called after him, but Mindwall didn't stop.

"Arthur, how long should we wait?" Celia said.

"The block starts about the tenth floor. A few minutes, at least."

"All right, then. In a few minutes, Dr. Mentis will put all of us to sleep. When he does a blanket offensive, he can't pick his targets. It will happen to all of us. He won't kill you, I promise. I guarantee you, there's no better way to stop a fight in its tracks. I've seen it done. Shall we simply keep talking until then? Keep trying to explain ourselves to each other? Or you can do . . . what, Mr. Majors? What's your next move?"

She was rather surprised that he had one. He reached into his trouser pocket and drew out a device that appeared to be a cell phone but had only two buttons on it. He pressed one.

"I've owned this building for a number of years," he said. "I've made many modifications to it, as your Dr. Mentis and his friends can attest. One of the modifications—the building's entire framework is rigged with explosives. I've just armed the system. The second button will trigger the explosives, collapse the building, and kill us all. That's how far I'm willing to go to stop you, Celia West. That's how dangerous I think you are." The spark in his eyes wasn't crazed; rather, it held the determined light of a martyr. He was convinced of his righteousness.

"Danton, no!" Sonic said, stepping forward. Shark stepped with her, but Steel moved between them and Majors, his weapons held ready to stop them.

Celia stared at the detonation device with a sinking feeling that she'd lost it all. Called his bluff, but he held the winning hand.

"Ms. West, I'm giving you one last chance: Sign over your company to me, submit to treatment at Elroy Asylum, and we all get to live."

"And you really can't tell who's the crazy one here, can you?" she murmured.

On one side of the room, Analise had her arms around both her kids' shoulders. Teia and Lew must have been too scared to breathe, much less try their powers on Majors—they couldn't stop him before he pushed that button. Nearby, Arthur and Anna were side by side, shoulder to shoulder. Anna stood tall and proud, glaring with anger. Not fear. Next she met Paulson's gaze, and even wounded and lying in an expanding pool of blood, he looked angry. That lifted her as well.

Shark inched toward Majors, arm out comfortingly, wary of Steel's blade. "Boss, don't do this. This . . . the situation here, it's not like you said. This isn't worth it. Put down the remote."

Majors glowered. "I thought you agreed with me. You've seen what these people can do! Who's going to stop them if not us?"

"Did you ever consider that maybe we could all work together?" Celia said—to Shark, to Sonic. "I mean, our football teams may hate each other's guts, but I never much liked football anyway."

Danton pointed at her. "You, stop talking, unless it's to agree to my terms. I'm going to detonate this building on the count of ten. One . . ."

Sonic pleaded. "Danton, Eliot is down there. If you collapse the building, he may not have time to get away—"

"Having powers means sacrifice. He knows that," Majors replied. "Two . . . three . . ."

Shark ran his hands through his hair, pulling. "Steel, bro, come on, this is crazy. Don't let him do this."

"He's right," Steel said, his jaw set and lips trembling. "We all agreed, he's right."

"Four . . . five . . ."

Please, Edgar, hurry!

Sonic again: "Danton. Put that down, let's talk about this."

"Tell her to say yes!" Danton said, pointing with the remote.

The woman took a breath and begged. "Ms. West, please. No one will hold you to it, we can work it all out later. You're the only one who can stop him."

"No, I'm not," Celia said, watching Arthur.

Whose eyes lit at the same time Anna yelled, "Dad!"

"There. There it is." Arthur scanned the room with a dark, fierce gaze, and a familiar voice called to Celia from the back of her mind: —*And there we are. I've got you all.*—

Majors fell first, his eyes rolling back as he dropped the remote and collapsed. Steel was next, and Sonic and Shark looked at each other, bewildered and comprehending. Then Celia smelled sage, an achingly familiar scent of imposed sleep. She got a glimpse of Anna folding, and Arthur catching her to lower her to the floor, before her vision went dark.

—*We'll be here when you wake, dearest.*—

TWENTY-FOUR

Anna awoke to someone shaking her. Her nose tickled, her head ached, and her brain was full of panic.

Gasping, she tried to sit up, but the headache rocked her sideways and bile climbed into her throat.

"Easy," her father murmured, propping her up. "Slow breaths. Good girl. I'm sorry I couldn't let you rest, but I need help. Will you be all right?"

She looked around. They were still in the empty office space in Horizon Tower. A few minutes of fighting had torn the place to pieces. She closed her eyes when nausea hit again, but her breathing steadied.

Her father was a mess, soaked with water, smudged with soot, face cut, eyes sunk with exhaustion. She clung to him.

"Dad, what's that about Mom having leukemia? Was that some kind of joke?"

He smiled. "Should have known that wouldn't get past you. I'm afraid it isn't, love. Can we talk about that later?"

Only a few moments had passed since Dr. Mentis knocked them all out. Having now experienced his mind control power, Anna could confidently say he'd never used it on her before. It was a strange comfort in the midst of the chaos. He'd already found a landline that wasn't shut down by whatever Majors had done to cut off transmissions and called the police and EMTs. They'd checked the elevators, deemed them safe, and should arrive any minute. Apparently, Mindwall had turned himself in once he reached the ground floor and told them how to disable the rest of the booby traps. Mentis collected weapons from the bad guys and ensured that the detonator was put somewhere safe until the bomb squad could disable it.

"Dad—Sam. Were you able to find out anything about Sam?"

"He's alive." And that was all he'd say about it. Anna had a bad feeling. She was certain he was alive—now that she was out of Mindwall's range, she could feel him. He was at the same hospital as Grandma, which was good. It should have been good. But Arthur wouldn't tell her how badly he was hurt, and Anna's powers couldn't give her any details.

But she was massively, hugely, vastly relieved that she knew where everyone was now. She could feel them all: Mom, Dad, Teddy, Eliot, Bethy, and Suzanne, everyone. All the holes in her awareness filled in. The world had righted itself.

The police and EMTs arrived, and Anna directed them to the aftermath. They went to Captain Paulson first. Anna was afraid he hadn't survived the wound on top of Mentis's mind control. But she could feel him, so he was still here.

When he could hand over authority of the situation to the police, Arthur went straight to Celia. Anna hung back.

The wig had been the biggest shock of the day. She'd imagined superhero battles. Not that the real thing was anything like she'd imagined, but none of what happened had been entirely unexpected. Until Celia took the wig off. Seeing her mother bald was just wrong. The expanse of skin made her look scrawny, bony. She had pale freckles on her scalp, mottled spots like an accidental splatter of ink. The shadows under Celia's eyes seemed so much larger, darker, without hair to offset them.

Suddenly, all her mother's behavior over the last few weeks made perfect sense, and Anna wondered why she hadn't figured it out on her own. She hadn't been able to conceive of the idea of Celia being ill, weak.

As Arthur shook Celia awake, Anna moved to join them, crouching at her mother's other side and taking her hand. Celia took a long time to wake up, and Arthur didn't rush her.

An EMT tapped his shoulder at one point. "Do you want us to look at her?"

"Not just yet," he answered.

Finally, she opened her eyes. Looked at them both for a long time before asking, "Did we win?"

"We did," Arthur said, stroking her forehead in a movement that would have brushed back her hair, if she had any. "Though you cut it very close there."

"I had a feeling."

"Mom," Anna burst, unable to keep quiet. "Are you going to be okay?"

Somehow, Celia knew that the question didn't mean right now, right here. She was asking about the long term. The illness. Would her hair ever grow back. Everything.

"I don't know," Celia said, squeezing Anna's hand. "But I hope so."

Everyone else started waking up on their own. Anna still had a million questions, but they'd have to wait.

By the time Analise walked over, Celia was on her feet, and the two women fell into a deep, rib-crushing hug. Anna eavesdropped.

"I'm so glad you're here," Celia said.

"And I'm so mad at you I could scream. When were you going to tell me about this?"

"I don't know. Never mind." Celia pulled away, held Analise's shoulders. "What happened? Typhoon?"

Analise just sighed. "I'm still working that out."

Led by a uniformed officer, Sonic passed by, in handcuffs. She pulled up short, glaring at Celia.

"Why didn't you just tell him yes? He would have stopped. He would have let everyone go."

"Are you sure about that?" Celia replied. "He'd taken it too far. Even if I'd said yes, he might still have pushed the button. Just to prove he was right."

"What are you going to do to him?"

On Arthur's advice, the EMTs had sedated Danton Majors when he started to wake up. They were strapping him to a gurney now.

Sighing, Celia looked around, taking in the shattered windows, the injured bodies, the exhausted, shadowed expressions. "Take him to Elroy Asylum. Let them decide what to do with him."

Teia, Lew, and Teddy were standing a little ways off. All here, all safe, if a little ragged looking and beat up.

"What are they saying about Sam?" Lew asked. "Is he okay?" The glint in his eyes had turned shadowed, and his shoulders slumped.

"He's in the hospital," Anna said. "Nobody will tell me how he is."

They were all so quiet. None of that strutting confidence they'd had during their practices in the park. Everything they'd done before this was just a game.

"I hope he's okay," Teia said softly.

They watched for a few more minutes, the comings and goings, bad guys arrested, the bomb squad taking charge of the detonator. Anna thought the four of them might be arrested for their vigilantism, but no one said anything.

"Thanks," Anna said. "Thanks for coming to help get my mom. We couldn't have saved her without you."

"Hey, teamwork," Teia said, her smile lopsided. Anna wiped away a stray tear. Exhaustion, that was all. But Teia caught her up in a hug, and she felt Lew's and Teddy's hands on her shoulders, and she started to think that everything really would be all right.

Night had fallen by the time they finally made it back to street level in front of the cordoned-off building. Analise, Teia, and Lew went home after giving statements to the police. The West clan was about to do likewise. Eliot had vanished. Anna focused and found him hanging around outside Elroy Asylum, where they'd taken his father. Not doing anything but watching, the way his presence remained stationary.

"You need a ride home?" Anna asked Teddy. They walked a little ways out by themselves while they waited for Tom to bring the car. Mom and Dad were still talking to the police. Mom had just spent ten minutes on the phone with Bethy, reassuring her that everything was fine. Except that she was sick. She told Bethy about that part. Celia'd left her wig back in the office. Bethy was going to be shocked at how she looked.

"My folks are going to kill me," Teddy said, sighing. "I didn't tell them where I was going."

"Maybe my folks can talk to them."

"Maybe I'll just put up with being grounded for a while."

She giggled. Walked a few more steps. The streetlights and twilight shadows made the skyscrapers look like towering monoliths. Who knew what secrets they all held?

Teddy said, "Hey, Anna?"

"Yeah?"

"Is this a bad time to ask you if you still want to go to prom with me?"

Maybe that warm flush in her gut was postbattle adrenaline. But she didn't think so. She didn't have to think about how to answer this time.

"No. I mean, no it's not a bad time. Yes, I'll go to prom with you."

"Okay. Yeah. Cool." He had such a goofy, great smile.

She grabbed his hand, touched his face to steady herself, and kissed him. His arms wrapping around her told her that yes, that had been the right call, too.

TWENTY-FIVE

News outlets the next day were filled with stories of the shocking nervous breakdown of Delta businessman Danton Majors, who'd collected his own team of superhuman mercenaries, captured beloved Commerce City icon Celia West, and held her hostage for the outrageous ransom of West Corp itself. That wasn't exactly what happened, of course, but that was the favorite spin. That was the sequence of events compressed into a simple, repeatable narrative. Even better were the tales of the heroic actions of Commerce City's own selfless superhuman vigilantes who came to her rescue: Dr. Mentis, of course, but also the Trinity, the two-member team known as Espionage, and a new hero the police had dubbed Weasel. Spark had emerged from retirement to save her granddaughters and become injured with a cracked femur in the process. The hospital had to ask people to stop sending flowers. And there was even, the *Commerce Eye* reported, a brief reappearance by the legendary Typhoon, who had often helped rescue Celia in the past. Few believed the accuracy of that rumor. The epic battle and its aftermath would keep a city full of reporters busy for a week. The Rooftop Watch site crashed its servers.

Despite all the news cameras that had shown up at Horizon Tower, the dozens of citizens who'd snapped cell phone pictures, the images that had been grabbed from traffic and security cameras, the only photos that appeared on any of the stories were generic shots of the building, of the glass-strewn street after the windows on the top floors had shattered, the swarm of police cars, and the aftermath: the Delta supers being led away morose and in handcuffs, Majors himself strapped to a gurney, taken away in an ambulance. Dr. Mentis gave a statement, and pictures of him appeared along with the usual quotes about Commerce City being safe once again. People observed that he was no longer the intense young man who'd been a member of the Olympiad back in the day. He was middle-aged, tired, and most concerned, he stated, with returning Celia West to her daughters.

The Trinity and Espionage remained as mysterious as ever, and some reporters murmured that police Captain Mark Paulson had a hand in that. Rumors said that unlike his predecessors, he might be working closely with the young superhumans, who might even be a new, secret arm of the police force. The idea intrigued many, who agreed that with villains like Danton Majors, the Executive, in the world, these new young superhumans might do well to protect their identities.

Majors spent a month at Elroy Asylum being treated by some of the best doctors in the world, specialists in various personality disorders related to megalomania and narcissism. Prosecutors brought charges against him and his entire team. The four members of his team, however, escaped prison when Monica Brooks—aka Sonic—shattered the walls of the city jail with her hypersonic power, freed her colleagues, and vanished. Notably, they did not try to rescue Danton Majors. Presumably, they fled back to Delta. Warrants for their arrest were issued, but no news was forthcoming.

Horizon Tower was disarmed, condemned, and torn down to make way for the city's new development plan,

recently voted on unanimously by the planning committee and spearheaded by West Corp.

Life in Commerce City goes on.

A nna steadied herself before entering Sam's hospital
room. She'd been told what to expect. She knew the
sight of him would shock her, no matter how much she
prepared, no matter how much she thought she knew
what she was going to see.

Celia came with her and kept a hand on Anna's arm,
a comforting pressure. Anna thought about asking her
mother to wait. Then she thought better of it.

"Ready?" Celia asked softly, and Anna nodded.

His parents, George and Melissa Stowe, were there,
sitting near the bed, talking quietly. They looked up,
blinked in confusion that never really went away, even
when recognition dawned.

"Is it all right if we come in?" Celia said, courteous,
always so deft in these awkward situations. She always
knew exactly what to say. She'd replaced the wig and
looked almost normal right now. Except that she was
losing weight—Anna could see her growing skeletal.
The Stowes wouldn't notice it.

Sam's father quickly invited them in, reached to shake
Celia's hand, thanked them for coming, et cetera. Anna
drifted to the bedside.

"He's getting better," Mrs. Stowe said. Her smile was
taut and her eyes red from sleeplessness and crying. "The
ventilator came out yesterday. He's woken up a few times
since then. Now he just has to heal."

Lew and Eliot had saved him, had cushioned his
thirty-story fall enough so that it didn't kill him. But he'd
crashed into the side of the building on the way down,
collapsed to the concrete below with too much force,
even with Eliot breaking the fall. Eliot had been strong

enough only to slow him down and catch himself, not stop them both.

Sam looked tiny lying on the bulky hospital bed, connected to what seemed like a million tubes and wires. A monitor clipped to his finger, IV tubes taped to his arms, oxygen tubes in his nose, sheets piled in messy folds around him. A plastic neck brace immobilized him, and his face was covered in cuts and bruises, swollen and purple. His left arm and leg were broken, his pelvis had cracked, his ribs had broken. His spine had survived, he wasn't paralyzed, but several vertebrae in his neck had cracked, and once he was more healed he would need surgery to repair them. He'd arrived at the emergency room with a head injury, a cracked skull, and excess fluid in his brain, but he'd gotten there quickly enough that doctors had been able to mitigate the worst of the damage. They hoped.

Sam would get better. Everyone said so. But it would take awhile. Anna gave a heavy sigh. She'd been holding an unconscious breath. This could have been any of them. Thinking about that made her numb.

"Can I touch him?" she asked, and Mrs. Stowe nodded. Anna lightly brushed Sam's hand, squeezing his fingers. Maybe it would help. His skin felt cooler than she expected.

"Mr. Stowe, Mrs. Stowe, I have some information that I think you need to hear," Celia said in her steady, calming voice. "Do you have a minute?" They did, they agreed. Would here be all right? They liked to be here for the moments Sam woke up.

"Mr. Stowe—"

"Call me George, please."

"All right. Your father is Gerald Stowe, yes? Do you remember him ever talking about a job he had when he was young, at Leyden Laboratories?"

"No—he had a lot of jobs when he was young. Kept bouncing around, you know?"

"This was a lab owned by my grandfather. The scientist in charge was Simon Sito, the Destructor, and there was an accident. A kind of radiation that affected everyone who was there, including my grandfather. Over the years we've found that the children of those affected have about a forty percent chance of displaying some kind of superhuman ability. I know you were probably asking yourself why this happened to Sam. Well, there's a reason for it. I bear some of the responsibility for this, I'm afraid. I've been tracking the families descended from those who were in the lab. Indirectly, I've been encouraging some of them to use their powers. Including Sam. Including my own children."

"Wait, what?" George Stowe furrowed his brow, baffled. "But I never—"

"No, but your nephew is Justin Raylen, yes? Breezeway? And you might ask your younger sister how much she really knows about Earth Mother."

"*Margaret?*" he exclaimed. "Margaret is Earth Mother?"

Celia put a finger over her lips. "You should probably keep that quiet, since she never went public. I'm trusting you with this information, George, because of Sam. You deserve to know. But it's not for public consumption. You understand, yes?" The Stowes nodded emphatically. "Also, all Sam's medical bills will be paid for. It's coming out of the Compensation Fund for Extraordinary Damages, the trust my mother established. Your family won't have any financial concerns, if that's all right with you."

"Yes. Thank you, yes."

Sam's fingers twitched under Anna's hand. His eyes were open, and he managed a smile with his swollen lips.

"Hey," she said. "How are you?" What a stupid question.

"Crappy," he murmured, his voice barely a scratch. "We won?"

"Yeah. But this . . . this sucks." She blinked fast to keep the tears back.

"Yeah," he said, the air going out of him in a sigh. He squeezed her fingers, but his eyes closed, and he slipped back into sleep.

This did, indeed, suck. But she finally believed he'd get better. Blaster would return.

Celia touched her shoulder. "We should probably get going, let him rest."

"Okay."

The leave-taking was awkward and drawn out. The Stowes seemed more stunned than when they arrived, not less, and Anna felt washed out. Just seeing Sam like that was exhausting. But she had to be thankful that he hadn't died. How much more awkward, to be standing at his funeral?

She didn't want to think about that.

They were in the elevator, descending to the lobby, when Anna felt a *ping* on her radar. "Mom, Eliot Majors is in the lobby."

"Oh?" she said. "That'll be interesting."

They couldn't help but meet him on their way out and his way in. Anna didn't show any surprise at all, but Eliot's eyes went wide, and he hesitated, as if thinking of turning tail.

"Hi, Eliot," Anna said. Any embarrassment she might have felt had faded to trivia. "I don't think you really had a chance to meet my mom?"

Celia smiled graciously and offered her hand. "So nice to meet you, Eliot. I never got a chance to thank you for what you did."

He had a bouquet of tulips, which he awkwardly shifted from one hand to another so he could shake Celia's hand. "Um. Hi. It . . ." His shoulders slumped.

"I wish I could have done more. I wanted to come visit."

Celia said, "He probably won't be awake. But his parents are there, I think they'd like to meet you." He blanched.

"So," Anna said, jumping in to fill an awkward silence. "Are you going to stay in Commerce City, at the university, or go back to Delta?"

"I think I'm going to stay. I mean, as long as my father is here, I think I should stay."

"A more urgent question for me, is Weasel going to stay?" Celia asked.

Eliot rolled his eyes. "I can't believe that's the name that stuck."

"Told you," Anna said. "You'd have been better off with Leapfrog."

"My advice?" Celia said, grinning. "Since you're never going to beat it, just own it. Put fur on your costume. Get a theme song."

He didn't look happy about any of those possibilities. "Ms. West, I'm sorry. For what my father did. If I'd had any idea, if I'd known what he was going to do, I'd have—"

"Eliot, it wasn't your fault. None of it. I speak with great authority when I say that children cannot be held responsible for the actions of their parents. Now, let it go and just worry about being a good person, okay?"

Nodding, he continued on to the elevators, and Anna and Celia continued outside.

"Not a bad-looking kid," Celia observed, smiling vaguely.

"I suppose," Anna said, realizing she hadn't actually thought much about Eliot over the last few days, beyond his superheroing. "We still going shopping for a prom dress tomorrow?"

"Yes. Is it all right if Bethy comes along? Girls' day out?"

Anna's first impulse was to argue. Bethy would talk too much and complain and she didn't know anything about prom dresses. But she stopped herself, because really, having Bethy along might be kind of fun.

"Okay," she agreed.

Among several news stories lost and buried amid the feverish reporting of the Executive and the battle at Horizon Tower was the report that Judge Roland had quietly resigned his position in the city court—and fled the country. The whereabouts of the criminal lowlife Jonathan Scarzen were also unknown. After his release, he, too, seemed to have fled. The *Commerce Eye* refrained from speculating that the two disappearances might be connected, and in refraining raised that exact possibility. The website Rooftop Watch had no such compunctions and praised the work of the superhuman vigilante Espionage in drawing attention to such activities when no one else could.

That was when Anna and Teia both realized that they had absolutely no control over what publicity they got. It was almost a relief.

Finally finally *finally*. West Corp won the planning committee bid, the development project was a go. Contracts issued, ground broken, construction under way. The weight lifted. Celia managed to delegate most of her West Corp duties until all she had left was facing the promise she'd made.

They went on vacation.

It hardly seemed fair, though, lying on a warm beach under a bright sun and feeling cold. She wore a hat and knit gloves, and held a blanket wrapped around her. More side effects of the chemotherapy—she was always

cold, always shivering. But she had only one more treatment, and the blood tests looked promising. The end
was in sight, the light at the end of the tunnel was bright,
and it wasn't the light of an oncoming train. They probably should have waited to take the holiday until treatment was finished entirely, but everyone was so tired, so
worn out. Not just physically but also emotionally, from
all the anxiety, the long nights, the uncertainty. Celia
wasn't going to make them wait on her account. She
needed this as well, and if she was going to be sitting
around bundled in blankets anyway, she might as well
be someplace beautiful, like Cascade Beach.

She wouldn't have missed this for anything.

The kids had found a volleyball net in the storage
closet of the beach house and set it up in the stretch of
sand out front. Bethy, Suzanne—wearing a leg brace
and still limping from her injury but gamely hobbling
through—Teia, Lew, and even Analise had joined the
current rousing match, not following any particular rules,
bumping and slamming the ball back and forth accompanied by much laughter. Celia wanted so much to join
in. Soon, she would. When she'd recovered. This gave her
something to work for. In the meantime, their laughter
warmed her.

There was a lesson here, one she reveled in: Suffering
and happiness weren't incompatible. She was in pain,
but somehow she was contented, lying in her lounge
chair. Happy, even. Her family was here, they loved her,
and they had survived. As soon as she got some energy
back, she'd shout her triumph to the skies.

Even Arthur had relaxed—as much as he ever did.
He'd abandoned his jacket and shoes, rolled up his trouser cuffs and sleeves, and walked on the beach, contem-
plative. Celia turned from the game to watch him. He'd
followed the edge of the water to an outcrop of distant
rocks and was returning now, hands in pockets, looking

over the sea. She couldn't read his expression from so far away, but she could mark the line of his jaw, watch his brown hair toss in the wind. His hair had thinned but was still brushed back from his face in scruffy waves. He was still handsome, in her eyes. He was hers, she'd never had to question it. From a hundred yards away he looked up, feeling her gaze and thoughts upon him. Raised a hand in a wave, and she smiled.

He wandered back, pulled up a chair beside her.

"You look happy," she said.

"I like it here. It's quiet. Not many people around."

He could lower his defenses here. He looked ten years younger. She reached for him, and he gently took her hand. He always knew exactly how firmly he could squeeze before hurting her oversensitive skin. She rested lightly against him.

The door to the beach house opened and closed, and Anna came out. Long tan legs, shorts and tank top, pure lanky youth. She stood at the edge of the porch for a moment, looking out, pensive, before dragging over another lawn chair and sitting by her parents. *She should be happy,* Celia thought. *I should tell her to be happy,* but she remembered seventeen.

"Hey there," Celia said, deciding to keep it simple. "You decided to come out."

Anna screwed her face up, tapped her foot. "I knew that Dad was back. I wanted to talk." She glanced at them both, tried to smile.

Celia looked at Arthur; this might have been a first, and she was afraid to move, in case the moment passed too quickly.

"We've been waiting for months for you to say that," Arthur said gently.

"Years," Celia corrected, then hunkered into her blanket, apologetic. Arthur rested his hand on her arm, a touch of comfort.

They remained quiet, waiting for their eldest daughter to find words.

"Dad, I can't read people like you can. But I still feel it. I don't think I can handle it. Mom, when I thought you were gone I didn't know how I was going to handle it, and then it turns out you're sick, and someday you'll be gone. And . . ." She looked at Arthur. "How do you keep from hurting when you lose someone?"

"You don't. It overwhelms you, and then you move on. You must move on or you die, and there's too much to live for for that."

She frowned. "You make it sound easy."

"Oh, no, it isn't easy. But the strength comes to you." He brushed Celia's cheek. "Though I would very much prefer it if you waited to leave until after I'm gone."

It would be better that way. She wouldn't have to sit there, watching his very mind fade. She would try to last long enough to save him from that. Sighing, she said, "I'm trying."

Anna's face had puckered, a young woman trying very hard not to cry. She'd asked how she would ever survive one of them dying, and what did they do? Gave her a picture of both of them leaving her. *I'm a terrible parent. I had nothing to do with my daughters turning out so well.*

Celia reached out her other hand, the one not claimed by Arthur. Anna might just as easily have walked away from it, but she didn't. She took it maybe just a little too hard, but Celia wasn't going to complain.

"What's it like for you?" Celia asked. "Knowing where we are, being able to feel us?"

"It's hard to explain. All I have to do is think of you and you're there, in the back of my mind. It's like the world is full, my brain is full. But that's okay—it felt worse when it was empty."

"The power means you're never alone," Arthur added.

"Yeah, it's like that."

"I can't even imagine," Celia murmured. She turned her gaze back to the volleyball game, which had degenerated into some kind of kickball-tag mashup that traveled down the beach. The kids ran ahead, and Suzanne and Analise trailed behind at a slower pace, side by side. They were talking—Suzanne giving the younger woman advice, Celia hoped. On how to be superpowered, how to be superpowered and a mom at the same time. How to get over losing a heroic husband.

Bethy stopped in the middle of sprinting, looked over, frowned. Arthur waved at her, and she stumbled through the sand to them. With a lack of self-consciousness that probably wouldn't last too much longer, Bethy flopped into her father's chair, half sitting on his lap and forcing him to make room for her. He put an arm around her, anchoring her.

The whole family. *My family,* Celia thought fiercely, proudly.

"What's up?" Bethy said. A loaded question that also asked: Is something wrong, is everything okay, and you're not leaving me out, are you? A teenage girl testing out her place in the world. For the first time ever, Celia wanted her babies back. The babies were so much easier to comfort.

"Family bonding," Celia said. Amusingly, Bethy wrinkled her nose. But she didn't run away.

Anna studied Celia's hand, and the screwed-up expression on her face meant another question was coming. She waited. Finally, Anna said, "Mom. Can you tell me about when Grandpa died?"

Oh, is that all . . . The family history that they all knew and never talked about. All those lurid biographies and exposés, and the poor kid had probably read them all, without any context. Celia never talked about it, she realized.

But she owed this to Anna. To both of them.

"I wish you could have known him. He'd have been so proud of you both—"

"Even if my power isn't—"

"Yes," she interrupted. "He'd have understood."

Clearly skeptical, Anna looked at Arthur, who would obviously know the truth about what Warren West had or hadn't thought. But Arthur was very good with other people's secrets.

He said, "We can't say exactly what he would or wouldn't have done now. I will say, he knew he'd made mistakes. He simply wasn't very good at expressing himself."

Celia rubbed at her eyes. Her father had never been able to admit he was wrong about anything during his lifetime. But maybe she just hadn't been paying attention. "Oh, no, he was excellent at expressing himself, as long as he could punch through a nearby wall."

"Well, yes. He was excellent at expressing anger and frustration."

Anna and Bethy both blinked at them in wide-eyed horror. Yeah, this stuff wasn't in most of the biographies.

"He sounds kinda scary," Bethy said.

"You would not be wrong," Arthur said, his thin smile showing clear amusement.

Anna said, "So you never actually, you know, talked to him about this. Powers, or what happened with you and the Destructor, or anything?"

"Oh, no, he was right there when the chief of police questioned me about the whole thing," Celia said, grinning.

"You know what I mean."

"Yeah, I do. And no, we never really talked about it. Seems pretty typical for me. Girls, I'm sorry. I didn't tell you because I thought I was protecting you, that it would be easier for you if I didn't tell."

"Yeah," Anna said. "Me, too."

Celia smiled, and Arthur's grip on her hand gave her the strength she needed, as he wrapped her up with the warmth of his mind.

"Anna, Bethy. We kept the command room and most of the other equipment operational for you. Just in case, whether you had powers or not. It's yours, if you want it."

They both looked like lemurs, processing that. Celia still didn't know if this was the right thing to do. They were too young. But it was out of her hands now, and that was okay.

"Do you want me to? Do the vigilante thing? I know that's what your dad wanted you to do and you didn't— but what do you want us to do?"

Be safe, be happy . . .

—You've done all you can on that score.—

—I know.—

"It's not up to me," Celia told them. "To either of us. You have to decide."

"I want it!" Bethy said, coming abruptly to her feet. "I know I don't have powers, but the Hawk didn't, and I can do it, I know I can!"

Celia winced. She was way too young. "You're still on an eight o'clock curfew, my dear."

"Anna?" Arthur prompted.

The young woman's face was puckered in thought. "I have to think about it," she said.

That was fair. Celia settled back in her chair. "Now, what else do you want to know about the family business?"

They talked for a couple of hours. Celia had ended up telling so much more than Anna had expected. Not just about the day Captain Olympus died, but about everything leading up to it, the years Warren and Celia West had refused to speak to each other, the fights, the reasons Celia joined with the Destructor, and why and how she left. All very sensational, and Celia told it all, only from her it was family drama, not superhero mythology. Celia had cried, some. It had happened so long ago, Anna figured it was old news to her, that all emotion would have been drained from the stories. But no.

Arthur added some commentary. Celia still partly blamed herself for the death of Captain Olympus. Arthur explained that this was a common result of the survivor's guilt that plagued her.

Survivor's guilt. That was what Anna had felt in Sam's hospital room.

And then there was the rest of it. Celia gave them the command room. Anna still didn't know what to think about that.

Telling the story had drained Celia, and she slept, right there in the lounge chair. Arthur stayed with her, Suzanne went in to start dinner, and the games ended. Thoughtful, Anna walked out to the beach to sit and watch the waves come in. She understood why her father liked it so much out here. The motion of the water cleared her mind like nothing else. She needed her mind cleared.

After a little while, Teia joined her. Two girls, sitting on the beach, staring out. Thinking too much.

"I wonder how much of it I could freeze, if I put my mind to it," Teia said finally.

"You going to try?"

"Maybe tomorrow. I have to admit. I'm kind of scared of what would happen if I really could do it."

"Maybe you'd better not try, then."

"Yeah."

The sound of it, Anna decided, the shushing and splashing, the roar that became a trickle and back again, was beautiful. Dark clouds were building on the horizon.

"Is that Lew?" Anna asked.

"No, that's just a storm."

Finally, Anna turned to Teia and said, "We're going to keep doing this, right? We have to keep going."

Teia pressed her lips together, nodded. "Yeah. We do. We will. But I think we need a new name."

Anna thought so as well, and the new name was on the tip of her tongue. She was afraid to say it, in case Teia's idea was different. The last thing she wanted was to argue this all over again. "Yeah. Me, too."

"You have an idea, don't you? You say your idea first."

She took a deep breath and said, "The New Olympiad."

And Teia smiled. "That's exactly what I was thinking."

Anna held her hand out, and Teia clasped it.

The waves rolled on.

TOR

Award-winning authors
Compelling stories